Beaumont's
Journey

Wolves, weather, wicked men
And war can't keep Walter Beaumont
from his Alaska home

Warren Troy
Alaska Wilderness Adventure Author

PO Box 221974 Anchorage, Alaska 99522-1974
books@publicationconsultants.com—www.publicationconsultants.com

ISBN 978-1-59433-598-3
eISBN 978-1-59433-599-0
Library of Congress Catalog Card Number: 2015960030

This is a work of fiction. Any
resemblance to persons living or dead, or to any
experiences others may have had is purely
coincidental, and not meant to disturb anyone.

Manufactured in the United States of America.

Dedication

I dedicate this book to all the Members of the U.S. Military for their service and sacrifices in so many conflicts all over the world, in order that we and many others might remain free.

Thank you

and

to my friend, Steve MacDonald, a long-time Alaskan. He was a good man

Contents

Chapter 1

The Journey Begins

When Walter Beaumont was born, it proved to be an easy birthing for his mother. He was her first child, and it could have been more difficult, but such was not the case. His mother, Hannah, was grateful for the relatively pain-free and smooth delivery.

The attending doctor was surprised when, as was the tradition, he smacked the tiny infant on his rump to get him jump started. The baby's reaction was unexpected. He was definitely alive and breathing well, but he didn't let out a cry at the smack. Instead, he had a look on his tiny wizened face the physician could only recognize as annoyance.

The doctor wondered for a moment if the newborn was actually irritated at his treatment, immediately dismissing the thought as foolish, a baby only a few moments into the outside world having a specifically directed emotion. Normally, the physician would have been correct, but not in Walter's case.

Rather than immediately wanting to feed when laid on his mother's breast, young Beaumont dozed off as if content, for the moment, to have completed his journey to a larger world, a tiny beginning to an adventure-filled existence.

Unfortunately, his mother developed an infection which flared up quickly, keeping her hospitalized for a week. The effects of the infection left her unable to have any more children. Walter was to be an only child, and this affected the way Hannah treated her boy during his childhood, giving him more leeway during moments of bad behavior on his part than might otherwise have been allowed. Still, he caused her and his father a fair share of frustration during his youth, that ultimately required a unique solution to resolve.

He was born Walter John Beaumont, in Manhattan, Kansas, where Fort Riley, General George Armstrong Custer's old stomping grounds, was located.

It was April 1942, only a few months after World War Two had begun, when the United States was still recovering from the horrendous attack on Pearl Harbor, and starting to arm herself for the combat to come.

His father had joined the United States Army after Pearl was devastated, leaving his young, pregnant wife to fend for herself and their unborn child. Fortunately, she had family all around her in the Kansas town that had been their home for several generations. They were solid, hard working Americans, so young Walter had good people to learn from and look up to as a toddler.

When the war was over, Walter's father came home whole and safe, to appreciate and enjoy the peaceful years to come.

Walter's parents were regular folks, his mother, Hannah, a housewife; and his father, Ben, an electrician, who also spent weekends repairing his neighbors' small appliances. Having served in the deadly Pacific Campaign, he was content living a simple, quiet life with his little family, earning a fair living, and helping his neighbors.

Being an only child never bothered Walter as it might another. He didn't seem to need a sibling. He had a few friends, and was sociable when required to be, but even when very young there seemed to be a little distance between him and his peers.

He was always roaming. Even when he was three or four years old, it was hard to keep track of him. Turn around for a moment, and the boy was out of sight. He drove his poor mother to tears with what she thought of as his aimless wanderings. At one point, she even wondered if there was something the matter with him.

Once, when he pulled his disappearing act and Hannah finally caught up with him a quarter mile down their road petting a neighbor's fierce-looking dog, who was smiling widely at him. In her frustration instead of saying, "Walter John, come here this instant!" what came out of her mouth was, "Weejer, you come here!" The spontaneous nickname stuck. It was a moniker he never appreciated. His mom knew it, and used it when the boy needed to be taken down a peg.

At age five, he discovered a couple of loose boards in the fence surrounding the back yard, which his father had put up to try to contain him until he was old enough to be on his own. When he was sure no one was watching, the inquisitive child managed to pull the boards aside until he could squeeze partway through.

There was a little draw behind the house. The sides were gently angled and covered with brush, while small willows and a few cottonwoods grew along the busy little creek at the bottom.

Being of a tender age, he didn't have a clue as to what existed in this new place. It was a wondrous thing for him, the newness of it all. He sensed this fascinating environment was as it should be, random and uneven, unlike the hard, boxlike houses on the street, flanked by straight-edged lawns, with their neatly trimmed grass and ruler-straight borders of flowers.

Even though there was a full row of houses along the street, the little gully with its clear-water creek had managed to remain untouched, as it probably had been before any streets had been laid out, or houses built, when the original inhabitants had lived there hunting and gathering.

He was drawn immediately to this wild bit of land, sensing its uniqueness in what was otherwise a flat, dry world for him. It might have been seeing this unspoiled environment as a toddler that stirred the desire in Walter to seek wild, untouched places later in life.

The animals traveling down the draw included raccoons, skunks, rabbits, and the occasional deer, coming through when humans were snug in their beds. His growing interest in these wild inhabitants caused the inquisitive child to eventually lose his newfound freedom outside the confining wooden fence.

In the early morning hours as the sun began to show, Walter would slip out of his bed and hunker down by the loose fence boards to watch, quiet as a leaf. He had a good vantage point, and saw all the denizens of the sparse woods as they hopped and skittered along, stopping sometimes to nip some grass or catch a frog.

From time to time, when a breeze flowed in the right direction, whatever animals he was observing would catch his scent, snapping their heads around to stare in the child's direction. These moments delighted him, ending when the critter, sensing no danger, would either go back to its business or move away if feeling edgy at his presence.

He was careful to keep his parents from finding out about his makeshift observation post, knowing it would be the end of the loose boards and early-hour observations for him.

His burning curiosity finally got the better of him, and one cool spring morning, with barely any light in the sky, he slipped all the way through the boards, pushed them back into place, and stood outside his little home world, breathing in everything now surrounding him. Aside from the row of houses, there were no structures as far as he could see, only some distant lights signifying another patch of civilization.

He took a dozen steps along the fence, one hand upon the boards. Sitting down in the damp grass, he stayed very still, hoping for a glimpse of a deer or raccoon. After a time, the child dozed off.

He was awakened by the unhappy sounds of his mother and father, who were loudly calling his name as they looked around the backyard for their missing boy.

Though he knew it was trouble, Walter arose from the outside place where he had drifted off to sleep, walked back to his secret door, and slipped into the yard. His mother, face wet with tears, spotted him first, then his father, who walked him by the ear into the house, emphasizing his situation with a firm smack on his backside as they reached the back door. Ben sat him down on his bed for a talk.

During their first serious discussion, Walter told his dad what he had been doing, and Ben explained to him how much worry he had caused his mother by disappearing, and made him promise never do anything like that again. It was the hardest part of it all, because Walter John Beaumont always kept his promises, even at that age.

But he didn't stay out of trouble through grammar school, though well behaved and quiet in classes. An intelligent boy, he found the lessons and projects in school easy to perform. The other kids, for the most part, found him a little different. There was something about his demeanor that caused them to give him some room. He didn't seem threatening; he just wasn't the kind other kids wanted to get close to.

They rarely invited him to play. For the most part, they simply left him alone.

Weejer discovered he had a knack for being sneaky, and people didn't notice until he was suddenly gone or showed up standing close to them. These unexpected appearings and disappearings were a little unnerving for his young schoolmates, but he liked doing it.

A few parents complained about him upsetting their children with his comings and goings, and he was told to stop sneaking up on them, though he still practiced slipping away, nothing being said about that. He had no specific reason for doing it, other than finding it amusing to be sneaky.

Walter's natural dislike for bullies came to the surface in fourth grade. Arthur Mueller, who was known to be a mean kid, tried to pick a fight with Walter at recess. Weejer stared directly into his eyes. At first, Arthur kept making rude noises at him. Then, he poked a finger in Walter's chest, who quietly said, "Don't, Arthur," continuing to stare at him with unblinking, firmly set eyes. Arthur's facial expression changed, all the meanness and anger gone out of him. Something in Walter's attitude had drained Arthur's confidence. He lowered his hand, turned, and walked away. Though he never challenged him directly again, one more incident between them had yet to play out.

There was a boy, slight in stature, who had sustained an injury to his leg as a toddler, leaving him with a pronounced limp. He was self-conscious about it. Most of the kids liked the boy, because he always had a smile on his face. Arthur, however, couldn't pass up any opportunity to bully him. While Walter figured it was none of his business at first, he eventually got tired of Mueller's cruelty.

One day, Arthur had the boy in tears, having trapped him in a corner of the playground. Half a dozen other children was standing around, simply watching.

Walter had appeared behind Arthur, grabbed him by the back of the neck, and pulled him away. This was the first time he had actually gotten physical with anyone, and Mueller found out how strong he was. He didn't even try to fight back.

Walter let him go after backing him up far enough to let the lame boy get away. When Arthur turned around and saw who it was, he froze, staring blankly at him.

Walter said, "Stop bothering him, it's mean."

Frightened, Arthur ran away into the school, and told a teacher Walter had grabbed him for no reason, hurting his neck.

The teacher came out and took him by the arm. He pulled away, not liking to be grabbed. The two stood still for a moment, facing each other. He had a determined look on his face, and the teacher wondered what she had on her hands. In a quiet voice, she asked him to come into the principal's office, and he followed her obediently.

When the teacher told the principal what had supposedly happened, he asked Beaumont what he had to say.

He said nothing, standing there resolute. He saw no need to explain himself to this adult. It was none of his business, as far as Walter was concerned.

Getting no reply, the principal called Hannah and had her come to the school and take her son home, expelling him for three days. Hannah was embarrassed, and didn't say a word until they got home, at which point all she could say was, "Oh, Weejer."

When Ben got home from work and heard what had happened, he asked his child why he had grabbed the other boy. All his son said was, "I did what I did, and I'm not sorry."

Though not happy to cause him pain, he took off his belt and gave Walter three smacks on the backside, then sent him to his room without dinner.

Late in the evening, the Beaumont phone rang. It was the father of the limping child. The boy had told him what had happened, and how Walter had stood up for him. The father told Ben what had occurred, and asked him to thank Walter for helping his son. He said it was good to know Ben had brought up his son to know right from wrong and how to deal with things.

As Ben sat listening, his chest tightened as he realized the truth of the situation. He felt terrible about punishing Walter.

Going to his room, he found the boy lying quietly on his bed, reading a book by one of his favorite authors, Ernest Thompson Seton. Ben looked at his son in silence for a moment, before telling him he'd found out what had actually happened. He apologized for punishing him, and told Walter he had done the right thing. Then he said he would never hit him again. In a rare moment of open affection, Walter got up, went over to his father, and hugged him. Ben got a big lump in his throat, and took the boy downtown to the soda fountain for a hamburger, fries, and a vanilla malt, Walter's favorite.

Ben kept his word, and never hit him again. He did go to the school the next morning with his son, and explained to the principal what had actually happened. Walter Beaumont was allowed back in school immediately. Arthur wasn't there a short while later, having been expelled from school for three days.

He behaved himself through middle school years, seemingly content to play with the few friends he had made after dealing with Arthur, and going places with his parents. His father would take him fishing and camping, things his mother never liked to do.

When he turned twelve, his father gave him permission to go for jaunts by himself, exploring the nearby open country around his neighborhood, if his chores were done and the family had no plans. This newly granted freedom allowed Walter to fulfill his desire to explore, which kept the youngster satisfied for quite some time.

By the time he entered high school, Walter had grown into a lanky young man, stronger than he appeared, topped with a striking shock of black hair with a mind of its own.

His wanderlust had fully resurfaced, and he took different routes to and from school whenever possible, never taking the bus, preferring to walk or ride his bike. He took to coming home a bit later than his folks liked, knowing how long he could stay out without causing serious concern. Walter sometimes missed doing his chores, riding his bike on the weekends, leaving early in the morning, exploring the patches of woods still existing in his hometown, and often missing lunch. He was driven to it, to be out and about in nature, but the boy always made sure he got home in time for dinner. His parents tolerated his absences as best they could, because scolding and grounding him didn't seem to help the situation. When they asked him to promise, he stayed silent. Eventually, he'd slip away again.

When he was home, Walter read books and magazine articles about woods lore, and stories about explorers and adventurers who had amazing experiences all over the world. He studied the animals of North America, learning their behavior and instinctive habits.

His father tried to get him interested in the Boy Scouts, but after several meetings he stopped going. He told his father he already knew or could learn on his own everything the Scouts offered, and he didn't need any merit badges or other rewards. Knowing his son's mind, all his father could do was shake his head and let it go.

Walter had another, more serious problem: he had lost interest in studying and his grades began to slip, though never getting bad enough to make him fail his classes. His parents were unhappy, of course, and wondered what they should do. They already knew punishing him didn't help. It only seemed to make him more determined to be himself, no matter what. Not knowing what else to do, and being familiar with his way of behaving, Ben sat his boy down one day, and angrily demanding an answer, made him promise to come home right after school, do his homework, and not to leave every weekend. Walter wasn't happy about it, because, as his father knew, he would keep his promise.

Chapter 2

Alaska Beckons

In late May, 1959, Walter's seventeenth year, his uncle, Aubrey Biggs, came to visit. Hannah's brother, Aubrey, was a rugged outdoorsman who lived in Alaska where he had moved right after World War Two. He made a living transporting supplies with his thirty-six foot, wooden-hulled boat, running up and down part of the Alaska coast, dropping off goods for folks living in remote locations. Aubrey felt the need for solitude, after fighting all through Central Europe for almost two years in World War Two. When the weary veteran returned home, he had made a beeline for the least-populated place he could think of, and had been there ever since. It proved to be perfect for him, and there were definitely fewer people around.

Most who came to the wild north didn't stay long, only a handful sticking to the life. As Aubrey put it, "People either love or hate the place. Regardless, if they can survive a full year, they can live there as long as they please, because they've proved up!"

To visit, Aubrey had driven all the way down the rough, potholed, Alcan Highway, which was a real test of a man and his machine in those days. He had purchased an old army ambulance, rigged it up as a basic camper, and made it all the way to Kansas without mishap, doing thirty-five to forty miles an hour when the road allowed. It was 1959, the first year of Alaska's Statehood.

Once Aubrey had arrived in Alaska, in early 1946, he spent the first few years camping, exploring, gold panning, hunting, and fishing for his food. He initially lived in a double-walled tent, and despite some rough times in bad weather and a couple of run-ins with bears, he loved every minute of it.

While he was working the mildly successful gold claim he had filed, Biggs built a cabin. It was a two-room log structure, sturdy and pleasing to the eye, and ample protection from the extreme winter conditions. After he quit gold mining, he moved further south in the state, where he made his living hauling freight by boat.

Walter loved listening to Aubrey's stories of Alaska, its animals and people, and the way he lived, in a rustic cabin on the coast. He would sit on the floor, quietly listening, soaking up everything he heard. He'd wait until his uncle was alone to ask him one question after another, until Aubrey begged off for a while, though glad his nephew seemed interested in his home, and nature in general. After he learned Walter's nickname, it was Weejer from then on, but when his uncle said it, the boy didn't seem to mind.

Ben and Hannah talked to Aubrey about the problems they were having with Walter. He understood immediately what they didn't seem to comprehend, having been much like his nephew when he was young, and Biggs reminded Hannah of his own youthful wanderings. An idea began to form in Aubrey's mind. He thought he might have a solution to the problem.

After having talks with the teenager, taking little hikes with him, and hearing the sincere enthusiasm as his nephew told him what he knew about the land and the animals living in the far north, Aubrey decided the plan he had in mind was the right one to follow.

He made his proposal to Ben and Hannah. At first they were concerned about their son's safety. After Aubrey promised to take good care of him and teach Walter things that would benefit him, they finally relented and agreed.

Several days before Aubrey left to head back north, he took a walk with Weejer along the creek behind the house, and told him what had been discussed. If he stayed out of trouble for the next year, helped his folks, and graduated with good grades, he could come live with him for the summer. Walter could only stand there, with his mouth slightly open, unable to speak. When Aubrey had made him the offer, he knew in his gut this would be something of great significance to him. Though he didn't think of it in those words, he certainly felt it.

"Well, what do you say, Weejer?"

"Okay, Uncle Aubrey, I'd love to, and I'll behave."

While the next year seemed to grind away slower than a glacier making its way down a carved-out valley, Walter minded his Ps and Qs as he had promised, and barely went anywhere beyond school and home. He came back on time, and did all his chores without a hitch. He even began working with his dad, helping fix small appliances.

His father was impressed with the way he quickly learned to put the toasters, irons, and small kitchen appliances back in working order. He had natural talent, and only needed to be shown something once for the process to be firmly set in his mind. Once he knew how a device functioned, Walter often found little ways to improve on the design, rerouting wires and reinforcing internal parts that seemed weak to him. His dad paid him a reasonable salary for a teenage boy, and after six months, Walter was allowed to spend time alone in the shop making repairs.

One afternoon, Walter was eating his lunch, sitting in the high school bleachers watching the track team practice. While he was never interested in team sports, one thing he did like was running. He knew he was fast, but had never wanted to try out.

It was his senior year, and even though the track team was already well established, he suddenly got a bug in his ear to join in. Setting his half-eaten sandwich on the wooden bleacher seat, he walked down to where coach Duncan was talking to a small group of athletes.

"Now, I know you kids want to get to the state finals this year. You also know we lost Lowery to a knee injury, so we need one of you to switch to the four-hundred-yard dash. Who wants to give it a go?"

None of the team spoke up, but a quiet voice behind Duncan said, "I would, coach."

Duncan turned to see the one boy he didn't expect to be there wanting to participate. He frowned and shook his head.

"Sorry, Beaumont, it's a little late to start training someone, considering you've never shown any interest."

Duncan had tried several times to get Walter to join the team, noticing how well he ran in regular P.E. classes. However, he needed someone he could count on.

"Well, I'm interested now, and I'd like to run for you. I'll do my best, Coach."

Duncan thought about it a moment. He knew the kid could run. Would he be committed enough when it got down to it?

"Tell you what, Beaumont, if you can beat two other runners in the hundred-yard dash, I'll give you a try. How does that sound?"

Walter knew immediately what the coach intended to do: pit him against two of his best sprinters. Smiling, he nodded his agreement.

"Okay then, young man, go suit up and we'll see how you do."

Walter was wearing levis, a clean t-shirt, and a scruffy old pair of Converse shoes. "I'm okay like this, Coach."

Duncan smiled and nodded, then picked out his two best sprinters, having the three teenagers go out on the track. The two runners stretched and did a few calisthenics while Walter, with his perpetually serious look, quietly waited. Coach Duncan had them line up, then blew his coach's whistle. He couldn't believe it when Walter left the two team members in his dust. To be sure it wasn't a fluke, he had them do the one hundred again. Warmed up, Walter did even better, to the dismay of the other runners.

Perplexed, Duncan had him run the four hundred once by himself, knowing, after two one-hundred-yard dashes, he would already be slightly winded.

"I don't want you to push too hard, just try to put in a good time. The four hundred can be a difficult distance to run, a long sprint. Go stand on the track."

When the coach blew his whistle, Weejer took off, setting a pace easy for him to maintain. Coach Duncan was amazed when he finished the run, coming in only three seconds behind the school record. He didn't tell the boy how well he had done.

"All right, you've got your chance. I want you here after school regularly to train with the team, and if you give me any guff, even once, you're out!"

"You've got my word on it, sir."

Something about the way he said it made Duncan realize he would keep his word.

Working with the team had a good effect on him. Though it took a little while to warm up to the situation, he came to appreciate being part of a like-minded group of people working for the same goal. The other team members took to him without hesitation, and he fit right in. Walter became more sociable as the school year went on.

Still, he needed his solitary time, so he would go for a run every night after dinner and homework. Not only did it keep him in good running condition, it also let his mind run free.

His parents were delighted with the major change in his attitude. Hannah wrote a letter to Aubrey, saying his plan was working well. She kept him apprised of Walter's results with the track team. Not only did he help the team go to the State Finals, winning his event, he set a new state record.

Walter thought regularly about Alaska, daydreaming about how it would be living there. He had learned from his research that it was like no other place, wild and vast. He had decided he would abide by whatever his uncle Aubrey told him to do, and learn how to behave in such a rugged, unruly place. Realizing the need to be tough and capable to live there only made him look forward to it even more.

After he had been told he could visit in Alaska, the country surrounding his Kansas home didn't hold as much interest for him as before. He had been reading many books about Alaska, and even wrote his final report for school in his senior year about the animals of the north country.

The land outside his home had served its purpose for Walter, drawing his mind and heart into the natural world, but, once in Alaska, he would expand his knowledge of things both naturally created and manmade beyond anything he'd ever dreamed of experiencing. There would be times when this would delight him, and times when it would tear at his soul, but it was all at the core of Walter John Beaumont's journey.

Walter never was much for spending time with the high school girls he knew. It wasn't because he didn't like girls or understand what he should do to get on with them. He simply didn't find one who grabbed his attention. He did most of the things he liked by himself, and didn't take time to develop a relationship. He also had no idea where he would end up, and this factor put him off from finding himself a sweet local girl. Maybe he'd find someone up north. The thought appealed to him.

Beaumont didn't graduate with honors, but his grades were respectable. Because of his prowess in track, he was offered an athletic scholarship to Kansas State University, right in his hometown of Manhattan.

His parents were delighted with the way Walter had turned out by graduation time, and the scholarship was icing on the cake for them. They all talked, and it was decided he would accept the scholarship and go to State to further his education after the Alaska visit. The athletic program there was excellent. Unknown to him, Coach Duncan, impressed with how well he performed and the positive effect he had on the team, had put in a word to the athletic department of Kansas State, his Alma Mater, hence the scholarship offer.

The big thing for Walter, of course, was the upcoming trip to Alaska. He agreed with his parents to go to Kansas State, for fear if he refused they might not let him go north.

Walter graduated on June 10th, 1960. By the 15th, he was winging his way to Anchorage. He had saved money from working with his dad, who gave him a bonus to make sure he would have enough for any supplies or equipment he'd need. He also got his son a present which totally overwhelmed him, because it was, actually, the perfect thing, his destination being what it was.

A month before Walter graduated, his father called him out to the garage. Ben had a rifle in his hands.

"I made a deal with our neighbor, Mr. Wills, in trade for servicing his appliances for the next year. This is a rifle he's had for many years, but no longer needs. I hope it will be the right one to have this summer. Your uncle said a .30-06 will work well enough if you do your part."

He handed Walter the gun. It was a sporterized Springfield Model 1903. Its wooden stock was reshaped and cut down from its military form, and the barrel had commercial sights attached, with a Lyman peep sight mounted on the back end of the action. The rifle had been blued, replacing the dull, gray-green parkerized finish that originally coated it.

Beaumont was stunned, though he had a .22 rifle already and knew how to shoot well. He was a natural with it, just as he was innately competent with other tools and equipment. He looked his father in the eye and said, "Thanks dad, I'll take good care of it."

Walter and his father took the rifle out to the local shooting range, which was an old quarry. Ben paced off approximately one hundred yards, after they had adjusted the sights to hit a large coffee can at about twenty-five yards. Walter locked his arm through the leather sling on the rifle to make it steadier, and touched off one round. From the way the can reacted, it appeared he had caught it at its top edge. He made a minor elevation adjustment on the rear sight. The next three shots sent the can flying each time he worked the bolt and squeezed the trigger. All three holes were well centered on the can. It was obvious Weejer could shoot whatever gun he was holding.

The second time, he went to the range by himself. When he was shooting he pretended the can was an angry bear, making the session a little more interesting. He only fired ten shots, not wanting to waste ammunition.

Chapter 3

Cheechako

During Walter's senior year, Uncle Aubrey had sent him several letters from Alaska, describing the place in detail to give him an idea of what to expect. In the last letter, he told his nephew he should fly to Anchorage, then make his own way down to Seward where they would meet and take the boat down to his cabin after making some deliveries.

While Walter wasn't concerned with getting to Seward on his own, he decided not to mention it to his parents, especially his mom, knowing she'd worry about her boy being alone in a wild and dangerous place. Unknown to him, Aubrey had written and told them about it, saying coming to Alaska would be a growing experience. His mom and dad never said a word to him about the letter.

Weejer said good-bye to his folks, who were sad to see their son go, but excited for him too. Soon he was flying from his Midwestern home in a DC-3. They made two stops along the way at small airports. Though Weejer had never left Manhattan, Kansas, except during the state track and field finals, he wasn't very interested in looking around, either in the air or on the ground. The only thing he was focused on was getting down to Seward.

In Seattle, he transferred to a larger plane, a DC-6, which was more luxurious and much quieter, with less vibration than the DC-3.

Walter's attention turned to the window as they flew over British Columbia. It was, even from the air, wild and rugged-looking country, and Beaumont wondered if Alaska was similar. He awoke after several hours sleeping, to look down upon a view of drastically rough country, full of black craggy mountains, snow capped and ominous looking.

He watched as the land changed to lake-dotted, open terrain. Though the reality of the country was concealed at high altitude, it looked smooth as a table top in places. The young traveler was mesmerized, and the stewardess had to tap him on the shoulder at dinner time, after asking if he wanted the offered meal.

The Anchorage airport wasn't much to look at as he stepped from the airliner, appearing pretty much as any other airport. Walter, standing at the top of the stairs from the plane, got the oddest feeling he had been there before. He held there, looking around, until the passenger behind him grumbled. Weejer walked quickly down, and out through the lobby. He wasn't bothered when there was no one to greet him, because it was expected, and he was glad to be on his own.

Beaumont started walking down the road from the airport, pack on his back, and soft-cased rifle in hand. He had hiked about two miles, when an old Studebaker pickup truck pulled over in front of him. As he walked up to the passenger side window, he observed a couple inside. The middle-aged man driving was a large fellow with a huge bushy beard, while the woman sitting next to him was petite, with her hair in one long braid. They both wore floppy brimmed hats. The woman smiled at Walter, said "Hi," and asked him where he was headed. He told them where he was going and why. The couple thought it was wonderful he was in Alaska to visit his uncle.

The man said, "You're a lucky young fellow. If you haven't got a place to stay, why don't you come spend the evening with us, and I'll take you to the Seward Highway in the morning to start you on your way. We've got plenty of room and there's a moose stew simmering in the Dutch oven right now."

Though he wasn't feeling like keeping company, when the man mentioned moose stew he nodded his head, and tossed his pack into the back of the truck. A large, furry, black and white dog jumped up and started barking at him, obviously annoyed to be thumped with the pack. He stood by the side of the truck quietly looking at the dog, who stopped barking and extended his muzzle towards Walter, who held out his hand for the dog to sniff, after which it smiled a wide dog smile. He placed his cased rifle gently into the bed and climbed in. The dog sat down next to him, leaning against the teenage traveler. They drove to the couple's home, talking and laughing with each other, the woman looking at Walter once in a while, smiling.

Leonard and Lizzie Patterson's home, at the south end of Anchorage, was hidden in a stand of spruce trees. It was a large log cabin, built by Leonard's grandfather, Eli, who had come north during the latter part of the Gold Rush and made a decent strike. He had built the cabin after selling his claim, and opened a small dry goods store, carrying all the basic supplies people coming to look for gold needed.

He'd married an Athabascan Indian woman and had six children with her, the eldest being Leonard's father, Joshua, who had always lived in the same cabin, as had Leonard. Leonard's father had made a living by trapping. His trap line had been deep in the Chugach mountains, where Joshua had several line shacks along his sixty miles of trapping territory. The area he chose was rich in fur-bearing animals: fisher, marten, wolf, and lynx.

He was killed in a territorial dispute, bushwhacked by the man who had intruded into his trapping territory, a man named Higgins. They had sabotaged each other's trap sets a number of times, and Higgins decided there wasn't enough room for the both of them, which was ridiculous, considering how vast and full of game Alaska was. He had shot Joshua as Leonard's father snowshoed up the trail, and then disappeared, never found and arrested for his cold-blooded crime. It was a senseless act, as he had to take flight from the area and never trapped there after all. Leonard's mom was badly affected by her husband's murder, and she took to drinking, leaving Leonard and his two sisters to take care of themselves. Leonard had started trapping, to follow in his father's footsteps. After marrying Lizzie, he began a trucking business that he still operated between Anchorage and Fairbanks, and down to Homer at the end of the Kenai Peninsula.

Leonard carried Walter's pack into the cabin, and Lizzie stoked up the fire. There was a big, cast iron, lidded pot on top of the woodstove full of wonderful smelling stew. Walter's mouth watered.

Lizzie also prepared something called bannock, which seemed like cornbread to him, except it had extra flavor and was richer tasting. Lizzie mentioned it was made in a skillet with bacon grease. For dessert, there was homemade blueberry pie. They sat at the table, eating the simple, yet delicious meal, cheerfully talking about their lives, and Walter's coming summer with his uncle.

Leonard was a skookum man, having spent all his years in the woods and on the tundra country of Alaska. He imparted some basic advice to Walter regarding the ways to do well in the wilds.

"I'm sure your uncle will have plenty to tell you too. I hope you don't mind me offering some advice."

He was more than pleased to listen to Leonard, and to Lizzie as well.

In the evening, after the wonderful meal, the three continued talking. Weejer mostly listened, as Leonard regaled him with stories of the old days, when his grandfather was searching for the yellow metal. He was totally immersed in what he was hearing, his imagination creating wonderful pictures in his mind as Leonard went on. To his surprise and delight, Lizzie stood, assumed a serious pose, and recited a Robert Service poem, *The Cremation of Sam Magee*. In later years Beaumont would read all of Service's works, along with Jack London and several others, and would, infrequently, recite them to interested ears.

Of course, there were a few bear stories, as in most recountings of Alaska. The tale he found most memorable was one in which Leonard's grandfather had risen one summer morning and gone to the outhouse, wearing only his long johns and boots. The outhouse was built behind his log cabin, the doorway facing out near the edge of a short slope. It was placed there because Eli Patterson enjoyed the view from the doorless privy, a vast forest with magnificent snow-capped mountains in the distance.

As he sat there answering the call of nature, he was startled by a cold, wet touch on his rump. There was a broken board in the back of the privy, that exposed the nether region of whoever was using it, and Eli had never bothered to replace it.

A large grizzly bear had come walking up to the back of the privy and stuck its cold nose into the hole in the back, poking Eli Patterson's backside. Half awake, the startled man let out a yell as he jumped up from the seat. He flew through the open doorway, tripped on his pants wrapped around his ankles, and rolled about fifteen feet down the little slope. He got up cussing and grumbling until he saw the old grizzly standing next to the privy, looking at him, at which point the man's attitude changed. He backed away and up towards the cabin, holding up his pants with one hand, relieved when he got inside and shut the door. Peeping out the window, he saw the bruin slowly walking away. From then on, when he went to the outhouse, he took his rifle with him.

"When Grandpa Patterson told the story," Leonard said, "he always ended it by saying, 'I swear I could hear that old grizz laughing to himself, pleased at his little joke on me, but I found no humor in it!'"

Before turning in, he walked around the property with Leonard and the dog called Runt, the one who had ridden in the truck with him. Leonard fed eight dogs, chained to their kennels behind the cabin. They howled, yipped, and barked as the two men walked up to them.

"These dogs are descended from the malamutes my grandfather used in the old days, though there are other breeds mixed in now. I run them in front of a sled for fun, and to keep them healthy. I guess you could call them furry family heirlooms."

"Why do you call this one Runt, Mr. Patterson? He must weigh a hundred pounds."

"As a little pup, he was always at the tail end of the food line when his mother was nursing. He wasn't growing much, so Lizzie and I started hand feeding him, making sure he got enough. The name Runt kind of stuck, even though he'd obviously made up for his early lack of size." Leonard chuckled, "He's not partial to strangers, but seems to have taken to you."

Walter left the next morning, eager to get down to Seward and his uncle. He regretted saying good-by to the Pattersons, never having met anyone quite like them, so open and helpful to a complete stranger. He hoped to meet more like them, but would come to realize Alaska had many different kinds of people living in her vast expanses, not all of them like the Pattersons.

Leonard drove him down to the Seward Highway, shook his hand after giving him a bag of food Lizzie had prepared, and wished him well.

"Remember what I said, Walter, while this country is neither a good nor bad place, it is wild and unforgiving of mistakes. One wrong move could be the end, young man. You trust your heart and mind to see you through. If you handle yourself well, Alaska will provide whatever you need. Good luck, and God Bless."

Leonard drove off, leaving Walter alone on the edge of the road. He had never hitchhiked, and knew Seward was a long way from Anchorage. Beaumont would have to depend on the help of others. Luckily, only three vehicles had passed by when a woman in a black Buick Roadmaster pulled over. He walked up to the passenger side, and looked in. A pungent smell of strong perfume assailed his nose. The woman was in her fifties, with bleached-blonde hair, and lots of make-up, wearing a loud, flowered dress.

"Where you headed, Honey?"

"I'm uh, going down to Seward to see my uncle, ma'am."

"Ma'am! Well, aren't you the polite young fella! Hop in, I can take you as far as the cut-off to the Sterling Highway. Heading down to Kenai myself."

Walter hesitated for a moment, not knowing what to make of this brassy woman.

"Oh, come on, I won't bite. It's good to have some company while making the drive. Get in."

Walter got in the big sedan, and the woman hit the gas, sending the car rumbling down the road. From the moment they started driving to the point where she dropped him off, Gloria never stopped talking. Walter didn't mind. He wouldn't know what he would say to her if given the chance. She wasn't like anyone he'd ever met before, and he was beginning to realize Alaska was full of surprises and new experiences, including its inhabitants. It didn't worry him, though. Quite the contrary. He looked forward to every new thing or person that came his way.

He found it interesting to listen to Gloria. Her folks had come up in 1920, when she was fifteen years old. They had opened a small bar in Anchorage, which had been their business when they had lived in Pennsylvania. Though they weren't particularly adventurous people, on hearing there was good money to be made, they had packed up and headed north on a freighter from the West Coast after traveling across country by train.

It turned out the rumors of good money were true, and they were successful from the start, running the Gold Pan Saloon for many years. Gloria had spent eight years in Anchorage before moving up to Nome, "For a change of pace," as she put it.

She had met a man, a trapper, and sparks flew immediately. She moved to the Kenai Peninsula with him, and they'd been together ever since.

"We never did get married or have any kids, but we've seen each other through good times and lean. We've weathered blizzards, floods, and troublesome bears. Now, we live in Anchorage, and I work in a small bar there, knowing the business as well as I do."

Gloria slipped a hand into her purse and pulled out a wallet. It was packed thick with currency. She saw Walter looking, and said, "I don't believe in banks, see, but nobody ever gives me any trouble." She dug deeper into her big purse and pulled out a small-framed, snub-nose revolver.

"I only had to pull it out once, never had to use it, though I would have if necessary." She took a photograph of her husband from the wallet to show him, somehow staying solid on the road through all her activity. The man was a stocky fellow, sporting a full beard, wearing buckskins and holding a strange looking fur hat with big ear flaps. The man's face caught Weejer's attention, tough, rugged, and fearless looking.

"Bob has been through it all. He survived two bear charges, killing them both, a rough fall down a mountain slope, and a terrible case of pneumonia. He's still kicking, thank the Lord, and everything still works!" Gloria let out a full-sized laugh, though Walter wasn't sure why it was funny.

At one point, Gloria talked about Alaska having become a state, and the pros and cons of the change. He got the distinct feeling she preferred it being a territory, a freer place with less government intervention.

Still listening, he smiled a little, finding himself liking this brassy woman.

"Wake up, young man, here's where you get off."

Walter had dozed off at some point. He wondered what he'd missed, figuring Gloria had probably kept talking while he slept. She bid him good-bye, slipping a couple of twenties in his hand, "Just in case," and roared off down the road, waving at him as she left.

The young cheechako, pack and rifle on the ground next to him, watched the car head out of sight. He looked around in awe. There was nothing in Kansas to match what surrounded him now. He was in a vast mountain range, the road to Seward before him. Everything was green and thick. Walter looked around him, taking it all in. Slinging the pack onto his back and taking the gun case in hand, he began walking.

He had been hoofing it for a couple of hours when a truck came by. He stuck out his thumb, but the flatbed was already past him before he got his arm up. He kept on walking, the pack wearing on his shoulders.

The heavily forested mountains seemed to go on forever, and he was delighted to be in a vast wilderness, blacktop road or not. He couldn't wait to go wandering in it with his uncle.

By now his feet were getting pretty sore. He thought he'd been smart, buying a pair of surplus army boots before leaving home. What he didn't realize was they were in new condition, and needed breaking in before being used for a long hike.

Walter walked past a noisy creek running across under the road, and decided to cool off his aching feet. He slipped down the little slope to the stream, took off his pack, boots and socks, rolled up his pant legs, and stuck his feet in the water. He was shocked at how icy cold it was, but it still felt good on his feet. He could only handle a few minutes of the chilling water, but it was enough.

Walter dried his feet with a handful of grass, put his socks and boots back on, and got up to leave. That's when he saw a huge, brown, furry head sticking out of the dense bushes to his left. There was no doubt in his mind it was a grizzly, a big one.

He couldn't read the look on the bear's face as it pushed easily through the brush and walked towards him, groaning and moving its head side to side.

He was going to run, but something stopped him. He remained where he was, and said in a firm tone, "There's nothing here for you; you go on now."

The bear stopped, hearing his voice. It got an uncertain look on its huge face, growled, and started moving ahead again, now only fifty feet away.

Walter said, louder, "You go on now, leave! Go on!"

The bear looked uncertain, and stopped moving towards Walter again, very close now. He could see the bear was confused. Quietly, he spoke one more time.

"There's no trouble here, bear, you go on your way, go on, it's all right now."

Standing still, the bear turned reluctantly and walked back into the bushes. Walter let out a big sigh of relief. He figured he could not have gotten his rifle out of the case in time. Besides, he hadn't put any cartridges in it. He was feeling pretty dumb for not having taken it out and loaded it when he began walking.

In his own defense, Weejer figured he had never been in a situation where a precaution like this was necessary. He vowed he would never get caught unprepared again.

Taking the rifle out, he reached into an outer pocket of his pack, removed five .30-06 cartridges from their cardboard box labeled "REMINGTON-UMC .30-06 180 grain," and loaded the gun. Walter climbed back up to the road and continued walking. Unknowingly, he had passed his first test for surviving in the bush, instinctively talking the bear away. Some might not have handled it the same, maybe becoming lunch for the grizzly, or at least getting mauled.

As Walter continued on down the road, he became more observant, watching the brush as he went. Any casual attitude in him had followed the grizzly into the bushes.

He had to fight his natural urge to explore, to walk off the blacktop into the forest on either side. It was as much a natural part of him as breathing, wanting to take off into the unknown. He disregarded his impulses, needing to get down to Seward and his waiting uncle. Besides, he wasn't equipped to wander off into some new, probably hazardous situation. The huge bear had instantly changed his perceptions of Alaska which, until then, were all from books and photos. No, he'd have plenty of time over the summer to see it in person.

Beaumont's feet were beginning to hurt again, when he heard the sound of a vehicle coming up behind him. He quickly stuck his thumb out and was heartened to see a Ford Econoline van pull over. Walking up to it, he saw another bearded, middle-aged fellow behind the wheel, with a huge mop of shaggy brown hair. The guy wore brown canvas pants tucked into tall, brown, rubber boots, and sported a thick old wool sweater, stained, with several holes in it. He told the man where he was going.

As soon as Walter got into the van, he was assailed by the ripe smell of fish. It seemed to mostly come from the driver. As they started to move, the driver glanced at the hitch-hiker's boots.

"You're lucky I didn't feel like hanging around Anchorage tonight. You might have done a lot more walking before you were through. Those combat boots look new. I'll bet your feet are sore."

Walter nodded his head. "Yeah, I think I have a blister or two."

"You ought to try breaking in a new set on the front lines in cold weather. They take some getting used to. Eventually, you don't even notice them. Best to wear a thick pair of socks with 'em though. Name's Tom. Tom Connelly."

"I'm Walter Beaumont."

"So, what you gonna do in Seward, Walter, lookin' for work?"

"No sir, I came up to spend the summer with my Uncle Aubrey."

"Wait, Aubrey Biggs?"

"Yes sir, do you know him?"

"I sure do, Walter. Your uncle is one hell of a skookum guy."

"Skookum?"

Tom let out a laugh. "You are new here, aren't you. Skookum means a smart, ready-for-anything person. You have to be prepared up here, Beaumont, and your uncle fills the bill. Your uncle fished with me a few years back, after panning for gold didn't work for him anymore, though it did buy him an old 36-foot boat. Biggs decided he didn't like commercial fishing, and he turned to hauling freight. I still see him from time to time when I'm on shore and he comes into Seward for supplies to deliver down the coast. Your uncle was a real hero in World War Two. He saw a lot of action, including D-day and the Battle of the Bulge, but you probably know that already."

"Actually, I don't know him well. He's my mom's brother, and invited me up for the summer when he came to visit."

Tom let out a loud, single "HA! Well, I'm sure you'll know all about him by the time the summer is over."

Tom and Walter conversed pleasantly, and the run down to Seward didn't seem to take long at all, helped along by the comfortable conversation, though it was actually late afternoon when they got there. Tom dropped him off on Fourth Avenue, and wished him well before cruising off to his destination. Walter unloaded his rifle, being in town, and slipped it back into its case. His stomach was talking loudly to him, and he started looking for a place to eat.

Since he'd come to Alaska, nothing was like what he knew back home, the people, the buildings, and definitely not the country. Seward seemed a snug little town, with lots of older-looking buildings. It felt like he'd arrived in a different country. The people he saw were all coming and going with purpose. He'd soon learn summer was the time when many here made a living, doing whatever they could in the winter to get by until summer opened up for them again.

He had crossed over to the next street, when he was attracted to the wonderful smells of seafood cooking. They came from a clean, brightly lit little place. He was soon chowing down on a big bowlful of local seafood, along with some delicious, fresh, sour-tasting bread slathered with sweet butter. Walter couldn't think of when he'd had such a good meal.

Chapter 4

Aubrey's World

He was sitting still, feeling full, and having no desire to move, when he felt a heavy hand on his shoulder.

"Thought I might find you here, Weejer, after a long trip like you've been on. Enjoy your meal?"

Beaumont turned to see Uncle Aubrey standing there, a smile on his face. He immediately recognized him, though he wasn't as neat and clean as he had been when he'd arrived in Kansas.

"Uncle Aubrey, hello! Yes, I loved it. Never had seafood before. The crab was delicious. I hope I didn't keep you waiting long."

"No, I got in last night. I have to pick up a load of supplies in the morning, food and gear for several of my regulars. We'll be busy tomorrow, help you work off the meal. Hey, Gracie, could I get a cup of coffee?"

"Why, Aubrey Biggs, did somebody say you couldn't? Coming right up. Who's the young man?"

"He's my nephew, Walter, come up to spend the summer with me."

"Well then welcome, Walter. I hope your uncle doesn't wear you out, or let a bear have you for dinner, ha ha!"

Walter wondered if all the people in Alaska laughed as loudly and freely as those he'd already met. He thought it was a sign of their good natures.

"I got a ride with a friend of yours, Tom Connelly."

"A good man, Tom, how is he?"

"Well, he smells like fish, if you don't mind me saying so."

Aubrey laughed, "And has, for a lot of years. He's a hard-working fisherman, and that's the smell of success here." Walter and his uncle sat and talked, while Aubrey downed several cups of hot coffee. Walter watched him gulp the hot liquid without hesitation, and figured he must be a tough man.

His uncle was beardless, though three or four days of stubble showed on his face, adding to the rugged nature of the man's looks. For a young person, Walter had good instincts, and he sensed his uncle was a unique man.

They drove in the same old army ambulance Aubrey had driven to Kansas, to a warehouse near the harbor to pay for the supplies Aubrey would deliver during their run beyond Resurrection Bay, south along the coast, and ultimately to his uncle's cabin. He had no idea where his uncle lived, or what his place looked like, but was eager to find out.

He listened while his uncle dickered with the man who was selling the goods he wanted. Aubrey was no easy mark, knowing what things were worth and exactly what he ought to pay for them. The two men talked, complained, yelled, and finally came to an agreement. He sensed a lot of what he heard was for show, perhaps to make what could have been a mundane transaction more entertaining for them, and perhaps himself as well.

The supplies would be delivered the next morning to Aubrey's boat. After money changed hands, they walked down to the dock where the "Mother Lode" was moored.

Beaumont gave the boat a visual inspection. He knew it was 36-feet long, and it seemed pretty wide for its length. The bow of the boat flared out at the top, probably to keep waves from breaking over it. There was a small wheelhouse close behind the bow, running almost the full width of the boat, with a flat deck from there back to the stern, clean of any equipment except for a small loading hoist on the starboard side of the deck, and a metal rail running along the top edges of the gunnels on both sides from the stern to just behind the wheelhouse.

There were four cleated six-by-six beams running across the open deck. He learned they were there to keep loads of lumber and other longer items just above the deck to make it easy to hoist them off the boat.

The *Mother Lode* was painted a bright white. Along the midline of the hull was a sky blue stripe tapering down gracefully towards the stern. The name, *Mother Lode,* was neatly hand-painted in black with gold edging on the transom. *Seward, Alaska* was printed beneath it. All in all, to his inexperienced yet discerning eye, it seemed a sturdy, capable boat.

They walked around the harbor after putting Walter's gear in the forward cabin. Later, they headed up to the same restaurant where he had eaten earlier. Beaumont ate another full meal of crab legs, clams, and mussels, as well as several more thick slices of the same tasty sourdough bread and butter. Aubrey smiled to see how enthusiastically his nephew devoured the delicious food, fresh from the Bay.

They called it a night afterwards, Walter giving in to the long, exciting day. Lying on their bunks in the boat's cabin, Walter told Aubrey what had occurred by the little creek when the bear appeared. The uncle was impressed with the way he'd handled the situation, and told him there would definitely be more surprises in store for him before summer was over.

Beaumont fell asleep with the smells of the harbor and the sound of water lapping against the hull of the boat.

When the supplies were delivered early the next morning, Walter jumped right in, helping his uncle get them into the hold. There were two sets of hatch covers in front of and behind the cleated beams, and watching his uncle work showed Beaumont he knew the best way to load everything into the boat, keeping things balanced and level.

As they were loading, someone yelled out: "Doing a little smuggling, are you Aubrey?"

Walter looked up to see a skinny old man walking down the dock towards them. He looked disheveled, dressed in well-worn clothes, looking like they needed a heavy-duty washing. He wore an old sou'wester foul-weather hat. As the man smiled broadly at Aubrey, Weejer was unsettled by the sight of a mouth full of bad teeth, something he'd never seen before. He didn't let on he was taken aback by the sight. The man was clean shaven with neatly trimmed hair, which seemed incongruous to his sorry mouth and dingy clothing.

Aubrey stepped up onto the dock and enthusiastically greeted the old fellow. They talked and laughed for a while, then Aubrey introduced Arnold Tuckerman to Walter. The young man was surprised at the strength of the skinny old man's grip when they shook hands, and Arnold noticed his reaction.

He smiled, and told him, "If a body isn't up for living here, he isn't going to last long, and I've been here for a lot of years!" Then he laughed, and Weejer couldn't help but grin broadly at the fellow's infectious personality.

"Well, Mr. Tuckerman, I guess I'll find out soon enough if I have what it takes."

Arnold stopped laughing and gave Walter a serious look, staring into his eyes. "Oh, I think you'll do, young man. I think you'll do fine."

Turning away, he said, "Aubrey, I got a good haul of clams this time. Would you like a sackful for supper?"

Aubrey said he would, and Arnold handed Walter the dripping burlap bag he'd been holding. "Put it in the seawater cooler below decks. You'll have a fine meal of these steamers. There are a few razors in there too."

When he took the sack of clams, it felt like it weighed eight or ten pounds. He went over to the stern hatch and lifted it, exposing the loaded hold and a lidded, water-filled steel tank in the port corner. Dropping down the short, ladder-like steps, he lowered the sack into it, and went back up on deck. He saw Mr. Tuckerman had left.

"I've known Arnold ever since I came down to Seward, Walter. He's a good man, real solid, despite how he looks. He has someone who goes clamming along the Bay for him, and sometimes drops a crab pot or two. You'll see him again. He likes you. Not always the case with Arnold and strangers. Well, let's get over to the fuel dock and top up, then we're heading out."

Beaumont's gut tightened when his uncle told him they were leaving the harbor soon. Though he'd already had a number of interesting experiences since coming north, he felt his summer was really starting now.

Chapter 5

On the Water

They took on fuel for the *Mother Lode's* diesel engine, then headed out of the harbor and down the length of Resurrection Bay. He loved the throb and sound of the boat's engine as they headed towards the Gulf of Alaska. It sounded as if it could run forever. His uncle had replaced the original, smaller engine with this one. It was more powerful, which meant higher cruising speed and better control in rough seas.

The craft had been built in 1928 for a wealthy gentleman who liked to go fishing along the coast, until the Great Depression had forced him to sell. Aubrey had ultimately found it in dry storage in Seward, looking the worse for wear.

He figured the boat, despite its neglected condition, would be a better way to make a living than mining. Having done some piloting of boats as a young man before the war, he knew this one could be refurbished, and would serve him well.

Aubrey had made a decent strike placer mining, but eventually tired of the harsh life. Seeking gold in the wilderness, with the rough living conditions and many disappointments takes its toll, even for a man of strong constitution, determined enough to seek his fortune in an extreme existence.

He had picked the boat up for a reasonable price, and the deal included letting him work on it where it was blocked up on the edge of the Seward Harbor. It had been a wise decision, and allowed Aubrey to live where and how he wanted, in a remote coastal location he discovered on his first run down the coast.

Redesigning the boat for use running freight had taken a lot of work. He'd gutted the several below-deck cabins for use as a storage hold. Aubrey was doing all of his own work, until Arnold Tuckerman had shown up one day as Aubrey was pondering some hull reinforcements. He looked as raggedy and underweight as the day Walter met him. When he started talking, Arnold proved to be an experienced boat builder.

Tuckerman was a former shipyard worker from New Bedford, Massachusetts, whose health was impaired by a ruptured appendix that almost killed him. Unable to work for an extended period of time, he was let go from his job in the yards. The Depression hit, and he couldn't get work when he was well. Arnold had started drinking. After losing his family and friends through his drunken episodes, Arnold took to the roads of America, wandering, as many others had in those times. He had finally gotten lucky, being offered steady work in Alaska as a rough-framing laborer, making good money for the times. At that point, he had quit drinking.

It was a place of great opportunity, and its grandeur and natural beauty strongly affected Arnold. His need for drink faded away, and eventually he became a finish carpenter. Once he had put some money together, Tuckerman did what he had been planning to do since coming north. Moving down to Seward, at the head of Resurrection Bay, he put up an open-walled shed to build boats, eventually closing it in. His brother in Massachusetts shipped him his tools, stored in New Bedford. Arnold's first boat was a seaworthy twenty-three-foot skiff with a snug little wheelhouse forward, and an inboard, three-cylinder diesel engine for power. It sold quickly. His business didn't take long to become reasonably successful, once the quality of his craft was known.

He'd learned of some rich clam beds along Resurrection Bay, hired a reliable man to work them and also trap crabs, and began selling clams, and Dungeness crabs to restaurants from Seward up to Anchorage. A number of locals began buying from him too. Arnold did well, and when he'd grown older and wasn't building very many boats, clamming served to keep him afloat, while he spent the majority of his time designing small craft, experimenting with hull designs he thought would work well.

When it came to refurbishing the *Mother Lode,* as Aubrey had renamed the boat, Arnold knew what to do, helping Aubrey turn the boat into a reliable hauler. It was Arnold who suggested getting a bigger and better engine. He knew people who could help with the refitting.

Arnold and Aubrey had been like brothers ever since, and they had helped each other through some difficult times, without hesitation.

Once the boat was fully refitted and the engine test-run, he stocked it for several weeks' travel, checked the charts he had purchased, left the harbor, and headed down Resurrection Bay out to the vast Gulf of Alaska. Aubrey pointed the *Mother Lode* south to find customers for his freight-hauling business, and to look for a good place to build a cabin for himself.

Though it would have been much more convenient, Aubrey did not want to live and work in Seward, or any other settled center, never caring for larger populations of people. One of his main reasons for coming to Alaska in the first place had been his desire for solitude.

Once he hit the Gulf, Aubrey had taken a deep breath and smiled to himself, loving the feeling of being alone out there, just himself, his sturdy boat, and the unruly waters of the Gulf.

This was a maiden run for him and the rebuilt *Mother Lode,* but he felt confident in her, knowing every board and fastener in her body. He knew she was sound. For necessities sake, and safety, he had a fourteen-foot skiff with a waterproof cover over it, in short tow behind.

Aubrey was his own man, ever the independent and self-reliant person he had been since childhood. It was what had made him offer to let Walter spend the summer with him, seeing the same traits in the boy.

Aubrey had met all kinds of men during World War Two, had seen some stand tall, scared yet resolute, while others kept down and out of harm's way whenever possible. He felt his nephew was of the first character. He aimed to teach the boy what he could, to help him find himself and put him to the test.

Though he had lived for years in the bush, Aubrey had never seen this kind of country until he first ran the *Mother Lode* down the coast. The islands were beautiful, full of rich forests surrounded by rugged beaches. He saw lots of animals, including moose, bears, and also plentiful numbers of deer, which he hadn't expected. They would provide him with excellent meat in the coming years.

On his first voyage, Aubrey stopped at a number of cabins and one village among the myriad of islands located all over Prince William Sound. There were Natives, as well as white people living all through them. Aubrey had the kind of personality that allowed him to get along with anyone who wasn't bent on trouble, and even a few of those had become more amiable over time, initially not caring for their solitude being disrupted by his unexpected arrival. By the time he'd returned to Seward, he had enough customers to enable him to start his business. All the arrangements had been completed with a handshake. For the people he'd met, it was enough.

He'd spoken to the distributor in Seward who was willing to sell him the foodstuffs and other basic supplies his customers wanted, at a fair resale price. He cautioned Aubrey there would often be times when some goods would not be available, or bad weather might make for long delays. Aubrey had already spoken to his new customers about these possibilities, and they understood. He hadn't left anything out in his planning.

After delivering the first load of supplies to his customers, Aubrey took some time to find a good site for a cabin. He methodically searched the islands of Prince William Sound, looking for a spot that felt right to him. He passed up numerous areas that many would have thought perfect.

On the third day of his travels, Aubrey was cruising along the east side of Hawkins Island, located on the south end of the Sound, when a small, hooked cove caught his eye and he decided to put in there.

Once he slipped past some rocks barely showing in the entrance to the little bay, he was surprised to see, off to starboard, a secondary hook, that seemed like a curved, rocky spit, and formed an inner break to the cove, holding a still, smooth pocket of water about one hundred yards across. He immediately realized it would be a secure, safe place to tie up. The water there was about thirty feet deep, checked by a depth line he dropped in the center, during what he figured was a medium tide.

Aubrey dropped anchor and rowed the skiff over to the far side of the inner cove. Climbing onto the rocks there, looking for somewhere to secure the skiff, Biggs noticed a corroded, old iron ring imbedded in a large boulder, a few feet up from the water's edge. Examining it more closely, he saw there were some letters crudely carved into the face of rock it was driven into. It was a name he couldn't make out well, though he did read the first two letters as "IV," and under it a date, barely discernible, reading "1852." He would look into this at another time, and study the history of the area.

He tied the skiff off, and worked his way up a slope covered with spruce, willows, and alders for about an eighth of a mile, when he walked out into a meadow, perhaps a half-acre in area, and surprisingly level. He sensed it was not a natural opening in the densely forested area, and the iron ring and carved letters might somehow be connected to it.

He explored the open place and found some traces of manmade timbers, rotten in the ground, in all likelihood hewn from the trees abounding there. There were young trees growing here and there in the clearing, but other than low bushes and grasses, it was quite open.

Seeing no other evidence of human activity, Aubrey still got gooseflesh all over, as he suddenly felt he had been guided to this ideal place for his home. Though he had found it after exploring for several days, if he hadn't stopped to visit potential customers along the way, he could have reached the little cove in one long day's cruise from Seward.

He did find several large piles of bear droppings, and he knew from past experience they weren't from black bears. Even so, he was comfortable about it being a good building site. He had dealt with bears many times in the past, and he wasn't overly concerned.

He heard a low rushing sound, and walking to the south end of the meadow, he found a small waterfall coming out of a rocky outcropping, supplying a steady flow of water. Though not an overly religious man, Aubrey smiled, looked skyward and said, "I sure appreciate the help."

Aubrey went back down to the cove, and rowed out to the *Mother Lode* for the night. He caught a rockfish, and had a fine dinner, humming to himself as he cooked. Sitting on deck afterwards, he sipped the one shot of whiskey he allowed himself of an evening, and smoked one of his favored Dutch Masters cigars. Before he went below to sleep, he looked up at the top of a hill behind the cove and could just make out a big bear standing there, looking down. He figured it had caught a whiff of the cooking fish.

"Sorry, Old Ephraim," Aubrey said, "you're on your own tonight."

"I will, uncle Aubrey. Thanks for having me come here. It's wonderful."

Walter went back to quietly watching, as the *Mother Lode* continued running steadily down the Bay, finally reaching the Gulf. The boy from Kansas was awed by the view of unending open water before him. He wasn't unnerved by it, as some might be. To him, it was more of the wonder that was Alaska.

They headed south, and, if anything, the coastline and the many islands, some quite small and others huge, were even more amazing to his quickly filling mind than country he had already observed. He didn't think of it as a wild, rugged place, however. All of it was perfect and pure, just as the little creek behind his family house had been to him, compared to the long-settled, domesticated row of houses.

Uncle Aubrey was talking to him about the scene all around them, imparting what he knew to his nephew. The young man didn't seem to be listening, but he was, all of it registering in his mind for future use. He was taking in all the new sensations, the sights, sounds, and smells, all at once, including the wonderful salt sea air, so alien to the Midwestern boy.

Already he was growing, his world expanding at an incredible rate. All of it, he sensed, was of value to his future. The feeling he'd had at the airport, of having been there before, grew even stronger, and Walter understood he was supposed to be running down the coast with his uncle, exploring and connecting to this land of heavy forest and rocky coast. This was where he was meant to be.

As would happen over and over again in his life, Beaumont didn't analyze what was happening, he accepted it in a natural way, no complicated thinking necessary, only intense observation. He had a quick thought, summing it all up for him. "I'm home."

Aubrey, watching his nephew's face, could see how this was affecting him, and he nodded to himself, his initial impressions of the boy verified.

The first place they put in to deliver some of their freight was Chenega Island, with its community of Aleut people. Aubrey was greeted by one of the elders who was smiling, openly glad to see him. Aubrey introduced Walter to the people standing around, who were pleased their supplies had arrived.

The older man standing next to Aubrey asked Walter where he lived. When he told him Kansas, the stocky fellow laughed, saying, "You probably won't want to go back, I can tell by the look in your eyes, young man. I seen it before. Ask your uncle, he'll tell you the same."

Walter smiled at the man's perception of him. He had been wondering what it would be like to live in this place full time. A young woman came walking up to them. She was not much more than five feet tall, but the way she carried herself made her seem taller. She had long, shiny, raven black hair and large, dark eyes. Her skin was the color of chestnuts. She had a serious look on her face. The girl said something to the man next to her, in a language totally unknown to Walter. The man laughed, responding in the same tongue. Her voice was surprisingly deep and firm for a petite, pretty girl. Aubrey asked the elder what she had said.

"Miriam wants to know where you found this skinny boy with the funny boots."

"This is my nephew, Walter Beaumont. He's going to be staying with me this summer, helping me with the cargo."

Miriam said, in English, "Maybe you could teach him it's not polite to stare."

Walter was caught admiring Miriam. He didn't react to her remark by looking away, but he did blink. Miriam said something else in their language to Mr. Rutoff, the village elder, before walking away. As she left, she turned and gave Walter a quick little glance, then picked up her pace.

Mr. Rutoff, who turned out to be her grandfather, laughed. Walter gave him a questioning look, wondering what she had said. Mr. Rutoff laughed again, seeing the look on Walter's face.

"Well, you may be in trouble, Walter Beaumont. My granddaughter, Miriam, said if you survive the whole summer with your uncle, she'll cook you a good meal, but she doesn't think you'll be around to eat it. This isn't a challenge she would offer easily."

Walter nodded, and slowly walked over to where Miriam was standing, talking to several other young women. She turned to look at him, a little surprised he had come over to her.

"I thought you should know I like crab, clams, and mussels."

After searching his serious, unsmiling face, she said, "Ok."

He nodded once and walked back to where his uncle was standing, smiling, and shaking his head.

Aubrey said, "Let's get done unloading, we have a couple more stops today. You can do some visiting another time." He looked at Mr. Rutoff, and noticed he wasn't smiling. Walter nodded, walked onto the boat, and got down into the hold, waiting for Aubrey to work the little hoist to bring freight onto the deck.

It wasn't long before they were cruising south to their next stop, beyond the south side of Montague Island, on a smaller, nearby island.

"Listen, Weejer, when we get to this next place, we're going to have to pack in about a half mile to an old fella's place. He's been there a long time. He used to have a fox farm there, raising them for the pelts, quite some time ago. Now, he lives there in isolation. He's gone a little bushy, meaning he's a little off in his head, from living alone too long. There are several people in Seward who help him out, take care of him with things he needs and can't afford. When we get there, set the dry goods in the little shed next to the cabin. If he comes out, which I doubt, don't say anything, just slowly walk away, got it?"

"Sure, Uncle Aubrey. Is he dangerous?"

"No, but I respect his situation and don't want to upset him."

When they got to Wooded Island and dropped anchor, they loaded some bags of flour, coffee, and beans, as well as a big piece of salt pork wrapped in oil paper, into two packs, then set out in the skiff. Aubrey had instructed Walter to load his .30-06 and bring it along. He himself had a Winchester bolt action rifle in 300 H&H caliber that he would carry.

The trail to the old man's place had heavy woods on both sides, all the way to the remote cabin. Walter was distracted by the sights and smells as they hiked. He saw lots of bear sign, tracks, and scat, all along the trail, and had no problem staying alert.

He and Aubrey talked about Alaska as they hiked. Walter noticed his uncle didn't try to be silent as he walked, and realized he was making sure they didn't sneak up on any bears in the neighborhood. He took to talking louder, until Aubrey told him he didn't have to yell.

"They can hear you just fine if you talk in a normal tone of voice."

Suddenly, there was a loud crashing off to their right. They both stopped, rifles at the ready just in case. Nothing bad occurred, and a minute later, they heard a loud roar at some distance. Walter sensed the power and raw energy behind the sound.

"Let's go, he's just letting us know he's aware of us and isn't happy about the intrusion."

Ten minutes later, they arrived at a little log cabin in a clearing. There was a small lean-to built onto the side of it, and an outhouse on the other side about fifteen yards from the cabin. Walter noticed the privy was leaning a little to one side.

There was a big, random pile of firewood next to a well-worn splitting stump in the front yard. A double-bit axe was lying on the ground next to it. Aubrey noticed fresh rust was growing on the blade.

Lots of small pieces of wood were scattered about, collateral damage from the splitting process. A maul was leaning against the front wall of the cabin, along with several iron wedges.

The roof of the cabin looked like the ones Weejer had seen in photographs of old homesteads, with grass and other plants growing from the sod covering it. All in all, the place looked like a real wilderness home, to his mind.

Aubrey was standing in front of the cabin. Anyone inside could see him through the single-pane window, with what looked like burlap curtains covering it. Aubrey saw one corner of the curtain move a little.

"Walter, he may come out. Don't say anything and be relaxed, okay?"

Walter nodded and stood still, wondering what kind of person the old man in the cabin was going to turn out to be.

When the door slowly opened, what Beaumont saw shocked him to the core. An elderly man, perhaps in his eighties, appeared in the doorway. The condition of his hair and clothing was shocking in itself, filthy and ripped. One of the legs of his old overalls was torn or cut wide open, and both sleeves of the flannel shirt he wore were missing. One suspender strap hung down. His right leg immediately drew their attention.

It was wrapped from a little below the knee to the foot, which was bare, in a heavily blood-stained rag. He looked at Aubrey with half-alive, red-rimmed eyes. In a thin, barely audible voice, he said, "Axe slipped." Then he collapsed on the ground.

Aubrey shrugged out of his pack, took two long strides, and reached the pitiful being lying on the ground. He found a pulse, then removed the miserable rag from the leg. There was an awful wound across it, with crude stitches holding it together. The flesh was swollen and discolored, and the smell from it was putrid, Aubrey knew this was serious. After going inside and tearing a strip from cotton sacking, he re-wrapped the putrescent limb and told his nephew, "We've got to get him to the boat, now!"

Walter dropped his pack, they lifted the unconscious man by his legs and shoulders, and started down the trail. The rough half-mile carrying the injured man was the worst distance Walter had ever covered. They had no time to worry about bears.

Beaumont's arms were burning by the time they got to the shore and gently laid the old man in the skiff and rowed him out to the *Mother Lode*.

Aubrey went to the boat's cabin and brought up several blankets and a pillow. They made him as comfortable as possible on deck. Aubrey checked, and there was still a pulse, though weak and uneven. He told Walter to stay with him, then they headed out and around Montague and back towards Chenega Island.

Walter kept watch over the poor fellow, hoping he'd be all right. At one point, the homesteader grasped Walter's wrist, though there was not much strength in the grip. He mouthed the word "Thanks," then fell silent again.

Aubrey got on the radio and called the harbor master in Seward telling him the situation. He knew there was a PBY moored in the harbor, and asked for it to be flown to Chenega to bring the old man to Anchorage for medical care. As he was calling for the flight, Walter came into the wheelhouse. Aubrey saw the look on his face, and even before his nephew told him, he knew the old-timer was gone. He cancelled the emergency call, shut down the engine to idle speed, and went out on deck. The homesteader's body lay there, all life gone out of it.

Aubrey checked for a pulse and breath, sighed, closed the man's eyes, then covered him with the blanket. He put his hands together and asked the Lord to watch over the dead man's soul.

Aubrey told Walter, "We'll stop in Chenega and talk to Mr. Rutoff. I believe he knows more about this man than anyone else does."

Walter nodded. He had never seen a person die, but he wasn't shocked or disturbed, as much as being aware of the somber moment. He stood by quietly as Aubrey tended the fellow, tucking the blanket around him. Then they headed to Chenega, at a steady, moderate speed.

Aubrey was right, Mr. Rutoff knew the old fellow well. He had, in fact, known him all the time he had been living on Chenega Island.

"Mr. Raney had been living on the island for as long as I can remember," Rutoff said. "He'd started a fox farm there in the late twenties. When the Depression came along, it was no longer worthwhile. After the farm failed, and he'd set the foxes free, Mr. Raney moved to Seward. He did any work he could find in Seward and even further north. For some unknown reason, in the early forties, he settled back on the island permanently, living off the land and the sea as best he could. We here on Chenega helped him out when we could, but he was a proud man. We took to leaving different things like tools, clothing, and food in the little lean-to next to his cabin, when he wasn't outside.

"We'll give him a decent burial here on the island and say some prayers over him. The Good Lord will receive him well. We appreciate you bringing him in to us, Aubrey, and you too, Walter."

Walter nodded to Mr. Rutoff, then he noticed Miriam standing nearby, half concealed by the corner of a building. He realized she was watching him. After looking back at her for a long moment, he nodded to her, and she slowly slipped back behind the building, without responding to his slight gesture.

Their somber task done, they bid Rutoff good-bye and left, the strong diesel engine thrumming steadily.

They had to stop at Wooded Island again to retrieve their packs. By the time they got to Mr. Raney's cabin, their packs had been thoroughly gone through, bags of coffee and flour strewn all over the area in front of the cabin, and the oil paper was shredded, the salt pork nowhere to be seen.

"Darned bears." Aubrey said. "Well, at least the packs will be lighter to carry. Let's go, Walter."

It was late in the afternoon when they stopped at the third and final location, to deliver a load of freight to a family living on Hinchinbrook Island, on the western end, inland from a long, curved bay.

When they anchored and rowed the skiff to the shore, Aubrey fired several rounds from the 45 Colt revolver he normally carried on his hip when island hopping. In a few minutes, a man, woman, and three children came out of the woods, along with two of the biggest dogs Walter had ever seen.

A pair of English Mastiffs came bounding over, barking loudly. Walter loved dogs and had a way with them, as he did with other animals. These two brutes were no exception. Walter went down on one knee, both hands out, palms up. The dogs sniffed his hands enthusiastically, then sat in front of him, tongues out, drooling from under their large jowls.

The man who came out of the trees with his family laughed, "They usually aren't friendly right away, eh, Aubrey?"

"Nope. They had me pinned against the skiff the first time I came here, and Seth managed to save me from these two. They're actually good dogs."

"Yup. They've twice run off big bears who got a little too curious."

Aubrey introduced Walter to the little family.

"Pleased to meet you, Walter. This is my wife Ellie, and our children, Christian, Cordell, and Rebecca."

"I prefer Becka," said the little girl standing in front of her mom, hands firmly on her hips, "if you don't mind."

Walter smiled, and nodded at her.

Seth and his family had been living on Hinchinbrook for three years. They invited the two men to come have supper with them, but Aubrey graciously declined.

"I'll have to take a rain check, Seth. Things went a little long today and we're running late. I'd like to make it home soon. Maybe next time, when I come for your new supply list, say in two weeks?"

"Two weeks will be good, Aubrey. We've learned to make things last, and harvest what we can from the island. We'll see you then."

As they rowed back to the boat and got aboard, Aubrey said, "Come on, let's get going. After everything today, I'm ready for home."

"I can't wait to see your place. Let's head out."

Once the skiff's painter was secured to a stern cleat, Aubrey cranked up the *Mother Lode,* and they headed around Hinchinbrook's western end, then to the inlet south of Hawkins Island and the little cove he had discovered years ago.

It was late by the time they anchored in what Aubrey had named Double Cove, and they stayed overnight on the boat, dining on fresh-caught rock fish, canned green beans, and cups of the powerful hot coffee Weejer's uncle seemed to love.

They sat on deck in folding camp chairs after dinner. Aubrey was having his one shot of whiskey, and a cigar. The night sky was full of Alaska summer light and, though it was well past ten in the evening, it seemed more like afternoon. Except for a barely perceptible breeze, there was no noise beyond the gentle lapping of water against the hull.

Walter was feeling a contentedness he had never felt before. Of course, he was young, and had so much more to experience. At one point, thinking of the vast country he found himself in, he felt small and insignificant, and told his uncle so.

"It means you're a wise young man. You're realizing we are insignificant bits of matter in the Lord's vast universe, but you can pack an awful lot of wonderful experiences in the short time we are allowed to be here."

"Like poor old Mr. Raney, right?"

"I wouldn't feel too bad for Mr. Raney, though I am sorry he had some pain at the end. He was living as he wanted, where he wanted, and for a long time, too. As to why he stayed alone all those years, I can't say. He probably could have gone back home, wherever his original home might have been. I have the feeling he loved it on the island, living in the trees with the deer, bears, and the foxes he set loose, which still inhabit the place."

"I think I would have done the same, if I was him."

"Well, remember, you're only here for the summer. Don't get too wrapped up in this place, at least not yet. When you get a little older, after college and all, you can decide for yourself."

Walter nodded. He already had some ideas in mind, not fitting in with what Aubrey and his parents were expecting. This wild, perfect place had already soaked into his soul, not something easily denied.

Beaumont woke up, startled. He had heard someone calling his name, clearly and close by. It was about four in the morning, and already getting lighter outside, after the few hours of semi-darkness the time of year allowed. He dressed quietly, not wanting to wake his uncle, picked up his .30-06 and slipped out on deck in his stocking feet, boots in hand. He saw no one around and decided the voice was part of a dream.

He had a strong urge to hike up to his uncle's cabin, and couldn't resist it. He looked over to where his uncle had pointed out the path to the cabin. Walter didn't think about or question his decision. He wanted to hike up to the cabin alone.

Putting on his boots and taking rifle in hand, he carefully pulled the skiff up to the stern of the boat, then stepped over and into it. Untying the line, he pushed it gently away from the *Mother Lode* with an oar and started rowing over to the rocks on the edge of the cove. Inside the boat's cabin his uncle smiled to himself, pulled the covers up tighter to block the morning chill, and went back to sleep.

Reaching the shore, Beaumont tied off, slipped a round into the .30-06's chamber, set the safety, and started up the trail. It was misty as the trail wound up the slope towards the cabin. The air had a fragrance to it, from the dense vegetation covered with the morning's dampness. The willows, alders, and grasses, as well as the spruce had their own distinct scents, and the mixture was intoxicating to the young man. His powers of observation had been growing since his first day in Alaska. Everything around him was registering strongly in his mind. Walter again felt he was where he was meant to be.

He was only about fifty yards below his uncle's cabin, and was passing by a large alder thicket. The alders were not large in diameter, and the trunks curved out and up, bending to all sides, creating what looked like a naturally growing maze. Walter thought it would not be easy, working through the tangled growth. He was peering through it, when he began to perceive a large dark shape a ways back. It took a few moments before he could make out what it was, then he wished he hadn't watched long enough to find out.

Weejer realized he was looking at the form of a huge bear, a brownie, as his uncle had called them. Though he had already been introduced to the species on his journey to Seward, he still listened to what his uncle told him.

"The big bears are what make Alaska, Weejer. They are, in a way, the heart and soul of the place, along with everything else unique to this country. They would rather avoid us humans whenever possible, to be left to live their simple lives. If one ever decides it doesn't like you being around, you'll have no doubt of its intentions."

Now, in the tight position he was in, Walter hoped this bear wasn't feeling vengeful. Staying very still, Walter fixed on one part of its huge furred head, and the eye staring directly at him. He avoided staring directly into the eye, looking instead at the edge of the bear's ear, much as one would look at the ear of a cat to prevent any perceptions of threat or aggression.

Walter then did something without thinking, strictly on impulse, though one might consider it an instinctive action. He whistled quietly, directing it towards the great beast. It was a three-note whistle, the first two notes the same, the third a lower tone. He whistled it slowly, over and over. Finally, the bear moved, fading into the dimness beyond the alders.

He let out a breath of relief and waited a few minutes. If, as his uncle had told him, the big bears were Alaska's heart, he'd better get comfortable with them, if such a thing was possible.

Walter felt it best to return to the boat, though he figured he was probably close to the cabin. Walking calmly back down the trail, he rowed back over to the *Mother Lode*, tied off the skiff, and climbed back on board. His uncle greeted him in the wheelhouse with a cup of coffee. "Well, do you like the cabin?"

Weejer told his uncle why he hadn't gotten all the way to the cabin. Aubrey slowly shook his head. "So, you whistled to the bear and it went away, no roaring, no bluff charge, nothing?"

"Yes sir, he disappeared into the brush."

"Well, I'll be. I guess you do have the right instincts. Doesn't mean it would have worked for someone else, though quietly talking to them has been known to have the right effect, as when that first bear confronted you at the creek. Whistling, now, that's a new one on me. Are you hungry? I'll make us some eggs and bacon, then we'll pack some goods up to the place. I hope old Ephraim is gone off somewhere else, but there's always bears around."

It took two trips up the trail to Aubrey's cabin to bring in all the supplies. Walter didn't mind, though the packs were heavy, holding large sacks of flour and beans, and smaller containers of salt, sugar, and coffee.

It was great to be hiking up to the log cabin Aubrey had built for himself along the trail he had cleared. His uncle told him it was an overgrown trail he had first followed, as it seemed to be the right way for him to go. He crossed it a short way up from the cove, and followed it to the meadow where he built the cabin. It had seemed a natural thing to do, as if it had been waiting for him to discover.

After the goods were unloaded, Walter took some time to look around. There were many interesting items hanging on the walls and stashed in the corners. The cabin didn't look as large on the outside as it did inside, because his uncle had arranged things well, building lots of shelves and cabinets on all four walls, except the area right behind the fine old cast-iron wood stove in the right rear corner. It was of the type called a Franklin stove, with cast-in decorations on the doors, which also had narrow windows of mica in them.

Walter was fascinated with the tanned animal furs, and a few old traps displayed on one wall. There was also a totally rusted old lever-action rifle on two wooden pegs driven into the log wall. Aubrey told him he found it near his old gold claim, deep in the Interior.

"I had been told the claim had been worked years before I started mining it. The old gun was under a pile of tailings I was going through, and I have no idea how or why it got there, though obviously it was there a long time. There are still some cartridges in the magazine under the barrel you can see through the corroded holes in it.

"It's a reminder to me of how one simple mistake or unhealthy situation can spell the end of it all. Remember that Weejer, and work on learning to always be alert. Discovering a situation at the last moment usually means you only get a brief glimpse of what might be your undoing. Being truly observant and knowing what you see might keep you intact. I know I've said all this before. You can understand how important I believe it to be."

Walter nodded, seriously absorbing the sobering advice his uncle gave him. He knew Aubrey'd had his share of exciting adventures. His mother, Hannah, had told him to pay attention to everything his Uncle Aubrey told him.

"He promised to keep you safe and sound, and I have complete faith in my brother's word. It's up to you to learn from what he teaches you."

"Come on," Aubrey said, "let's go clean up and we'll have dinner soon. I've got a jar of moose meat, and some fresh potatoes, carrots, and onions. Tonight we'll have moose stew."

He followed his uncle out of the cabin to the little waterfall at the far side of the meadow. Walter was pleasantly surprised at what he saw. There was a small wood-framed shower with canvas-tarp walls.

A moveable wooden funnel was used to divert water into the shower from the little waterfall.

"Okay, nephew, skinny down and step into the shower." Walter did as he was told. Then Aubrey moved the wooden water feed over the shower and a fast stream of cold water engulfed him. Walter let out a yell when the water hit him, making him catch his breath. Aubrey moved the water feed back over and told him to soap up. Then Aubrey rinsed him off with the water feed, until he was clean and covered with gooseflesh, shivering slightly.

"Okay, now it's my turn."

Walter did to his uncle what had been done to him, then they dried off with two big pieces of cotton cloth hanging on a spike by the back wall of the shower. Aubrey hadn't reacted to the cold water at all, and Walter vowed to himself, he would eventually be able to do the same.

After they had dressed, his uncle said, "Come on, I'll race you back to the cabin, it's only about forty yards." He took off like a shot. Walter was surprised when his uncle handily beat him to the cabin door.

The moose stew Aubrey made for dinner was the best stew Walter had ever tasted, even better than the one the Pattersons had fed him. It had savory and unusual flavors, that Aubrey said were from naturally growing, dried herbs he had added.

Sitting out in front of the cabin after dinner, Aubrey asked his nephew if he'd ever drunk any hard liquor. Walter told him he'd had a beer with teammates after the state track meet, and didn't like it.

"Well, it's an acquired taste. I'd like you to have one drink with me tonight, then you can say you've tried it."

Aubrey poured two glasses of his favorite bourbon, and handed Walter one. The uncle made a toast, that went: "Here's to the ships on the sea and the women on the land, may the one be square-rigged and the other well-manned."

They clinked glasses, and both took a drink. The whiskey burned all the way down, but then Beaumont caught the flavor of the liquor, and found it to his liking. He gulped down the rest.

"Interesting taste. Sure is powerful though, isn't it."

"Well, yes it is. If people let it take control of them, it can and has ruined many a life. If you drink it in moderation, like the one drink I have in the evenings, it can simply add a little enjoyment to things."

"I understand. Our neighbor in Manhattan was a drunk, I heard my dad say one time. It sounded like a bad thing, and he was a funny sort of man, always saying things I didn't understand."

"Well, Weejer, and this is only my opinion, I think people give up the abilities and power they are given, often for trivial reasons that don't give anything good back to them. I hope you find a better path to walk on."

Walter digested his words. He understood much of what his uncle had said, and he needed to apply it to his own life. "Since I've tried whiskey now, maybe I could try one of your cigars?"

Aubrey chuckled. "I think you've had enough new experiences for one day. Another time, perhaps."

A bear, some distance away, let out a roar. Walter went on alert, not out of fear, but from his newfound desire to be aware of everything in this new environment. A little shiver of excitement went through him, realizing there must be a lot of bears around. Aubrey saw the look on his nephew's face and smiled, sensing his thoughts. The two men, one experienced and the other just starting to understand the magnitude of things, sat there in silence a while, listening to the wilderness around them. Aubrey sensed this was going to be a satisfying summer for him, too. Walter was, in a number of ways, making up for the son he'd never had.

They called it a day then, leaving the evening to the other creatures living in the forest.

When Walter woke the next morning, his uncle was already up and out of the cabin. After dressing and drinking some water from the bucket by the cooking area counter, he went outside. He walked around to the side of the cabin, and was surprised to see his uncle doing what looked, at first, like a strange dance. After seeing the hunting knife Aubrey had in his hand, Walter watched quietly, observing him going through what he realized must be knife fighting practice.

After several minutes, in which Walter was impressed with what he saw, Aubrey saw him standing there and motioned him over. He turned the knife's hilt towards Walter and offered it to him. Walter took it without hesitation.

"Weejer, there will hopefully never be situations when you'll need to defend yourself, though it's something you can expect as time goes on, since there are bad people in the world. Some of them do others harm for no reason other than they feel compelled to do it, or they may even like it. If you're willing, I'll show you what I've learned about hand-to-hand fighting."

Walter, after giving it a moment's thought, nodded his agreement. For the next hour, his uncle talked to him about the art of self-defense, showing him how to use a knife properly. He found his nephew was a natural, quickly picking up all the instructions he gave him. As for Walter, he'd been carrying a pocket knife since he was nine years old, a gift from his dad, but he'd never considered using one for self-defense. Once he started trying what his uncle was showing him, the knife felt natural in its new role.

It was the first of many sessions in his education on self-defense. His uncle shared with him all he had learned when training in the army, and some fighting techniques he had studied on his own, having plenty of time to read, especially in winter.

Walter's instincts were excellent, and beyond what his uncle told him, they lent a natural aspect to his movements. At the end of the first hour, both of them feeling the effort, Aubrey told his nephew to try and stab him. At first, Walter hesitated, then he made a move towards Aubrey, and found himself flat on his back, his uncle standing over him, the knife in his hand. The fierce look Aubrey assumed made Weejer hesitate before rising, until Aubrey grinned, offering him a hand up.

"You've still got a few things to learn, but we've got plenty of time, long as we get all our other business done first. Let's go cook up some breakfast."

The two spent several weeks at the cabin, and Aubrey took Walter on some hikes to show him the country. As they walked, Aubrey imparted to his nephew all the knowledge he had gained after years living in Alaska, hunting, fishing, trapping, and simply living in remote areas. He pointed out animal sign, tracks and scat, hair stuck to tree bark, and the animals themselves as they momentarily appeared and disappeared.

Aubrey noticed slight changes, as time went on, in the young man he was coming to know. He saw alterations in the way he handled himself in the forest, how he moved and observed the world around him. Aubrey began hatching a plan to make sure Walter achieved a high level of skill in understanding what goes on in the wilds, no matter where he was, or what he was doing. Having been through everything life had thrown at him, Aubrey knew how important what he was teaching Walter would be one day.

Chapter 7

Hunting and Tracking

"Take the wheel for a while, I need to go below." Aubrey had called to Walter who was leaning on the port side railing, watching arctic terns flying above them. He knew how comfortable his nephew had been handling the boat in the past, as he stood behind him keeping an eye on things. He felt it was time for him to go it alone.

Walter jumped at the chance to run the *Mother Lode* by himself for the first time. He knew how big a deal it was, his uncle letting him take over.

"Keep it out some from the island's coast. Lots of rocks to make trouble if you get too close."

They were rounding the north end of Montague Island, after getting the list of needed supplies from Seth and Ellie on Hinchinbrook. Ellie had insisted the two take a loaf of homemade sourdough bread with them. They had been tearing off pieces to chew on as they cruised along, headed to their final stop at Chenega Island, then back to Seward. Though their watery route was long in distance, Walter never noticed. The longer the run took, the better he liked it.

They had made one more stop, new customers on the eastern end of Evans Island. A man and his brother were building a cabin to live in. They wanted a frame cabin, and had contacted the company in Seward who sold Aubrey all his customers' supplies. The distributor passed on the information to Aubrey over the boat radio. They would stop at Evans Island to discuss what was needed.

"Head down Montague Strait, Weejer, then down around the south end of Eleanor Island along the Passage, and Evans Island will be off to port. I'll be up by that time, and we'll go see the Craig brothers. Later, we'll put in at Chenega, maybe even stay there for the night. You good for heading around now? The charts are under the bench to your right, if you need them."

"Yes sir, I'll let you know if anything comes up."

"Okay, I'll be in the cabin for a while."

Walter was alone in the wheelhouse of the *Mother Lode*. He breathed in the salt air, letting it fill his lungs. His mind was crowded with thoughts of what he planned on doing at summer's end. He had been with his uncle for over two months, and had learned a lot from him. He felt he had changed, seeing things differently now after what Aubrey had taught him, and he had spent much time out in the wilds, on the land and water.

Walter's memory went back several weeks to when he had taken his first game animal for food. His uncle had awakened him, and said, "Get dressed, it's time to hunt for meat."

Walter slipped into his clothes, splashed cold water on his face, took his .30-06 from its corner, checked to see the magazine was loaded, then waited for his uncle, who handed him a pack frame with a large cotton bag tied to it. Then he gave him the same knife Walter had been learning to fight with. He slipped the sheath on his belt.

"This blade will serve another important purpose today, if we have any luck."

They went down the trail and out to the boat, started the motor, hoisted the anchor, and ran out of the cove following Hawkins Island's coast, keeping about a quarter mile offshore.

Several times Aubrey shut the motor down, and scanned the coast for animals. After about an hour of running the boat and glassing, Aubrey handed his nephew the binoculars and pointed to a large rock outcropping extending out from a slope and down to the beach.

"Look about twenty-five yards to the right of those rocks, and tell me what you see."

Walter looked intently through the glasses until he saw what Aubrey was talking about, a herd of deer, six or seven, close to the beach, browsing on grasses. He looked at his uncle and nodded.

They ran the boat back around until they were able to anchor about fifty yards offshore, one hundred yards from the rock outcropping, knowing the deer wouldn't see them.

They rowed to the beach, and slowly crept up to the outcropping, stealthily working their way around. Aubrey put his hand up balled in a fist, a sign to stop. Taking his hat off, he slowly moved his head around the rock in front of him. He could see three deer within thirty yards of their position. He waved Walter back. In a hunting whisper, he said, "As soon as we show ourselves at all, those deer will be gone. We're going to climb up this outcropping to get in a good position to take two of these deer without them seeing us. Are you up for it?"

Walter nodded.

Slinging the rifles onto their backs, the two men carefully worked their way up the rocks. It turned out to be fairly easy, and within ten minutes of slow, careful going, they arrived at the top.

No sooner had Walter lifted his head above the top, when he saw something he couldn't believe. He ducked back down and whispered to his uncle below him, "Bear! There's a bear lying up there watching the deer!"

Aubrey thought a minute, then asked, "Is it a black bear or a grizzly?"

Walter took another peek. The bear was definitely black in color and didn't appear to be a grizzly. It was lying at an angle, its head peering over the far edge, below which the deer were grazing. "I'm pretty sure it's a black bear. What should I do?"

"It's good eating. Shoot it, but be careful and place your shot right."

Walter nodded again, and with extreme caution, he slowly slipped his rifle off his shoulder. He had his feet positioned securely on a narrow ledge of rock, and felt comfortable making the shot. His uncle pressed his hand into Walter's lower back for support. Once he had the rifle in position, he slowly worked the action, gently pushing a round into the chamber, trying not to make any sound. He was all set.

Something had spooked the bear. Walter hadn't been making any noise, and he didn't know if the wind had changed directions.

Whatever it was, in a flash, the bear was up and standing on its hind feet, its head moving back and forth, nose working the air for a scent.

In an instant, it locked onto Walter, who pulled the trigger with the open sights centered on a small white patch on the bear's chest. When the gun went off, sending a one-hundred-and-eighty grain bullet right where Walter had aimed it, the bear roared once, turned, and to his amazement, jumped right off the far edge of the rocks.

He turned and told his uncle what had happened.

"Well, we'd better get down there, and see what's what. Be careful when we get to the bottom."

They worked their way back down the fifty-foot outcropping, and walked carefully around it. Though it was a long fall, even for a bear, they didn't know what to expect. As Aubrey figured it would be, the bruin was lying dead, flat on its belly, all four legs spread, snout jammed into the soft earth.

"I think it was dead when it hit the ground."

"You're right, Weejer, and those deer must have had quite a surprise when it came down. They're probably still running!"

This was Walter's first actual hunt, and he had a number of thoughts running around in his head.

Aubrey put his finger into the little pool of blood on the grass by the bear's mouth, and made a red smear on Walter's forehead. "You're officially a hunter now. We've got meat to last a good long time. Now the work begins. Unsheathe the knife, and I'll show you how to dress out a bear."

Walter followed his uncle's instructions once again. It seemed a simple, straightforward process, and though it was a messy task, with smells he'd never experienced before, he took it in stride. Aubrey had talked to him about hunting before, how a hunter looking for meat takes responsibility for the whole process, instead of simply purchasing meat wrapped up in a butcher shop.

"Besides, fresh game meat is a lot healthier for you, being wild, not domestic."

When Walter asked him what he meant, Aubrey told him there was a lot of good energy in game meat. "It will revitalize you after a long day of physical work, and it has richer flavor than domestic meat, too."

The only thing that put him off momentarily was the bear, skinned, lying flat on its back, legs splayed out, looked curiously human. His uncle nodded when Weejer mentioned this, long aware of the fact.

"Everything living out here, including us, is food for someone else. It's nature's way. Come on, let's cut up the bear, then get the meat back to the boat. We'll leave his innards for someone else to eat."

Heading back to the cove, the bear meat in muslin bags on deck, sea birds wheeling above hoping for a few morsels, the two were bonded closer than before, as sharing a hunt can do.

Returning to the cove, they washed down the deck, strapped the bags of meat to the pack racks, and hiked up to the cabin with the heavy loads.

Once there, they got busy canning the meat in quart jars as stew meat, ground meat processed with a small hand grinder, and small steaks tightly packed in the jars. It took hours for the two of them to do the job, but bear meat spoils quickly, and it all had to be processed right away. It took twenty-five jars to do the job, minus a roast they cooked on a spit outside the cabin in a small rock fire pit over an alder wood fire, after it had burned down to hot coals. Aubrey told Walter bear meat had to be thoroughly cooked because of parasites, which made him wonder what it was like to eat. When he took a first, hesitant bite, it was the most delicious meat he'd ever had. He liked the strong flavor of the roast, figuring a bear wouldn't taste like a cow, pig, or even a deer.

Afterwards, the two shared one shot of whiskey and Aubrey had a cigar. Walter tried a few puffs, but found it wasn't to his liking, and he never did take up cigars as a past time.

Now, piloting the *Mother Lode*, happy to be alone in the wheelhouse, Walter poured himself a cup of coffee from the big thermos. Sipping and thinking, he carefully watched the water ahead.

On the last run from Seward, they had narrowly missed a huge floating log lying heavy in the water, barely showing above the surface. Walter had been sitting on the bow in front of the wheelhouse writing a letter to his parents, when he looked up and saw a strange, uneven black line in the water, directly in front of the *Mother Lode*. They were doing about eight knots at the time.

Getting up, he went to the wheelhouse door and said, "There's something in the water ahead of us."

Aubrey saw it as he spoke. In a rare moment of inattention, he hadn't spotted it himself. He yelled, "Oh, Good Lord! Hang on!" Aubrey spun the wheel, forcing the bow hard to starboard, then cut the engine to slough off speed. They were now parallel with the giant log floating there, so close, its great mass rubbed along the port side of the boat, luckily causing only some loss of paint.

Aubrey breathed a sigh of relief, watching as the forty-foot log slid past. Shaking his head, he brought the engine back up to speed.

"Like I've been saying, all it takes is a moment of inattention, and that's all there is to it. Good eye, son."

His uncle had been calling him son a lot lately, but Walter didn't say anything. He didn't mind, and besides, though he loved his father, Aubrey had taught him more about the things he was interested in than his dad ever had.

One skill Aubrey had been teaching him every time they'd had a chance to go hiking was how to read sign, to track wild game, and understand what was going on around him in the forest. He pointed out what to be aware of, disturbed ground, broken branches, twigs, leaves, and fur caught in tree bark. He taught him about listening to the sounds, or lack of them, in the woods. "Sometimes," he said, "silence tells you the most."

The furtiveness Walter had developed as a young boy came to the fore as he stalked through the wilderness. He didn't always do it intentionally. Sometimes it was just instinctive. His nephew's uncanny ability for moving around in total silence was not lost on Aubrey. Several times Walter had gotten the drop on him, for a bit of fun, which his uncle understood. But he told him, in all seriousness, sneaking up on people for fun was not a good idea.

"If you have to deal with someone where extreme stealth is necessary, chances are you are on some kind of mission, and either you complete the mission by taking someone down, or by slipping away to take back important information. You have to treat this ability as a tool, not a toy, understand?"

"You mean like in the army, when you're doing a, uh, what would you call it?"

"Recon, a reconnoiter, out on patrol to study enemy activities. You know, Weejer, a couple of years in the military, honing your skills, and learning new ones, could be a real benefit to you even when not in service. The mental discipline required can be applied to many situations."

"To tell the truth, Uncle Aubrey, I never thought about it. I did sign up for Selective Service right after I turned eighteen. Dad made sure I did."

"Well, it's nothing for you to think about right now, even though it's a worthwhile endeavor. You learn things in the service you can't learn any other way."

Beaumont was silent for a moment, then he asked, "Why did you come up right after the war, if you don't mind my asking?"

His uncle considered the question, and though he rarely spoke of it, he responded, saying, "I was in the service, in the war, for a little over three years, including extensive training, until I was wounded, taking me out of combat. My war was over."

Walter had noticed several scars on his uncle's back looking like ragged sealed-over holes, and decided they must be gunshot wounds. The corresponding holes in his abdomen were much smaller, less noticeable.

"I didn't mind being a soldier, but I saw too much, horrible things, the brutal treatment of people, civilians. I couldn't understand how anyone could be so evil, and it caused me to lose faith in mankind. I helped liberate one concentration camp, and never ask me what I saw. Later on, after I recovered from my wounds and was discharged, I wanted to get as far away from people as I could. I eventually came to see and appreciate the good qualities most people have. But it took a while. I suppose you could say living up here helped heal me."

"So, you didn't buy the old ambulance to remind you of the army."

"Nope, I bought it because it was a cheap buy as surplus, in like-new condition. Tough old rig if you keep it maintained and aren't worried about getting anywhere quickly. I'll let you drive it sometime."

Walter stood silently by his uncle, watching the water in front of them. Finally he broke the silence, curiosity getting the better of him.

"Uncle Aubrey, have you ever been married?"

Biggs stood at the wheel a while, until he decided to answer his nephew.

"No, never did tie the knot."

"How come?"

Aubrey sighed. "I had a girl before I entered the army. We were together through most of high school, and were making plans when we graduated, but the war came along. I had been in about two years when I got the letter from her." He went silent for a moment. "She had found someone else, and we were through. End of story."

"Must have been difficult for you, being far from home and all."

"I figured she wasn't as much in love with me as I was with her. Now, go find something to do, okay?"

One morning, Walter told his uncle he was going to do some exploring to see what he could find. Aubrey thought it was a good idea, and told him to take a few emergency supplies and his rifle, then watched his nephew as he hiked up the slope behind the cabin, and went quickly out of sight. He had no grave concerns, knowing this was a good thing for the boy to do, to gain some first-hand experience by himself. He knew it was, quite often, the only way to fully understand some things.

Walter slipped up to the top of the ridge above the cabin, and started working his way along it, finally dropping down into the thick forest on the far side. He was applying all the training Aubrey had given him, closely observing everything around him, looking for signs to tell him what animals were around and how they were behaving. He drifted like a ghost through the forest.

He had hiked about two miles from the cabin when he spotted a print in a spot of clear ground. It looked similar to a lynx print, but larger. He'd never seen a track like it before, and had to find out what had made it. By the time he had gone another couple of miles following the track, he knew it was not a tall animal, as all the visible evidence of its movement was only about two feet above the ground. He stopped to examine some grass that looked like it had been chewed on, and his curiosity was heightened. What was this creature he was following?

Ahead of him, a fallen birch tree had deep, fresh claw marks on it. The gouges were wide spread but didn't seem like bear claw marks, judging by their size and depth.

He was considering the marks when he started getting a "being watched" feeling. He stayed still, listening to the forest, hearing nothing unusual, though there was something indefinable, an intangible he hadn't felt before.

Walter decided it might not be the best thing to continue his tracking. While the claw marks weren't from a bear, they certainly were from a predator. Not knowing what it was, he headed back towards the cabin.

The woods were dense, with many tall old trees. He saw several toppled cedars, manipulated by natural events, storms and heavy rains, into odd shapes, their roots rising high above ground like buttresses. He realized these formations made for many hiding places, and he could be walking right past this mystery animal and never know it.

As he continued walking, Walter stopped and turned to look at the slope above him. Some internal warning he had never felt before told him to be ready. As he continued watching, he flipped off the safety, and waited.

After several minutes when nothing occurred, he decided to move on. He was only a mile from the cabin. Beaumont figured he and his uncle might go out the next day to track what had made the prints. As he started to turn, he heard something scream. It was a long, drawn out, high-pitched sound, and it unnerved him. He turned in the direction it came from, and stood watching, though he was torn between wanting to see what made the noise and needing to be back in the cabin.

A tawny colored form came streaking out of the trees toward him. He immediately recognized the beast from pictures he'd seen, but there was no time for prolonged observation. It was moving very fast, its movement making it a hard target to lock onto as he raised his rifle. The large cat leapt just as Walter got his sights lined up and fired. It was a close shave, the animal slamming into his shoulder after the shot. Fortunately for Beaumont, the bullet had found its mark, and the animal was dead when it hit the ground. He was spun aside by the impact, and if it were still alive, he would have been hard put to get off another shot.

What lay before him was something he hadn't expected to see in Alaska, a full grown mountain lion, a male. He waited a moment, a fresh round in the chamber, making sure the creature was dead. He studied the cat for a few minutes, before field-dressing it. Walter continued on to the cabin, holding it by its front paws, the cat hanging off his back, its tail dragging on the ground behind him.

His uncle was standing in front of the cabin, waiting, after hearing the shot. He was amazed when he saw what Beaumont was carrying.

After laying the cat on the ground and allowing Aubrey to inspect it, Walter told his uncle all about the episode. Aubrey nodded as he listened. He told Walter he had never seen a mountain lion in Alaska, never heard of one either.

"Things change over time in nature, nephew. Species come and go, or change location. Apparently this cat got the urge to head north, maybe from British Columbia. I know there's a large number of them there. The deer were possibly a draw for it, or maybe it was curious, as all cats can be. We'll likely never know.

"Let's get this critter skinned out and the hide salted down. Congratulations, you did well."

Walter was glad he'd handled it too. He knew what he would do with the skin. He wanted Aubrey to show him how to prepare and tan it properly.

"I'd be happy to, and I'm curious about what this creature tastes like cooked. Fancy a cougar stew?"

"Well, I'm game if you are. Let's give it a try."

Chapter 8

Chenega and Miriam

The core of life for Aubrey and Walter that summer was to continue making regular deliveries of goods for all their customers. On one trip, before going to Chenega, they had made their stop on Evans Island. The Craig brothers had stood up two crossed pieces of drift wood on the beach as a signal, with a piece of red cloth hanging down in the middle. By the time they had anchored and rowed the skiff to shore, the brothers were standing there, having heard the boat approaching.

Walter was interested to see the two men were dressed like some of the old time adventurers he had seen in photographs, with high laced leather boots, wool pants and shirts, and big suspenders. One of them wore a fur hat, and the other had on what Aubrey later told him was a campaign hat, brownish-green with a hard, flat brim, the crown concave on four sides.

He listened and watched as Aubrey spoke with the two. The three men seemed to be cut from the same cloth in some way. They followed the brothers to their camp, a quarter mile inland from the shore. Walter was impressed with the solid way the camp had been set up. The tent was tautly stretched on ropes over a wooden frame of crossed end poles and a ridgepole, with a little sheet-metal cook stove within.

They sat on little stumps outside the tent, drinking coffee, discussing what they would need.

They did indeed want to build a frame cabin, which made Walter wonder, because the island, as were all the other islands, was covered with wonderful trees to build a log structure. Of course, a man had the right to build his home any way he saw fit.

Aubrey wrote down the list of supplies and equipment they wanted, and though he couldn't give them much more than a rough estimate of cost, the Craigs seemed satisfied they could depend on him, and gave him more than enough money to buy what they needed, saying he could bring back any funds left over.

"We have enough food to last us a month, Mr. Biggs, which should be fine until you get here with the goods."

"Well, Mr. Craig, after this, I'm going to Chenega Island to get a list of supplies. Afterwards, we'll go up to Seward to get all needed items. I'll have to go to a wood mill to get you the lumber you'll need to get started with your building, and I should be able to lease a small barge to bring all the wood at one time. Whatever it takes, I'll get your goods here as soon as possible."

Aubrey shook hands with the men, before he and his nephew hiked back to the *Mother Lode*, and were soon on their way to Chenega Island.

As they headed out on the boat, Aubrey said they were probably going to be doing business with the brothers a lot in the future. When Walter asked him why, his uncle responded by saying the two men seemed the ambitious type.

"I think they plan to build something larger there, perhaps some sort of money-making proposition, like a lodge for fishing or hunting. So, this may prove to be lucrative for us until something changes. For now, we'll keep bringing them what they need."

"You said us, but this is your business."

"Walter, do you think I wouldn't pay you for helping me? A man's time is worth something. We'll settle before you head home at the end of August."

Walter didn't respond beyond a small nod, thinking to himself, "Home? This *is* home." The thought stayed with him and grew stronger as the summer rolled by. He knew he was where he should be, and before summer ended, Walter had made a major decision, not part of the original plan laid out for him. It would, however, allow the determined young man to follow his chosen path.

Walter looked forward to Chenega Island. He liked the Native people there, and he was curious about Miriam Rutoff. She was different than the girls he had met in Kansas, more serious, more mature somehow, definitely not the giggly type. While he didn't consciously think about her all the time, she came to the forefront of his thoughts whenever they headed to Chenega.

The last time he and his uncle had stopped to deliver supplies there, Miriam wasn't around. He gave her grandfather a journal to give her. He had bought it in Seward. It had colorful flowers on its edges, and in the middle of the front cover it said, "My Dear Diary." Walter didn't want to give her anything too personal, but he wanted to bring her something. His choice seemed right, in his mind. He wrote something on the first page. It said, *"Miriam, this is for you to write down any interesting and important things. I hope you like it."* He signed it, *"Sincerely, Walter John Beaumont."*

Her grandfather didn't smile. After a long moment, looking at Walter with serious, unblinking eyes, he said, "I'll see she gets it." It felt as if the wise old man had been staring right into his heart. He hoped Mr. Rutoff was satisfied with what he saw.

On their way to the cabin after dropping the last load for Seth and Ellie on Hinchinbrook, Aubrey had a serious talk with Walter.

"Walter, unless you have serious feelings for her, you shouldn't be giving any more gifts to Miriam Rutoff. I wish you would have told me about it. This is more serious than giving a girl back home a nice little gift like the diary. Here, it's a big deal, and Miriam is not a young woman you would only want to have fun with. Giving her a gift is announcing your serious interest in her, with marriage in mind, something I'm sure you didn't intend to do. I would let it drop, if I were you, since you're leaving in a couple more weeks. I'll let Mr. Rutoff know you were only being friendly."

Walter thought for a minute. He said, "I understand. Miriam is an interesting girl, different from the ones I've known back home, though I've never had a girlfriend. I wouldn't want to do anything to make problems for her. I kind of think she's special. I'd thought about giving her the mountain lion skin. Now I know it wouldn't be smart."

Walter stood silent a moment, before saying to his uncle, "I wanted to talk to you about me leaving. I've thought about it long and hard, and I can't go back to Kansas. I love it here, and this is where I want to live. If I go back, I won't do well there, and I'll find a way to come back. Would you let me stay here with you? I'd work hard and help with the business."

Aubrey had half expected this. He could see how being in Alaska had affected Walter the way it had touched him, though the circumstances were different. He knew people either loved or hated Alaska, with its rugged, wild land and constant testing of a man's abilities. Walter had become a competent woodsman in a short time, as if being here had allowed him to grow into who he was meant to be. He told Walter he'd think about it, and give him an answer the next morning.

When Aubrey woke early, as was his usual practice, Walter was already up, splitting some firewood out back of the cabin. The young man looked like he belonged there, swinging the axe with a smooth, easy motion. Aubrey smiled, knowing his decision was right. He went back inside to fix breakfast, calling his nephew in when it was ready.

The two men spoke not a word as they ate their platefuls of eggs, bacon, and potatoes, cut up and cooked together in the one big cast iron skillet Aubrey used for almost all the food he cooked.

Walter was obviously waiting for his uncle to tell him what he thought about his desire to stay. When they were finished with their meal, Aubrey poured them both another cup of strong black coffee, very hot as usual. Now Walter was drinking it right down, like his uncle.

"All right, if you feel so strongly about it, we'll call your folks when we get back to Seward, but you can be sure they won't like it. You're grown up enough to know your own mind, and I'll do what I can to smooth their feathers. Hang onto the big cat skin for a while. If you do return to Kansas, leave Miriam alone. If you stay, proceed with honesty and sincerity. The Aleuts are proud, capable people, who suffered during the war, being displaced from their homes because of possible invasion by the Japanese. They weren't treated well, and they have some hard feelings towards other Americans, though they don't usually speak out about it, understand? Like I said, Miriam is a serious young woman. Things may not work out the way you want."

He nodded his understanding and agreed to Aubrey's plan. His heart was beating a little faster at the prospect of staying.

Arriving at Chenega, they were met at the dock by Mr. Rutoff and several villagers, including one of Miriam's aunts. When Aubrey and his nephew stepped from the boat, Aubrey had him stand back while he talked to Mr. Rutoff and the auntie. They talked seriously for a few minutes, ending with smiles and handshakes. They even seemed to chuckle a little, and Walter assumed they were laughing over his youthful error. Finally, Aubrey nodded and walked back to the boat, the needed list of supplies in hand.

"Come on, let's head out."

Walter started to question him, until his uncle fixed him with a look, and he kept quiet. They went aboard the *Mother Lode* and got under way immediately. After they'd been cutting a wake through the choppy water for a while, Aubrey spoke.

"Remember what I told you about the Aleuts? Well, after we'd left last time, Miriam's grandfather had called a family meeting to discuss the diary you got for Miriam. I told you this was a big decision. Well, Mr. Rutoff, knowing you are supposed to stay just for the summer, was concerned you were only trying to get Miriam to like you for the wrong reasons. I told him you wanted to stay permanently, and you're an honorable young man who didn't understand the importance of the gift. He acknowledged my words, and said, if you did stay, they'd be okay with you visiting. If you were going to leave, you weren't to come back again. So, the situation has become hard-edged, and we will abide by his wishes."

Walter nodded his understanding. He said, "So, if I stay, I can go to Chenega with you, but, I should hold back about Miriam, unless my feelings for her are sincere?"

Aubrey nodded. "I told you this was a serious situation. These are not people you can treat lightly. Unless you're willing to be committed to her, let it go."

Walter, his head bent thinking this over, searched for his true feelings. Finally he said, "What if Miriam decides to like me?"

"You'll have to find out for yourself, and I'm sure you'll know exactly how she sees things, and if she finds you worthy." Walter's uncle flashed a funny little grin after he spoke. "Let's see how the call to your parents goes. I think you'd better be the one to talk to them first, okay?"

"Sure, and thanks."

The run up to Seward was different this time, Walter's mind on the situation in Chenega. His staying had taken on a different aspect. He was learning how life can throw you a curve ball, put you in an unexpected situation to make decisions you didn't know would have to be made.

As always, he was resolved to do what he thought right. His gut was telling him staying in Alaska was the thing to do. Maybe he'd find someone to share his life, which would likely make it better. Perhaps Miriam Rutoff was the one. Only time and fate would reveal what was to be.

He had never considered anything on this serious a level. Before now, it had been a matter of doing things spontaneously, without much thought involved.

The young man got a chill down his back. His scalp actually crawled with the intensity of his sudden awareness, considering what unknown experiences might lie ahead of him.

Looking around at the rich, beautiful land and the water flowing beneath the boat's hull, he was overwhelmed with its perfection. He remembered hearing the old saw about someone thinking a certain place was God's country, but now, the full meaning of the words came to him.

He turned from looking out over the railing to observe the unique and capable man who was his uncle. Aubrey turned his head to look at Walter, who realized his uncle understood exactly what he was thinking and feeling at that moment. He nodded at his uncle, who smiled knowingly. They went back to watching the water ahead, finally turning to starboard, running up into Resurrection Bay towards Seward.

Chapter 9

Doing the Right Thing

Arnold Tuckerman happened to be at the dock they moored to, so he caught and tied off the lines. Once the *Mother Lode* was secured, he and Aubrey shook hands and talked quietly together. Walter stayed at a distance to give them some privacy. He did hear Arnold say in his gravelly voice what sounded like, "Yep, like we figgered."

They walked up to the restaurant, the three men from different generations, to eat what had become their traditional seafood meal. Though Walter was eager to make the call to his folks, he kept his outward appearance calm, and waited with as much patience as he could muster. He knew better than to pester his uncle, and having Mr. Tuckerman there made it easier to maintain his composure, knowing the tough old man would make some sort of remark if he tried to push things along.

When they had finished their meal of local fare, Aubrey went to the restaurant manager, who allowed them to use the office phone to call the Beaumont home in Manhattan, Kansas. The phone rang several times before Walter's father answered it. Aubrey began the conversation, making a little small talk before handing the phone to Walter, who said hello to his dad, a hard lump in his throat. He was amazed when Ben breached the subject of him staying in Alaska.

He told him even though they had concerns about him staying there instead of going to college, if he was set on it, they'd have to accept his decision. "I know you well enough, son. If your heart is set on something, no one is going to stop you."

Ben said Aubrey had written them a letter explaining what he thought was probably going to happen, knowing how Walter felt. He had assured Ben and Hannah their boy would be fine. Walter cast a glance in his uncle's direction, but Aubrey avoided his eyes.

Ben said, while he and his mother had accepted what they knew was an inevitable situation, they had agreed with Aubrey he needed some kind of responsible foundation. If he stayed, he would agree to join the military when he was twenty-one years old.

At first Walter thought it unfair, even if it would only mean leaving temporarily to serve, but what his uncle had taught him made it seem a good thing to do. Walter gave them his word, and it was settled. He then spoke with his mom, who had one more thing for Weejer to agree to, promising her to visit at least once a year, no matter what. He accepted her request, saying he would have wanted to visit even if she hadn't asked him to do so. He said his good-byes, promising to write and let them know how things were going.

After spending the night on board the *Mother Lode*, Walter and Aubrey drove up the highway to obtain the lumber and other supplies the Craig brothers needed for building their place. Aubrey had borrowed a large trailer to haul behind his old army ambulance. It was a heavy-duty one capable of handling a large load, which is exactly what it was carrying after the visit to the mill. Aubrey kept the old truck in lower gears, running at slow speed all the way back. The truck did fine, though the way the engine was working revealed it was pulling a lot of weight. It took a long time to reach Seward.

It was hard work getting all the lumber and other building supplies loaded onto the small barge Aubrey was using for the run. It was a thirty-five-foot, open barge Tuckerman had actually built years before, for the man who rented it to Aubrey. Judging from its appearance, it had seen little use.

Aubrey walked the docks at the harbor, and hired two out-of-work men to help load the lumber. The barge was visibly lower in the water by the time they were done. Aubrey had concentrated on stacking the load evenly. Still, he'd have to be cautious. They'd only go if the water was calm enough. He hoped this would go well, though he knew sometimes you don't find out until you get to it.

It was late in the day by the time they were finished. Arnold had shown up to help as best he could, but the old boat builder was dealing with some sort of respiratory problem, and he had to sit and rest when the coughing got bad.

Beaumont had come to respect the old New Englander for his capabilities and for his wise advice, though he'd had to get past Tuckerman's cranky attitude to realize it.

He had once asked Arnold if he'd ever gone out on the boat with Aubrey, and the old fellow got a strange, distant look in his eyes and walked away.

He had questioned his uncle about it, and he had told him during World War One Arnold had served on two ships, both sunk by German submarines. He had been more than fortunate to survive, though many of the men he knew had not. He swore he'd never go out on the sea again, and Arnold Tuckerman was also a man of his word.

They'd had their evening meal together, and sipped coffee afterwards, discussing various subjects concerning the future, as was their way.

Tuckerman looked at Aubrey with a twinkle in his eye, before speaking to Walter, "So, your uncle tells me you will be staying on permanently."

"Yes sir, this is where I want to live. It's a wonderful place."

"Well, I felt exactly the same way when I arrived here, a long time before you were born. Are you gonna raise a family here?"

"Uh, I guess I might, Mr. Tuckerman, if it's meant to be."

"If your Aleut girl decides you're the one she wants, you won't have any choice in the matter!"

Arnold started chuckling, which made Walter's face turn red. His uncle couldn't help laughing too, and soon both men were enjoying the situation. Beaumont didn't find it particularly amusing.

The next morning, Aubrey and Walter were headed out Resurrection Bay on the way to Evans Island, the water calm and smooth, which suited Aubrey, considering the load they were towing. The *Mother Lode* was running steadily at about four knots, and it took a while to reach Evans Island. They passed Chenega in the process, because Aubrey wanted to unload the supplies and lumber the Craig brothers ordered, before heading to Chenega.

When they came ashore, Aubrey fired off three rounds from his revolver, and in a few minutes, the Craigs came out to help offload the barge. The four men strained and sweated, pulling on the painter until they were able to bring the loaded barge up to the shore, making the unloading easier. They made two good stacks on the beach above the high water line. The tide was in, and Aubrey had anchored the *Mother Lode* as close to the shore as possible. The tide started back out about an hour later, and soon the boat was high and dry, making it more difficult to unload the other goods.

Unloading all the wood and other supplies off the boat and barge was heavy work, and the men were hot and sweaty, and became caked with fine sawdust from the rough-cut boards.

When they were done, all four stripped down and went splashing in the cold water off the east end of the island. They weren't in the water long when they'd all had enough, but it was refreshing, and all the sawdust had been washed away.

They had all dressed and walked up to the Craig's camp with some of the supplies, making small talk, waiting for the tide to come back in. Suddenly, Walter raised his hand to catch the others' attention, and pointed into the trees. All the others stopped conversing and looked in the direction Walter had indicated. There, about fifty yards away, was a large bull moose, quietly watching them, half hidden in the undergrowth. Beaumont had seen moose before, but none like this, however. It was a large-bodied bull, with truly massive antlers, the largest he had ever seen. The eldest Craig brother, Johnson, spoke in a normal tone of voice, "Oh, he's been around before. Biggest moose I've seen here. Might be our source of meat this coming winter."

Walter nodded, not saying anything. The bull was in his prime, and Beaumont felt it shouldn't be taken, though he wasn't exactly sure why. He spoke to Johnson Craig.

"Mr. Craig, he's probably the head bull here, and maybe it would be good to leave him be."

Aubrey looked away, knowing his nephew had overstepped his bounds. Johnson Craig, as if in response to the young man's suggestion walked over to his tent, took out a fancy lever-action rifle, worked the lever, took careful aim at the moose, but didn't shoot. He gave Walter a harsh look. "Young man, when it's time to take our winter meat, if that bull or any other one is within range, they will be taken. Meat's meat. If you don't agree, keep it to yourself!" Craig's face was quite red when he stopped talking.

Beaumont was smart enough to refrain from saying anything else. Aubrey was giving his nephew a look, but he stayed out of it. If Walter caused trouble for himself, he would learn from it. As long as Craig didn't threaten him, he'd leave the situation alone. Aubrey had enough respect for the young man, despite his inexperience, to keep out of his business, unless he knew Walter needed support, as with the situation with Miriam.

The rest of the visit was awkward. They had a plateful of beans and salt pork with the Craigs, and Aubrey carried on a conversation with the brothers. Beaumont remained silent.

The tide was finally high enough to float the *Mother Lode*. Saying good-bye, they'd come back in a few weeks to see what else, if anything, was needed.

The empty barge following obediently behind, they headed out to Chenega Island. It was late by the time they'd arrived, and no one came down to the dock, so the uncle and his nephew stayed on the boat, settling in for the night.

Aubrey hadn't said anything to his nephew about the incident with the Craigs, and Walter didn't bring it up, either. He had learned a lesson, and no more words were necessary.

Just after six the next morning, Walter awoke to a knocking on the wheelhouse door. He answered it, and it was Mr. Rutoff and two other Aleut men. Aubrey had awakened, and they both dressed while the men waited on deck to help unload the village supplies. It was drizzly raining, and they were soggy by the time it was all done. Aubrey spoke to Mr. Rutoff, while the two men he had brought, sturdy fellows with serious looks on their faces, stared at Walter. Walter, being who he was, simply stared back at them, with the same degree of intent as they were sending in his direction. It turned out one was Miriam's cousin, and the other was her Uncle Teddy.

In a little while, the three men left, pulling the carts they had brought to haul the supplies. Aubrey related to Walter what Mr. Rutoff had said, after he told the Aleut elder Walter was indeed going to be staying on. Rutoff had invited them to a meal at mid-day, in the village center.

"I think they want to make it official, as they did for me a while back, because they know you're staying." Aubrey smiled, adding, "I'm glad you intend to handle this properly, because you're in it now. I hope you can stay the course, otherwise I'll have to take you elsewhere to live." Aubrey laughed quietly, watching Walter thinking and hoping it would all turn out.

In early afternoon, they went up to the village center and went inside a long wooden building. They had washed up on the boat as best they could and changed into clean clothes.

There were about forty people there, talking and laughing. When Aubrey came in with Walter, they all became quiet. Beaumont noticed the people were dressed in what must have been their traditional clothing. There were interesting smells coming from the pots of food being cooked, some of which he couldn't identify, rousing his curiosity.

The young man knew this was an unusual situation, opening a door for him, a sharing tradition from people who had been here for a long time, according to what his uncle had told him. He kept his outer appearance calm, but inside he was excited. This was another welcome to Alaska, as a number of his experiences since coming north seemed to be.

Mr. Rutoff came over and welcomed them, saying they were invited to share their food. Walter took this with appropriate seriousness. He held out the large cotton muslin bag he had been carrying towards Mr. Rutoff.

Aubrey looked questioningly at his nephew. This was not quite what he expected to happen.

Mr. Rutoff stood waiting for an explanation.

The young man took a deep breath, and spoke loud enough for everyone in the room to hear. "Mr. Rutoff, I want to thank you for accepting me in your village. I know I'm a stranger here, and you have been concerned with my intentions. I want you to know I have only respect towards your people, including your granddaughter. I hope you will accept this, given in respect."

Aubrey and Mr. Rutoff both stared at the bag, not speaking, surprised at the excellent little speech, spoken with sincerity. Truly, there was a lot more to his nephew than Aubrey had yet to discover. He felt a rise of pride for the young man.

His speech over, Walter handed the bundle to the old Aleut chief. When Rutoff opened the cloth and let the mountain lion skin unroll, there were many sounds of questioning surprise. None of the people had ever seen a mountain lion, knowing it wasn't a normal Alaskan animal. They came over to look at this unusual fur.

When Rutoff asked him where he had gotten it, Walter told him what had occurred. The older man nodded, smiled, and offered him a chair at the long wooden table where they would eat the meal. It was made from a cedar tree, one wide slab about twenty-four feet long.

Walter glanced at his uncle who was smiling broadly. The look on his uncle's face let him know he had done the right thing.

As the meal was served, Walter looked around at all the people. He could sense there was a strong bond among them. After a while, he wondered if Miriam would make an appearance. She didn't show until near the end of the feast. They had served many different bowls of traditional food. Mr. Rutoff told Walter what each bowl held, including caribou from further north, moose meat, black bear, some sea lion, fish, and shell fish.

Just when he thought things would end without him seeing Miriam, he looked up to see her walking directly towards him, holding a beautifully painted wooden bowl. Walter swallowed hard, a lump forming in his throat. She was beautiful, her long black hair combed and shiny, her face needing no make-up. She was wearing a dress made from tanned deerskin, almost white in color, with bands of blue and red cloth around her waist, and another band of the same colors running across the bodice, then up and over her shoulders, running across the back. There were thin strips of fur sewn onto the cuff of each sleeve. Walter thought it beautiful, in its perfect simplicity.

Miriam kept her head bent as she approached him, their eyes making no contact. Walter sat there, mesmerized, realizing in an instant everything his uncle had told him about this situation was true. His feelings crystallized, and he knew what would happen, just not when or how. When Miriam reached the table, she looked up and held the bowl out to him as an offering. He hesitated, and she whispered, the expression on her face unchanging, "Take a piece of meat with your hand, Walter, eat it and smile your approval."

Walter did as she told him, smiling broadly after eating the rich-tasting meat. All the people who had been watching intently also smiled, and nodded. Miriam walked along the table, offering the meat to others.

When the meal was almost done, people got up, some with drums, and a dance began, quickly growing in the number of dancers and the loudness of the drums. Then singing began, in the same language he had originally heard Miriam and Mr. Rutoff speaking.

Walter realized many of the movements of the dancers must be mimicking animals they were familiar with. After several hours, all the activity started to wind down. It had been a terrific experience.

He saw Miriam walking around, talking to others. She didn't seem to take any notice of him. After looking around, smiling at various villagers who nodded, some men shaking his hand, he turned and almost bumped into her, she was so close. They stood there, looking at each other.

She was the first to speak, "Walter, thank you for the diary. What you wrote in it was very nice. I have already been writing down important things I will want to remember later. I don't know you well yet, but I think you are a man of honesty and good heart. I would like to get to know you, no matter what I might learn. Maybe I want to see if my thoughts about you are right. Since you're going to be living in our part of Alaska, perhaps I'll get the chance to find out."

Walter was struck by the straightforward, open way she spoke to him, and the serious look in her eyes. There was something else in her look, and it stirred him. All he said was, "Okay."

Miriam laughed at his simple response.

Trying to find something interesting to say, he asked her what kind of meat had been in the bowl she carried.

"It was fox meat. Every meat has its own energy. The fox is a clever, quick animal. You might find such energy useful."

Walter had a strong desire to kiss her, though he knew how foolish and inappropriate it would be. He saw she knew what he was feeling, and what he wanted to do. The expression on her face didn't change, though she continued to look directly into his eyes, some unknown thought in her mind.

"Well," she finally said, "it's been very pleasant, and I hope we'll see each other again."

She walked away, leaving Walter to his own thoughts. Truth was, he didn't know what to think. Finally he went outside, after saying goodnight to Mr. Rutoff, and walked down to the boat to sit on a dock piling and let his mind clear.

Uncle Aubrey came down a few minutes later. "You handled things well, son. You are welcome here now. So, what do you think of Miriam? Think you can only be friends with her?"

Walter saw a sparkle in his uncle's eye. "Well, yeah, I guess. She seems like a nice girl."

"A nice girl? Nothing more?" A little smile broke out on his face.

Walter didn't know what to say, knowing his uncle had his own thoughts about things, though he didn't know what. So after a moment of silence, he said he was tired and went below to sleep, while Aubrey stayed topside and had his evening whiskey and cigar.

Everything seemed right to Biggs, all the wheels in the universe spinning smoothly together, life flowing as it should. He knew one thing for certain, he had a good partner in his nephew, one he could depend on. He decided to talk to Tuckerman about something he wanted to do for Walter. The project would take time. He knew nothing would change the way he felt about his sister's boy, and time was of little importance, since Walter wasn't going to be leaving at the end of the summer.

Tossing the stub of his cigar into the water, Aubrey turned in. Though he'd never admit it, work was starting to wear on him a lot more than it used too.

Standing up and stretching, he mumbled, "Man, this getting older is not for the weak of heart, no sir."

Waking up on the boat the next morning, they dressed, had some coffee and bread and butter, and prepared to head out. As they were warming up the engine, Miriam came running down to the dock, slowing to a walk when Walter turned and saw her. She had come to say good-bye, and brought the two men a hand-made basket full of food. Though she had prepared it herself, as a gesture of humility she told them her auntie had made it.

Walter knew she had fixed the basket herself. He told Miriam to thank her auntie, and smiled, causing her to turn away. A moment later, she turned back, with the same look in her eyes that had rendered him speechless before. The two young people, both their hearts opened, needed no words.

Aubrey waited patiently, not wanting to intrude on their time. Before Walter turned to leave, Miriam put a hand on his shoulder and told him to stay safe. As they headed out from the dock, Aubrey mumbled something about "one of many moments to come."

His nephew asked what he meant. His uncle smiled, and continued steering the *Mother Lode* away from the island.

Chapter 10

Working the Sound

There were still several loads to be delivered, and Aubrey needed to get back to his cabin soon. Besides his freight business, there was still firewood to be split for the cold months of the fall and winter to come, and they were way behind in building a good reserve.

Aubrey and Walter had talked, and it was decided a small cabin of his own would be a good idea. There was a smaller patch of level ground about one hundred yards northeast of Aubrey's log home. It would make a good building site.

The two worked well together, Walter having grown stronger and more experienced. Aubrey realized what a blessing his nephew had actually been to him. He wasn't getting any younger, and having a capable partner was proving to be more important than he had anticipated. Still, Aubrey was a healthy and tenacious outdoorsman, ready to deal with whatever was presented to him.

They made their deliveries to Montague and Hinchinbrook islands. There was a U.S. Fish and Wildlife team on Montague, doing some research on the big bears. They had been dropped off, and were spending the whole summer among the giant bruins. Aubrey was asked to check in once a month to see what supplies were needed. He was being paid well to do so, the "easiest money he'd ever made," he said.

"All I have to do is get in touch with them over my boat radio, and even if they're all right, I get a check every month."

When they made their delivery on Hinchinbrook, the two found a sorrowful situation. Seth and his wife Ellie met them on the shore after the three pistol shots signaled their arrival. The dogs came out as usual, calming down when they got close, familiar with the two men. Seth and Ellie came walking out slowly, with two of their three children. Cordell was not with them.

The little family all had long faces, and it was obvious something had happened. Seth shook hands with Aubrey, who turned to smile at Ellie. The woman started to cry and fell to her knees on the beach, her two children clinging to her, also crying. Seth hung his head. Finally, Aubrey spoke quietly: "Cordell?"

Seth nodded. "We were hiking up to a high meadow where berries grow well. We were busy picking when we heard Cordell scream. I looked up to see him falling from the edge of a steep drop-off. I ran down and around to help him while Ellie stayed with the other children, waiting. There was nothing I could do. There were big rocks everywhere. He had been badly broken up, and was gone." Seth turned away and the sorrowful man's shoulders shook, as he quietly cried, grieving deeply.

Aubrey and Walter could only look at each other, feeling helpless. Beaumont went over to Seth and told him whatever was needed, they would do what they could.

Seth looked over at Aubrey, who nodded his head in confirmation of what his nephew had said.

"We've buried him a short ways off from the cabin. I made a cross out of split spruce limbs. Ellie and I have talked, and we can't live here anymore. When do you think you will be coming back this way?"

Aubrey told him they'd be by in about two weeks. Seth asked if they could go with them, back to Seward. Aubrey told Seth it would be fine. They would have to make several stops on the way to get supply lists from other people, which was no problem for Seth.

"We're fine with whatever you have to do, Mr. Biggs. We need to leave the island, to go somewhere else and make a new start. A couple more weeks may make it easier to leave our boy behind."

They agreed to a specific day, barring any problems, and unloaded the supplies they had ordered. Aubrey and Walter headed out to their cabin. On the run towards Hawkins Island, the two spoke little.

They arrived at their protected cove, took the small load of supplies up to the cabin, and had a quiet evening before turning in.

As they were dozing off, Walter said, "This is a place where a person can do or be whatever he feels is right, but he needs to know anything can happen, and whatever happens, you need to be prepared to deal with it, no two ways about it."

Aubrey smiled a little. This was the longest bit of philosophy his nephew had ever spoken to him, and he answered, "You're right. You do what you can to survive and stay well, keeping in mind at any moment something can come along and swat you like a mosquito. This country makes you realize how small and vulnerable people are. Even though you might be tough and smart enough to survive just about anything, you can't always escape what nature, God actually, has in mind. Best to not dwell on it. Appreciate everything in this world, and keep on moving along."

As he dropped off to sleep, Walter's mind focused on the girl who had apparently captured his heart. She was special, all right. He knew she was more than a little interested in him, too, and understood what his uncle had told him. With a girl like Miriam, well, there was only one way to go. His mind wandered into areas that made it hard for him to sleep. He made himself think of other things, and managed to doze off.

For the next week they gathered firewood, felling trees, cutting them up with a two-man saw into eight-foot lengths, then dragging them together to the cabin to be bucked up into rounds they would split and stack for the wood to season.

They also gathered enough logs of the right diameter to be stacked for building Walter's cabin come next summer. As with most all things to be done in the wilds, these were tedious, necessary tasks.

Every day after work was done, they'd go over to the little waterfall and wash off, the icy cold water energizing them. They'd cook a basic meal of fish or game meat and fry bread or homemade sourdough bread, if Aubrey was up for making the dough. Eventually, his clever nephew learned how to bake bread and even biscuits. He would wake up to find Walter already quietly preparing dough. He appreciated the effort Walter was making. The several partners he'd had in the past during his gold-mining days were different, and none of them ever worked out for long, human nature making for difficulties that always ended in a parting of the ways, including the time when he had to run one man off at gun point.

The fellow had gone a little bushy over the winter they had cabined together, and Aubrey had gotten into some dangerous situations with him, including once when the man pulled a knife. After disarming him, he had actually locked the guy out of the cabin for an hour, in twenty-below-zero weather. It worked, the man promising to behave if he would let him in again. The effects of the incident lasted several weeks.

The weather had become downright awful, with heavy snows and high winds half covering the little cabin with drifts. It put the situation into a clearer perspective, the two miners playing cards and rationing what food they had left to eat, until an old cow moose came by as Aubrey was out bringing an armload of firewood from the dwindling stack next to the cabin. He pretended to ignore the animal, grabbing his rifle as soon as he got inside, slipping right out again and shooting it.

The fresh meat certainly saved them from greater difficulties, and though they were being careful with each other, an atmosphere of distrust hanging around the cabin, they managed to keep a truce between them, knowing another bout of trouble with each other would not end as well.

When spring finally came, the two parted ways, Walter's uncle following him away from the claim, rifle in hand, looking over his shoulder as he walked alone back to the cabin. Aubrey left soon after, tired of living the life. He never did find out what happened to the man who had been his partner.

Walter, however, was always ready to help out and easy to get along with. Aubrey was glad he had decided to stay, and the young man seemed sincerely interested in the freight-hauling business. Aubrey fully intended to make him a partner soon. Knowing he and Miriam would likely end up together, his nephew was going to need something to build a good foundation for their lives.

As the days rolled on, however, he could see Walter was getting restless. He had come to realize his nephew often needed to get out and about, always in need of a chance to explore, hunt, or track some wiley critter.

One morning after they'd been back at the cabin for well over a week, seeing he was getting restless, Aubrey told Walter he wanted to play a little game out in the woods. His nephew gave him a quizzical look, and the uncle explained, "I'm going out in the trees, and I want you to track me down and find me where I'll be hiding. It's good practice, and fun, too."

Walter smiled, "Okay uncle Aubrey, but you know I'll find you easily enough."

"Maybe so, maybe not. We'll see how good you are, or if you're just being cocky. Go inside, give me about half an hour, then come find me."

Walter gave him a quick little salute, and Aubrey slipped out the door and was gone. The confident young man sat and sipped a cup of hot, strong coffee. He put on the olive drab fatigue jacket Aubrey had given him, and walked outside latching the door behind him.

He slowly walked around the cabin looking for sign, and found several fresh footprints heading off to the east up the slope behind the cabin, not the direction they usually walked. Walter went into the mindset he had developed, partly from experience in the forest, and partly by his instinctive thinking. Everything grew sharper in his mind, the shapes and patterns of things naturally growing contrasting with anything out of place. It might be some displaced grass, or a leaf half-broken from its stem, revealing where something had moved through the brush, leaving an "off" look to the vegetation. And there were also his heightened senses of hearing, and even smell. Beaumont had become a well-tuned tracker, and a natural element in the woods.

He followed sign for about three quarters of a mile, and figured some of the things he was seeing were intentionally created by his uncle. Walter moved cautiously, as he sensed his quarry was close.

He was standing beneath a large old spruce tree, looking down at a clear heel print, made in what looked like a scuffed-out area in the soil. He was pondering this, when a little bit of bark falling from the tree above him hit him on the shoulder. As soon as he felt it, Walter tensed to jump off to the side, realizing what was about to happen, but too late. Something large knocked him off his feet, though not hard enough to do any real damage. He rolled over quickly onto his back to confront what turned out to be his uncle standing over him, the fierce look on his face Weejer had seen before when they were practicing hand-to-hand combat. Walter let himself relax, knowing the game was up.

Aubrey leaned down and offered him his hand. When they were both standing, he said, "One thing to always remember, most people never look up."

Walter wouldn't make that mistake again. He'd already learned being fully alert was hard work, though his natural abilities made it easier.

Something about the little episode he'd gone through with his uncle made him realize he existed in a world where being on guard might mean the difference between surviving, or succumbing to the bad intentions of someone or something bent on taking him down. The full impact of what his uncle was teaching him became clear. Living in the wilderness, and having to be cautious in dealing with predatory animals was one thing. Having to handle dangerous situations with other people was something very different. Beaumont looked forward to a time when he might fully discover his own capabilities to deal with them, and at the same time hoping he'd never have to find out.

Seriously considering the possibilities, Walter unconsciously crossed over onto a higher level of understanding. He would never see things quite the same again, always in the back of his mind maintaining a heightened awareness of the world around him.

As they walked back to the snug log cabin, Aubrey gently extended his arm out to the side, and put the palm of his hand against Weejer's chest. They both stopped moving. Walter cast his eyes around, wondering what his uncle had seen to make him stop their forward motion. Slowly, Aubrey moved his arm and pointed a few degrees to their right. Walter followed the direction his uncle was pointing, and saw a brown bear feeding on the edge of a small opening in the trees, a little meadow covered with young plants, grasses, roots, and pushki. The bear busily grazing on the wild greens presented an odd scene, considering it was a vastly powerful predator, heavy and wide, feeding like some bovine in a pastoral setting.

They remained watching this scene for a minute or so until, because of a slight shift in the air currents, or some sixth sense, the bear rose up on his hind legs to sniff the air, turned around, and saw the two men standing barely thirty yards away. The boar let out an incredibly loud roar, angered at being disturbed while eating, not pleased with the human scent and presence. He took several quick bounds, stopping close to them popping his jaws, and bouncing up and down on his front feet, clearly displaying irritation. It was one of those uncertain confrontations between man and bear, when the humans involved don't know what it intends to do, and neither does the bear.

Walter did as he had during the encounter he'd already experienced when he'd seen the big bear in the alders: he started whistling in a calm, and actually pleasant fashion. His uncle gave him a quick glance, wondering how this bear would react, remembering Walter telling him about doing this same thing to the other bear, and he watched to see what would occur, not having any other choice. He had his 45 Colt revolver on his hip, but it wasn't much of a gun for dealing with a huge bear, and this bruin certainly qualified. Beaumont hadn't brought a gun with him, either.

After perhaps a full minute of Weejer serenading the animal, it seemed to have lost the anger and aggression it had first shown. Though it still had an unhappy look on its face, the bear slowly turned and walked off out of the meadow and into the trees. After it had been out of sight for several minutes, the bear roared again, a reminder he was still there.

Aubrey turned towards Walter, to ask him how he knew whistling would calm the bear and defuse the situation. But his nephew had already started walking back to the cabin. Aubrey could only smile and shake his head. He thought to himself, "Who is this nephew of mine?"

Chapter 11

Tragedy, Love, and Tuckerman

Time moved in a steady rhythm over the next few months. They had taken Seth and his little family off Hinchinbrook Island with the few personal items they were taking with them. It was a somber journey, with Ellie resting down in the forward cabin with her daughter, while Seth stayed up top with his remaining boy, Christian. There was little conversation, though they did talk a bit about Seth's plans for the near future. He intended to settle in Anchorage, find a job and a place for his family to live, their days living remote over. Ellie would go back to sewing, and taking in clothing for alteration and repair. She had done well at it before they had gone homesteading.

Seth went down to the cabin, and some yelling ensued. Though the two men tried to ignore it, there was no place they could go where they wouldn't hear. The distraught wife apparently blamed Seth for talking her into homesteading, and made it clear she felt this was why they had lost Cordell. Seth came back up on deck, walked to the stern, and just stood there, his remaining son clinging to his leg. Aubrey and Walter looked at each other, and said not a word.

It was quite late in the evening when they reached Seward. Seth and Ellie were obviously weary from the run out from Hinchinbrook, just sitting and thinking. She had come out on deck with her daughter, shifting from watching the land and the sea as they made their way along the coast, to bouts of quiet crying. Seth was holding himself together well, because he had to do so, being the one to start getting their lives in order once they reached Anchorage. Seth's son had to be constantly watched as he walked about the boat having fun, not paying attention to his place near the railing and by the stern of the *Mother Lode*. Becka sat close to her mom. Aubrey wouldn't allow any of them ahead of the little wheel house, to play it safe.

When Seward came into view and they were finally moored at the dock, Seth and Ellie couldn't get off the boat fast enough. It wasn't because they didn't appreciate Aubrey's help, for which he refused payment. They were simply desperate to start over, and let the past fade away.

Aubrey and Walter did something unusual, for them. They stayed at the hotel in town, taking long hot showers and scrubbing themselves with sweet-smelling soap, before dressing in clean clothes and going out for dinner, after which they went back to their unfamiliar room and quickly fell asleep.

The next morning, as they would be going out in a few days to their remaining customers to learn what supplies were needed, Aubrey and Walter drove north of Seward several miles, stopping half a mile from a spot where Aubrey had occasionally seen deer grazing early in the morning. It was rare to see deer in the general area they had driven to, and Aubrey hadn't mentioned it to anyone. There was no guarantee any deer would be there, but when they carefully worked their way through the trees to the edge of a little meadow, as luck would have it there was a fat, healthy buck, perhaps four or five years old, grazing on the far side, perhaps twenty yards away. It seemed unaware of their presence.

Aubrey whispered to Walter to take the shot from there, as the surrounding woods might make it hard to get closer without being seen. Walter told him in the same low whisper he would make his way around, and Aubrey could wait there in case the deer was wounded and headed his way. He smiled at the smart plan, and nodded at his nephew.

Twenty minutes after Walter had slipped away, vanishing into the trees, Aubrey heard the loud report of his .30-06 coming from somewhere on the side of the meadow where the buck was browsing.

The animal humped up in reaction to being hit by the shot, before running across the meadow headed in Aubrey's direction. Halfway across, the mortally wounded animal hesitated, its legs buckled, and it went down. It thrashed around a few times, trying to raise its head, finally lying still, its life extinguished.

Walter walked out of the trees towards the downed buck. He saw Aubrey heading towards him across the meadow. When they were both standing over the deer, Aubrey patted him on the back. Without a word, they got busy field-dressing the animal. Walter did most of the work, Aubrey helping, to make it easier. He told Walter it was good the animal had fallen out in the open on dry ground.

"A deer's not so bad, but there's nothing worse than having to work on a moose stuck between tight trees, or after it has fallen into a lily pond. This is as good as it gets."

It took little time to get the buck gutted before they dragged it out by its antlers, one man on each side. They loaded the buck into the ambulance and took it over to their favorite restaurant. They stopped at the back door. Aubrey knocked, and spoke to the owner when he opened the door. Walter saw the man smile and nod. He held the door open, and they brought the deer in and hung it in the restaurant's meat cooler. When they were ready to head out to the sound, they'd come get the deer, and when they got home to the cabin, they'd hang the meat from a cross pole tied between two trees behind the cabin, after skinning and quartering it to let it age. They would rub the meat with vinegar, and spread pepper on it. This would create a quick rind on the flesh and keep bugs out.

The next afternoon, they hauled the meat down to the *Mother Lode* and stashed it in the hold. Aubrey never had to explain to Walter why they shouldn't have taken the deer as they had, because his nephew never asked. Aubrey was an old sourdough, and needing meat meant going out to get some. It wasn't a sporting event for him, it was survival, and though he wasn't homesteading as he had in times past, relying only on the wilds for food, the process never changed for him.

Heading out on the boat the next day, they stopped at the several islands where people would have supply lists ready to be filled, including the Craig brothers on Evans Island. They were pleased when they saw Aubrey handing a hind quarter of deer down to his nephew. It was intended to be a peace offering after the last visit when Walter overstepped his bounds with Mr. Craig. Fresh meat was always welcome. Johnson Craig shook Walter's hand, thanking him for his thoughtfulness. Their connection seemed amiable again.

The Craigs needed only a small load of supplies next time they made a delivery. Both Aubrey and Walter noticed a tenseness between the brothers when they talked to them. Aubrey knew living remote can affect people in different ways, bringing things out in their personalities not normally revealed in more populated, civilized areas. He said as much to Walter later, when they were alone on the *Mother Lode*.

"I'm thinking the Craig brothers may not work out well together on Evans Island. Maybe the solitude is getting to them. We should probably be cautious around them whenever we put in there."

Walter nodded, his thoughts aligned with his uncle's.

They stopped at Chenega to get the village's needs list, and headed up to Seward. Miriam had not been there, and Mr. Rutoff seemed preoccupied with something, so the visit was brief.

When Walter awoke the next morning, there was a deep chill in the boat. Walking on deck, he saw a light covering of frost on the *Mother Lode*, on the docks, and the other boats moored around them. He shivered slightly, as much from knowing he'd soon be in his first Alaskan winter as from the actual chill in the air. Certainly he'd experienced winter in Kansas, but he was sure it wouldn't match what Alaska would be like. He would find out soon enough.

When Aubrey awoke, he saw a fire in the little oil stove in the boat's cabin, and smiled. "Need some hot water for coffee, Weejer? No other reason to heat the place up, right?"

Walter had become accustomed to and appreciated his uncle's sense of humor. "Nope, no other reason. The weather is fine, maybe Indian summer. Hey, why don't you go take a dip in the harbor while I get breakfast ready?"

"Are you kidding? It's getting frosty enough, I'll be washing up indoors from now on. You can go ahead, if you'd like."

They smiled at each other, enjoying the little game they played. The two had become as comfortable as two men living together could be.

After breakfast, they headed over to the distributor to buy the supplies they needed for the return run. They found prices had increased greatly in only a few weeks. Aubrey tried to work out a better deal with the distributor. It did no good. The man held firm to his elevated charges. When the transaction was done, they shook hands. But, the good connection between Aubrey and the man he had dealt with for several years was gone. They fueled up the boat at the oil dock and headed down Resurrection Bay. Aubrey spoke little, concerns for the business on his mind.

When they arrived at Evans Island and Aubrey fired off a few shots to let the Craigs know they were there, no one responded. After a while, they started walking inland to the cabin site without the supplies. When they arrived, neither brother was there. They walked around, calling out, not getting any response. It looked as if little, if any building, had been done since their last visit.

Walter went over to a spruce tree, and picked something up near its base. It was the hat Johnson Craig was always wearing when they came to the island.

Staring at the hat, Aubrey said, "I think we'd better search for a while, Walter, and see what we can find."

The two started to look around, when Beaumont heard his uncle say, "Mr. Craig, we were wondering where you and your brother were keeping yourselves."

Walter turned to see Johnson Craig had come from behind the partially built cabin. They had looked in that direction only a minute or two ago. Craig didn't say anything in response to Aubrey. He just stared at them both, a blank expression on his face, his eyes empty. Aubrey noticed a small cut on the side of the man's face. Aubrey spoke again, as amiably as possible, "We have your supplies. Say, where's your brother?"

A change overcame Craig's face. It was as if a sudden surge of powerful emotion passed over it, until he contained himself again. "Oh, he's around somewhere, don't worry about him. Why don't you leave the supplies on the beach. We can pick them up in a while, and you can just continue on your way."

Walter walked over to the man and held out his hat. After a moment, Johnson grabbed it out of his hand without a word of thanks, and walked away, behind the unfinished cabin.

"C'mon Walter, let's get back to the *Mother Lode*."

Walter glanced back several times, feeling edgy about the strange interaction with Craig. His uncle quietly told him to keep walking back to the boat.

After they were under way again headed to Chenega, Aubrey called the harbor master in Seward and told him there was something wrong on Evans Island. He suggested the authorities should take a run out and do an investigation. He told the master he thought the Craigs had a bad case of bushiness, and he was concerned for the younger brother. The harbor master said something to him, and Aubrey said, "Well, you could call it a hunch, it's up to you." He signed off.

When he saw his nephew giving him a concerned look, he asked Walter what he thought.

"I think Mr. Craig was acting pretty strange. It felt like he wasn't telling us something. He gave me the creeps."

"Well, from what I could tell, you saw your first case of cabin fever. It can be a lot more serious than it sounds, as in this case. One or two people living alone in a remote place can sort of, well, lose their mental stability, depending on who they are. The dark side can come out, like with my old gold mining partner. I hope the authorities come check out the situation. I'm thinking the worst for the missing Craig brother, though I hope I'm wrong. Let's head to Chenega and hope for the best."

Beaumont sat thinking. He said, "Is there always a lot of trouble up here? Seems like something's going on all the time."

"This is a wild and tough land, Weejer. Many people who come here aren't up for it, like we've talked about. They aren't ready for what they find, and the place has no sympathy for unprepared folks."

"Well, I probably would never have come up here if it wasn't for you. I'm glad you're an experienced Alaskan, or I might have ended up on the list of people who couldn't survive here."

"It's possible, son; however, you've got a lot of natural abilities, instincts I think, that would enable you to come here on your own and survive." He gave Walter a little smile. "Of course, you'd probably end up with some rough edges."

The stop at Chenega was a brief one, as the last time they had been there. Walter found out Miriam was staying in Anchorage with friends, and they didn't know when she would be back. It bothered him more than he had expected. Miriam had been on his mind quite a bit since the dinner they shared with the community on Chenega.

After dropping off the goods, they headed out to check with the Fish and Wildlife team on Montague Island. Aubrey had a feeling it was getting to be time to bring them off the island, so they could return to their offices back east.

Sure enough, when they arrived in the little cove where the camp was located, the head of the team asked if Aubrey could come back in three days to take them up to Seward. Aubrey assured them there was no problem. He and Walter headed home to lay up for several days before returning to Montague.

The weather had definitely turned colder. The first morning back at the cabin the temperature had dipped well below freezing, and the frost was heavy.

Over breakfast, Aubrey told his nephew they'd soon be shutting down the cabin and heading up to Seward to stay for a while. This wasn't something they had discussed before, and he questioned his uncle about it.

Aubrey explained, "When winter comes, we won't be able to run freight anymore, not in these waters. Besides, this cove freezes up in the coldest times, and the snowfall here can get heavy, so it's up to Seward until we get provisioned for running my trap line. We'll stay with Arnold until then. He's got plenty of room."

Trap line? Walter thought his uncle had trapped in the past, but not any longer. Apparently he was wrong.

"Do you think you would be interested in trapping with me? It's not an easy way to live, and I don't run dogs. We'd be snowshoeing anywhere we go. I live basically, just having the essentials to keep it together over what can be a hard winter season. Fur prices right now are good, so with any luck we'll have a grubstake put together when we bring furs in to Anchorage. What do you think?"

"I can't think of anything I'd rather do, Uncle Aubrey. When do we leave?"

Aubrey smiled at Walter's statement. He knew his nephew wasn't trying to sound tough; he did think of Alaska as his home, and was definitely trying to prove his worth.

"All right, we'll go soon. I have all my gear at Arnold's place, and I might have a few things for you by way of warm clothes, but you'll need good footgear, heavy pacs to keep from freezing your toes, and a few other things. We can get them in Seward."

That night, Walter didn't sleep right away, tired though he was. He kept trying to envision how things would be through the winter, harvesting furs with his uncle.

In the morning, they began prepping the cabin for shutting down the next time they were there. During the night there had been a light snowfall. The land looked amazing, with a light layer of snow crystals all over it, and the trees sparkling in the sunlight. The snow didn't remain long, the sun quickly melting it.

About six a.m., they were on the *Mother Lode*, warming the engine for the run to Montague and on to Seward. By the time they reached the Wildlife team's camp, they were all packed up, ready to embark.

The five-man research team sat below, crammed into the small cabin staying warm and drinking coffee, discussing their time on Montague. Walter didn't hang around with them, not because it wasn't interesting to him, but his senses, including his sense of smell, seemed to have sharpened, and these guys had been living without any luxuries for quite some time.

The trip to Seward was uneventful. The water flowed smoothly around the boat, and the coast slipped by in all its natural beauty, with the lush, forested slopes looking grand, many animals visible on the shores and in the sea. Beaumont felt as though he'd been traveling through this northern land forever.

One of the team from Montague eventually got seasick, and spent some time leaning over the side, with Walter standing nearby in case he lost his footing. By the time they got to Seward harbor, the fellow was looking quite green, and swearing he'd never set foot on a boat again, before leaning again over the rail. Walter and his uncle looked at each other and tried not to smile, without much luck.

It was late by the time they went up to their favorite restaurant to eat, and the place was closed for the night. Jim Bigelow, the owner, saw them starting to walk away and called them back. He insisted they come in, and fed them both a large meal of seafood not useable for the next day. They ate mussels, shrimp, crab, and cod until they couldn't eat any more, as well as some of his tasty sourdough bread, as always. Walter loved the chewiness of it.

Jim wouldn't take money for the food, making the two promise not to mention it to anyone, saying, "You know what would happen if the free-loaders in this town ever heard about this. Why, I'd have a line a mile long every evening after closing!"

Arnold Tuckerman was up in Anchorage after some needed boat hardware, according to the note pinned to the doorway. The two men got both wood stoves going to heat the large shop. By the time they fell asleep, it was warmed up enough to be comfortable. Glad to turn in after the busy day, they talked about what to expect that winter while trapping, and about life in general, as had become their tradition at end of day. The subject of the Craig brothers came up again. Aubrey told Walter he had seen enough men acting odd before to seriously wonder where the younger brother had ended up.

Aubrey was not happy the next morning, after talking to the man who sold him the supplies he required. His prices had gone up again, to the point where Aubrey would have to charge his customers more than he knew they'd want to pay, or should have to pay, in his judgment.

While trying once again to get the man to drop his prices, the fellow told him there was a man in Seward who was starting up a supply service using airplanes, two De Havilland Beavers, rigged with floats. The planes were stable, the supplier said, and could carry quite a load, as well as passengers. Aubrey was not pleased to hear this news. He sensed this was going to be a successful means of bringing supplies to people down in the islands. Bush pilots had been in the north country for a long time, transporting people and their goods to remote areas, but this was hitting close to home.

The supplier finally dropped his prices, "just this once," to what they were the last time. Aubrey nodded his head without comment, begrudgingly paying the high prices once again, planning on taking the loss this time, instead of passing it on to his customers, charging them what was fair.

Aubrey knew he had some decisions to make. He wasn't one to put things off, and this time was no different. He didn't plan on losing money instead of adding to his reserves. While he and Walter waited at the *Mother Lode* for the supplies to be delivered, he explained the situation to his nephew.

"I have the feeling we'd better consider some other way to make money after the winter trapping is over. Things are changing, and I need to go talk to this fellow with the planes to find out what's up."

They drove over to where the man, a former fighter pilot, had his two planes tied down in a corner of the Seward harbor. The planes' floats had wheels attached so the Beavers could be run on dry ground from the water's edge.

The Dehavillands were sturdy aircraft, and though Aubrey knew they might mean the end to his business, he couldn't help but admire them. He could tell they would work well for flying supplies out to people living remote.

The pilot said he'd already been out to Chenega, and had flown as far as Sitka, making deals along the way to bring gear and deliver goods as well as transport people. Aubrey was bothered Mr. Rutoff hadn't mentioned it to him. He'd have to talk to him when they brought the requested supplies, probably for the last time.

He appreciated the pilot being square with him about what was going on, even though the situation was still disturbing. But, the old soldier had been through worse times and he'd figured out how to survive. This time would be no different.

After breakfast, Aubrey and Walter discussed the future. They'd arrived back at the cabin the day before. The stop at Chenega restored Aubrey's faith in human nature, though it wouldn't be enough to keep the freighting business going. Mr. Rutoff, in response to his question about the pilot coming to arrange a supply run, had told him yes, the pilot had made him a fair offer. Even though it would be a quicker way to get supplies at a slightly better price, the old Aleut said he told the flier he already had a deal going for getting his goods from Seward.

He smiled at Aubrey and told him, "Some things are more important than saving a few dollars, like helping a friend to keep going. Aubrey, you know as well as I do life can be difficult. I won't make things any harder for you, and that's all there is to it."

Aubrey Biggs' chest tightened up when Rutoff spoke to him. They both understood and appreciated true friendship and loyalty. "Thank you, but you might as well accept the pilot's offer. Even if you stick with me, I won't have enough business to keep going. After trapping this winter, I'm going to find another way to get along. I'll still come to visit, but you'd be best advised to go with the plane service."

Rutoff was sorry to hear what Aubrey told him. He nodded slowly, shook his hand firmly and walked away into the village. Now Aubrey would have to change his situation once again. He had an idea he thought would be a good answer to the situation. He'd have to talk to Arnold Tuckerman about it, since it would involve using his skills to make it work.

While his uncle was talking to Mr. Rutoff, Walter went looking for Miriam, who hadn't come down to the dock. He finally went to Mr. Rutoff's house where Miriam's Grandma Joy answered the door.

"Hello Walter. Miriam's here, but she has a bad cold and needs to rest. You should wait for the next visit to come see her."

Walter understood, though he was disappointed. He said good-bye and started to leave, when he heard Miriam call his name. Going around to the side of the house, he saw her looking out an open window. He was glad to see her, and walked over to talk. Even though she was sick, he still saw her as beautiful.

"I must look a mess, Walter."

"You look fine to me, Miriam. I hope you get well soon."

"Oh, I'll be fine, Walter, don't worry. I have something important to tell you. I'm going to live in Anchorage soon, with my Cousin Mary. I need to get a good education, and I have to go there to get one. Even though it will be harder for us to see each other, I don't want you to worry, because I don't plan to lose touch. But, if you don't want me to go . . . ."

"No, Miriam, it sounds like something you need to do, and anyway, I wouldn't try to stop you. Besides, I'll be trapping with my uncle this winter, and I won't be around either. We'll have to be patient." He stopped talking, not wanting to say what he needed to say. "Remember what I told you, I'll be going into the army when I turn twenty-one. I don't know what will happen. I think you're special, Miriam, and it would be swell if we can stay in contact."

Miriam smiled, "If I didn't have a runny nose, I'd kiss you, Walter Beaumont."

Walter smiled, "Well, You could kiss me on the cheek."

Miriam did kiss him on the cheek, grabbing Walter around the neck, burying her face in his shoulder. In a little voice he could barely hear, Miriam said, "I love you, Walter Beaumont."

Walter pulled away and, looking straight into her eyes, said, "I think I love you too, Miriam, and hope we are given a chance to find out how far it could go."

Miriam Rutoff smiled brightly despite her cold, and hugged Walter's neck again, until they heard Grandma Joy say, "All right you two, enough of this monkey business. Walter, go away now. You'd better come back again later, so this silly girl doesn't pine away!"

As Walter walked down to the boat he had a lump in his throat, and a lot of thoughts and feelings running around in his mind. He struggled to settle down, and by the time he reached the *Mother Lode*, he'd pretty much gotten himself together, though when his uncle saw him, the old soldier grinned.

"So, I take it you saw Miriam?"

"Yeah, she's going up to Anchorage for school, and since I'm going trapping all winter with you, I better put things right in my mind, cause I don't know if and when I'll see her again. Besides, she's a pretty girl, and might meet somebody at school. I'd better not make any plans, right?"

"Well, one never knows where life will take us, so you might be right. I think Miriam is a loyal girl who knows what's in her mind and heart. Let's keep on moving, and we'll see how things go."

The temperatures had dropped well below freezing by the time they were ready to head up to Seward and Arnold Tuckerman's place. They'd stay there and prepare their gear until the time came to head north.

The water in the calm little cove where the *Mother Lode* was anchored had developed a light layer of soft ice on its surface. The little skiff slid right through it as they rowed out to the boat to begin their voyage up to Seward. They could hear the sound of the water outside the cove. It was obvious conditions were not going to make for a smooth run. There had been snow falling on and off for several days, and the boat had a pure white coating all over it. A half hour of brushing and sweeping had it cleaned off well enough to head out.

Walter was thoroughly enjoying his first snow in Alaska. As far as he was concerned, though he had no idea how heavy winter was going to get, this would be a great time for him. His uncle didn't seem too happy with winter coming in, though he didn't appear displeased either. He was all business, getting ready to go. When Walter asked him about it, he shrugged and said, "Doesn't matter much to me what season it is, if I can survive in good shape."

Heading out amongst the now-familiar islands, the water was rough and choppy. The *Mother Lode* handled it well, though she rocked and rolled through the waves, revealing the one drawback to her round-bottomed construction. Neither Aubrey nor Walter were prone to seasickness, however, and it was no problem. They both wore heavy rain gear, including the tough sou'wester hats boatmen had worn for ages.

As they slipped past the point where they would turn off for Chenega, Walter had a strong urge to ask his uncle to put in there for a short visit. He held back, knowing it wasn't the way it was to be. Besides, he was sure Miriam had gone up to Anchorage already.

It was getting quite dark by the time they reached Seward harbor, the long daylight hours of the summer gone. They tied up to the dock where Walter assumed the boat would remain while they were trapping. But, such was not the case, as he would soon learn. When they had their packs in hand, they walked around to where the old ambulance was parked, as usual, behind the bar where Aubrey occasionally had a sandwich and beer, Walter content with a sandwich and a glass of milk.

The bar was owned by an acquaintance of his uncle, another World War Two vet. Walter was surprised at how many veterans were living in Alaska. He figured a lot of men must have had the same desire as his uncle, to be where there weren't too many people, and they could live a relatively free existence.

They drove around the north end of the harbor and pulled up next to a long, wooden building with a tall peaked roof in the middle, that appeared to be some sort of shop. There were several partially constructed boat hulls outside, including one covered with a large canvas tarp. Walter walked over and started to lift a corner of the tarp when a gruff, gravelly voice behind him said, "Somebody give you permission to go snoopin' about, young feller?"

Beaumont turned to see old Arnold Tuckerman standing there. He was wearing what looked like an old military parka, with wool pants and a pair of bulbous white rubber boots, grimy with various stains.

"Hello Mr. Tuckerman, how are you, sir?"

"For heaven's sake, boy, call me Arnold, so I don't go falling asleep while you run through the formality of your greeting."

Aubrey grinned at the old man's faked crankiness. Tuckerman had come to appreciate Aubrey's nephew. He also knew Walter was an exceptional kind of person, already well seasoned after one summer. He told Aubrey, the last time they had been together, it was a good idea for Walter to spend his first winter out in the forest, learning to trap.

"There's nothing interesting under the tarp, only another open-water boat I'm working on when I'm not doing repairs on the abused ones the coarse characters around here don't maintain properly. Come on in."

Inside, the long, wide building was toasty warm despite its size. The woodstove Arnold used was constructed of two fifty-five-gallon barrels, connected, one on top of the other, with two large pipes welded between the barrels. The bottom barrel had metal legs and a frame of iron strapping resting on the hard-packed dirt floor. The door for feeding firewood into the stove was on the front of the lower barrel. In its middle was a small, round opening with a disk of metal that could be screwed open or closed to control the air coming in, and a damper in the stove pipe extending up out of the upper barrel to control the heated air going up the pipe. It was putting out a lot of heat, keeping the large space in the shop warm. Tuckerman had designed it himself, using what he had on hand, getting a welder to put it all together in trade for some boat work. Along one inside wall, was a long, high stack of firewood.

The back of the shop had two smaller rooms sectioned off with plywood, one a kitchen and eating room, the other Arnold's bedroom and living area. It had stacks of all sorts of interesting looking items, almost all of them related, in one way or another, to boats and their hardware. Walter kept his curiosity from causing another cranky outburst from Arnold. Against the outside wall of Arnold's living space were two cots, made up with military surplus wool blankets. Walter learned they would be using them until they went trapping.

Ironically, despite the obviously grimy condition of Tuckerman's clothing, the tool benches full of woodworking tools and gear for boat work were spotless and well organized. There were many specialized fixtures and jigs, though most of what he saw were well-kept, old woodworking hand tools, ready to do what they were intended for.

On the left side of the shop was a boat about the size of the *Mother Lode*. It turned out to be a boat Arnold was refurbishing for a man from Anchorage who wanted it put in seaworthy condition and equipped for long lining. He intended to commercial fish for halibut and cod.

After getting settled in, they shared a wonderful fish stew Arnold had been preparing. It was tasty, a little spicy, and the cod and halibut in it came from the waters of Resurrection Bay. When the savory potful was almost ready, Arnold plopped in some quartered potatoes and short ears of corn. The potatoes were common fare, but the ears of corn were a treat, and Walter appreciated them. Arnold said, as he served the food, it was a "true New England meal."

Walter was caught off guard when Arnold said grace before eating. Aubrey sat quietly as he gave thanks for the food, and the good life they were given to live. It made an impression on Beaumont. His family never said grace when he was a child, and they only went to church on holidays.

After dinner, glasses of bourbon and one cigar in hand, since Walter and Arnold had passed on the smoke, the three men discussed the plan for trapping. Aubrey was returning to the area where he'd had a trap line some years back. He was pretty sure the types of fur-bearing animals he'd trapped there before were still available, though in what numbers would have to be discovered, once he and his nephew got there. He didn't expect anyone else to have been in the cabin, although that too remained to be seen.

The trap line was in the vast, heavy forest and mountains on the Kenai Peninsula, north of the town of Kenai. They'd have to drive up the road from Seward, turn onto the Sterling Highway, and head south through the Kenai Peninsula towards Skilak Lake.

It wasn't time to go yet. Aubrey wanted a deeper snow base to snowshoe in on. As he had told his nephew, they were going on foot.

Aubrey had never liked the task of running and maintaining dogs. He thought they were a hassle and unnecessary. Walter was disappointed, expecting to have the experience of using a dog team to travel out into the wilderness. He assumed it was the traditional way it was done. Aubrey explained it to him.

"People have traveled by foot in this country for a very long time, which is how I like to do it. I don't need the extra work of feeding and caring for a dozen or more howling dogs. We'll have enough to do as it is. Besides, the presence of even one dog can spook what we're after. We'll be fine."

"Yup," said Arnold, "and you'll probably find out why an Indian your uncle once knew named him 'Iron Legs,' though I sure can't pronounce the Indian words for it."

Aubrey looked at his almost-empty glass and smiled a little smile.

"An Indian?" questioned Walter.

"Yeah, someone I met in my early days here, gold panning and getting along out there. He helped me learn the ways to survive in the country. I never knew his Athabascan name. He told me to call him George. I'd hear him talking to himself in his own language around the fire sometimes when he was lost in thought. It got a little eerie, but he was a good man. He was bothered I could out walk him though, being a cheechako, a dumb white man. So, he gave me the name, as some kind of joke for himself, though I never quite figured out why it was supposed to be amusing. One day he didn't come around anymore, never did find out why. I was grateful for his help; he taught me a lot. Well, time for me to turn in. Night."

As Walter lay in his cot, the big shop feeling like a cave in the darkness, his mind flickered from thoughts of trapping to wondering what they would do next spring and when he might see Miriam again. He could be patient, a valuable trait.

Two weeks had gone by since they had arrived at Arnold's shop. Walter had gotten some lessons in working with hand tools and a little knowledge about boats. Arnold was happy to mentor him in these things. The old boat builder saw Beaumont was a natural in more ways than most. Whatever Tuckerman showed him once he'd absorb, and the knowledge would stay clear in his mind.

About ten days after they had arrived, Arnold took him outside and pulled the big tarp off the boat he was working on. It was an unusual hull, running twenty-six feet long. Wide in the beam, it had a surprisingly high bow, spreading out almost like a stylized pair of bird wings. The main hull was deep for the length, not a shallow-draft boat at all. It had several sharply angled fins in the bottom to help stabilize the hull in rough water, Arnold's own design. The small wheelhouse was back towards the rear, with enough room around it to get anywhere on the deck. There was a short ladder descending into a hatch located in the wheelhouse floor. You could step down into the hull and walk around almost upright. There was a surprising amount of storage space and a cozy little cabin in the bow, with a small, round porthole on either side, equipped with old-looking, brass-rimmed, heavy glass port covers.

"I've been working on this for about three months, and it's turning out the way I want. It's a smaller craft, but capable of handling some pretty rough water. It's a design I've been perfecting on paper for some time now. What do ya think, young fella?"

"Well, you're the boat designer, Mr., uh, Arnold, but even with my unknowing eye it sure looks good, it definitely does. Someone should be happy with it."

"I believe so, Walter. Listen, you take care of your uncle out there this winter, all right?"

Walter smiled. "I figure he'll be watching out for me, Arnold."

"Nah, I think not, young man. You're a natural in the wilds, according to your uncle. You mind what I say, watch out for him. Promise me to lend him a hand. He's the best man I know. This is between you and me, eh?"

"Sure thing, and I promise. Don't worry."

As if to help them on their way, it snowed hard most of the night and half the next day, over a foot of hard, dry snow. Aubrey told Walter he felt it was time to head out. They spent that night and the next day getting all their gear together, whatever would fit in two packs, except for the short, almost round snowshoes they had for the trek. Aubrey had gone over them, redoing some of the sinew lashings, and applying another coat of varnish to them. He had replaced the pivoting leather bindings, making new ones himself. They were ready for the trail.

Arnold came up to Beaumont the night before they left, with a little package wrapped in a clean cloth, and handed it to him. When he opened it, Walter was surprised to find a small, short-barreled pistol. It looked like an old-fashioned gun, in good condition, cleaned and oiled. He gave Tuckerman a questioning look.

"A trapper needs something handy to finish off an animal still alive in the trap. This little thirty-two is perfect for the purpose. You don't want to mess up a pelt any more than necessary. Take care of it."

Arnold also gave him a full box of ammunition.

Aubrey and his nephew drove the ambulance over to the food distributor's warehouse. They bought the basic food they would be taking with them, bags of coffee, salt, sugar, beans, flour, and a slab of bacon. Walter knew they'd be living simply. Instead of feeling he'd be deprived of the things most people considered essential, he was glad things would be fundamental, and they'd have to gather meat for themselves. Beaumont looked forward to being in the deep wilderness during winter, even though any little mistake could mean the end of things.

By evening, they had all their gear packed up for their trip into the woods. Some equipment was supposed to already be at the cabin they'd be staying in, if the place had survived the years of being left unoccupied.

Walter never even considered asking his uncle if he remembered the way there. He had no doubt they'd get to the trapping cabin without a hitch, his skookum uncle leading the way. He managed to get some sleep, lying on his cot, thinking of wandering through a snow-filled forest. It was a wonderful way to drift off, thoughts turning right into dreams.

Chapter 12

Trapping

"Pull up in the turn-off to the right, Arnold. This is the place where we'll start out."

The three men had been traveling for hours, from Seward up to the turnoff at Tern Lake where they'd head south on the Sterling Highway, until they reached the spot on the Kenai Peninsula where they'd head into the forest on foot.

The veteran four-wheel-drive ambulance was a steady running vehicle, though slow, and the road surfaces being inconsistent, speed was not important. The old rig was stable enough when driven cautiously, though the back end did wiggle on occasion. They all wore their parkas, gloves, and boots, because the vehicle had no decent heating.

When Arnold pulled off, he left the engine running while they all stepped out and stretched. Walter was struck by the views all around them, snow-covered trees and mountains in the background, the crisp, cold air making his nose hairs crinkle. He was in heaven, not caring one whit for the possible dangers ahead of them, feeling totally alive and ready for anything.

His uncle had talked to him about the way things would be, how it always was in winter. He described the best ways to deal with frozen rivers and deep snows, and showed his nephew how to make shelters to survive in if he got lost. Aubrey told him how to create snow caves and spruce branch shelters, with banked fires in front of the spruce shelters to reflect heat into them. He taught Walter how to build a wind block in front of the entrance to a shallow snow cave where body heat alone, sheltered from the outside air, would help keep him alive.

Aubrey untied and pulled the wooden drag sled off the roof of the ambulance. It was fairly narrow to easily slip between trees, and long enough to carry a decent load. He had built it years ago out of birch, steamed, bent, and lashed with sinew. It would service their needs over the coming winter. He and Walter loaded it up without delay. Being inactive in this weather was the wrong way to go, even wearing good, cold-weather gear.

Walter was still getting used to the wool pants and shirt he was wearing. Even though he found them itchy and rough, he wasn't going to mention it to his uncle, who smiled a little when he saw Walter adjusting his clothes a few times.

Aubrey had the old 300 H&H rifle he had bought when he first came to Alaska, from a man who decided he wasn't suited for the life and was leaving the state. He sold Aubrey the rifle for fifty dollars, and included a hundred-and-twenty rounds of ammunition. Aubrey still had forty rounds of the ammunition left, which he figured would last for years, since he only used it for hunting or protection. He had the old, double-action, 45 Colt revolver on his belt, and also carried a short-barreled twenty-two caliber semi-auto pistol in his parka, for finishing shots on trapped animals.

Walter carried his .30-06 Springfield with several boxes of 180-grain factory ammo. He had the .32 in his pack, leaving it there until it was needed.

When they were set to go, the two men said a quick good-bye to Arnold, who they wouldn't see again until a short time before breakup, at the same spot on the road. The date had been arranged. They all shook hands, and Tuckerman drove back up the highway. They stood there watching until the old ambulance was out of sight.

The sled had a double harness on it for the two men to pull at the same time over open country, but they would take turns pulling it through the forest, maneuvering between the trees.

"You ready to go, Weejer?"

"Yessir, I sure am."

As they worked their way into the forest, heading west off the highway towards a distant range of mountains, Walter was full of excitement, which soon faded when they ran into places where they had to work the sled around to get it through the woods. Aubrey took the first shift pulling, while Walter would push on the rear uprights to help out in tight spots. This made it much easier on Aubrey, but it wasn't easy. Walter was pleased when they came out onto an open area of tundra. But it was small, and soon enough they were back in thick forest.

His uncle never made a sound of exertion, complained about the bad spots, or cussed the difficult traveling as some might. Walter wasn't one to bemoan his own problems either, so the two men worked their way silently through the spruces.

After several hours, Walter took his turn at the harness, slipping the pull strap over his head, and under his right arm, pulling the heavy sled along. Once he had some momentum moving forward, it went easily enough. He was actually enjoying the process, feeling like an old-time character out in the wilderness doing what had to be done to make it through.

Snowshoeing while pushing or pulling the sled took some getting used to. It was more complicated than just shuffling along, without the sled threatening to catch him up, causing a fall and possible injury. He did as he always did, using his natural abilities to quickly learn the right way to move.

His uncle let out a quiet little whistle. Stopping and turning partway around, Walter saw Aubrey pointing off to the north. Following his arm, he saw a truly huge bull moose standing still about sixty yards away, watching their movement through the trees. It had an enormous rack of antlers. The moose didn't move, and they continued on, leaving him to live as a free-roaming animal, with few concerns, unless a full pack of wolves might try to bring him down.

After several more hours it was growing dark, time to set up shelter for the night. They had brought a canvas tarp, and after cutting and tying a small pole between two trees, laid the tarp over it, tying it on by the corners. Walter cleared off some snow from the ground beneath the tarp, and laid down a thick bed of spruce branches, while his uncle built a fire in front.

Cooking some thick pieces of bacon on sticks over the fire, then laying them up on some slices of bread from a loaf they had brought, the two settled in for a much-needed meal, with cups of hot coffee to drink afterwards.

They talked for a little while, mostly about trapping in the country they were already crossing, but the long hours caught up to them, and soon they were tucked into their sleeping bags, resting in preparation for a new day.

As would be his way in the years to come, when Walter was in the bush and other wild places, he'd wake up now and again, look around, and go back to sleep. Though he wasn't immediately aware of it, his uncle did the same.

Waking up with the land still cloaked in darkness, they took their time warming up and getting the kinks out of their joints. Even Walter had sore, tight muscles after the previous day's travel through uneven country with the loaded sled.

It was noticeably colder in the morning than on the day before. Beaumont looked forward to getting on the trail again, knowing the activity would help warm him up. There was enough light to see by when they finished their simple breakfast of oatmeal and coffee.

Beaumont offered to take the first shift pulling the sled, but his uncle said he'd start off, preferring to let Walter take over in the afternoon.

The trees thinned out soon after they started, making traveling easier. As they made their way, Walter noticed blaze marks on trees made by chopping away chunks of bark with axe or hatchet. After spotting half a dozen of these markings, which were about three feet over his head, Walter mentioned it to his uncle when they took a ten-minute break. Aubrey seemed weary, and Walter realized he was old enough for pulling a load to be taking their toll. He was glad he was there to help and realized now what Arnold had been talking about.

"Actually, those are trail markers I cut years ago, when I was first out here. Figured it was better to have them until I got used to the trail. There was a much heavier snow layer when I did it, which is why they're high up the trees. The man I took over the trap line from brought me out to the cabin in winter. He didn't want to wait until spring to head back to civilization, after trapping out there for years,

118

weary of the isolation. The old trapper needed to get back amongst people again, to get his mind right. He told me one more winter alone might have proved his undoing."

His uncle's story about the old trapper reminded him of the Craig brothers on Evans island, and how they, or at least the older brother, seemed to have gone off. He wondered if the police had followed up on Aubrey's call to the harbor master in Seward about his suspicions regarding the younger brother possibly having come to harm. He made a mental note to find out when they got back to Seward in the spring.

Now his mind turned again to Miriam. Walter thought he had managed to put the situation in proper perspective, to keep it from causing potentially dangerous distractions out in the wilds. He knew he needed to keep his mind on what was happening in the present. But, in quiet times, he couldn't help thinking of her.

As they traveled along, he searched the snow on either side of the trail for sign, and saw a number of different tracks along the way. He identified rabbit, marten, fisher, ptarmigan, and a track of paw prints he hadn't been shown by his uncle. They were three or four inches across, with five widespread toe prints and a wide pad behind them. The clearly visible claw marks showed they were made by some predator. Aubrey told him they were wolverine tracks.

"I hope we take some. The pelts are paying well right now, from what I've gathered."

It turned out Aubrey had been right. They reached the cabin as the light was failing in late afternoon. The little structure had several feet of snow on its peaked roof. It had been built on the ground out of spruce logs about eighteen inches in diameter. For its small total size of twelve-by-fourteen feet, the logs seemed quite large. It certainly looked like a place able to survive many a winter's snow. They stepped up onto the front porch, protected by about a four-foot overhang created by leaving the roof logs long in front. Two poles with the bulbous shapes of burls on their lengths were used to hold up the porch roof. They took their snowshoes off and hung them on long wooden pegs driven into the front wall, and pulled the sled up onto the porch.

There was a thick wooden peg keeping the door latch locked. The wood had swollen over the years, and it took several hard yanks to pull it out. They walked in, leaving the door open for a little light.

There was a thin layer of frost throughout the cabin, because the interior temperature was the same as the outside temperature. The atmosphere inside gave the impression the long-unused cabin was in hibernation. It would soon be waking up.

Aubrey walked over to a kerosene lantern hanging on a hook in a cross pole overhead. He shook it and found it still held fuel. Taking some matches from his parka pocket, he raised the glass globe and lit the wick. It took a while for the ice-cold lamp to take the flame. He adjusted it once it was burning well, and closed the globe again. The frost crystals on the glass globe suddenly disappeared as the heat from the flame spread, allowing the light to bring the cabin interior into better view. Walter closed the door.

He saw a snug shelter, its walls covered with the necessities of cabin life, skillets hanging from spikes driven into wall logs, and a small shelf supported by wooden pegs driven into holes bored into another log. On the shelf were a number of dishes and cups, a coffee can with what looked like hand-carved wooden spoons, along with several metal knives and forks sticking out of the open top.

There was a large, lidded, iron pot, a Dutch oven, sitting on a wooden box. Two heavy flannel shirts and a pair of worn loden-green wool pants were also hanging from wall spikes, and there were several animal pelts alongside the clothing. His uncle told him later they were the first two pelts he'd taken, martens, and he kept them for luck. Two narrow bunks were placed across the little cabin from each other. Rolled-up pads to be used as mattresses were lying on the wooden bunks.

The cabin interior was pretty dim, the quality of light given off by the kerosene lantern dulled by the smoky glass globe. There were two small windows, each placed on opposite walls of the cabin. They didn't, Walter considered, give an impression of openness to the small log dwelling, minimal portals to the outside.

"There should be some kindling in the stove, Weejer. Let's get this place warmed up."

The small pot-bellied stove was in one corner of the cabin, inside the front wall. There was about a foot-and-a-half space between it and the wall, and there were sheets of thin metal held away from the log wall by some sort of spacers, to protect the logs from the heat of the stove. Walter realized later, on closer inspection, the sheet metal was from large square tin cans cut open and flattened.

Aubrey was right about the kindling. He said, "I could be wrong, but I do believe these are probably the shavings and sticks I put in the stove before I left, years ago. It doesn't seem like anything has been disturbed or used since I was last here. It's a good sign."

After a few minutes of the dry kindling burning, he threw in four pieces of larger wood from the small stack of split firewood next to the stove. Being quite dry too, they also took to the flames quickly.

"There's a stack of wood outside, against the cabin wall. Once the fire is going, bring a couple of armloads in. Use the shovel in the corner there to clear some of the snow away."

Walter went outside. It was dark, only a sliver of moon showing in the night sky. He could clearly see vast numbers of stars, identifying the Big Dipper and Orion, before clearing snow away from the head-high stack of split wood running most of the length of the cabin. He took four armloads of wood into the cabin, stacking it neatly near the stove. Walter knew right away things had to be kept as orderly as possible in such a small space, occupied by two people. He sensed the little cabin would prove to be a cozy home for them when they weren't spending time trapping in the bitter cold and deep snow.

Beaumont felt no pleasure at the prospect of killing animals for their skins, but it was a traditional way people made a living in these forests, so he was willing to accept the process, and was looking forward to his uncle teaching him the proper way to obtain and work the furs to prepare them for market.

Above all, he had a great desire to spend time out in this incredible country. On the way in, he focused on observing and mentally noting landmarks for future reference. They were deep in it, and there was a whole new world to experience.

It took several hours for the little place to develop enough warmth to warrant removing their parkas. Aubrey was busy preparing a stew for dinner. The Dutch oven was on the stovetop with two potatoes, a couple of carrots, a small onion, and a pound of cut-up meat they had brought in. It was the last "outside" meat they would have while trapping. They had also brought several cans of Spam and one of corned beef, for a little variety, and if no other meat was available. Walter had never eaten either. His father hated canned meat, having had his fill of it in the army, so there was never any in the Beaumont home. Aubrey had actually enjoyed the stuff while in the military, and still used it fried in sandwiches, as breakfast mixed with eggs, and for corned beef hash.

While Walter did not share his uncle's enthusiasm after the first time he tried it, he would eat it all the same.

Aubrey told him they would hunt for a moose the next day, their meat for the winter.

"There were always moose around when I was living here. Hopefully the population is still good."

Walter had seen several sets of moose tracks running through the snow nearby while they were coming in on the trail. He hoped they could obtain one without much trouble, and get on with the trapping. As if reading his mind, Aubrey told him things changed in the bush without notice, and getting a moose might take some effort.

The stew tasted delicious after the long day of snowshoeing. Soon, the store-bought bread would be gone, along with the bacon and the few vegetables they'd brought.

They would get down to the business of trapping in the bush, their days and nights reduced to the basic process of survival, staying warm, and eating regularly. Their priorities would trim down a great deal before all was said and done.

There were a few old books on a shelf above one of the bunks. One was Mark Twain's book about his time in the Old West, called *Roughing It*. Beaumont figured the title could be applied to where they were now, and how they would exist.

The next morning dawned clear and very cold. The fire had died down, and the frigid temperature outside had found its way in. While Walter didn't want to leave his warm bed, he needed to get things going, instead of his uncle having to do so. Walter felt it was his obligation, being younger, to help out in any way he could. Besides, he had promised Mr. Tuckerman he would do so. After slipping on his wool socks and pulling on a flannel shirt, he got the fire restarted. As the wood began putting out heat, he got fully dressed and went outside to put snow in the metal bucket sitting next to the woodstove. He packed it full, brought it back in, and set it on top of the woodstove. Walter was surprised to see how low the level of the water was in the bucket when the snow had completely melted. Still, it was enough to make a pot of coffee.

His uncle had awakened, and was sitting on the edge of the bed, stretching and rubbing his arms. Walter knew from past experience to let his uncle speak first, meaning he was awake enough to interact. Walter brought him a cup of coffee when it was ready, and Aubrey nodded his thanks. By the time the cup was empty, he was ready to start the day.

Two hours later, they were out in the trees again hunting for moose, snowshoes on, rifles slung on their shoulders, and pack frames on their backs.

It quickly became obvious there were still moose in the area. They crossed a number of sets of tracks, several of which Aubrey knew were made by a cow moose. He had told his nephew this was, of course, hunting for the sake of survival, not for sport. They would take either a bull or a cow, which ever they came across first. Even though the cows were smaller, they were still big enough to supply plenty of meat. He said, "Better to find a cow moose instead of no moose at all. Besides, you can't eat antlers."

As if to settle the issue, they found hoof prints made by a large bull, which could provide enough meat for the whole season.

They followed the prints for about a half mile when Aubrey suddenly put his hand up, causing Weejer to stop immediately and search the area for sight of the huge animal, and huge it was. About seventy yards away, visible in a small opening in the trees, the moose was standing by some willows, eating his fill. It was a massive bull, going sixteen- to eighteen-hundred pounds.

The animal had a truly majestic set of antlers. The brow tines were long, despite the points on the top and sides of his paddles being well rounded. This meant the bull was slipping past his prime. Yet he would still be a force for younger bulls to reckon with during the rut.

In a low whisper, Aubrey suggested they get closer to make a clear shot.

They were able to close the distance to about fifty yards when the moose stopped browsing and looked around. It knew something was up, and was trying to find the source of concern, but too late. Aubrey already had the 300 H&H up to his shoulder, and a moment later he fired. The bull didn't seem to react to the bullet's impact, even though Aubrey knew he had made a good shot. The moose moved off through the snow at a steady trot. Less than two minutes later, he stopped, let out a moan, stumbled, and fell on his side. He struggled to rise again, but didn't have the strength. He was done.

Aubrey thumped Walter on the back, saying, "Now we're good. Let's get him dressed out."

Though Walter was pleased, he soon learned the truth in the old saying, "After you kill a moose, the real work begins."

The moose was lying against a birch tree, and it was a real task to get it into a good position to field dress. It was no different than gutting any other game animal, deer or black bear, except it was a lot larger. Aubrey was certainly no stranger to the process, and he told Walter what he needed to do to help. It took about an hour to dress and quarter the bull. They loaded both their pack frames with meat and started back to the cabin. The loads were heavy. To carry lighter loads now would mean more for them to pull in the sled, which they would bring back to make transporting the rest of the meat easier. It took two sled loads to bring all the useable meat back to the cabin. Pulling the loaded sled was definitely harder than Walter anticipated, even with Aubrey pulling beside him. No matter, they got it done.

Darkness overtook them before they got the final sled load to the cabin, but there was enough light from the partial moon for them to follow their own tracks back. Luckily, each time they had returned to the kill only a few ravens and jays had come to help themselves to the meat. They flew off a short distance when the men arrived, noisily declaring their annoyance at having their meal interrupted. The men knew as soon as they left again the birds would return to the kill. Hopefully nothing else would discover the site. There was enough offal left behind for birds and predators to clean up. They took the heart and kidneys back with them, along with a good-sized portion of the liver. Beaumont had never cared for beef liver. Moose liver fried in bacon grease, however, proved to be firm and tasty.

Aubrey had set several leg-hold traps near the remains, staking them into the ground and covering them with a light coating of snow. He scattered some small pieces of meat over them, and would return in several days to see if there was an animal in the trap. He had cleaned the traps and boiled them the night before, to kill any human scent.

Walter and his uncle had hung the quarters and ribs on a pole lashed between two nearby trees, keeping them from the reach of predatory animals. The hanging meat was well frozen by the time they returned to the cabin. It would be a simple matter of lowering the meat and cutting off a piece with the Swede saw when needed. They had handily provided themselves with meat for the winter. Now it was time to place the traps and snares where they would be best set to catch furbearers. Aubrey set up traps at the bases of tilted trees martens and fishers were using as part of their natural paths. He used bits of bacon and moose meat for bait.

Walter didn't realize how long the trap line was, until Aubrey told him to take the thick old wool blankets out from under the beds. They would sleep out while working the line, setting enough traps to make it worthwhile. He and his uncle snowshoed for miles, pulling the empty sled. Walter was weary after keeping up with his uncle as they worked the line. He wondered if what Tuckerman had said was true. Aubrey seemed energized, being out in the territory he obviously loved. The old Indian his uncle had known had apparently named him right in calling him "Iron Legs."

He had also taught Aubrey how to make pemmican, and he had brought a ten-pound bag of it with them, keeping it in the freezer at the seafood restaurant until it was time to go. It wasn't too bad, though the fat in it took some getting used to. But it provided a good source of energy while trapping, out in the freezing weather.

Walter was cold the whole time they were out, though not to the point where he couldn't function. He found it better to stay on the move and keep the blood flowing. The wool blankets and the camp fire at night thawed him out enough to be all right the next morning, when the process began all over again.

His uncle impressed and motivated him to do his best. The man always did what he had to do and kept on going. Walter thought Aubrey's military experiences fighting in the dead of the European winter, poorly equipped, had enabled him to press on regardless.

Three days later, after warming up at the cabin and eating more meat and fry bread than he thought he'd ever want or be able to, they headed back out again. They had found a few caught animals on the way back to the cabin, and reset the traps. There were a large number of traps holding marten and fisher, and a fine mink, perhaps twenty-four inches long, when they worked up the line again.

To Aubrey's delight, there was a mature lynx, still alive, in one of the leg holds. Aubrey had spread bacon grease on a stick and placed it over where the trap lay in the snow. The big cat was lying quietly, and didn't seem to have struggled much once it was caught. Walter thought it a beautiful animal, with its thick, finely marked pelt.

Aubrey walked up as close as was safe and killed the animal with one head shot from his .22 pistol. He laid the carcass in the sled with the others, and they continued on down to the end of the trap line. They slept there, and headed straight back to the cabin in the morning. It took them a day to return. Aubrey said if they were going to work the line regularly, they'd build a small line cabin at the end, perhaps the following summer.

Back at the cabin, Walter watched his uncle as he skinned and processed the pelts. It seemed easy for him, though Beaumont knew there were years of experience and skill behind what he did. He watched every detail closely, planning on doing his best to emulate his uncle.

As with many other things, Walter was a natural, and the first time he skinned out a marten, a small animal requiring skill to do, Aubrey shook his head in wonder, as his nephew cleanly and carefully did what was necessary to create a marketable pelt, needing only a few suggestions.

The second time they ran the line, Beaumont was surprised to find two trapped coyotes. While he knew there were coyotes in Kansas, he had never thought to find them this far north. His uncle didn't think much of them, their value as furs not much compared to the other furbearers they were after. But he didn't want to waste the animals or their pelts, so he worked them also. Aubrey was disappointed they hadn't caught any wolverine, with their beautiful, thick fur.

There were several light snows the first month they were trapping, a foot or eighteen inches overall. Aubrey would have been happy to get more, but at least they would not have great loads to push off the roof and from around the cabin.

The nights were spent working pelts, and eating plenty of moose meat prepared in a number of ways. Walter never tired of moose. The taste was excellent, even though it was an older bull they had taken, and their spices to flavor the meat were limited to salt and pepper, chili powder, and some dried garlic.

There was spruce-needle tea to drink, though it took Beaumont some time to get used to the flavor. Some bags of Lipton tea were in the cabin, sealed in a metal can. Drinking tea helped make the coffee last. They restricted their intake to one cup of coffee in the morning, and one at day's end, when they were not on the trap line, and some old instant when they were, whose only benefit was that it was hot.

Aubrey taught Walter to make bread in the Dutch oven. It was a simple recipe: flour, salt, baking powder, and water. They had cut some thin strips of moose meat and hung them on a wire near the woodstove to make jerky, and would sometimes break up a strip into small pieces and put it in the bread dough for flavor. Walter loved the taste.

The food they ate, Aubrey had eaten for years in the past, and while it was satisfying, he had no great love for it. It was fuel to him, and he was glad they were well supplied.

Aubrey taught his nephew to play gin rummy and dominoes. They spent pleasant hours at night trying to best each other at the games, once their necessary work was done. They talked about wilderness living and trapping, the uncle telling his nephew some of the stories he had heard, and about the interesting characters living in the northland. Most were tales of hard work, disaster, disappointment, and wrongful behavior.

Aubrey told him one story of a man in the Yukon who met his end in an unusual way. Aubrey began the story:

"He was not a good man. He had a mean streak, and a total lack of love for his fellow human beings. He had treated a number of men, and several women, badly and violently. He was also known for treating his dogs harshly.

"There was one dog he owned, a malamute mix, who seemed to accept the beatings and lack of food as normal. He never became aggressive towards the man who treated him cruelly, even though he was a large, tough animal who managed to survive the heartless treatment.

"One day, the folks who dwelled in the small village where this fellow lived had enough of his antisocial behavior. He had mistreated one man's young daughter, and it was the final straw. They had a community get-together and decided he had to go.

"Half a dozen men went over to his ramshackle cabin, broke in with drawn guns and subdued him, tying his hands behind him. They walked him to a tree with sturdy, horizontal limbs. All of the villagers were there, including mothers with their children.

"They had a brief, to-the-point conversation with the fellow, before they tossed the rope over a big tree limb, stood him on a tall wooden box, put the noose around his neck, and were going to kick the box out from under him, when someone came running, yelling that the church was on fire. All the villagers ran off, leaving the man standing on the box, right at the point of meeting his maker. He yelled for someone to let him down, hoping he might somehow make his escape, but no one came to his aid.

"He waited, trying not to move, when who should come trotting up the street but his big dog, the malamute mix. The dog stopped right in front of the box and stared up at his abuser, a strange look in his eyes.

"Standing on the box, his head still in the noose, the cruel man got nervous about this dog staring up at him, knowing there was no love between them. The dog put both his front paws on the top edge of the box and pushed. The box rocked back a few inches. The man yelled at the dog to get away, and tried to kick at him. This only served to throw him off balance. When he managed to get square on his feet, the dog pushed against the box a second time, putting the man off balance again, and he started to fall sideways. Before he could restore himself, the dog shoved once more and the box fell from under him. The canine backed up a few feet, as his former owner struggled against the inevitable, and watched until the man stopped struggling, having met his intended justice. Only then did the dog turn and trot away, never to be seen again."

It wasn't a particularly light-hearted story, and Walter wasn't sure if it was true, but he figured it certainly could be a real tale from Alaska.

Another month had gone by, and the two trappers had harvested a thick stack of hides. Winter was still solidly frozen in, the temperatures sometimes reaching thirty-five below. On those coldest of days, they would only do what needed to be done, bring in firewood, melt snow for water, work on hides, and maintain their gear.

Beaumont had cleared a path to the outhouse, located a short distance behind the cabin. It was a sturdy structure, made of short pieces of logs fitted together, with a sod roof like the cabin; however, there was nothing pleasant about having to slog through deep snow in the middle of the night to answer the call, sitting on the icy-cold, wooden seat. So, at Walter's suggestion, and Aubrey's amusement, his nephew made a coyote-fur seat cover to sit on. After using it a few times, Aubrey had to admit it was a worthwhile idea.

One night, as Beaumont left the outhouse to walk back to the cabin, he heard a wolf call. The howl sent chills down his back, though not out of fear. He had hoped to hear the sound before now. Knowing wolves were a major creature in the northern wilderness, he wanted to experience hearing them. They had found tracks while on the trap line, though they had yet to see or trap a wolf. Several times, there were prints all around a number of the traps in one area, and yet a wolf had never tripped a pan and been caught.

As he stood listening, there were answering calls, and at one point, in Walter's mind, the eerie song was all there was. Hearing it added an important part to the amazing puzzle of Alaska. It fulfilled something within him, and made the reality of being in the northern wilderness much more complete.

When he walked back shivering into the cabin, the wolves finally ending their communications, Aubrey looked up and saw something had affected his nephew. He figured it out within moments, knowing how Walter felt about Alaska, as he, himself, was bonded to the place.

"The wolves sing Alaska into you, did they?"

Beaumont smiled, his uncle's remark hitting home. "They did, it was amazing."

"Well, that about sums up everything here, doesn't it?"

"Yes sir, I believe it does."

The two men had been out on the trap line for a full day. It had been lengthened about three more miles since they had started trapping, to cover fresh ground and not take all the furbearing animals in one area. They had turned off to the north from their usual trail, and managed to take a number of marten and ermine, and a large wolverine which had almost escaped the number-three trap it was in, the caught paw partway out of the jaws when they showed up. Walter walked up and quickly fired a round from the .32 pistol Mr. Tuckerman had given him to use. It was doing a good job of dispatching animals not yet dead in the trap. The wolverine was an amazing looking animal with truly gorgeous fur. No wonder his uncle had wanted to harvest them.

They would have to spend the night out, the darkness making it a difficult trek back to the cabin.

Under a shelter of spruce boughs with a good fire going in front, they lay there quite comfortable in their winter gear. The crackling fire lulled the two men into a peaceful mood. They had finished their simple meal of moose jerky and fry bread, using handfuls of snow to wash down the food. There was no coffee to drink.

Aubrey sighed, and pulled out a cigar from his shirt pocket beneath his parka. He bit the end off, and lit it with a burning stick from the fire. Getting a whiff of it, Walter had a desire to smoke one himself. But he had learned the taste didn't live up to the smell, and ignored the impulse.

"So, Weejer, is this like living in Paradise, or not?"

"Sure is. There are so many places in the world I've never been, but I have the feeling they wouldn't match up."

"Well, you'll see new country when you join the army, and you'll have a chance to find out if it's true."

Walter had forgotten about his promise to spend time in the military. He wasn't happy about it, not wanting to leave for any reason, but he had promised. He considered what his uncle had told him about doing his service, before putting it out of his mind again.

Back at the cabin, Aubrey went out to chop some dead trees for firewood. He had gathered his share over the years, and this would be one more time when he'd work to keep warm twice, once when he cut the wood, and again when he burned it in the woodstove.

He had Walter to help this time. He'd come out after his uncle cut down the trees, to help him process them into firewood.

He had brought down two dead trees cleanly, but the third one got caught on a live spruce. He needed to cut pieces off the bottom of the hung-up tree, allowing it to fall. But when he started to make the second cut, the tree was released by the one tangled with it, and its base slid directly against his lower right leg, breaking it. The pain was intense. In a sitting position on the snow, taking off his snowshoes, he pulled up the torn wool pant leg as high as possible, and saw one end of his lower leg bone pushing out below the skin's surface. The flesh over the break was lacerated by the rough surface of the cut tree impacting it.

He was about one-hundred-and-fifty yards from the cabin. Pulling his 45 revolver out, he fired three shots, to signal for help. In a few minutes, his nephew came snowshoeing up to him.

"Leg's broken. Help me get back to the cabin."

They got him up with his arm around Walter's shoulders, and slowly made their way to the log structure. Sitting him on his bed, Walter helped his uncle out of his parka, and carefully removed his pacs.

When Beaumont helped his uncle out of his pants, he could immediately see the injury. The break was obvious, the leg raw and becoming swollen. As he cleaned the area with warm water, Walter listened to his uncle talking about the way they would proceed.

"I won't insist you set the bone, Walter. You might get it right, or, moving the bone the wrong way could cause more internal damage. I would be willing to let you try, but I don't want you to have any regrets."

Walter was unsure of himself, and worried he would make it worse for his uncle. But, he had the feeling leaving the leg as it was could be a bad thing. "Well, if you know how to do this, I'll make the attempt, if you think I should."

"I do, son, and yes, you should."

Beaumont nodded, then did as his uncle asked and got the partial bottle of whiskey from the cooking area shelf. Aubrey told him what they needed to do, pull the foot straight out to let the ends of the broken bone slip together.

They talked a while, and Aubrey took half a dozen good gulps of the bourbon. When the whiskey seemed to have dulled his senses, he reached his arms over his head, grabbed the uprights of the bed, and nodded. Beaumont, holding onto Aubrey's foot, studied the broken lower leg, until, without warning, he pulled as hard as he could, and the bones shifted. He had to do it one more time, to make things right.

This time, his uncle passed out, instead of grunting loudly as he had the first time. The bone seemed right where it should be, as Beaumont felt along it on both sides of the break. Pulling the wool pants back on his uncle, he went out to gather some small willow branches as Aubrey had instructed him, to make into a splint, which he tied around the leg with strips of flannel from one of the old shirts in the cabin.

His uncle regained consciousness a short while later, and Walter told him he thought it had gone all right. Aubrey nodded, and let himself drift into sleep, aided by another shot of bourbon. As he dozed off, he said, "See what I mean, Weejer, let your focus slip a little, and all hell breaks loose."

Walter didn't get much sleep, waking up to check on his uncle numerous times during the night. He had decided what to do, come morning. He would put Aubrey in the sled with one of the thin mattress pads to lie on. He would cover his uncle with the heavy wool blankets from the cabin, then haul him out to the road, and get him the help he badly needed.

When the light in the morning sky brightened as much as it would, he prepared for the journey. The mattress pad fit well on the sled, curving up on each side, which would cushion Aubrey against the many bumps and bangs on the rough trail, and shield him a little from the cold. Once he was settled in and well covered, Beaumont placed a pack in the bottom end of the sled. It carried what food and gear he and his uncle figured would be needed to make it out.

They started down the trail, Walter pulling the sled with both tump lines crisscrossed over his shoulders. He carried Aubrey's pistol in its holster on his belt, leaving the .30-06 and the 300 H&H stashed in the cabin.

Aubrey had tried to convince Walter to leave him and go get help, but he would not leave his uncle behind. He knew the leg would be much worse by the time he brought help back to the little cabin, and he wasn't willing to chance it.

As he pulled the sled, Walter kept glancing up to locate the blazes chopped into the trees. His uncle's advice to look up while out in the forest paid off.

It was fairly easy going for the first several hours. Walter was fit, and the more open sections of widespread trees they passed through helped. But the forest turned thick again, making traveling more difficult and blocking some of the winter daylight.

The several snowfalls that had come while they were trapping completely hid the sled and snowshoe sign they made coming in. Walter, in addition to seeing the blazes up in the trees, had a sense of the direction to follow. He had noted the way in carefully, but a trail walked in the opposite direction for the first time can look totally different. Beaumont managed it well enough though, turning around occasionally to see the blazes on the opposite side of the trees.

He had been pulling the sled steadily for over four hours, when he heard his uncle calling to him.

"Weejer, you need to stop for a while," he told him, "so you'll have something left at the end of the trail, understand? Make camp for now."

"We've still got a little daylight left, and I want to push on a while longer, then we'll make camp. You lie back now, okay?"

The injured man nodded. Walter dug around in the pack and pulled several pieces of moose jerky from a cloth bag. He gave Aubrey one, and chewed on the other as he continued to drag the sled over the snow-covered trail. Aubrey took only a couple of bites, and then fell into a state of semi-consciousness brought on by fatigue from his now infected injury. He had said nothing to his nephew about how he felt, knowing it could only worry him. Walter pushed on.

An hour later, daylight fading quickly, Walter tied a tarp between two small spruce, protecting the sled as best he could. He built a fire, and melted some snow in a pan. When it was boiling, he made a cup of spruce needle tea, and had his uncle drink some. He tried to get him to chew some jerky, but Aubrey had no appetite, dropping off again after swallowing several gulps of the soothing drink.

Walter was concerned about his uncle's condition though he knew he was doing as much as possible to help. He ate some of the remaining jerky and a big piece of fry bread. Beaumont figured he'd need at least another full day to get to the road, and intended to get there any way he could. Though he wanted to stay awake in case Aubrey needed something, after stacking more wood on the fire he dropped off to sleep, done in from his efforts.

In the wee hours of the morning he woke up, hearing some scratching sounds. Carefully pulling the big pistol from its holster, he saw, in the glow of the fire, two wolves near the bottom of the sled, pawing at the blankets covering his uncle. Pointing the pistol over their heads, he yelled at the top of his lungs, firing a shot in the air at the same time. The wolves instantly disappeared into the surrounding darkness.

Aubrey jerked upright at the sound of the shot, barely glimpsing the fleeing wolves, then fell back again. Looking at Walter, he said, "Thank God for you, son. I'd be a goner right now, if it wasn't for you."

Seeing a glistening on his uncle's face in the glowing firelight, Walter put his hand on Aubrey's forehead. It was hot. His uncle's condition was worsening.

For the first time he could remember, Walter was truly scared, fearing he might not get his uncle out in time. He knew now, anything could happen in the bush.

He got little rest for the remainder of the night, bringing himself around to stoke the fire, and keep watch in case the wolves came back. If they did, he'd shoot to kill.

The moment there was enough light to see, Walter headed out again. He roused his uncle enough to urge him to drink more tea, but the injured man had no desire to drink or eat anything. Walter managed to get him to sip a little, and no more. There was nothing else he could do but continue on.

He ate more jerky, and had a big piece of pemmican, slipped the lines over himself again, and started out. His feet were numb from cold as he began walking. Feeling soon returned, and the pain of them warming up made him growl and move even faster.

Beaumont thought of nothing else but the trail in the next hours, and getting his uncle to the highway. Time lost significance, and he had no idea how long he had been pulling his precious cargo. He was exhausted, his shoulders and back hurting constantly, but he ignored the pain and pressed on.

He didn't stop until he saw the raised roadbed right in front of him. Straining with all he had left, he pulled the sled up to the shoulder of the highway, and checked on his uncle, who was unconscious. Walter felt for a pulse, and put his ear to Aubrey's mouth. He was still hanging on, though Walter knew he needed help badly. Uncovering his injured leg from under the blankets and unwrapping the cotton cloth bandage, he saw the wound looked raw. There were several short red lines coming from the wound itself. Walter wasn't sure what it was, but he knew it wasn't good. Rewrapping it and covering his uncle as best he could, he sat on the end of the sled and waited. A large bull moose came up to the road from the other side, looked both ways as if watching for traffic, and crossed over the road, disappearing into the trees. In a brief moment of humor, Walter thought how handy it would have been to have a moose to pull the sled. He was weary, and nothing seemed right.

He was half dozing, trying to stay awake in case a vehicle came by. There had been no sign of a car or truck since they'd arrived over an hour ago. His uncle lay still in the sled. Hearing a noise overhead, Beaumont lifted his eyes to the sky. A single engine light aircraft came sliding through the air, barely two-hundred feet up. The Cessna 180 flew on a short ways, banked, and came back around. As Walter watched, the pilot was looking out the window, and obviously saw him, and his uncle in the sled.

Coming back around again, he landed on the road, stopped a few yards away, and shut the engine off. The pilot stepped out, dressed in a World War Two fleece flying jacket, gloves, and a wool cap, and trotted to the sled to see what the situation was. He talked to Walter, who explained what had occurred. The man pulled back the blankets and inspected the leg.

"Did you set the leg, young man? If so, you did a fair job of it, and splinting it as well, but the flesh is looking bad. It appears some blood poisoning is setting in. Come on, let's get him into the plane, and I'll fly you both to the hospital in Seward."

His uncle safely in the plane, lying flat inside where the rear seats had been removed, Walter hauled the sled back into the trees, brushing the snow with a spruce branch to hide the activity. Watching him, the pilot smiled at the young man's thoroughness.

They took off, and the pilot, a doctor from Soldotna, set his course for Seward. "I've got some coffee in my thermos," he yelled when they were in the air. "You're welcome to some."

Walter accepted the man's offer, even though he nodded off halfway through the cup. Despite wanting to observe the land below them, exhaustion had caught up to him. The pilot glanced at the sleeping young man, and shook his head. He had been living in Alaska for many years, and had seen plenty of things happen. He was glad it was 1961 and he had a plane to get them to proper medical care. Twenty years ago it would not have worked out so well. He gave the Cessna a little more throttle, concentrating on getting the man to the hospital quickly.

Walter slept until they reached Seward, shook his head, and stretched to wake up. The pilot radioed in, and there was an ambulance waiting when they landed.

Walter thanked the flying doctor, and asked if he could do anything for him.

The doctor smiled and shook his head. "I'll send you a bill one of these days," he said.

Walter was fully awake by the time they reached the hospital. He followed his uncle, now being wheeled on a gurney into the depths of the hospital building. Walter knew this was where Aubrey would get the help he needed, but it was strange being there after coming out of the wilderness only a short time before.

A team of medical staff got Aubrey out of his clothes, and checked the injured leg and his vitals before taking him away to X-Ray. All Walter could do was stand aside and watch. He took off his parka and waited.

He'd been told after his uncle was x-rayed, that they'd decide the best course of treatment, and talk to him later. Walter was shown the way to the cafeteria, and asked to wait there or in the waiting room until they came to find him. Though Beaumont wanted to stay by his uncle's side, he left the doctors alone to do their job.

Despite all his concern, Walter was ravenously hungry, so he went down to the cafeteria and got served a roast beef sandwich, some potato salad, and coffee. Not done, he ate another sandwich and a piece of apple pie. He sipped the coffee slowly, his mind far away.

Walking back up to the waiting room later, he wasn't sitting there ten minutes when a doctor came in to talk to him.

"Your uncle is going to be all right, Mr. Beaumont. One more day without help might have been much worse for him. The infection in his leg is pretty bad. We've repaired the damage to the leg, and done all we could to take care of the flesh wound. We had to remove quite a bit of dead tissue from the laceration, but it should heal well. We've given him a large dose of a general antibiotic, and when blood tests come back, we can treat him with a more specialized type. We'll keep him under observation for a while. What are your plans?"

"I don't know. We were out at his trapping cabin and I had to haul him in on the sled."

"Oh, where is your dog team right now?"

"Oh, no dogs, I pulled him out myself."

"By yourself? How far in were you?"

"Oh, maybe twenty miles or so. Not exactly sure. I got him to the road, and a man in a small airplane spotted us, landed, and flew us here from down on the Kenai Peninsula."

The doctor looked at the weary young man. He was impressed by his story and what he had done. He understood what the sick man must mean to him. "Who is the patient to you?"

"He's my uncle; I live with him. He's a good man."

"Yes, I'm sure he must be."

The doctor thought for a moment. "Tell you what, I'll have a room made up for you to stay in while your uncle is here. You can shower and get some sleep. How does that sound? We'll keep you informed on how things are going with your uncle."

Walter had considered going to Arnold's shop to let him know what had happened. He decided instead to stay near his uncle for the night. "Sounds great. I sure appreciate it."

The doctor went off to get a nurse, while Beaumont remained in the waiting room, letting the worry and burden of the last few days drop away.

Soon a nurse walked in and told Walter she'd show him where he could stay.

The hot shower felt wonderful. He tried to remember the last time he'd taken one instead of bathing with cold water or taking a sponge bath. It had been quite a while. He thought about using the disposable razor in the bathroom to shave off his beard, but left it alone, deciding it looked fine.

Beaumont lay down on the bed, and almost immediately fell into a deep sleep until a nurse woke him in the morning. His uncle had come around, and seemed to be responding well to his treatment. The first thing he asked was how his nephew was doing.

His uncle would probably be released from the ICU the next morning, though they wanted to keep him in the hospital for a while longer. Walter knew he would recover, knowing his uncle's disposition.

Later that morning, Walter called the Seward harbor master and asked him to give Mr. Tuckerman a message letting him know what happened, and asking him to come over to the hospital.

Arnold was a little peeved when he found out Walter hadn't contacted him the day before. He shook his head and asked to see Aubrey. Both he and Walter were allowed to see him a short while later. It was a happy reunion, to be sure. Aubrey was still drugged and fell asleep again, so they let him be.

After they left, Beaumont told the old man he would appreciate it if Aubrey could recuperate at Tuckerman's shop.

Arnold gave Walter a hard look and said, "You didn't even have to ask, young man." He wanted Walter to stay at his shop too.

Beaumont agreed, telling Tuckerman what he planned to do. The skins he and Aubrey had harvested were still out at the cabin, and it would be weeks before winter was over. He intended to go back to the cabin and run the trap line until the season was done. Walter wanted to leave Seward before his uncle felt better, or Aubrey would try to keep him from going out alone.

After he told Arnold his plans, the old boat builder nodded. He could see Walter had come of age out there trapping with his uncle, and dealing with the broken leg situation. Arnold took Walter out for lunch, and they returned to the hospital later. Neither of them let on to Aubrey about Beaumont's plans.

Afterwards, Arnold took him to the grocery store to buy some foodstuffs for his stay at the cabin. Beaumont included, besides more coffee, a jar of instant, bacon, salt, and flour. Arnold dropped a big jar of peanut butter in the cart. Walter grinned broadly, and patted Tuckerman on the shoulder. Arnold smiled back at him, and Walter decided when he could, he'd definitely get the old man's teeth fixed.

Next morning, Arnold took him to the turnoff for the Sterling Highway, and down to the place where the sled was located. It wasn't difficult to find.

Wishing him well, Tuckerman said, "You be sure and come back in one piece, boy. I darned well don't want to be the one to tell your uncle you've been chewed up by a wolf."

Walter smiled, shook Mr. Tuckerman's hand, then watched him drive the old ambulance back towards Seward.

An inch or so of light snow had fallen since he'd been there, which actually had kept the sled safer and harder to spot from the road. He had doubled the tarp before laying it over the sled to protect the blankets and mattress pad, and they were fine when he pulled the tarp back. He placed the pack in the sled, slipped the line over his head and shoulder, and was set to go back into the forest.

Though the trail itself would be no problem, the sky was heavy, threatening snow, and he needed to keep a steady pace heading back.

It was a rough go, despite the several good nights' sleep he'd had. Four hours into it, he was feeling fatigued, but he kept the pressure on himself to maintain a steady speed, going another two hours before stopping for the day. He made a shelter as he and his uncle had, though it felt different being there alone. He didn't mind, being familiar with the area now, but his uncle's absence did make things feel a bit off.

Beaumont put the tarp up over the sled as before, then built a fire. After eating a thick peanut butter and bacon sandwich, the bacon cooked sizzling on a stick over the campfire, followed by a cup of instant coffee, he enjoyed an unexpected treat. While going through the food to get what he needed, he found a large pack of Oreo cookies, something Arnold had apparently sneaked in. He pulled out half a dozen, and did what he always had as a child, carefully splitting them and licking the cream off. He smiled. This one little act somehow made everything okay, thanks to Tuckerman.

In need of some much-deserved rest, he climbed onto the sled and snuggled into the mattress pad, two wool blankets over him.

The next morning, he awoke to four inches of fresh snow, with more coming down. Though the fire had been snuffed, the shelter had protected him from most of the falling snow. He got up, shook the sled free of loose snow, broke camp, and continued on, chewing on moose jerky when he got hungry as he pulled his way towards the trapping cabin. After a half hour moving at a steady pace, his muscles had loosened up, making the task easier.

The old tracks were buried by the new snow. Even so, Walter had been over the trail several times now, and knew the way. The snow fortunately let up in about an hour's time, and the temperature was almost up to zero, which made it much easier to travel than in the well-below-zero temperatures when he had come out with Aubrey.

With the lighter sled weight and the early start time, Walter made it back to the cabin by dusk the second day. He got the lantern and the woodstove going, and made an easy meal for dinner, too tired to make anything fancy. Fried potatoes and Spam along with some bread did the trick.

When he went outside later to answer the call, he was disturbed to find only scattered debris, and a few bones below where the remainder of moose meat had been left hanging. He thought something had chewed through the lines holding the meat out of reach, devouring it where it had fallen. There were tracks and disturbed snow everywhere. Walter knew a pack of wolves had come in and taken his food. But he couldn't figure out how they had got to the lines, until he noticed the light rope had snapped, not been bitten through. He realized the wolves had jumped up and grabbed the meat, hanging on until the lines broke. He marveled at the intelligence and perseverance of the wolves, even though their marauding meant he'd have to hunt again, and soon.

Sitting back after eating, the woodstove warming the cabin, he went over in his mind what he would do: run the trap line and process whatever hides he got, and leave when break-up seemed imminent.

Going outside to look around before going to bed, Walter saw the aurora borealis in all its glory, showing yellow and green, streaking and sliding around in the night sky. He thought it the most beautiful thing he'd ever seen, making him ponder what could create such an amazing sight. He concluded it couldn't merely be some random natural event due to atmospheric conditions. It had to be more.

Before he turned to enter the cabin, he heard a wolf call, then another, and another. They weren't far away. He thought they might have come back because they had gotten to the meat, thinking there might be more. He'd be ready if they did, and he'd add several pelts to the harvest. He went back inside, set the stove, and lay down. All was silent, save for the gentle crackling of the fire. He thought to himself, "Home is where the wood stove crackles, and moose meat sizzles in the skillet." He smiled and drifted into a much-needed night's rest.

Aubrey had taught Walter well in the ways of the woods, including the trapping he was doing on his own while his uncle recovered. Beaumont was a seasoned woodsman after a short period of time, needing only to experience whatever was to confront him in the wilderness to know what to do. He missed his uncle's company, but was fine by himself. The woods, the cabin, and having satisfying tasks to do were all he needed. At times, his mind did dwell on the Aleut girl, Miriam, wondering where she was and what she was doing. He still thought she might find some smart young man while going to school, and would forget all about him. It wasn't because he didn't trust her feelings for him; he had learned life had a way of quickly changing people's situations, often in a mere moment of time. His Uncle Aubrey's mishap was a perfect example.

It seemed he only thought about Miriam in those quiet moments when all his chores were done. He came to look forward to those times when he felt close to her. For now, though, he had plenty of other things to keep his mind occupied, including a hunt for more meat, which he'd go on the next morning.

He awoke early, well before light, and roused himself with cold water from the bucket inside the cabin. He always kept water handy, melted from snow. He had learned to sleep with his wool socks on, not enjoying the feel of the cold wooden floor on his feet to start a day.

After breakfast he would begin hunting. He fully expected to travel for a distance and spend hours hauling the meat back to the cabin. But when he went outside to strap his snowshoes on, a large cow moose, without a calf, came walking out from the trees and stopped in the clearing off to the west side of the cabin, barely fifty yards away. She stood still as if waiting for something to happen, looking straight ahead. As slowly and quietly as he could, Beaumont picked up his .30-06 from where it leaned on the cabin wall, carefully worked a cartridge into the chamber, took careful aim, and fired. The cow started to run, stopped, turned around, and began to run the other way, collapsing about where she was when he shot her.

Walter was elated. Not only did he not have to spend time looking for moose, perhaps traveling several miles or more, but the cow had fallen, basically, right in front of the cabin.

In two hours' time he had gutted, skinned, and quartered the fallen animal, placing the meat onto the roof of the cabin, using the pole ladder to climb up. He laid spruce boughs down on the snowy roof, and covered the meat with more boughs. In the low temperatures, he figured the meat would keep well, and this way wolves, coyotes, or even wolverines would be hard put to get to the moose meat, at least not without his knowing about it when he was inside.

He brought the moose heart into the cabin, sliced it thin, and fried it, lubing the skillet with bacon grease saved in an empty spam can. It was delicious.

Beaumont left the moose innards where they lay. If anything came for them, he'd have a chance to get several more hides. It only took another day for wolves, probably the same pack that had taken the moose meat from the hanging pole, to come around, chasing off the ravens and jays gathered for a gory feast.

Walter was surprised to discover the two wolves caught in the leg-hold traps he had staked deep into the frozen ground, right up against the gut pile he had left there under a layer of snow. Even though he knew they were smart animals, and could sense when something wasn't right, perhaps hunger, as it did with other species, dulled their sense of caution.

The sound of wolves growling and yelping brought him out of the cabin. Three other wolves took off when they saw him. He watched a while making sure they were well caught, walked over, and dispatched the two animals with the little .32 pistol. The two wolves had paid dearly for the meal they anticipated when they had caught the scent.

Beaumont spent the next few weeks working the trap line and trying to stay warm. He was always focused on his surroundings as well as the specific tasks he had to do. Nothing out of the ordinary happened. Even so, the way he was living would have been extraordinary for most people who lived a mainstream life in a civilized area. For Walter, now, this was normal living. The way he had felt since a toddler in Kansas, constantly wanting to explore the natural world, had come to fruition in Alaska. His early impression of being home by coming to Alaska, only grew stronger as time went on, and he became established in the wild heart of the place.

Walter had decided to only spend one night, at most, out on the trap line. He did set more traps in different directions within an area requiring only a one night's stay in the forest. He didn't want to be away from the cabin for a longer stretch.

The first time he returned to the cabin after trapping by himself, he found numerous wolf tracks in front of the dwelling, some actually showing on the first of the two steps leading to the front porch. Disturbed snow about ten yards out showed several wolves had lain there for some time. Walking around the little log structure, he saw a lot of disturbed snow on the ground below where the moose meat was cached on the roof, but they had not been able to get to it. Beaumont smiled.

Out of curiosity, late in the night Beaumont brushed the snow smooth with a spruce branch. The next two mornings showed no wolf sign. On the morning he returned again from the traps, the wolves had been all over the place. He smiled a little, now knowing they only came when he was gone, and he didn't think it was coincidence. Finally, they stopped coming completely, giving up on getting another free meal. He had several weeks of good trapping, and his days and nights had settled down to a steady routine. Walter was disturbed to find some traps had evidence of animals being caught, except there were no animals left in the them. They had been literally ripped from them, several times leaving a severed foot behind. There was a bloodstain near each trap, disturbed snow, and nothing more. At each trap site, he saw wolf tracks, and always three animals.

Beaumont came to the conclusion these were the wolves from the small pack out of which he had trapped the two wolves at the moose kill, a male and a female. The theft at the traps continued. The only two animals the wolves didn't take was a wolverine, which showed numerous fresh wounds, and a lynx, untouched for some reason. He had no choice except to shoot the wounded wolverine, which had obviously fought off the wolves despite being caught in the leg hold. He had no way to release the animal without getting chewed up, and didn't want to leave it as it was, so he put a .32 bullet in its head killing it instantly, though it took a little time, the animal struggling to get at Walter, not to escape, making it hard to place a clean, quick shot.

This was the first time he had experienced the ferocity of the skunk bear first hand. It had fought off the wolves, was pretty badly torn up, and was still willing to sink its teeth into Walter, given half a chance. Beaumont studied the wolverine for a minute, amazed at how tough this beast had been. The hide was ruined and unsellable. Out of respect for the spirited animal, he removed the body from the trap, and took it back with him to try and salvage it for some small usage.

Lying in bed, Walter gave a thought to ending his season. He and his uncle had harvested a fine pile of prime pelts. There were marten, fisher, mink, wolf, lynx, wolverine, and the lone coyote hide. His food was running low, except for the moose meat still on the roof, though some had been pecked at by camp robbers, magpies, ravens, and smaller birds wintering in the area, which had found small openings in the boughs covering the meat. Besides, he wanted to see his uncle, to know he was all right. So, after spending one more day on the line, gathering the few animals that had been caught, and retrieving the traps, he got ready to leave, afterwards taking a short snowshoe hike through the area once more, just for the pleasure of it.

The next morning he headed out, pulling the sled loaded with the skins and his equipment. He had placed the remaining moose meat out in the clearing by the cabin for others to have, except for one full quarter he brought out with him for Tuckerman and Uncle Aubrey.

The night before leaving, Walter had gone out under a full moon, and walked to the snow-covered tundra meadow where he had taken the moose for food, and the wolves had been trapped. This night, there was no evidence of the violent life required for survival in the wilderness, a light covering of fresh snow concealing any sign of it.

As Beaumont quietly looked around, the eerie quality of the moonlight casting a surreal aspect upon the surrounding forest, he felt as if his own existence had come clear in his mind, and he understood what he loved and needed, including the perfection of the Alaska wilderness. It was a rare moment, and he had moved once again onto a different level inside himself. Walter had come to real fulfillment, and realized how fortunate he was, at his age, to have reached such a place.

Before taking the remaining moose meat into the little meadow, he'd sawed off several pieces to take along. Beaumont wasn't going to rush the trip to the road. He wasn't keen on leaving the forest, but he had other things to deal with now.

The trip took three days, with Walter savoring the nights he spent out under the trees. The crackling fire, flames reflecting strange images against the surrounding trees, always put him into a peaceful reverie, though he never completely lost an awareness of his surroundings.

The weather was warming, breakup close to turning the snow into watery mush, making travel difficult. Walter had barely left in time.

On the third day of travel, still several miles from the ribbon of road, Beaumont stopped to examine some huge prints cutting across his intended path. A brown bear had come out from its winter sleep. It was clear by the size of the tracks they were made by a very large animal.

It was okay with him, not seeing the maker of the tracks. He was respectful of the big bears from his past experiences with them. He was fine with leaving them to their solitary lives, and wanted them to do the same for him.

Beaumont was glad to finally reach the highway. He was weary from the constant strain of pulling the loaded sled, and was dreaming of another hot shower and a seafood meal in Seward.

It was several hours before an appropriate vehicle stopped to give him a ride up the highway. He needed a lift in a truck of some sort in order to transport the sled also.

Eventually, a man in a stake bed truck stopped, and said he could drop him off at the Seward turnoff before continuing on to Anchorage. Walter was glad to take him up on the offer. The fellow didn't talk much, which was fine with Beaumont. He had never been a big talker, and living in the woods had put him out of practice. Still, there was no awkwardness in the silence between them. Both had a destination to reach and business to attend to. The man did mention the fine furs Walter had with him, saying his father had trapped further north, in an area west of Fairbanks.

"It was, from what my father said, very remote country."

Walter nodded, to confirm he had heard.

There was a couple with a pickup truck stopped at the turnoff when the stake bed pulled up. They were having a snowball fight, which didn't impress Beaumont. When asked, they said Seward was their destination, and agreed to take him there, which was ideal. He didn't feel like having to sit and wait for another ride. The woman kept looking out the rear window of the truck at Beaumont. She seemed impressed by this rugged looking man with the sled full of furs. He ignored her numerous glances, sitting still in the bed of the pickup next to the sled, half dozing. It didn't seem to take long to reach Seward, and Arnold's shop.

A minute after they had arrived, the couple in the truck had driven off. Aubrey and Arnold came out of the shop, and greeted the bearded young trapper heartily, with slaps on the back and hugs from his uncle.

His uncle put a hard look on his face. He said, "Pretty sneaky, leaving me in the hospital. I was not too happy about it."

"I figured it was the easiest way to get back to the cabin without you trying to stop me. I knew you needed to recover, and didn't want to take a chance on you getting sicker, Uncle Aubrey."

Giving him a hard stare, Aubrey said, "Why the heck did you think I'd stop you, Weejer? I knew you would be fine, and besides, those furs had to come to market."

Arnold spoke up. "You wouldn't believe how much griping and complaining I've had to put up with, babysitting this cranky so-and-so. You owe me a good meal, young man."

"Well, I'd be happy to, Mr. Tuckerman. In fact, the sooner the better."

His uncle smiled and said, "Miss the luxury of a good meal, Weejer?"

"Well, sir, even though I'd love a seafood dinner, I'd rather have a hot shower first."

Aubrey chuckled. "You don't have to tell us; it's quite evident. Come on, let's get you cleaned up. After dinner, we'll check out the furs. Looks like a good season, after all."

Aubrey was pleased with the pelts Walter had added to what they'd taken before he'd injured his leg. It had made their season successful, although trapping was never a way for a man to get rich, only to keep going and hopefully survive until something better came along.

When Aubrey saw the torn-up wolverine hide, he questioned Beaumont about it, who told him the story of finding the wolverine after it had fought off the wolves, and his uncle nodded, understanding why he kept it.

After Walter had cleaned up, they headed over to the seafood restaurant, Aubrey using a crutch, obviously unhappy about the necessity.

Beaumont didn't speak much as he ate a large meal of cod, mussels, and shrimp. He didn't realize how much he'd missed the flavors. Finally full, and sipping a beer he'd decided to have, he talked with the two older men, discussing what plans they might have made for the spring and summer.

While Walter was still in the woods, Aubrey and Arnold had talked about what to do with the *Mother Lode*, since his freighting business was at an end. They had decided to convert it to a long liner to catch cod and halibut for selling to restaurants and private citizens. It was already being converted, a long line winch situated in the stern of the boat, and the hull refurbished to contain a fish-holding compartment.

"When the season gets closer, Weejer, we'll gather up all the fishing gear we'll need, and head out towards the far end of Resurrection Bay to try our luck fishing. Are you up for it?"

"You bet. Can't think of anything else I'd rather do than fish with you."

Over time, they discussed all the ins and outs of long lining. Aubrey had fished with other people a time or two, and knew what was needed to be successful, if the fish were willing, of course.

Chapter 13

Miriam Returns

Walter had taken a walk into town to buy some groceries. He was picking out some canned goods when a familiar voice he hadn't heard in far too long spoke behind him. He turned to see Miriam and another young woman her age standing there. He was surprised, and as was normal for him when around her, he remained silent. Miriam laughed, surprising him once again by grabbing his arms and giving him a big kiss, with feeling. He didn't respond at first, and she pulled back with a look on her face, as if she thought something had changed in the way he felt, until Walter embraced and kissed her with equal passion. After a while, the other girl cleared her throat. They stepped apart, both flushed with the moment.

"It's wonderful to see you, Miriam. How come you're in Seward?"

"I'm on break from school, Walter, and it is wonderful to see you too."

Miriam's normally serious expression had broken out into a wonderful smile, and Beaumont's heart skipped a beat.

"Oh, I'm sorry, this is Kathy. We met at school and have become good friends."

He shook Kathy's hand, and she said, smiling mischievously, "Hi Walter. Miriam has told me about you, lots of times." Kathy giggled, and Miriam poked her in the ribs.

"Walter, I'm staying with Kathy's family here in Seward for a while, before going out to stay at Chenega. Maybe you could come by for a visit. Would it be okay, Kathy?"

"Kathy giggled again, "I better say yes, or you two might not survive being apart."

Miriam pushed Kathy's shoulder, and gave her a pleading look. Kathy told him where her family's house was, and to come over about six. Walter and Miriam hugged and kissed again before parting.

Back at the shop, Walter told the men about seeing Miriam and his invitation to have dinner with her.

Arnold laughed loudly, saying "Ha!" He said to Aubrey, "Looks like you're not going to get much help out of the boy with his girl here in town!"

Walter blushed, feeling his neck get hot. but then the three men smiled at one other, Aubrey and Arnold pleased because Walter was happy.

Walter barely kept up with the conversation at Kathy's house. Her parents were interesting, the mother a Native woman from Illiamna, her father a Norwegian man. The mother had always lived in Illiamna until Mr. Halverson had found her there while teaching in the village. Married a few months later, they were always teasing each other, smiling and laughing together.

Walter, in a stray moment when he wasn't looking at Miriam, wondered what it would be like living with her, and if they would tease and laugh with each other as the Halversons did. Miriam cast a glance his way as he was thinking those thoughts. They looked into one another's eyes. Walter felt as if she was reading his mind. She gave him a quick wink, they both smiled, and everything felt perfect.

All too soon Miriam had gone back to Anchorage and her studies. Walter found it was even harder now to see her leave, but he knew by the way she had acted around him during this visit that she had set her mind and heart on him, and he needn't worry about that any longer.

Chapter 14

Kansas Visit

Walter had finished getting all the long lining gear stored away, and was washing down the deck. He and Uncle Aubrey had brought in an excellent catch of halibut, ling cod, and a few sablefish. The 1961 summer fishing season was over.

Despite the rough waters just outside Resurrection Bay, the boat had handled it well, as expected. The men had no trouble working together, Walter doing his job like an experienced fisherman, much to Aubrey's satisfaction. The fishing had brought them a goodly sum of money, and they planned on long lining in the future.

Walter loved being out on deep water. He was at home there, as much as he was in the forest. His uncle didn't actually care much for fishing, but it was a decent way to make a living, and with his nephew's help it had gone well. What he hadn't told Walter was his healed leg had been giving him a lot of pain, the fishing proving to him the leg wasn't ready yet for hard work, as Beaumont had already figured. Biggs was wondering if it ever would be good enough again.

They had unloaded at the fish processor in Seward, and collected their money. Now they were sitting at their favorite eatery, having steaks and French fries instead of the seafood they usually ate there.

After a full season long lining and partaking of their catch for many a meal, they preferred beef for this dinner.

Walter broached the subject of Arnold Tuckerman's bad teeth to Aubrey. "I sure wish we could do something about Mr. Tuckerman's teeth. Wouldn't it be a swell thing for him?"

"I don't know, but I have the feeling Arnold is afraid to go to the dentist. Yeah, it would be a good thing to do. Let's kick it around some more and see what happens, okay?"

The evening after their fishing season had ended, while at Tuckerman's shop, Aubrey reminded him it would soon be time to join the military. Walter didn't say anything, only nodding slightly. Miriam was back in Seward now, with a beginning position teaching at the grammar school. Walter and his girl spent as much time together as possible, and their relationship had grown and matured. To those who knew them, it seemed they were meant for each other. Knowing he was going to spend several years in the army in some unknown location, more than likely in the Lower 48, they had held back from committing to marriage, even though the idea felt right to both of them.

With fishing over, before the weather turned too cold and snowy, Aubrey and Walter worked on a sixteen-by-twenty-foot cabin for Walter and Miriam in the small clearing up beyond Aubrey's place. They kept it secret from her, wanting to wait until they were married, and surprise her with it. Beaumont didn't know if she'd want to live remote on the island his uncle had chosen for his home. If not, they could use the new cabin for their own enjoyment. Either way, it seemed like the right thing.

The winter trapping season in 1961 had been very poor, bad enough for them to pack it in early and return to Seward. Though Aubrey didn't let on, Walter could tell the leg was giving him grief, after time spent snowshoeing and trapping. Pulling the sled on the trail into the cabin had tired Aubrey, and he had spent a full day resting up. It was a disappointing time, but the two men didn't let it get them down. Something else would make things good again.

In Seward, when he wasn't spending time with Miriam, Walter worked around Arnold's shop, while Aubrey patiently waited for winter to be over.

In March, 1962, Walter and Miriam had flown down to see his parents in Kansas. He continued to see them once a year as he had promised, and bringing Miriam this time seemed like the right thing to do.

She had said, when he brought up the idea of a visit, "Do you think it's time for me to meet your parents, Walter? There isn't any reason why I shouldn't, is there?"

"No, not at all. I'd love for them to get to know you."

Flying down to the Midwest fascinated Miriam, who hadn't flown except for short distances in a small plane. It was a thrill for her to be seeing new country.

Wherever they went, it seemed everyone dealing with them were being considerate, as though their love, which was plain to see, affected those around them.

When they arrived at the small airport in Manhattan, Kansas, Walter's parents were waiting for them. From the moment Ben and Hannah met Miriam, they were taken with her. They knew she was unique, as well as beautiful, and it was obvious to them she loved their son.

Ben looked at him and said, "It's about time you showed up." He grabbed Walter in a big bear hug. While holding his boy, Ben realized he was no longer a teenager. He felt strong and mature, and Ben knew Alaska had helped him come of age.

Walter had considered shaving his beard off before visiting, but Miriam would have none of it when he told her he was going to be clean shaven for the visit.

"You look fine, Walter, with your beard full. I like you the way you are."

So the beard stayed, though he trimmed it a little to look neater. While his father barely paid attention to it, his mother mentioned, though only once, she wished she could see his whole face.

Ben and Hannah were fascinated with the stories Walter told. He left little, if anything, out. Miriam was amused at the changing expressions on their faces as the conversation covered it all, from wonderful scenery to grizzly bear encounters. Ben and Hanna were also interested to hear Miriam speak of her people, and what it was like growing up in the tiny village of Chenega.

After dinner the first night, Hannah and Miriam went into the kitchen, while Walter and Ben sat in the living room, each with a glass of whiskey. Aubrey wasn't the only one who savored a drink in the evening.

Father and son discussed entering the army. This would probably be the last time they could do so, face to face, before Walter enlisted. Ben shared what he could of what Walter might expect, though he admitted things might have changed since he had served.

He said, "To get through your time in the service takes a few simple rules. Do what they tell you to do to the best of your ability, but never volunteer for anything. Stay out of trouble with the other soldiers. If you have to take care of some business, do it where your sergeants and officers can't see, and make sure you come out on top. There are all sorts of men in the military, and while most of them are good eggs, there's always a few bad ones. When you first get in, your drill instructor will treat all of you like crap. It's the nature of the training. Never get too cozy with the officers and non-coms, or the other guys won't like you.

"If you do go into combat, though I pray you won't, I think you'll be okay. The most important thing is to back each other up. Your very survival depends on it. Listen to what your sergeants tell you. If you are offered a promotion, take it and say 'thank you, sir.' Every promotion brings you more responsibility, but I think you're up for it."

Walter told Ben about Uncle Aubrey teaching him self-defense and other useful things that would benefit him in the military.

"He also taught me a great deal about how to live in the wilderness too, dad. He's quite a skookum guy."

Ben gave him a quizzical look. Walter laughed and explained the term skookum, as his uncle had told him. Ben smiled and nodded.

"Your uncle and I spent some time together before he went north. He and I reached some understandings about what we had both been through, though we fought in different campaigns. I'm sure he taught you well, and I know it will come in handy."

"Between the two of you, dad, I don't see how I can go wrong."

"Well, I can't think of anything else to tell you. I know you'll do well, son. I'm proud of you."

Ben gave Walter another hug, and they joined the women, who were chatting away as though they had known each other their whole lives.

They talked about Walter a lot, and by the time the visit was over, Miriam cared even more about him.

Later the same evening, the night before the visit ended, Walter and Miriam sat in the old-fashioned porch swing enjoying the beautiful evening. She told him how much she liked his folks, and he said they felt the same way about her.

"Looks like we're going to have to stick together, so they won't be disappointed," he said.

"Oh, you can count on it, Mr. Beaumont," Miriam replied, and snuggled up to him. They sat quietly together not speaking, loving the moment.

Early the next morning, Walter went to the spare room and woke Miriam, told her to get dressed, and took her out back of the house to show her where he used to keep watch by the old creek. Walking around behind the fence, he was dismayed to see the creek had dried up, and most of the trees were dead and broken. It was obvious from the lack of sign that few if any animals came through there anymore. He could also see houses in the distance that hadn't been there before. Miriam took his hand, sensing what he was feeling.

"The world changes, and there's not much we can do about it. Even Alaska has changed since I was a little girl. But since it's so big and wild, it will probably take a long time before any real change is seen. At least I hope not."

He nodded, gently kissed her, and they went into the house.

They had spent a pleasant week with Ben and Hannah. Walter's father had a small store now, about a mile from the house. He was always busy there. Besides repairing appliances, he also sold new stoves and refrigerators. He was doing well, and Walter was glad for him. He knew his father to be a fair and decent man who deserved to prosper.

The four of them were saddened to say good-by at the airport. Walter told his parents he'd let them know where he would be stationed, when he found out. Miriam had given them her address in Seward, to keep in touch.

On the plane ride back from Kansas, Walter brought up the subject of his going into the army. He told her, "I told my folks and Uncle Aubrey I would go in when I turned twenty-one, but, I'm thinking of going in a little earlier. It would only be a matter of a few months, but it would mean I'd be back that much earlier. And I don't want to wait any longer than necessary for us to start living our lives together, which I'd like to do right after I get back from the army. What do you think?"

Miriam sat listening until he was done. She loved the idea of him being back sooner, and she had never heard him speak so many words at one time, which made her smile.

"I think it would be fine, Mr. Beaumont. Since I'm going to miss you whenever you go, we might as well get it over with, as you said. I trust your judgment." She took hold of his arm and leaned against him.

Chapter 15

Beaumont's Journey

It was April, 1962. When they returned from Kansas, Walter explained to his uncle what he and Miriam had decided. Aubrey saw no problem with it, telling his nephew he was as ready as could be to enlist. He never brought up the next season's fishing, thinking he'd found something easier to do. He would hire his boat out for the summer. The head of the team that had done research on Montague Island had gotten in touch and asked if his boat was available for more research teams to use, and he jumped at the opportunity.

Uncle Aubrey drove Walter to Anchorage, where he enlisted in the United States Army. He never considered the navy or marines. Both his father and uncle had been in the infantry, and it seemed appropriate for him to follow in their footsteps.

He listened patiently to the entire talk the recruiting sergeant gave about the benefits of serving in the military. When he was done, the soldier asked what he thought about joining up, and Beaumont told him he had already decided before he got there. After staring at Walter for a long moment, he handed him the necessary paperwork to fill out, and sent him to a nearby clinic where he received a complete physical. The doctor there told him he was in better condition than most of the young men he examined. "Try to stay that way," the doctor told him.

Returning to the recruiting office, Walter handed the sergeant the completed medical forms. The soldier smiled, shook his hand, and congratulated him on his decision.

When they got back to Tuckerman's shop, he told Arnold how it went. The old man nodded and continued working on the hull of a skiff he was building.

His uncle said, "I've tried to teach you all I know to help you get through whatever you experience with the least amount of trouble, but it's up to you, Walter, to keep yourself safe and sound, and to help your brothers-in-arms, and they *are* your brothers, or will be by the time all is said and done."

Walter was to report to Ft. Benning, Georgia in two week's time. When he read the documents he had received, a chill ran down his back, not from fear but excitement. He knew this was a big step for him, and he was ready to do what was necessary.

When he showed his uncle the paperwork, Aubrey nodded, a solemn look on his face. All he said was, "Well, you're on your way."

Mr. Tuckerman, standing nearby, looked at Aubrey and said, "What do you think, should we do it now or wait until he comes back?"

"Oh, we better do it now, in case he turns into a lifer and never comes back."

"Come on now," Walter said, "you know I'm coming back. Nothing could keep me away." He smiled, realizing they were teasing him.

"Come on outside, boy," Tuckerman said, "We've got something to show you."

Walking out and around the side of the building, Walter saw what was obviously a newly completed boat. He realized it was the boat Tuckerman had shown him before. It was finished now, and was beautiful. It was twenty-six feet in length, with a nine-foot beam. There was a large wheelhouse running from six feet ahead of the stern to eight feet before the bow, with a short ladder down into the forward hull. There was a door in the upper cabin to reach the bow, as well as the stern.

The hull was extra deep for the boat's length, with a shallow sleeping area in the bow end, and a small galley between it and the steps to the upper cabin, with a little table and a fixed bench seat on the hull side of the table. The seat could double as a narrow bed.

Walking around the boat, Walter saw the bow was fashioned high and wide to handle choppy water, similar to the *Mother Lode*, and it was painted the same way too, white with blue trim. There was a low brass rail around the bow, and on each side of the open stern area.

Tuckerman said, "Come on up, boy, I want to show you something."

Climbing up, he swung his leg over the rail. The engine compartment hatch was open, and there was a new-looking V-8 engine nestled inside. It had the necessary manifolds and other parts needed for marine use.

Aubrey said, "Arnold found a 283 Chevrolet engine, and decided it would be perfect for this boat. He bought it, and had a marine mechanic he knows convert it for marine use. It should push her through the water at a good clip. Probably do fifteen to eighteen knots with no problem, once it's broken in. We thought you ought to spend a little time on her before you go. Give you some incentive to stay whole and get home safe and sound. Come on down now. Got something else for you to see."

Walter was walking on air. He was stunned over this beautiful craft Mr. Tuckerman and his uncle had put together for him, but he was concerned about it, too. It must have cost a pretty penny to build.

Climbing back down the ladder and walking to the stern of the boat, he saw there was a strip of heavy paper covering the transom, below which was a fine, three-bladed bronze propeller. Walter stood still, for some reason, unable to take off the paper to reveal what lay beneath, until Arnold said, "Well, you gonna take all day? Pull the paper down."

Reaching up, Walter peeled away the paper, and was amazed at what he saw, a lump forming in his throat. The name of the boat, hand painted in gold lettering with black edging as on his uncle's craft, was *Beaumont's Journey, Seward, AK.*

A tear formed in the corner of his left eye, and rolled down his cheek.

Aubrey noticed, and put his hand on Walter's shoulder, while Tuckerman looked on, nodding with a slight movement of his head.

Aubrey spoke: "You've been a help and a blessing to me, son, and I'm happy to be able to give you something you'll use and appreciate for a long time to come."

Tuckerman said, "I feel the same, boy." The taciturn old man turned away, his eyes getting misty. He was not one to easily show his feelings.

Walter smiled and said, "You two are the best friends a guy could have, and I will never be able to do enough to deserve this. Thanks."

Chapter 16

In the Army

The droning of the bus engine put Walter in a thoughtful state, as he and the other raw recruits took the final leg of their journey to boot camp at Ft. Benning.

His mind wandered back to the last night he had spent alone with Miriam. It was a quiet time, both of them sad he would be leaving. They had previously made several trips together on the *Journey*, exploring Prince William Sound, getting to be with each other a little more in the short amount of time they had left. They stopped at Chenega, of course, where they were openly welcomed. Everyone knew Walter and Miriam were a couple, and were happy about it, except her uncle Teddy. He had been moved in the Aleut relocation, during the Aleutian campaign, and held hard feelings. He would have preferred it if Miriam had been interested in an Aleut boy.

The last trip they had made, ending up on the little island located between Perry and Naked Islands behind Chenega, proved to be wonderful for them both. It was a beautiful cove they anchored in, to relax and eat the lunch Miriam had made. Before they started eating, Miriam said to Walter, "So, this is the last boat ride we'll be able to take before you go, right?"

"True, and I don't like thinking about it."

"And we know we love each other."

"Well yes, of course."

Miriam leaned close to him, their faces inches apart. "Walter Beaumont, there's something I'd like to do before lunch. If you'd want to."

Walter sat looking at Miriam for a moment, uncertain of what she was saying. When the meaning behind her words, reinforced by the look in her eyes, suddenly hit home, he didn't know what to say, though he could feel his heart pounding.

"Are you sure, Miriam?"

"Surer than I've ever been of anything, Walter, and it will remain our secret. No one will know of this, except you and I."

In response, he took her in his arms and kissed her. He knew this was a perfect moment, with a wonderful woman, his woman. They spent the rest of the afternoon with each other in the way only those truly in love can do. There was no awkwardness from either of them, though neither had experienced this before, another affirmation of their rightness together.

The rest of their intimate adventure was spent quietly enjoying each other's company, talking and laughing, though tinged with sadness as they ran the boat back in to Seward.

Walter had driven her to Kathy's home, where she was staying. They sat together in the old ambulance, soaking up all they could of each other. Finally, Miriam hugged him tightly, slipped out of the vehicle, and watched as he headed back to Arnold Tuckerman's shop.

Walter shut off the engine and sat there in front of the shop, letting things settle down inside his mind.

"Don't worry, you'll have many years with your sweet girl, count on it."

Walter turned to see his uncle standing outside the ambulance door, a look of understanding on his face.

"I hope you're right, Uncle Aubrey, I truly do."

The three men spent the rest of the night together, eating and drinking a few beers, with the two older ones trying to tell Walter whatever they could think of that they hadn't before. He felt they had given him a good backlog of their past experiences to learn from. He knew he was ready to go on this journey to another world so unlike Alaska, and probably not like Kansas either. He knew he'd miss it greatly. It had captured his mind, heart, and soul completely.

The bus came to a stop, with a loud hiss of air from the brakes. Immediately, an older soldier, a sergeant, appeared in the doorway of the bus yelling for everyone to get on their feet, grab their gear, and get off the bus. He had them stand in a straight line, their gear in another line two feet in front of them. Everything he said to them was in an extra loud voice, yelling instructions to the new recruits, some of them thrown off by all the noise and sudden activity, some smiling to be there. Walter followed instructions straight faced, but he observed all the human activity going on around him. He had arrived, and intended to keep clean and get through basic as best he could.

The sergeant, wearing what Walter knew was a campaign hat, introduced himself and told the boys lined up in front of him exactly what they would be doing, and what they should expect if they screwed up. He ran them over to the reception center for their paperwork and medical to be done. They were stripped down and examined as though on a production line. Afterwards, they jogged in their shorts and shoes to the supply room to be issued their uniforms and personal supplies. The recruits were given three minutes to dress in uniform, and go get their "boot cut" as the sergeant called their military haircut. As soon as they were done, the men were sent to their barracks to be shown how to put their gear away properly. If the recruits thought they were through for the first day, they were mistaken. As soon as they were done stocking their foot lockers, which were inspected and dumped out if done improperly, they were set out on a three-mile run, with physical exercises mixed in. The sergeant had two lesser sergeants assisting him, as loud, if not louder, than the drill sergeant.

Beaumont knew to expect all this in essence, if not in specifics. His uncle and his father had explained to him how most recruits needed to be reprogrammed to fit in properly to the army way of doing things. Fortunately for him, Walter was capable of adapting easily. The tough life he'd been living, as well as his own natural fitness made things easier for him than most, though not easy. He did as he was told, and took what was required of him as a challenge to do his best.

He recognized what the drill sergeant had to do with these young men in the next nine weeks: make them into solid, basic soldiers. He could see it wasn't going to be easy, and he had only himself to depend on these first weeks.

That night, amid the quiet moanings and groanings from most of the young men, sore and tired from being worked hard, he let his mind take him to Seward, and the other places he already missed. Ft. Benning was a big facility. He could see wooded areas within the camp's perimeter during their run, and hoped he might get a chance to explore before leaving. What he didn't know was he and all his fellow recruits would have plenty of time to see what comprised the base.

When he received his military field manual to memorize, Walter absorbed it like a sponge, his mind always ready for new material to make use of. Some of the other boys had a lot of trouble, and he found himself being asked for help. At first he hesitated, until he realized if there was ever a time when these men would all be trying to survive combat together, they needed to rely on each other. His mind made up, when he could, he tutored a couple of the men.

The sergeant was aware of Beaumont helping out, and he didn't say anything to him, though he made a mental note of it. He had been in the army many years, and recognized a man with desirable qualities and character. It was obvious to him Beaumont was one of those. As time went on, and Walter never skipped a beat in either PT, basic training in the use of small arms, and the way he interacted with others, he knew he had a potential leader.

There is always someone who can't let things be smooth and trouble free. They always have to stir things up and make problems where there are none. Stanley Bucks was one of these. He had already found a smaller man lacking in confidence, and Stanley hassled the guy every chance he got, making him miserable. He verbally abused the fellow, whose name was Sandler. Bucks called him Sandbox.

Sandler had trouble dealing with his training because of the treatment Stanley gave him. He once stole Sandler's boot laces, and Sandler was given extra PT for losing them, and made to wear his boots without laces for a time, making running and other activities more difficult.

Walter saw what was going on, and while many of the men found it amusing, Beaumont's dislike for bullies hadn't changed since he was a child. Late one evening, after lights were out, he went over to Stanley's bunk while he was sleeping and grabbed his trachea with his fingers the way his uncle taught him. With enough pressure, he could have crushed the man's windpipe, but instead, when he had

Buck's attention, he told him he was not to bother Sandler anymore, or there would be consequences. Once Bucks nodded his understanding, Beaumont went back to bed.

The next morning, his sergeant called him into his office and asked him to explain what Bucks had reported to him. As the sergeant expected, Walter didn't deny or lie about it. He simply told the sergeant it was something he had to do, since no one else was doing anything. Sergeant Drucker growled that he didn't appreciate him doing the sergeant's job, and he alone would decide what to do. He had Beaumont give him thirty push-ups, and sent him away.

What Beaumont didn't know was, while the sergeant was aware of the problem, he chose to let Bucks and Sandler get squared away themselves. As time went on and nothing changed, the sergeant had decided to do something soon, but Walter had acted first.

One morning on a day when Sandler was free to work through his military training without any hassles, the sergeant called the men to order, and announced it would be a good idea to have a boxing match for the men's entertainment. They all looked at each other questioningly. He asked for volunteers, and even though a dozen men raised their hands, he picked Beaumont and Bucks, even though neither had volunteered.

All the men trotted over to the base gym, where there was a boxing ring for unit competition. The two men stripped to their fatigue pants, and put on gloves.

"Remember, this is not serious, this is just to let off steam. Let's go!"

When Walter went up to touch gloves with Bucks before fighting, Bucks caught him with a pretty good right cross. While it hurt Walter, the punch served only to make him angry. Two minutes later, Bucks was flat on his back, out like a light. Walter glowered at him, not even breathing hard. He could have put him out quicker, but he wanted to make it last a little longer.

Nobody cheered, stunned by the speed with which Beaumont had finished the match, though they were all impressed with how well he took care of business. Walter glanced at the sergeant, and Drucker saw a look in his eyes he had seen before, in the field during combat. The sergeant sent them all, except for Bucks, who was not steady yet, on a five-mile run. Stanley never bothered Sandler again.

Running was something Walter excelled at, but he held back when running with the other recruits, to keep things even. He wanted to do well at everything he was required to do, but not to excel in an obvious way. Still he always kept at the head of the pack.

One thing he couldn't help doing well was the use of small arms. He was a crack shot, and it showed. They used Springfield 03-A3 rifles initially, plus some training with the Colt model 1911 .45 ACP semi-auto pistol. The weapon Walter liked the best was the M14 rifle. It was a fine firearm, and accurate. If ever there was anything that made Walter smile, it was shooting the M14 at the range. He qualified as Expert, the only one of his unit to do so.

Walter was the first to make PFC in his barracks, too. Nobody cried sour grapes over it. He was well respected and liked by everyone, except Stanley Bucks, of course, who still disliked him for knocking him cold. Even so, he gave him begrudging respect.

A week before basic ended, Sergeant Drucker called Beaumont into his office. "Beaumont, I'm not supposed to be giving you your orders quite yet, but you're going to Ft. Polk, Louisiana for advanced combat training after basic. You'll be leaving the morning after you're finished here, at 0600 hours, and you will be entering Ft. Polk as a corporal. Live up to it. You've been exemplary in basic. Don't screw up and make me look bad. Keep this to yourself. Dismissed."

A week later, he was running with a platoon at Ft. Polk. He fit right into the system there as he had during basic training, and his knowledge and abilities grew with each new assignment in combat training. Among a mass of new information, he learned what was required for forward recon missions, how to stay in potentially hostile areas for weeks on end with a minimum of equipment and supplies, how to gather intel with precision and accuracy, how to strike the enemy when necessary, and slip away without being taken.

Of course, Walter had no trouble with any of this. While what his uncle had taught him helped him, his own natural abilities and intelligence took over at Polk. Having a group of men around him who were of the same mind set helped him be a team member, just as joining the track team in high school had taught him to be part of a cohesive unit.

The afternoon before he left Benning, Walter was glad to get a letter from his mom. Things was good with them, and they were hoping he was doing well. He wrote a quick letter, letting them know he was well and being transferred to Ft. Polk for advanced training. He told them he'd get in touch as soon as he could. It was like Beaumont to not mention his promotion to corporal. He wasn't the kind to blow his own horn.

When he had first arrived at Ft. Polk, after settling into the barracks he was assigned to, a Captain Ricks had him report to his office. What transpired there was not expected.

"So, you're Sergeant Drucker's golden boy. He seems to think you're a gem. Well, I'm telling you, you're no better than anyone else training here, understood?"

"Understood sir, and appreciated."

"Meaning what, corporal?"

"Meaning I'm not looking for any special treatment, sir, I'm like everyone else here, as you said. I want to learn from my training and become a better soldier, sir."

"I don't know whether to take you at your word, or consider you a sarcastic, s.o.b., which is it?"

"I gave an honest statement on how I feel about being here sir, no more, no less."

"All right, get the hell out of my office; you've got a long day ahead of you."

Walter, with his platoon, spent the day doing physical training, running, and exercising, building their stamina and strength. This went on for three full days, starting early in the morning until sundown, with their DIs yelling and berating them about everything and nothing. Beaumont saw immediately how his instructors and officers intended to weed out the weaker men, to end up with only the best. He intended to stick it out to the end.

On the third day, they were introduced to the obstacle course, and told what was expected of them by the time their training was over. The DI stated in no uncertain terms if any trainee couldn't do the course under the maximum time allowed, they would be sent packing, to be a regular grunt, instead of joining one of the special units the training would qualify them for. As usual, Beaumont did well, actually enjoying the different elements of the course. A month later, he had an interesting experience.

The weather was crappy, rainy, hot, and humid. It didn't matter. They had to do their forced marches with full packs, through woodlands and swamps, day and night, having to utilize what they learned in their classes to remain unknown to their assigned enemies during combat exercises, as well as making it through physically.

At night in the barracks, the troops interacted as men from many different backgrounds would, learning to relate, knowing they would need to depend on each other, when the time came, for survival. Beaumont understood clearly now what his uncle Aubrey and his dad had told him about learning things in the military he wouldn't learn anywhere else. They were right.

One day during maneuvers, the hot sun bearing down, humidity high, the DI, a tough southern man, was issuing orders about the day's exercise. In a moment of abnormal behavior, Walter raised his hand and suggested they enter the area they were to reconnoiter from a different direction than the sergeant wanted to follow. Beaumont was right in his thinking, but the sergeant did not appreciate him undermining his authority.

"So, you dumbass moose screwer, you think you can out plan me? You think you know this area better than me after a few weeks here, you little maggot? Tell you what, boy, I'm going to give you one hour to relocate yourself in the section I'm apparently totally ignorant about. When that hour is up, I'm sending your squad in after you. And if they find you, they can do anything they want short of killing or making you unserviceable to the army when you're found, and they will, because these other men believe in me, am I correct?"

"Yes Sergeant!" was the chorused response to his question.

"So, you move out, soldier. Get your ass out into the field, and you better hope you're lucky. Move!"

Walter headed out at a quick trot, wishing he had kept quiet, though he actually was glad this had come about. He knew the sergeant would continue to treat him with prejudice even if he excelled at what he had to do. Still, he relished the challenge, though there were better ways of being given one.

About a mile and a half in, he came across a swampy area he had seen before on earlier exercises. He waded out into the murky water until he was waist deep, and headed north, deeper into the heart of the watery environment. At times he was up to his neck, as he continued on.

At one point he froze, as a water moccasin swam by close to him. Fortunately, it had no interest in the man wading through his territory.

Walking out onto dry land, he headed for the thickest brush he could find. Removing his shirt and dropping his pants, he took enough time to feel all over his body and remove the dozen or more leeches now attached to him. It was obvious they had gotten blood, judging from their bloated bodies. He rubbed his back against a tree, removing several more. Dealing with them, he missed and appreciated his Alaska home more than ever.

Dressed again, he covered as much of his uniform as he could with smears of mud, and some large leaves to break up his shape, tucking them into his belt, pockets, and anywhere else they would stay in place, covering his face with streaks of mud as a final touch. Leaping to keep his footprints as far apart as possible, he looked for and found a perfect tree. It had a large trunk and heavy extending branches starting about ten feet off the ground. There was a lot of foliage further up the tree. Hiding his pack and rifle carefully, he jumped onto the trunk as high as he could reach, and worked his way up until he was thirty feet above the soft ground beneath. He got into a good position to keep his shape concealed, which would also give him a useful vantage point of the surrounding area. He waited for well past an hour, until he heard a segment of whispered conversation. Pressing flat against the tree, he waited. Sure enough, several minutes later four men he recognized from his squad came slowly walking down through the area beneath him. They stopped for a few minutes, looking around, searching for any sign of Walter's location. He had left none, even having tossed the leeches back into the swamp. He listened to the men quietly talking.

"You know, Beaumont is pretty damn good on maneuvers. He's a stealthy guy. He must have learned stuff in Alaska."

"I thought it was all snow and ice and wide open spaces."

"No, dummy, there's lots of forest there too. He said he'd hunted and trapped up there. So, we've got our work cut out for us. Better get to it."

The men continued their search through the land, looking for the man they never did find, even after he climbed down and started stalking the men who were supposed to be hunting him. He trailed them, noting their positions and who were in the two groups looking for him.

Night was coming on, and Beaumont decided he'd made his point. Skirting the area where he figured the guys would end up, he avoided the road they were trucked in on, and slowly made his way back to base.

Reaching the barracks, he reported to the guard at the post, to record when he got back. He stripped down at the barracks, took a quick shower, and redressed. He decided to sweep the floor, and was most of the way through when the squad showed up.

The sergeant had kept them out well past dark, hating to admit a grunt had outsmarted him.

They stood there, dirty, sweaty, and tired, while Walter, looking clean and fresh, nodded at them and finished his sweeping. A moment later, the sergeant came in and started to dress Beaumont down for sneaking right back to the base. Walter told him he had returned to base less than a half hour before, reporting to Gate 3.

"I was far from where we were last situated when I came out of the heavy stuff, sergeant. It seemed the best choice to head back to base."

"All right, report on your actions during the afternoon, corporal. Enlighten us as to how you avoided capture and the ensuing pain."

Walter went into a specific and detailed report on how he had avoided detection and capture. He included the several hours of his tracking and observing the other men, stating who was in the two separate search groups.

The more he said, the less harsh was the look on the sergeant's face. He actually ended up giving Walter a little praise. Finally, he told the squad to clean up and hit the sack. As he was walking away, he told Beaumont, "Not you, mister sneaky. You clean the head first, and it better be spotless!"

All Walter said was, "Yes, sergeant!"

The sergeant never pushed Walter again, except when he thought he could do even better. Training went on for the soldiers, honing them into fine fighting men. Two months after the swamp incident, Beaumont and one other man who was second only to Beaumont in his competence and advanced combat abilities, were called into the CO's office. They had no idea what was up, and didn't question it.

When they got there, they found the commanding officer, Colonel Rexforth, Captain Ricks, and a sergeant who had a long run of hash marks on his sleeve. He was obviously an old war dog.

The colonel told them the reason they had been called in was because there was a small unit being put together for service in Southeast Asia, as an experimental forward recon group.

"You men have been chosen for this recon unit. You'll be given specialized training and, if you complete it successfully, you will be sent into Southeast Asia to gather intelligence on communist activities there, to determine if they are building up men and supplies, and preparing to take over territory in the southern parts of the area. As far as the rest of the army is concerned, the unit will not officially exist. You will not, I repeat, not make any mention of this to anyone in your current outfit, and you will be relocated without advance notice. You will write to your family, telling them you are being given an assignment making it impossible to communicate, after which you will not communicate with friends or relatives about this assignment, ever. Do you understand?"

After they left the office, the man who had come in with Walter grumbled he'd planned on signing up for Ranger training for a chance to see some real action. Beaumont suggested to him this unit they were being trained for sounded like it was going to see plenty of action, maybe more so than a Ranger company.

For Walter, the die was cast. He would soon begin what would ultimately define the rest of his service. Though he didn't know it at the time, it would almost be his undoing. Only time would tell what was to be.

As instructed by the Colonel, he wrote a letter to his parents, Uncle Aubrey and to Miriam, simply stating he was to be in a service situation where communications would be impossible. He loved them and would get in touch when it was again possible.

He could have lain in his bunk that night pondering his destiny, but Beaumont saw it was of no value to do so. He shut his eyes and grabbed what he already knew to be a most valuable thing, some sleep.

Walter was sent to an unnamed facility, and underwent three more months of training, enabling him to do high-level reconnaissance, gathering vital intel, to observe and counteract communist efforts to invade and dominate expanding territory, including a crash course learning basic Vietnamese, to interact with locals when necessary. As usual, he was successful at everything. Three months wasn't a lot of time to prepare for this duty, but it was a small unit. Two dozen men starting training, all of them highly competent already as combat personnel. By the time training was over, one dozen of them were still in place.

At the end of training, Beaumont was given the rank of Sergeant. Despite being the youngest member of the unit, over half of them having had much more time in the army, he had proven himself in training, and none of the other men lacked confidence in him. They were all ready to begin the duty they had been selected and trained for.

Chapter 17

Nam

F our days after training had ended, the new unit had been flown to and landed in Viet Nam, at a facility outside Saigon. There were, Beaumont noted, as many men dressed in civilian clothes as there were military personnel. He was curious who they were, but had no time to find out. After going into a major briefing the same day, they were immediately loaded onto several UH-1 "Huey" choppers, and flown out to their drop-off points. As soon as the men hit the ground, they faded off into the jungle. Once concealed, they spent a short time getting all their ducks in a row, and headed out in three different groups. It would be almost a month before they returned to the Saigon facility for debriefing, which was done by both military and non-military personnel. A week later, they were out in the field again.

The team had been given free rein to pick their personal small arms and other gear. The main asset of the group was the ability to travel fast and light, living off the land as much as possible.

Beaumont was perfectly suited to this kind of duty. He adapted to the jungles of Southeast Asia as he had to the northern forests, though he disliked the heat and humidity, the bugs and snakes. The nature of the action he was involved in changed Walter's personality, bringing forth a focused, serious facet of him that had never needed to be as fully utilized as it was right after he was in country.

Over a period of six months, he and his teammates gathered vast amounts of important data, aiding U.S. Army intelligence in their efforts to monitor North Vietnamese activity, at the cost of four of the initial team members, including the man who had first been selected along with Beaumont, who had wanted to be a Ranger. At the end of that time, the original unit was disbanded, having become too well known to the North Vietnamese.

After the original unit was broken up, Walter and one of his original team mates, Guthrie, a Native American from Oklahoma, were partnered together, and sent to a forward observation base to do further recon work. It was a small base, manned by a company of men, its purpose solely to observe any action in the surrounding area. They weren't supposed to cause any open hostilities, unless unavoidable. The two scouts reported to Captain Hanover, Base Commander, who didn't seem pleased to have them there. After eyeing them a moment, he said, "Nothing I can do about it; you're assigned here, but you're under your own orders. I'm to provide basic enemy activity reports and let you have at it, to fill in the spaces. This is your place to lay low when not in the boonies. I've heard you two are great at gathering intel, and you're both kind of nuts from too much time in the bush. You might get us screwed out here, and bring in heat from your recon efforts. Do I have to be concerned?"

Guthrie said, "Captain, the Viet Cong already know about you being here. Your base doesn't present a real threat, so for now you're golden. We'll do our best to keep the situation from changing, sir."

"Let's hope so. Go get settled in. There's an empty dugout you two can use, keeping to yourselves as I expect you'd prefer. Report back tomorrow at 09:30 for briefing on your first recon. Dismissed."

The two men found the dugout, cleaned out the debris from the last men who stayed there, and were settled in a short time later. They didn't talk much. They'd been through some high level action together, missing being caught by a matter of minutes several times, having had their share of close brushes with the enemy, and death.

While eating some C rations, Walter asked Guthrie, "You still up for slipping through the trees, man, haven't had enough yet?"

Guthrie smiled, knowing Walter was giving him a hard time for fun. He moved close to Walter and said, "In the trees? You kidding, white man, I'm full blood Kiowa/Comanche. Been hunting and tracking my whole life. I'm good to go. You know, the only time I feel good is out there. I do better slipping around with the snakes and bush pigs, instead of sitting somewhere waiting to get nailed by a mortar. Out there, I can keep myself safe. You good for it?"

"Absolutely, G, I've got your back, like always."

Guthrie and Walter sat there staring into one another's eyes, as they had done many times before. If anyone had seen the two G.I.s standing eye to eye, reading each other, it might have seemed like a scene played over and over through human history. Two warriors sizing each other up, needing to know if the other is going to be there for him in time of need. As always, they both saw what they needed to see, a man still resolute and willing to put himself on the line, one for the other.

They both got some shut-eye that night, before Walter woke, nudged Guthrie, and said, "C'mon, let's report back to Hanover and see what he has for us."

Captain Hanover told the two men there were reports of enemy activity about twelve klicks to the northeast of the base. They'd head there, sniffing things out along the way. As they left, the officer shook his head, hoping these two were as good as he had been told, and wouldn't bring a firestorm down on them.

The two men put together what they would take with them, not even having to think about it, having prepared many times before. Both of them were skookum enough to travel light, living off the land while they were out. It might be a couple of days or two weeks. There was plenty of natural food out there if a man knew where to look, and what was safe. They had no flak vests or helmets, wearing only their fatigue hats, sleeveless shirts, and pants instead, hating the extra weight and heat retention of the vests, and the noise helmets made when contacting branches and other vegetation. Guthrie took four extra mags for his specially modified M-14. It had a fourteen-inch barrel, converted by the armorer on their training base. It also had a lightweight stock.

Walter had his Ithaca twelve-gauge shotgun. It too had a short barrel, 18 inches, with an extended magazine tube holding four extra rounds of double-ought buckshot. It was an effective arm in dense foliage for close-up action. Each man had a Colt Model 1911 .45 ACP pistol on his web belt. Both of them had personal knives, Guthrie's a long skinny-bladed piece, apparently homemade, while Beaumont had the knife his uncle Aubrey had given him. Both had seen use for every purpose a knife might be needed for. The two men would always prefer to use their blade instead of the noisy firearms they both carried, the silence of the knives a key to survival more times than not.

About five the next morning, the two men slipped away. No one saw them go, except for Sergeant Panko. He was an old veteran, a lifer, having served in World War Two and Korea. Nothing ever got past him. He said a little prayer for the two, though most would not have thought it a prayer. He was a hardened man, and there wasn't much he hadn't seen. He had lost two toes to frostbite in Korea, and had several healed-over bullet wounds in his torso.

He said, quietly, "Stay safe, you crazy bastards. I've got a feeling you're gonna need all the help you can get."

During the first six klicks, the men moved swiftly, and silently. The jungle felt peaceful, with no tension around them. Birds were singing. The two moved parallel to each other about fifty feet apart. Both traveled like shadows, instead of flesh and blood soldiers. Their initial team had been given the name Ma Ru Ng, the Forest Ghosts, by the VC. They would be given the same moniker by those they now stalked.

The two American scouts had now covered a total of ten klicks. Though he focused his full attention on the land around him, Beaumont was not the one who first spotted movement. Guthrie stuck his hand out in Walter's direction in a fist, and they both dropped flat to the jungle floor.

The two lay there for several hours, observing the enemy troops around them, both of them smeared with streaks of camo paint, war paint as Guthrie called it. Forest debris was stuck in their clothing to break up their shapes. Both men saw these were NVA regulars, not VC. This was the first time either had seen NVA this far south. Something big was up.

Guthrie realized Walter had slipped up to his side. The two conversed silently in sign language. Walter signed the number sixty and Guthrie nodded, both having observed a short company of men.

There were no fixed structures, meaning they were on the move to some unknown location.

Guthrie tapped Walter's shoulder, and pointed to a specific spot on the right. At first Walter couldn't see what it was, until a figure stepped back from behind a tree, and he saw it was an NVA officer. He and Guthrie looked at each other, and they knew what the other was thinking. The two men smiled at each other, not what one would consider pleasant smiles.

They waited until it was dark, moving around to a place where they had a good view of the mass of soldiers, including the officer. They knew where he was bivouacked, and would make their move when the time was right.

It was one in the morning. Time had come. Two guards were posted, one at each end of the officer's tent. There were several small fires in the regulars' camp, enough light to make things out, but not enough to give them away.

Guthrie slipped up behind the guard at the back, and killed him without a sound. He whispered in Vietnamese, "Come here, I need help." The guard at the front slipped cautiously around, SKS at the ready. Unfortunately for him, he had chosen the wrong side, and Walter took him down.

Dragging them into the bushes, they slipped into the tent at both ends. The officer was sleeping soundly, unaware of what was occurring. Before he fully woke up, he had a blade at his throat, with the man holding the knife shushing him to silence. Walter carefully bound the man's hands behind him, and gagged him. They half dragged him out the back of the tent and headed as quietly as possible in the general direction they had come from.

At one point in their movement, the officer tensed up to try and make a break. Walter sensed what he was thinking, and tripped him, the Vietnamese soldier falling forward onto his face.

Putting his knife to the man's throat and drawing a little blood, Walter spoke in English, saying, "Try to run again, I'll finish you right here, understand?"

The officer, though not understanding English, knew exactly what Walter was saying and nodded slightly. He made no further effort to escape.

The return to the base went without a further hitch, though a bush pig came bursting out of the jungle across their trail, squealing loudly, pumping adrenalin through them all.

They had barely slipped under the wire, when small arms fire started up around them. The VC had discovered the officer missing and the guards dead. They knew where the American base was, and figured it was where whoever had invaded their camp had headed to. They moved quickly, trying to catch them up before they got back, but they were a little late. The base opened up on them with machine gun and rifle fire. The action only lasted about three minutes before the Vietnamese backed out of the area, leaving their officer to the enemy.

Guthrie and Beaumont took the officer to Hanover, who stood there, agitated by what they had done.

"Are you frickin' nuts?! I said nothing about any prisoners. This is what I didn't want you to do!" He stopped and looked at the two men, looking like the jungle, smeared with mud and camo paint, their eyes revealing nothing to him.

Walter took the haversack they had brought from the officer's tent, and handed it to Hanover, six or seven men now around them, smiling broadly at the furious, though silent enemy officer, ashamed of his present situation.

"There are some maps and communications in there might come in handy, Captain. This NVA officer was delivering them to someone, probably VC, which means they're working together now, maybe under one head command. Mind if I go shower off now?"

"Yeah, get the hell out of here, the both of you, I've got some calls to make."

As they walked away, Hanover called out to them. With a barely discernible smile he said, "Outstanding, you two, just fricking outstanding."

Washing off in the base shower, Guthrie and Beaumont said nothing until they were clean and drying off in the sun. Finally, Guthrie said, "You did pretty good out there Walt, but you were too damn noisy most of the time. I can't believe they didn't hear you and do us in."

Understanding the man's wry humor, despite his poker face, Walter smiled slightly and nodded. Only time would tell how long the two could continue with what they were trained to do and stay safe. While they knew the odds would steadily build against them after this mission, they didn't dwell on it. It was what they did, and they were heavily into it. They wouldn't be happy doing it any other way.

A chopper landed on the base, remained in place for less than a minute, and took off again. Walter and Guthrie looked at each other and smiled. They knew the haversack full of intel and the NVA officer were headed to Saigon.

The two recon men went out on a series of missions over the next few months. They developed a reputation among their fellow American soldiers on base for being the wild and crazy G.I.s who would go it alone and always manage to come back with the goods. New troops coming in to replace those leaving would get the lowdown on them, and always looked at them as men to be respected, but not interacted with. The established base personnel would tell some pretty tall tales about them to the replacements. They were nicknamed "Tanto and the Lone Ranger." Walter and Guthrie didn't mind, though Guthrie enjoyed it more than Walter, who took it in stride, figuring he was only doing his bit the way he preferred to serve.

Several units of VC were committed to catching and killing the Forest Ghosts, to stop them from finding and reporting their positions, their numbers, and all other pertinent information. Beaumont and Guthrie had taken out some of them too, usually by knife, to be able to complete their missions. They worked at psyching them out, often leaving a calling card right in the enemies' camp, a figure made of sticks and leaves lying on the ground out in the open, easily seen. It creeped out the Cong, and also made them more determined to stop the American "ghosts."

Activity in the near vicinity of the base was growing, and getting closer. The two kept track of any VC activity, taking out one five-man squad reconnoitering less than a klick away, without a sound.

Sometimes, when there has been unfailing success, people tend to become overconfident, a false sense of security emboldening their activities, as it did with the two scouts. Truth to tell, they were amazingly competent at clandestine operations, the two of them given natural gifts for functioning with stealth in the wilderness, no matter where. Near the end of their missions, they never let anyone know when they left and returned, except when they reported to Hanover, who relayed it up the chain of command.

It was hard for Hanover to keep from getting a chill down his back whenever the two would suddenly be standing near him or appear in his dugout without a sound. He still felt in his gut they would eventually bring a firestorm down on the base, and they did seem like ghosts.

One night, back on base from another foray into enemy territory where they discovered major troop activities, Guthrie and Walter were resting in their dugout, and Panko came by with warm beers. The old veteran wanted to have a serious conversation with them, which he hoped they would heed.

"You know, you two sneaky bastards, no matter how good you are at what you do, at some point your number is going to come up, and your war will come to a bloody halt. You two have already overextended yourselves, in my estimation. Hell, you've got the enemy actively after your asses with a price on your heads. Doesn't that tell you something?"

"Yeah," Guthrie said "it tells me we've done a real war dance on their heads, and they're scared of us."

Panko shook his head and looked at Beaumont, who sat there with no expression on his face, as usual.

"What about you, Sergeant, don't you think it might be wise to give things a rest, at least for a while? I know Hanover would be fine with it, though he'd never admit it right out. Doesn't it feel like maybe you've already done what you can?"

"You might be right, Sergeant Panko, except there's a lot of activity going on, and things are definitely building up. I wouldn't feel good about leaving off now."

Panko rose, shaking his head. He'd had his say. "Young damn fools," was the last thing he mumbled, before walking out of their dugout.

"Maybe Panko has had enough of this business, eh Walt?"

"I don't know, G, I don't know. he's a wise old GI, seen it all. Doesn't matter though, we know our job's not done yet."

"Ah, I'm going to bed. I'm beat."

Beaumont's partner had only recently told him Guthrie wasn't actually his name. He had come from Guthrie, Oklahoma when he enlisted. His white name was Everett Beeman, and he never told Walter his Indian name. He might have done so eventually, except Panko had been right; he never got the chance.

The two men laid low to rest and throw the enemy off, who were waiting for them to show up again. The two scouts never repeated the same moves twice in a row. Several mornings went by, and they slipped out before dawn after a briefing with Hanover, heading directly east this time.

They had been out for two days, about twenty klicks from base, and were now squatted down under a large, tropical plant with enormous leaves, like a pair of giant frogs dressed in camouflage. They were sipping water and eating some packets of peanut butter, whispering occasionally about where to go next. The sharp sound of a small branch breaking underfoot put them on full alert, both of them slipping their weapons off safe.

As they listened, the jungle around them seemed to come alive with all sorts of minute sounds, the little splats of sandals on wet ground, something bumping a wooden rifle stock, and the occasional sound of Vietnamese being spoken softly. All they could do was to hunker down lower and deeper into the vegetation.

After about five minutes, the sounds seemed to fade out, and the two decided to continue on, away from all they had been hearing, after making notes on what they thought had passed around them. They slipped out from under their leafy sanctuary.

Everett chanced standing up to look around, and he saw a VC soldier standing thirty feet away, staring right at him, his mouth open in surprise. Everett made an instant mental observation on how young the guy looked. The man lifted his SKS carbine, too late. Unable to get his knife out quickly enough, the American scout shot first, putting the enemy soldier down. All hell broke loose.

The VC were in two groups with some distance between them, wide enough to have lulled the boys into thinking they had left.

For the next several hours, there was a running firefight, with a few quiet moments when the VC were trying to sneak up on them, while the Americans used all their talents in going to ground unseen. Mostly, Walter and Everett were continually moving, firing only when necessary. They knew trying to stay in one location was certain death for them. Their enemy knew who they were, and would do everything they could to bring them down. A tossed grenade landing close by rattled Walter and Everett badly, but didn't stop them, only serving to make them move even faster.

Bullets were flying past them, virtually inches away. Now the boys concentrated more on getting away than fighting. Both of them were quick, and adrenaline was pumping through them. Finally slipping out from under the enemies' view, they managed to place themselves in relatively safe cover under an overhang of vegetation by a stream they had jumped into off a four-foot bank. The foliage hung down to the water completely concealing them, an enemy soldier passing by unaware only a few seconds after they had hidden themselves.

They lay in their hide, head to head, controlling their heavy breathing, the adrenaline still coursing through them. Walter and Everett remained there for some time, hearing enemy soldiers searching all around them, until the sounds again faded away, yet they remained where they were.

They were beginning to feel a little safer, until a soldier dressed all in black pushed aside the screen of vines with his carbine, exposing them both. Everett started to bring his M14 to bear, but the soldier fired several quick shots at point blank range hitting him twice, in the groin and right hip. Walter pointed his shotgun and killed the soldier, then turned his attention to Everett.

He gasped, "Walter, get back to base, man, let them know about this, go on, I ain't gonna make it back, brother, GO!"

Walter hesitated for several seconds, even though he knew Everett was right. "I'll come back for you," was all he said. He slipped upstream, hugging the bank. A minute later, he heard the sound of an M14 and several SKS', and then, silence.

Walter never knew how he got away. He had used most of his ammo by the time he got clear of the enemy. A rifle bullet had cut a grazing wound along his left cheek an inch above his jaw line. Burning like fire, it only served to keep him going.

The enemy kept the pressure on him, coming close several times to shutting him down. Utilizing everything he knew, he managed to give them the slip, killing several out of necessity with his knife, chancing it for the sake of silence. Finally, instincts alone were keeping him out of harm's way. He ran and hid like a desperate animal, for that was what he had become, thinking only of survival, knowing his enemy was intent on one thing, ending him.

His attempts to escape capture or death became a blur of activity, and time had gone completely subjective, only the falling of night

letting him know the day was over. He burrowed into places difficult
to discover, lying amid mud, insects, and rotting vegetation.

Beaumont slipped away just before night was over. He didn't want
to chance blundering into his enemies in the dark. To throw them off,
he headed south for several klicks, came around in a wide semi-circle
and reached the base almost a full day later. But the ruse had worked.
There was no one on his trail.

After almost three days of this struggle, with no potable water except what
he could glean from plant leaves, and only what he could literally dig up to
eat, he was squatted down just outside the wire, scanning the area around,
feeling like screaming out all his anger and frustration at having to leave his
partner, his brother, to the enemy. Finally he entered the base, unseen.

When Hanover saw him, he sent him immediately for medical
attention, the wound on his cheek already infected. Walter had
developed a fever, and he ended up staying low for three days after
making it back, the base medic treating his wound and fever.

He briefed the captain while lying on a cot, relaying information
in a flat, emotionless voice, after first telling Hanover, Guthrie was
gone. The officer said nothing, knowing what this meant to Beaumont.
He'd wait a while before asking for details. Hanover had radioed the
information to Saigon, and put the base on full alert to deal with the
enemy troops who were sure to come.

There was no attack however, no retaliation. Perhaps they felt killing
one of the two ghosts was enough to stop the recon missions.

The lack of enemy retaliation against the base didn't give Beaumont
much satisfaction. He would have been happy to deal with the troops
who had taken out his partner, and left him wounded and sick.

Several days later, he wanted to go back out to find Everett, knowing
it would have been madness, guaranteed to fail.

Hanover refused to let him go, and Beaumont's loud, threatening
reaction to his refusal, partly brought on by his feverish state, caused
the captain to put him under guard until a chopper came to take
him out for medical treatment in Saigon and some R&R afterwards.
Hanover made sure Beaumont's superiors in Saigon knew he needed
to be kept out of the boonies until he settled down.

In bed in Saigon, he was debriefed by staff from the facility where he
had originally arrived in Viet Nam. They pressed him for every small

detail, and he told them what he had learned, his excellent retention aiding them in their mission. He was glad when it was over, after describing what had happened to Guthrie.

Sitting in a lush garden in Saigon with a cold beer after he'd recovered, the illness and infection gone, all Beaumont could think about was finding Everett, though he wouldn't find him alive, and would probably die in the attempt. He knew having to leave his partner there would haunt him forever if he didn't make an effort, no matter what. He had convinced his superiors he could still be of use if he went back to the forward base to gather more information, since the VC would doubtless think he wouldn't return.

Heading towards his base in a chopper, Beaumont reflected on what Panko had said, torn between wanting to curse the sergeant out for jinxing their luck, and feeling like crap for not listening to the grizzled old soldier.

He was planning on slipping away right after getting back to base, but on the way in, less than half a klick from base, the chopper took a direct rocket hit, and it crashed outside the compound. Beaumont survived in spite of taking several pieces of shrapnel in his abdomen. He was rescued along with one other man, even though the damage done by the jagged pieces of metal meant his war was over. His guts were badly torn up and he was evaced out an hour later. He ultimately needed several surgeries.

The vagaries of life can either save or destroy us. The grievous wounds he had received probably saved Walter Beaumont. The next day, the VC attacked the base, causing almost seventy-percent casualties. The two main dugouts were destroyed, and Captain Hanover was badly wounded, losing his right arm. Sergeant Panko was killed outright by a mortar shell. He had been right. Eventually, time runs out for those who continue on past their allotted call, including him.

American combat involvement in Vietnam hadn't formally begun yet, though the situation was soon to change. The base was shut down and cleared off, all action there ending up in classified military files.

When well enough to function, Beaumont was assigned to the Saigon facility to man a desk. The staff and activities there had increased, and they knew his experience would be of benefit, but Walter proved to be of little use. Unwilling to give what they wanted, he finally requested, and was granted, a transfer back to Ft. Polk, and was put on light duty while he continued to recuperate. They had offered him an opportunity to become an instructor when he was well enough, but he declined. His current tour of duty was almost over. All he wanted to do was go home, homesickness constantly gnawing at him.

He suffered a relapse, due to several small pieces of shrapnel still inside making trouble in his bowels. They had to come out, which required going back under the knife.

While hospitalized, he wrote to Miriam, his parents, and his uncle Aubrey. The only ones who responded were his parents. In their letter, after writing how wonderful it was to hear from him and know he was all right, they asked if he had heard about the huge earthquake Alaska had suffered through. When Beaumont read what they wrote about it, a fearful chill ran down his back. Using a hospital phone, he called his parents, who were overjoyed to hear from him. They told him what they could, finally saying they had not heard from Aubrey or Miriam after sending repeated letters to them both. The quake had occurred at the end of March, 1964, two months earlier. Beaumont had been existing in a totally different world, a rarified reality, and knew nothing about the '64 quake.

He went to the base commander and told him there was a family emergency, and since his tour was up in less than a month, asked for extended leave, without pay if necessary. The commander, knowing some of what Walter had gone through, sighed and sat back in his chair. He didn't want to lose a good soldier like Beaumont, but looking him in the eyes, he knew he'd been through enough, and was of no further use to the army.

"All right, Sergeant, I'll see to your leave, with pay, ending with your discharge. Hopefully, you'll change your mind."

Walter Beaumont was going home.

Chapter 18

Coming Home

When the airliner touched down in Anchorage and taxied to the terminal, Beaumont, standing at the head of the stairs leading down to the concrete apron, taking in the panorama before him, could see damaged structures beyond the airport, and the airport itself undergoing reconstruction.

Beaumont felt strange wearing a uniform there. He craved the feel of anonymous civilian clothing. His military service would soon be over, at least on the outside, the changes of location and clothing only masking the internal turmoil he constantly felt.

He was not the young man who had left less than two years ago, in love with Alaska and a young Aleut girl, looking forward to future adventures the North land held in store.

He took a taxi downtown, and was shocked to see much remaining damage the monstrous earthquake had caused. On the last leg of the flight in, he had spoken to several passengers who had been in Anchorage when the Good Friday quake hit. He sat there shaking his head as they described how it had been, structures broken into piles of rubble, fires, roads collapsing, and the earth splitting apart. The power nature had displayed made the efforts of men seem fragile and insignificant by comparison.

Walter ate at a diner, a late breakfast of real eggs, bacon, home-fried potatoes, and sourdough bread. The meal tasted like a bit of heaven after military food, processed for storage and quick cooking.

He watched people as he ate, trying to feel like a civilian again, but it wasn't coming. He wasn't home yet in his mind. He had to be patient, to leave all the tension, violence, and strangeness of his experiences behind. Beaumont ran two fingers along the rough edge of the long scar on his cheek. It would always be a reminder of what had transpired in that far-away world of breath-taking beauty and death, and an intimate memorial to Everett. A wave of emotion came over him, and he lost track of his surroundings. He looked up suddenly. The young waitress was asking him something.

"More coffee, sir?"

"Oh, yeah, thanks."

Sitting long enough to finish the cup, Walter went out, got another taxi, and went to a functioning car dealership. He saw a 1961 International Harvester Travelall he liked. He wanted his own set of wheels, independence from needing others to get around. The lot still showed several cracks with freshly poured blacktop sealing them. There were two crumpled cars, most likely damaged by the quake, sitting in one corner, as though a reminder of the catastrophe.

While going through the paperwork, Walter asked the salesman about the extent of the damage.

"Was the rest of the state affected?" he asked.

"Oh, my Lord, yes!" replied the salesman. "There's huge damage all along the coastal areas, Seward down to Homer, Prince William Sound down through Southeast. Valdez got hit hard. The little Native village on Chenega Island was wiped out."

The salesman described general damage along the coastal areas all up and down the state. It was a lot to take in.

When the man had mentioned Chenega being destroyed, Beaumont felt his heart tighten in his chest, and found it difficult to take a full breath. After all he had been through in Viet Nam, this hit him harder than he could have imagined. He could only pray Miriam wasn't there during the destruction, but he wouldn't find out for some time.

"Was Seward hard hit? I have people there, and really need to get back and see if they're okay."

The salesman stopped writing, and sat staring at Walter. Tears flowed out of his eyes, and his voice cracked when he spoke.

"Yes, sergeant, it was badly hit by the earthquake, and several tidal waves, the second one much more powerful. I lost several good friends there."

The salesman sat looking at Walter, thinking a few moments before he spoke.

"I would love to sell you a vehicle, but you know, the highway isn't passable all the way to Seward yet. It won't be for a while. If I might offer some advice, find someone with a useable boat or small airplane, and go down there to decide what you need to do next. When things are closer to normal, I'll be happy to give you a good deal on a car or truck."

Walter's concern had grown stronger listening to the man describe how entire piers, boats, and houses, as well as much forest growth along the shorelines were devastated. He had a desperate need to head down to Seward to learn what had happened to his loved ones. He wouldn't feel right until he did, even though he wasn't sure what he would have to deal with there.

Slowly riding through the downtown area of Anchorage in another taxi, having taken the car dealer's advice, Beaumont saw all the construction going on, the massive rebuilding to restore Anchorage to full function. The cab had to detour several times where damage to the road still made it impassable, even with repairs going on all the time. Stores were at all angles and in different states of collapse.

He found an outdoor supply store open for business, despite the conditions all around it. Walter went in to get some tough clothing, canvas work jacket and pants, work boots, and wool socks. The size of the clothing he bought was one step down from what he was used to wearing. He had lost weight during his military service, though in truth he was stronger than before in some ways, despite the bodily damage he had received.

The store was still undergoing restoration from the quake damage. The walls were being repaired, and the lighting was only partially functioning, but he could see it would soon be back in good condition. The spirit of Alaska was at work here, a strength of character enabling people to live in and develop the wilderness state, and to recover from disasters, natural and otherwise. It gave Beaumont pause to wonder if being back might heal the sadness, anger, and frustration he felt from what he'd been through, and the dark side of human nature he'd experienced, and yes, shared in, though for the right reasons, just as many veterans before him.

Walter was feeling better in a number of small ways since returning to the land he loved. There were some deep-seated thoughts and feelings needing more time to heal, and though he didn't realize it yet, finding Miriam and having her back would help make him right.

Forsaking the taxi, Beaumont walked, and talked to many people as he wandered through different parts of Anchorage. He asked if anyone had a plane or knew someone who might help him get to Seward.

Finally, a man overhearing him said he had a plane still in good working order. He quoted Walter quite a high price for taking him there. Though he knew it was a lot, Walter agreed, so great was his need to get to Seward. The man drove him over to a remote corner of Merrill Field. The roadways were still rough and uneven, large fissures in them still visible. Twice they had to carefully avoid bad stretches, but made it through.

The man's plane was a newer Cessna 182, equipped with tundra tires. Beaumont waited and watched while the man did a visual inspection of the plane, checked fuel levels, and loaded his duffel into the plane.

Walter could see some damaged planes nearby, and some bad fissures in one of the runways. The man, Artie, seeing him looking at the surroundings, told him not to worry. "One of the perks of having a small plane is maneuverability. We'll be fine."

In a matter of minutes they were in the air, after Artie had radioed to the men who were directing air traffic from a ground-level building, the control tower not yet repaired.

In no time they were at altitude, headed down to Seward. The flight gave Walter a chance to see the incredible damage to, and change in the land from their vantage point. The differences to terrain Beaumont would have recognized easily before the quake, were amazing and disturbing.

All along the coast, and inland, the damage to manmade structures and natural terrain was often hard to comprehend. The full force of nature had been unleashed. He could see where landslides and huge tidal waves had wiped away and permanently altered the land. Some of the coast looked like it had collapsed, while other places looked like they had been raised up into new high ground. Artie flew over some of the Seward Highway, and Beaumont saw the car salesman was right. The area thirty to forty miles south of Anchorage had collapsed, the Seward Highway devastated and partly submerged by the waters of Turnagain Arm. Already the task of rebuilding the roadbed was under way. It was obvious vast amounts of fill were going to be needed. There was no way he could have made it down to Seward by car or truck.

It didn't take them long to fly down to and over Resurrection Bay. Walter was stunned by what he saw. The pilot made several turns over the Bay where a thriving town and harbor had been. There was virtually nothing left of the waterfront. The docks were gone, and the boat harbor non-existent. The city itself was almost a total ruin, and it looked like everything at the head of the Bay had been shoved inland by the huge tidal wave the earthquake had caused. Walter felt as if the upper Bay had somehow slid away. His perceptions were right. There were also signs of a large fire. Things looked charred everywhere. He decided the oil tank farms must have been destroyed and ignited after the quake and tidal waves hit. There was no sign of Tuckerman's old shop, but Walter saw a structure being built near where the shop had been, and he was amazed to see what must be his uncle's old military ambulance nearby. Beaumont's heart started beating faster, and he asked the pilot to see if he could find a place to land.

There was a relatively clear patch of ground about a quarter mile away, and the pilot was able to touch down with little room to spare.

Walter and Artie had talked on the flight down, and Beaumont mentioned he had been in Vietnam in the military, but offered no real details. When his duffel bag was in his hand and he was out of the plane, Artie told him he wanted a much smaller amount of money.

Walter gave him a questioning look.

Artie smiled and told him it would cover costs. "You'll probably need what you have to get set up again. I know it took me a while to get situated after Korea, in more ways than one. Good luck to you."

Facing the Cessna into the wind, Artie throttled up, short taxied through the muck, and flew off back to Anchorage. Walter watched him go, turned, and walked towards the new construction. He had no idea what he would find, and he had no choice but to find out.

As he got closer, Beaumont realized the half-finished building was larger than it appeared from the air. He heard hammer blows from inside the wooden framework. Standing in the open front, he saw a familiar figure whose back was to him, standing on a ladder nailing an inner wall into place.

"Need any help, Mr. Tuckerman?"

The man on the ladder froze in place and didn't turn around right away. He slowly climbed down, and hung the hammer from a rung before turning. Seeing Walter, he slowly walked up without saying a word, reached out and took hold of his arms. Walter could feel the tough old man trembling slightly, and saw tears roll from his eyes. "Oh, Walter," was all he said. Putting his white-haired head against Walter's chest, he quietly cried.

Beaumont knew immediately why Arnold was grieving. His uncle was gone. By impulse, Beaumont put his hand on Arnold's hoary head, patting it gently. Walter stood silently, tears running down his face too. He wouldn't allow himself to become more emotional. There was too much loss inside him, and he wasn't sure if he could stop, once he started.

After a minute Tuckerman had composed himself, and took Walter over to a white wall tent actually set up inside the unfinished shop, sat him on a stump, and poured him a cup of coffee. Walter sat, quietly holding his mug while Arnold told him what had happened.

"I was coming up from the Kenai after seein' a man about some fishing gear to install on a boat I was rigging. The boat's gone now, destroyed. The quake hit when I was driving back to Seward. I stopped the ambulance, but it kept bouncing and shaking for what seemed like forever, until the quake finally let up. The rig was right on the edge of the road, and would have slid off the roadbed if the quake had gone on.

"I knew this was a bad one, to go on and on like it did, and hard, too. Just like that, it seemed to be over. Figured I'd start slowly drivin' back to Seward. In several places I barely got around huge fractures in the highway. Once, I had to leave the road and work my way through the brush until I got to solid roadway again.

"By the time I come close to Seward, there was huge billowing clouds of black smoke. From the smell, I figured the oil tanks at the head of the Bay had ruptured and exploded."

Arnold went on, describing the ruination and general destruction. Finally, Walter asked Arnold point blank, "What about Uncle Aubrey, Mr. Tuckerman?"

Arnold's lip quivered, the old man finding it difficult to tell Aubrey's nephew what he knew. "Your uncle was out on the *Mother Lode* when the quake hit. He was headed out to his cabin." Arnold paused, took a deep breath and said, "I don't know where he was when the tidal waves hit. He's never returned in the last two months. I fear the worst, though Lord knows I wish I could say otherwise. We need to accept it, Aubrey is gone."

"You don't know for absolutely sure, right?"

"Well, no, but my gut is telling me no one, even on a big ship, could have survived such intense waves, if they was on the water. The one come up the Bay here was truly big, and come in at a horrible speed. If you run out the Bay, you'll see how high up the wave took out trees, clearing the lower slopes off."

"Were you able to search for him?"

"With what, Walter? There was no seaworthy vessels here for some time afterwards. Lord help me, I'm no good out on the water anyway, as you surely know. By the time there was some boats, those searching along the coast turned up little, and nothing connected to Aubrey or his boat.

"A couple of search planes flew over the coast for some days. A few survivors was located, and some who didn't make it. Your uncle was a true friend. Don't you think if there was something I could have done, I would have?"

"Of course you would have, Mr. Tuckerman, I know you would. Uh, by any chance did you ever see Miriam here, before or after the quake?"

"Your girl come by a couple of times before, asking about you. As you should know, there wasn't much I could tell her. You weren't communicatin' with us. I guess you had your reasons."

"It was beyond my wanting, Mr. Tuckerman. I had orders. I was doing some classified work. I'm glad it's over now."

"Hmmm," said Tuckerman, giving Walter's scar a once over, "looks like you got into some sketchy situations over there."

"Yes, I did," was Beaumont's only reply, and Tuckerman let it drop, except to say,

"Well, it's all right now, and I'd rather you call me Arnold."

Arnold looked at Beaumont, smiled, and said, "It sure is great to see you."

"Wait, smile again, please."

Arnold hesitated, before flashing another big grin. Walter was amazed. Instead of the oral catastrophe Tuckerman used to have, he now had a set of beautiful, straight, white teeth.

"You look great. When did this happen?"

"Well, you're partly responsible. Aubrey told me you had suggested helping me. One day, you must have been gone a year or so, your uncle told me there was some boat gear down in Kenai he wanted to look at, and he needed my help. I agreed, and we drove down there. He insisted we go on Wednesday, for some reason.

"We drove down into Kenai, right to a dentist's office. I got pretty hot, Aubrey pulling something like that on me, but he insisted I come in with him.

"I was standing in the front of the office, giving him a pretty hard time, when a woman's voice said, 'What is all this, what's the fuss?'

"I turned around and there was this redheaded woman standing there, in a pure white doctor's coat, a real looker, too. She was the dentist, a Doctor Bailey. Push come to shove, she somehow got me into the chair, spent about an hour examining my mouth and talking. Told me she had lived in Bangor, Maine, in her childhood. What could I do?

"She said to me, straight out, 'You need full dentures Mr. Tuckerman.' My own chompers were a total loss. It took half a dozen sessions to get rid of the old teeth, and make me a very comfy set of plates. So, here I am, all thanks to your uncle, you, and the pretty dentist. Always been partial to redheads." He smiled widely again.

Tuckerman stopped smiling, and said, "If you've got the time, I'd like to show you something."

They got in the ambulance, and Arnold drove carefully through and around the debris piled up around the head of the Bay, and a fair distance beyond.

At one point, Beaumont saw three boats all jammed together, good-sized fishing boats, two right next to each other, keel to keel, and one sideways, on its side, on top of them. He could only shake his head at a power capable of doing all this. He never could totally comprehend it.

They drove about a quarter of a mile inland, and had to walk a hundred yards farther to see what Arnold had been referring to. There, hidden by Arnold with light debris, to Walter's amazement, was *Beaumont's Journey*.

Tuckerman watched as Walter made a lengthy and minute inspection of his barely used boat. It seemed in surprisingly decent condition, though it would need lots of detailed work to be seaworthy again.

Arnold finally spoke up, "I waited to see if you were gonna come back before endeavoring to get her right again. If you hadn't, I would have let her be. What do you think, would ya like to help me with her? You can stay with me, help me get the shop weathered in."

Walter smiled. "I think we've got some work ahead of us, Arnold. We'd better get busy."

Arnold nodded, a renewed twinkle in his eye.

Beaumont made several attempts to find Miriam, with no success. The school where she had been teaching when he had left was gone, destroyed like most of Seward. Reconstruction was going on in town; however, it would be some time before it would be fully functioning again. Many of the people living there had existed on a primitive level before, no running water, no electricity. They would carry on until things were shipshape again. They were Alaskans, after all. At times he saw and spoke with locals who came by to share information. He'd always ask them about Aubrey and Miriam.

There had been a number of smaller quakes that occurred after he had returned home. He and Tuckerman, when they felt them, would look at one another, wait for the shaking to subside, then resume whatever they were doing.

About two months after coming back, he saw Miriam's cousin Jimmy, from Chenega. His stomach tightened as he approached the Aleut man. Shaking hands, they talked. He told Beaumont about the massive destruction on Chenega. They had lost twenty-six of the less-than-seventy, full-time residents, many of them related in some way, and how they were all scattered now, relocated.

Jimmy told him, "Miriam wasn't there when the quake hit, Walter, and none of us have heard from her. We believe she might have been in

Anchorage at the time, but that's all we know, I'm sorry to say. We pray every day for the ones of us who didn't survive, and we ask for a better life for those who did. It is a sad time for our people, and rough on us. As always, we'll get on with living, and heal in time, God willing."

Walter went back to the shop, all enclosed now. They had managed to get the *Journey* down to it, dragging it on a skid they built from salvaged wood, using a small bulldozer run by a Seward resident they knew, who had lost all his property in the oil fires except for the dozer and some clothes. He had been busy ever since, helping others get back on an even keel.

The *Journey* was starting to look like it did before things turned upside down.

One day in June, as they were finishing up final repairs to the boat's wheelhouse, two Alaska State Police officers pulled up in an International Travelall. It had seen better days, and Walter suspected much of the wear had come since the quake.

Arnold had seen and talked to them before, as they were assigned to the Seward area. There had been some incidents of looting and theft of private property.

They all introduced themselves, and sat with mugs of coffee. The two law enforcement officers looked like experienced men. Beaumont decided they'd seen their share of action.

The older of the two men inquired of Walter if he'd had any experience running the waters in Resurrection Bay, and those outside, to the north and south. Walter, curious as to the question, replied he had, to the south, and also hunted and explored the land in the general area around Prince William Sound. He asked if there was a specific reason they were asking.

"We need people to help in the continuing search for survivors of the quake along the coastal areas, civilian search and rescue people. There is still a lot we are unsure of, and evidence keeps, uh, coming to the surface, in a manner of speaking. You would be paid regular wages, and if you have your own boat you'd be paid for its use, including fuel. We do need help, even at this point. We're pretty understaffed. By any chance, are you ex-military?"

Beaumont nodded, "I am, and my training would come in handy. Still, not knowing what I might encounter out there, I'd prefer to have an official title, and I'd want to be able to use my time as I see fit when I'm not needed for running the coast."

"Well, even though I'd have to check with our supervisor, I'm sure we could arrange something suitable. Let me get your information and I will definitely get back to you."

Without being aware of it, Walter Beaumont had set into motion an action that would guide his life for quite some time. Though it had not always been a happy time, his experience in the military had taught him the importance of working with dedicated and determined men. He had come to have a definite need for it, though not as a conscious desire.

It took another several weeks before his boat was once again shipshape. It looked as sweet and clean as the day he had first seen it. Tuckerman had a mechanic in Seward, familiar with Chevy engines, strip the 283 down to do a complete inspection of its condition. Invading water had created some corrosion inside, but the damage had been minimal. After a thorough cleaning and replacing of a few unusable parts, the reinstalled engine was ready to run.

Walter was warming it up and he told Arnold to come aboard for her second maiden voyage.

Arnold shook his head, "I made a vow many years ago, I would never head out to sea again, no sir."

"Arnold, I'd consider it an honor if you'd join me. Without you, and my uncle, I'd never have this fine boat. Please come aboard."

Walter could see Tuckerman going through some powerful inner turmoil.

To his amazement, Arnold said, "Fine, young man, I'll do it for Aubrey's nephew, and no one else. Let's head out and speak no more of it."

They had managed to fill several barrels with viable gasoline, stashing them under a tarp partly hidden by some debris. It would be a tempting target for the few looters who still came around. The tank was full, and the boat ready to set out.

The engine sounded healthy as they slowly cruised down Resurrection Bay. The boat was as steady and smooth running as Walter remembered, and after a brief time out on the water, Beaumont felt the inner tightness in his mind loosen, allowing him to enjoy the run.

Tuckerman, after a time, seemed to settle into it. By the time they were nearing the mouth of the Bay, both men found some relief, being out and away from the debris and destruction around them in Seward.

Still, there was evidence of the changes in the terrain on both sides of the Bay. The tidal wave had stripped most of the vegetation far up the sides of the slopes climbing up from the water's edge. There was lots of natural debris along the shore, broken trees and exposed boulders, but also, there were pieces of manmade lumber and other flotsam scattered along the coast.

The devastation caused by the earthquake and tidal waves would probably be visible for years before nature finally healed things over, returning a more normal look to the place.

When the open water beyond the Bay was clearly visible, Arnold asked Walter to turn about and head back. Walter nodded and they started back in.

Part way back up the Bay, Arnold spoke up, "Mebbe you and I could look for your uncle some time, or at least the *Mother Lode*, or what's left of her. I'd be willing to go with you, young man."

Walter knew what Aubrey meant to Tuckerman, and how much he missed him, for the old ship builder to suggest going out on deep water again to try and find him. Walter simply nodded, and let it go for the time being.

Since he had returned to Seward, Beaumont had turned his mind often to Miriam, and what might have become of her, but, he never got any news, not from anyone he talked to.

Chapter 19

Searching

There was plenty for Walter to do once he started working with the State Police, searching the coastline for anything or anyone to report or save.

His first assignment was to search the entirety of Prince William Sound, circling the coastlines of each island, and there were a lot of islands. He took an extra tank of fuel bolted down to the deck, and enough food for an extended voyage. He brought his recently acquired rifle with him.

It was on a trip up to Anchorage with Arnold to purchase some supplies, when Walter had bought the new rifle. The .30-06 he'd gotten from his dad had disappeared with his uncle, who'd had it on the *Mother Lode*. He bought a custom-built rifle based on a Mauser action in a heavier caliber, a .35 Whelan. The cartridge had been developed in the twenties, and was a .30-06 cartridge case necked up to hold a heavier bullet, .35 caliber. It was a potent round, able to handle anything, including the big bears. He had gotten five boxes of custom ammo, because it was not readily found as commercially loaded ammunition. They were loaded with heavy, 275 grain bullets. The rifle had a two-and-a-half-power Lyman scope mounted on it, appropriate for the kind of shooting Walter would use it for, and the scope could be detached quickly, allowing the open sights to be used. Beaumont would come to use and rely on this firearm for many years, rarely carrying it with the scope mounted. With his sharp eyesight, even longer-range shots were possible without optics.

While in Anchorage, Walter was impressed with the amount of new building and general repairs which had already been done. He smiled, once again appreciating the Alaskan spirit.

The morning he headed out on his first search, the water of Resurrection Bay was smooth, with only a slight swell rolling. The V-8 engine in the *Journey* rumbled steadily along. Beaumont felt good as the boat slipped through the water, though he had a bad moment because of his uncle not being with him. He missed him a great deal. It was Aubrey who had made it possible for Walter to come to Alaska, a defining part of his destiny.

Headed south, coming to the outskirts of the Sound, Walter began his search at Evans Island. He could have gone right to Chenega Island, but he needed to hold back. Even knowing Miriam wasn't there when the tidal wave hit, it would still be hard for him to face the tragic scene.

Arriving at Evans and searching around its coast, he saw the island was clearly changed, with much of the outer perimeter unrecognizable, due to the loss of vegetation and some reshaping of the land by the tidal waves.

Curious, Walter dropped anchor in the general area where he and his uncle used to bring the Craigs their supplies, until things had gone wrong between the two brothers. He had questioned Tuckerman about the Craigs, and Arnold recalled reading in the paper that the authorities had found the partially eaten remains of one of the brothers, predators making use of the body. They found no trace of the second brother. They actually didn't know which one had been eaten.

"Might as well write it off to the way of life here." Arnold had said.

Wandering about the area where the Craigs had been building the large frame structure, there was no sign of anything there created by the hand of man. The giant wave had removed every trace of human efforts.

Content there was nothing of importance to report, Walter returned to the boat in the little rubber inflatable, hoisted the anchor, took a deep breath, and headed to Chenega.

He wasn't prepared for what he saw. The docks, the buildings by the shore, in fact, almost all human structures were gone, wiped clean,

There was no one there as he scanned the area. Walking around, a knot in his gut, Walter only saw one house and the school still there, and they were of no value any longer, just hollow structures. The village center with its wonderful cedar table had vanished.

He sat on a low concrete wall by the school gazing at the ruin, and the small amount of debris scattered around. Beaumont was relieved Miriam hadn't been there. He thought of Mr. Rutoff, Miriam's grandmother, Joy, and all the others he had come to know. He knew a third of the village's residents were dead or missing, many of them related. The survivors had been relocated. He knew they had been living in the village for many, many years, but were all gone now. Walter left Chenega Island, its destruction too much for him to deal with further, knowing villagers he knew had been lost to the destructive event. He headed over to Eleanor Island, and ran around its outer edge for about an hour, before putting into a small cove for the night. He could have spent more time searching, but Beaumont needed to be in the Sound, surrounded by the natural beauty just for its own sake, and, hopefully, to find a little peace. It was powerful medicine for his mind.

In the afternoon, he baited a hook on the hand line he had brought and tossed it over the side of the *Journey*, wanting some fresh fish for dinner. In a few minutes he had brought up a small cod. It would do.

Evening found him sitting on the front deck, the summer light prolonging the day well into the night. He sat with a glass of whiskey he had poured after dinner. Beaumont had started drinking bourbon again since returning. It helped him relax, and he kept the drinking to one glass in the evening after dinner, as his uncle had done. It helped him feel closer to Aubrey, though he knew he'd never see him again. The loss never left him, as with his guilt about not saving his partner Everett, though he managed after some time to put the memories in a place which enabled him to live with them.

Dozing on deck, Beaumont dreamed he was back in the jungle. Standing in front of him was Everett, with two VC holding his arms. Everett was smiling, and nodded at Beaumont. Walter lifted his shotgun and fired it directly at Everett, who burst into a red vapor and disappeared. Beaumont snapped awake standing up, sweat on his brow, breathing hard. He let out a yell, seeming to come from his core, then leaned over, hands on his knees, shaking slightly, until his mind and heart were cleared. He knew it would come again, but for now he had collected himself, and went inside the cabin to rest, but not to sleep.

Morning found him slowly cruising along the western part of Eleanor Island's perimeter. He came around to the south side of the island, running about one hundred yards out, when he saw the wreck of a wooden-hulled fishing vessel. His heart skipped a beat, and he came as close as he could, anchored and paddled the inflatable to shore. The closer he got, the more he tried to make it the *Mother Lode* in his mind, but it wasn't. It was a fishing boat called the *Dyer Straits,* out of Homer. The hull was stove in on the port side. Walter figured a tidal wave had slammed it up onto shore, though he had no definite idea what had actually occurred.

There was no one on board, no remains at least, and what was left inside the hull was a mass of tangled gear and personal items. He wrote down the name of the vessel, its location, and condition. He was required to report whatever he saw on his search, no matter how insignificant seeming, and hand it in to the State Police.

Finishing the run around Eleanor he found nothing else of importance, only typical small debris, natural and otherwise, washed up on shore. He decided to bypass Montague and head over to Hawkins Island, where his uncle's cabin was located, on the trail above the double-hooked cove.

He arrived late in the day, and was stunned to see the cove was gone. There was no more protected water, only a rounded piece of coast, typical of what Walter had been seeing, lower levels stripped bare, except for tangles of uprooted trees.

Running closer to the inner edge of the now-collapsed cove, he looked carefully at the rock face still standing below the base of the trail to his uncle's cabin, and spotted what he was looking for. Dropping anchor, he was surprised to see about seventy feet of line slide into the water. The inside area where the cove had been was about forty feet deeper than before.

Paddling the rubber raft towards the place he had located, Walter tied it off to the old iron ring pinned into the rock. He could still see the faded letters he had noticed when he had first arrived with his uncle, with the date 1852 carved crudely into the stone below the ring.

202

Lifting the .35 Whelan from the raft, he shouldered it and started up towards his uncle's cabin site. The lowest portion of the trail had been washed away, but he knew it well, and about fifty feet higher up, the trail showed again, although he had to work around a number of fallen trees.

Beaumont found himself getting tenser the closer he got to the cabin, and soon saw it was for good reason. The home his uncle had built was ruined. It appeared the quake had shaken it apart, and it looked like a set of Lincoln Logs all in a pile. A spruce tree had fallen across it, as well.

Walter gave an involuntary shudder, looking at the ruin. He walked towards it to see what might lie beneath the logs. To his relief, there were no human remains under the debris. Still, the collapsed cabin was bad enough for him.

Beaumont sat on a log end thinking for a few minutes, until he had made a decision. He would rebuild the cabin. Almost all of the logs were still useable, collapsed in a random pile. Yes, he would rebuild it, and live here as his uncle had done, when it was restored. He couldn't think of a better place to live, and had already accepted that he would probably be living alone.

He was going to check on the condition of the partially built cabin he and Aubrey had started building for him and Miriam to use, but thought better of it, and headed back to the boat.

Next morning he cruised around Montague Island. He planned to check out Perry and Naked Island, before making a run farther down the coast to Kayak Island, a place he'd never been to before, but always wanted to see. It was supposed to be an unusual place, geographically, with most of the island being a tall mountain rising up from sea level. It wasn't part of the search plan, but he'd go there, nonetheless. There was enough fuel for the run to Kayak, and for getting back to Seward.

After finding nothing of interest at Montague, he returned to Hawkins Island, anchored close to the former inner edge of the now-destroyed cove, and spent the night there.

Strange noises woke him up about three in the morning. He looked out the side window of the boat's cabin to see a pod of Orcas leaping and splashing close by. He had never seen them cavorting around like this, and went out on deck to watch. After a few minutes, one of the Orcas came up very close, parallel to the boat, rolled slightly and floated there, its visible eye looking at Beaumont. Walter was transfixed by the sea mammal, and the obvious intelligence in its unblinking eye. It's curiosity apparently satisfied, it slowly slipped beneath the surface and reemerged near the others.

Walter went back to bed, and for the first time in a long while, slept peacefully and dreamlessly. Alaska was indeed healing him. The land and its creatures would make him whole again, filling the dark void inside with what he needed to be right. He didn't need a lot of friends to feel good, and most of the ones he was already close to, he'd never see again.

When he woke again he dressed, ate a quick breakfast, started up the motor, and headed south, still watching the water and the land off to port as he went.

Kayak Island was in view now, and even though it was still some miles away, the mountain comprising its core already loomed large, rising straight up from the island's shoreline.

He enjoyed watching the island as it grew larger, like some magical land rising from the sea. It was an odd-looking place, and Walter's impulse to explore the island grew stronger, the closer he came to it.

Through his binoculars, the base of the mountain showed what was now an expected scoured ring around its base where the tidal wave had come across. The zone seemed to have reached higher up, and Beaumont figured the direction it was coming from had allowed it to develop more speed and height. But he was no scientist, though he did have a good mind for analyzing situations, enhanced by his military training and experience.

As he approached within a few hundred yards, Beaumont saw a storm, perhaps a squall, approaching from out in the Gulf, and he decided to head back for the west side of a smaller island a few miles north of Kayak. Running north and south, it looked as if it would afford some shelter from the foul weather definitely coming his way.

The wind and rain were almost on him when he slipped to the lee side of Wingham Island. He got the *Journey* anchored firmly with its bow facing the island, and settled in to wait out the weather.

There was a strong, steady wind blowing, at least thirty-five knots, Beaumont estimated. The island protected him and his boat from the worst of it, though the rain was coming down in sheets.

Walter sat in the *Journey's* cabin, eating some smoked salmon on homemade bread, compliments of Arnold Tuckerman, who counted smoking fish, as well as baking, among his many talents. He spread the bread with butter after toasting it on the tiny oil-burning stove that served for cooking as well as warmth, then he laid a good thick layer of the smoked salmon on top. It was delicious, washed down with some hot coffee. He had a can of peaches for dessert, before sitting back contentedly with two fingers of bourbon. The way the storm made the boat jiggle and twitch bothered him not at all. The anchor was holding firm.

The wind made strange music on all the corners and edges of the boat's hardware, putting him into an introspective mood. Being out of the reach of the full fury raging on the other side of Wingham, he felt very content where he was. Certainly something could turn the situation around, putting him in a threatened position. But he disregarded the possibility, even though he would respond immediately if things worsened. For now, he sat listening to the wild and powerful music nature was producing, and felt at peace.

The storm had completely subsided by early morning. Beaumont had actually dozed off in the night, getting some needed sleep. His ability to catch a quick nap whenever possible, still came in handy.

In the morning, he had a cup of coffee and a thick slice of bread and butter. After securing the anchor on the bow, and cranking up the Chevy engine, he headed over to Kayak Island once again.

There was a thick layer of high fog around the island's peak, the lower levels showing clearly. Beaumont motored slowly around the west side of a knob extending out from the island's north shore.

The island was about twenty miles long, and the mountain was over sixteen-hundred feet high, Walter estimated, the lower half covered with dense vegetation above where the tidal wave had scoured it. To the west of the mountain was a large rock formation looking like a ruined castle, while on the other end of the island was another monadnock. It was a mysterious-looking place.

Beaumont was surprised at how clean the low-lying beaches were. There was little debris there, either natural or manmade, the water currents and wind keeping the shore cleared off. He did see a few pieces of shattered boards and beams buried in the beach sand, probably from an old wooden-hulled vessel, but nothing worth reporting.

Walter decided to come about and motor towards the eastern end of the island, going by the mountain again close enough to see anything worth investigating.

He saw a lighthouse and several outbuildings on a natural terrace about forty feet above the lower beach. It looked functional, yet he saw no signs of people as he went by, and wasn't inclined to stop. It was obvious the lighthouse was of very sturdy construction, and had indeed survived.

Beaumont decided he had seen enough of Kayak for this trip, and he headed north, skirting Wingham Island on its west side. When he was halfway past, he heard what sounded like three evenly spaced shots, and they could only have come from the island. He backed off the throttle, and scanned the shore with binoculars.

He was about three hundred yards out, and his eyes locked onto what looked like a person on the beach. He spun the wheel to starboard, and headed closer. Sure enough, a man stood there, waving his arms above his head. Walter headed towards Wingham, dropped anchor, and paddled the raft in to shore. He had his pistol belted on, not knowing what he was heading into.

The man he saw looked rough. His clothes were torn and filthy, his beard and hair unkempt, and he appeared thin. Beaumont realized this fellow must have been on the island for quite some time. He saw the man was using a homemade crutch under his right arm.

The guy came up to Walter, chattering away, dropped his crutch, and hugged him, still babbling. Walter would have felt more compassion for him if he didn't smell as bad as he did. He obviously hadn't bathed for some time.

"Oh, God, I'm so glad to see you! I haven't seen anyone for a long time. Thank you, thank you for coming in."

"Not a problem. Who are you and what are you doing here?"

"I'm Billy Weaks, and I've been here for over a month. Come on, I'll show you where my boat is."

Beaumont followed him and they walked into the brush on a little foot trail. About fifty yards in, they came upon an amazing sight. There, resting upright, was a fishing boat about fifty-feet long. The hull looked good, as if the boat could be hauled back to the water and set afloat.

"We were running about a mile out into the Gulf off the west side of this damned island when the boat's movement suddenly felt weird. It seemed as if we were being drawn out further.

"My two crewmates and I were wondering what was going on, when Jeff saw a high wave coming towards us. I tried to put the bow into the wave, but before I could, it carried us close to the island. The water pulled away again, into the Gulf, leaving us stuck on the exposed bottom. We looked at each other, knowing what was next. A wave at least forty or fifty feet high came running hard at us. It was moving fast and lifted us up onto the island. I was in the wheel house, Jeff and Chuck were on deck. All the windows were smashed out when the water struck and we were driven inland. I dropped and tried to hang onto the wheel pedestal, but when we hit a couple of trees, I lost my grip and got slammed into the front wall of the wheelhouse. It knocked me cold, and when I woke up, I saw my leg was broken. The boat had come to a stop and the water must have subsided while I was out.

"I lay there hurting a lot, then after a few minutes, I pulled myself up and looked around. There was nothing on deck. It had been swept clean, and there was no sign of Jeff or Chuck. I had no idea where they were, and they never showed up again. I'm pretty sure they were taken back out when the water ran off. It all happened so fast. I don't know why I made it."

Beaumont spoke, "Well, fortunately, you were able to survive with what food and water you had on board. I'd say you're pretty lucky all the same. No way to explain why things happen as they do. So, you were never able to contact anyone while you've been here?"

"No, the radio antenna was torn away and the radio itself wasn't functioning. The boat batteries were torn loose and I couldn't make anything work. I'm a pretty good fisherman, but don't know squat about engines, electricity, or anything else. Jeff was our engine guy, and Chuck covered the rest. The few boats coming by were too far out to see me."

"You set your leg. Must have been rough."

"Heck, yes. When I finally got it set back into position, I passed out from the pain. I tied my right foot to the upright of one of the bunks down below, pushed with my left foot, pulled back with my arms, and gave a jerk as hard as I could. It took three tries, the third time I blacked out, and when I came around I splinted it as best I could. I had a good first aid kit with antibiotics, which I took, in case of infection.

"There was a lot of food and potable water on board, and once I could get around again I dug for clams, and there were mussels on the rocks down the beach at low tide, and some small game, like the birds I was able to snare. I knew I might be stuck on this damn island for a while, and I rationed the food and water we had brought, having to boil the water later on, 'cause it started tasting pretty foul. I managed to make a rig to catch rainwater, except it didn't help much with the small amount of rain there's been. Besides, the storms blew it away anyhow.

"I did a little exploring, but this thick brush made it hard to navigate through, especially with my bum leg. I did find a small pool of pretty fresh water, and managed to bring some back to the boat. I'm thinking it was a good thing you showed up when you did. Where are you from?"

"Seward, and I think we'd better gather up whatever you think necessary to take along, Billy, and get you out of here."

Beaumont helped the man with a few armloads of things he wanted to bring out, got him settled in the cabin, fed him, and headed north. He hadn't anticipated something like this happening, but this was why the searches were needed. Now, it felt more worthwhile to do them.

His passenger didn't talk much once they were under way. Several times, Walter saw his shoulders shaking and heard a few quiet sobs. He realized the man had been through a lot and considered the difficulties he'd managed to overcome.

"I'm sorry Mr. Beaumont," Billy said, "Jeff, Chuck and me went through a lot together. We knew each other since we started fishing years ago. It's hard to lose them."

"I understand, Billy. Been there, and I don't know if you can truly get over it. I put things away in my mind and move on from there."

"Well, I've got fishing buddies in Cordova who will be glad to take me in, and help me get back on an even keel. I would appreciate it if you would take me there."

Beaumont was happy to take him to Cordova. He didn't know how much damage the little fishing town had sustained, though they'd soon find out. Cordova was around the other side of Hawkins Island from where his uncle had found the cove.

When they cruised into Cordova along the shipping channel, the place didn't look too badly damaged, certainly not as much as Seward. When they pulled up to a boat dock, several people were visible, working on a boat hull. Billy saw the three men and yelled out to them. The three dropped their tools and came running over, obviously amazed to see him. He explained to them what had happened, and there was a lot of head shaking as he told the story. These were fishermen Billy had known and worked with for years before getting his own fishing vessel, and they all knew Jeff and Chuck. The sadness on hearing they were both lost was strong on their faces.

Once Billy was unloaded along with his gear, he and Walter said good-bye, and Billy told him to come visit.

They parted ways, Beaumont heading out, going north to Seward.

Chapter 20

Together Again

It felt good turning to starboard and heading into Resurrection. Despite the harsh physical changes the Bay had gone through, he still found pleasure in watching the shore as he headed towards home.

After he moored the boat and made it secure, he headed over to Tuckerman's shop, looking forward to seeing Arnold, and telling him about his travels around Prince William Sound. Though he barely tolerated being out on deep water himself, Arnold would enjoy hearing about it.

There was a light rain coming down as Beaumont neared the shop, but he stopped walking, stunned by what he saw. Coming towards him was someone in a rain coat, hood up. It could only be one person. She walked slowly, using a cane to support herself, an obvious limp revealing she had sustained some injury to her left leg.

When they were a few feet apart, Walter thought his heart would burst out of his chest. The woman had pushed the hood back. There before him was his sweet girl, Miriam, her raven black hair dampening in the rain, those deep dark eyes of hers looking directly into his soul. He couldn't speak, and finally, Miriam said, "Walter."

Closing the narrow distance between them, he took her in his arms and held her close. Her arms were around him too, the diamond willow cane falling to the ground. They clung to each other without a word for several minutes.

He could feel Miriam sobbing, and thought he knew why. What happened on Chenega was a tragedy for her. He didn't realize seeing him again meant the most to her, until she said, "I never thought I'd see you again, Walter, never get to live with you, sleep together for all the nights. God has given you back to me, and I know life will be good now."

Walter held her at arm's length, looking at her, and she at him. Simultaneously, she noticed the rough scar on his left cheek, and he saw the smaller, yet similar one on her right cheek. His heart tightened to see she had been hurt, not wanting to think of her in pain. She felt the same.

They heard Tuckerman's gravely old voice. "You two gonna come in out of the rain, or does love mean you have to get a cold to prove it?"

They smiled at each other, and walked to the shop, Arnold unable to hide a happy grin at the two of them coming over, hand in hand.

Late at night, as they lay together in the tiny bow cabin of the *Journey*, for privacy, Miriam told him about how she had been at her cousin Mary's house in Anchorage when the quake hit. Before they could get out, the structure partially collapsed. Miriam had been pinned by a fallen wall, and lay there for a whole day before being found. Her cousin Mary had not been as fortunate. All Miriam could see was one of her hands, where it was visible from under more debris.

"My hip and leg were broken pretty badly, and something cut my cheek. I was flown down to Seattle for medical care and I got back about two weeks ago. I've been in Anchorage, trying to contact anyone I could. I was lucky, Walter. Do you know about Chenega?"

"I went there, a short while ago. It was too much to take in. I had been told you weren't on the island when the tidal waves hit."

"But I lost family. No one lives there anymore. They're scattered among a number of villages."

Miriam stopped talking, put her head against Walter's shoulder, and lay there quietly, until she fell asleep. Beaumont could feel her heart slowly and steadily beating against him. He had a surge of emotions, and could only lie next to her until it subsided. He knew what should be. He would never again be parted from Miriam, if life allowed.

Miriam and Walter spent every moment together for a full week, staying at Mr. Tuckerman's shop and running the boat around Resurrection Bay. She loved the *Journey*, and told Mr. Tuckerman he was a wonderful boat builder and a sweet man. Walter smiled when Arnold blushed at the unexpected compliment from her.

Arnold and Walter were talking one night about what Beaumont could do to make a living.

"This job with the police doing coastal searches won't last much longer. You need to find something of your own, I reckon, maybe chartering your boat out to people wanting to explore this part of Alaska. I've always figured Prince William Sound would be a good place to take people on tours. Something to think about, anyways."

"Not a bad idea, Arnold, though I wonder if the *Journey* is big enough and properly outfitted for charters."

"I thought about it too, Walter, and we can make her good. Right now, though, I want to show you something you ought to think about."

Walter went inside the shop, and told Miriam, Mr. Tuckerman wanted to show him something interesting. "You want to come along?"

"Not right now. I'm feeling a little tired. You two go ahead and tell me about it later."

Beaumont drove the old rig up the road out of Seward a couple of miles, until Arnold told him to turn right on a rough dirt road. They had gone about half a mile, when he pointed to the left. "There's what I wanted to show you, what do you think?"

Beaumont saw a small log cabin, with a couple of frame outbuildings and an outhouse. The structures, on closer inspection, all seemed to be in surprisingly good condition, unharmed by the quake, untouched by the tidal waves. The cabin had two rooms, a combination living room and kitchen, with a smaller bedroom. The only damage Walter saw inside was a cracked window in the bedroom.

"This is a great old place, Arnold, and I'm curious why you wanted to show this to me?"

"'Cause it belongs to me. I bought it a few years back. It wasn't something I needed, since I live in my shop, but it was so darned pretty lookin', I couldn't resist. The cabin's solidly built on a decent piece of land, and I got it dirt cheap. The original owner, whose wife had died, was elderly. He was goin' to Oregon to live with family. What I have in mind is for you and Miriam to live here. I know you want to rebuild Aubrey's cabin."

Tuckerman became silent for a few moments, looking down at his feet until the emotion passed, and he could speak again. "But I don't know how Miriam would do way out there, her not being a hundred per cent, and maybe not going to be for some time. Besides, if you had a little one, being nearer a town might not be a bad idea."

"You're a wise man, Arnold, and that makes a lot of sense to me. Give me a minute to consider."

Walter wandered around the buildings, getting a sense of them, how it might feel to live there. It didn't take long for him to realize it would be a good thing to do. He told Arnold, who offered him the land for the same price he had paid, one hundred and fifty dollars.

"You can pay it off working for me at the shop. I'm at the point where some good help is a necessity, and I think you'd do fine. Maybe I'll teach you to put some boats together on your own."

When they got back to the shop, Miriam was cooking a pot full of slumgullion for dinner, along with some sourdough bread, the way her Grandma Joy had taught her to make it. Tuckerman had supplied the sourdough, glad to let someone else cook for a change.

Arnold busied himself with some preliminary work on a boat he was starting to build, with no specific person in mind. Walter would help him, learning as he did.

Beaumont spoke to Miriam about the place Arnold had shown him. He told her it would make a fine home for them. "And we could add a room on if we have a kid or two." Done talking, he sat and looked directly into her eyes, waiting for a response.

She smiled and said, "Why, I think it would be a wonderful thing to do. Can I see the place tomorrow?"

The next morning they drove over to the property, walked through the cabin, and looked around at the land. She loved it, and told Walter it would be perfect.

Talking together later, they both thought this was a way to rebuild some of what had been lost, an attempt at renewal.

A minister in Seward married them a week later. It was a simple event, with only a few people attending. Afterwards, they had a small reception at Tuckerman's shop. Jim Bigelow, the restaurant owner, had made food, and Arnold had bought a cake from a woman who had remained in Seward after the quake, restoring her little home bakery to functioning condition. It was a sweet little cake, shaped like a boat, doubtless Arnold's suggestion.

The wedding was attended by Arnold, two of Miriam's cousins from Kodiak where they had moved after the quake, the lady who baked the cake, and Mr. Bigelow. Halfway through the little gathering, two Alaska State Policemen came along to speak with Walter, and ended up taking part as well.

The first night in their new home, Walter and Miriam talked about what they wanted to do. Miriam's wishes were few. She wanted to live with Walter, have a family, and try to live a peaceful, decent life. It seemed simple and righteous enough.

For his part, Beaumont knew he had the ability to live in Alaska and prosper. He could hunt and trap, build whatever he needed, and, if necessary, deal with any potential challenges, even dangerous situations, the types of things more likely to happen there than in other, less-remote places.

He had come to regard his military training as an enhancement to his life in peacetime as well as in war, improving his ability to track animals as well as people, and to move stealthily in the wilds.

Walter awoke to the smell of coffee, and noises of breakfast cooking. He lay motionless, taking in the delicious smells and sounds, aware his wife was making life the sweet experience it could be.

Though he appreciated his good fortune, the extreme situations he had gotten into and escaped from, particularly in the army, had planted a seed of cynicism, an expectation of something unpleasant and potentially deadly always coming along to turn things around. He didn't allow it to actively control his life, but it was always in the background. He never explained it to Miriam, and made sure she'd never know.

Chapter 21

Life is Good

I t had been a productive and prosperous first year since the Beaumonts had gotten married. He started advertising, with Miriam handling most of the work, for doing tours of Prince William Sound to see the wildlife and gorgeous wilderness country there.

It had taken two months before they got their first reservation from a couple and their son in California. Miriam quoted them a price, and they sent a deposit. She had better business sense than Walter did, and handled all the details, while he took care of the actual tours, having set up the boat for a better level of comfort for tourists. She figured day tours would work best, allowing people to experience the comforts of a real bed and good meals, when not exploring the Sound.

Walter had built a small frame cabin with Arnold's help, a short distance from his and Miriam's own log home. It was good for four people, with a tiny kitchen area, their own outhouse nearby, and a gravity-feed water system for washing up. Miriam was right. She told him people would love staying on what appeared to be a traditional homestead. Even the mosquitoes and no-see-ums, though annoying, were part of the experience.

Beaumont took them around Montague, Hinchinbrook, and several of the smaller islands. There was always some sea life there, including orcas, sea otters, sea lions, and many different birds. They could see deer on shore and the occasional bear. People took photographs, and thoroughly enjoyed being in Alaska, realizing it truly was the last frontier.

Beaumont entertained them with stories about the people and animals, making sure what he told them was true.

They had installed a little refrigerator and a hotplate in the frame cabin once electrical service was available, perhaps not in the realm of an old homestead, but certainly not a luxury for the folks staying there. Their little charter business blossomed over the next several years. It seemed their simple life was full of success, though occasionally they had some downright irritating clients. There were a few who considered themselves as some sort of aristocracy, with a lot of attitude, demanding to be waited on hand and foot. Several insisted on being put up at the one decent hotel in town, which was fine with the Beaumonts. Mostly, their customers were regular folks, grateful for the adventure they could take part in, often excited like kids on an outing.

Walter wanted to pack it in several times, his tolerant wife always convincing him it was worthwhile to hang on.

In the third year of their marriage, Miriam informed Walter he was going to be a father. He was rendered speechless, as he often was with her. Miriam anticipated his response, or lack of it, and laughed softly at his silent smile.

After six months of pregnancy, Miriam started having serious pain. First visiting the local doctor, Walter took her up to Anchorage to see an obstetrics specialist for an in-depth exam.

It turned out her healed pelvis, broken in the quake, and the way she had been put together again, made it difficult for her hips to expand properly. She would have to take it easy and rest when possible, and a Cesarean would be performed when the baby was due. The doctor told her it would be best if she only had the one child and no more.

She told Beaumont what the doctor had said, except for his opinion about having only one child.

The obstetrician set her up for the Cesarean procedure. Miriam had a substantial amount of pain as the birth drew near, but refused to take pain medication, for the baby's sake. She complained little, though Walter knew she was hurting.

The time for their child to come into the world had arrived. The birthing went well, with no complications, and the Beaumonts had a sweet baby girl, Emma Joy, in the cold, rainy month of October. Walter's parents, who had never been before, came to Seward for their grandchild's birth. Walter had invited them and Miriam was pleased they would be there, along with her two cousins from Kodiak. Ben and Hannah arrived, and they were wonderful to have around, always helpful, but never pushy. They stayed in the guest cabin, which they found very cozy.

Walter took his father out to fish after the baby was home, leaving the women happily to themselves. Ben enjoyed their time together on the boat, though it turned out even a little choppy water made him queasy. But after he caught his first halibut, a twenty-pound chicken, he accepted seasickness as part of the deal.

Rapidly approaching rough weather cut their fishing short. They ran back in, docked the boat, and sat in its cabin, sipping glasses of bourbon, rain coming down hard, wind blowing, the boat thumping her rubber bumpers against the dock.

At one point, Ben asked him about his experiences in the army. Walter told him all about basic training, and a little about Ft. Polk, then he left off, telling his father he couldn't talk about his actual duty. Ben sat a moment, considering this.

"Have you been keeping up on what has been happening in Viet Nam, how deeply we are involved now, with more of our people going over there all the time?"

"Well, I've heard about it, Dad, but I don't read the papers and I don't listen to the news on the radio. I've experienced what I needed to tell me what was and is going on. I don't need to know more."

Walter got a faraway look in his eyes, and turned to look out the boat's cabin window. Ben knew the look, having had his share of combat, though he'd not seen it for some time.

"So, why did you leave the service? Were you badly wounded?"

On impulse, Walter pushed his raincoat back and lifted his shirt front. Ben had seen enough wounded men to know the scars he saw now were from serious wounds and surgery. He was grateful his son was talking to him.

Walter suggested they go over to Tuckerman's shop, which they did, and the two never spoke of Nam again.

Winter always put a total halt to Beaumont's charter tour business, and he spent a lot of time in Tuckerman's shop. Arnold was teaching him how to build a New England-style dory, perfectly suited to the waters of Alaska. Arnold had changed the design to handle a small inboard engine, instead of an outboard on the transom, if the length of the dory was eighteen feet or more, for better steerage in case of rough weather.

Arnold was impressed with how well and quickly Walter learned to build a simple boat, and thought he could, with time and interest, become a competent boat builder. Sadly, Tuckerman was quite old and losing his health, worn down from his long, often difficult life. The years of drinking had not helped either, though he had given it up a long time ago. If Walter wanted to learn what he could from Arnold, time was their only obstacle.

Chapter 22

This is For You, Walter

Winter was running mild, with moderate temperatures and thin snow cover. Walter continued to work with Arnold. His first boat was done and would be available to anyone who wanted it. It was a fine, handy skiff, 18 feet from bow to stern, with a strong keel and ribs set tight and hard. While the two-cylinder diesel engine installed wouldn't allow the craft to develop a lot of speed, it was reliable, and a practical source of power. Tuckerman patted Beaumont on the back as they admired the boat where it was held upright on its blocks.

"She's a fine dory, Walter; you've done well. Next one, you'll build all on your own."

Kidding, Walter said, "What's the matter, Arnold, you getting lazy?"

"Nah, nah, boy, I'm only getting tired quicker than before. Maybe I need to take 'er a little easier. Come here, I want to show you something."

They walked over to the workbench where Arnold kept all his fine hand tools, and opened a deep, wide drawer. In it was a thick stack of heavy paper, and on top of that was a wide, bound book. Tuckerman took out the book and opened it. He talked as he turned the pages.

On them were wonderfully drawn diagrams of different steps in the process of designing and building a number of different styles of boats.

Beaumont was absorbed and fascinated as the old boat builder went through the book.

He heard Arnold saying, "There's not much missing in this notebook and on the other papers here, for you to build some fine boats, which I know you can do with your good mind and hands. There is a bunch of specifics in the back concerning what wood and hardware to use in making a seaworthy craft.

"Anything happens to me, and it will as it comes to everyone, all of this is yours. You can continue building or sell it all, up to you. You're the nearest thing to family for me, so, well, there it is."

Beaumont was speechless, finally saying a simple, heartfelt "Thanks," to Tuckerman, gripping his hand as he said, "But, don't be in any hurry, Arnold."

"Oh, I'm not, but don't ever think we have the control to decide these things, it's all in the wind."

Chapter 23

Boats

The following summer, Walter's charter/touring business was more successful than the year before. Even people living in Anchorage and other Alaska cities, as well as folks from out of state, made reservations to sight-see around Prince William Sound with him.

There were times when the wildlife in the Sound seemed to appear as if on cue. The people who took the tours were always pleased with all the animals they were able to view, on the land or in the water.

One client kiddingly asked Walter if he had hired the animals to make the trips more interesting. Walter smiled and told the man, whose wife was standing by her husband's side with an innocent look on her face, he had an understanding with the deer, bears, sea lions, and killer whales, and they had been known to want one or two travelers for their fee.

"I don't understand," the man's wife had said. "What would they possibly want with people?"

"Well, ma'am," Walter said, "the animals who live here can always do with some extra food."

The wife's face showed she didn't understand, until, a moment later, her mouth opened, and her eyes got big.

Walter was suddenly sorry he had made the joke to this poor woman, who had come many miles to participate in an exciting trip, and had gotten more than she'd bargained for.

The husband rolled his eyes, nodded at Walter, then took his wife a few feet away, to explain it was a joke. One thing the charter clients always loved was when pods of dolphins swam and played in front of the boat's bow. They were full of energy, and appeared to be having a lot of fun, entertaining the passengers on the *Journey* until they disappeared, going elsewhere for their own purposes.

Sometimes, humpback whales could be seen surfacing, spouts of mist-filled air spewing from their blowholes. Walter always hoped the people might see the whales catching small fish by surrounding schools of them with a net of bubbles they blew, coming up through the middle of the "net," swallowing huge mouthfuls of the fish. It had only happened once, and the clients were thrilled.

Walter came to love the tours he conducted. It was a perfect way to share his love of Alaska.

The second season proved so successful, the Beaumonts made enough money to carry them through the off season.

He had been asked to take people hunting, but he never agreed. While he obviously had no problem with hunting for food and survival, sport hunting never appealed to him, and he felt it would change things with his business in wrong ways.

Though Walter was satisfied doing the charters, nothing topped coming home to Miriam and Emma. He always made sure to pick up his daughter, hold her above him, then give her a big hug and kiss her face. She always laughed with delight.

His little family had gone far to heal the pain and losses he had suffered. He, Miriam, and baby Emma were a part of the natural flow of things. Everything they did together happened in harmony, as if preordained by some higher power, taking them along a trail with few obstacles and knotholes to work through.

He and Miriam never had cross words with each other, and they always discussed anything important, figuring out the best way to keep things moving along smoothly. They loved one another as only people who have deep loyalty and trust can. The thought that one might intentionally do something wrong, something hurtful to the other never occurred to either of them.

The second season was over, *Beaumont's Journey* made ship-shape, polished, and cleaned completely, readied to be idle for the winter. It had proven to be a rugged, reliable boat. Still, Walter was having thoughts about building a longer, wider boat with more room for clients and extra storage space, a boat tourists could spend the night on, to prolong the time they could spend on the waters of the Sound. He also wanted to have a large skiff to tow behind, in case of trouble.

He had voiced his ideas with Arnold, who brightened visibly at the thought of a new project. He had gone to his design drawer and pulled out half a dozen pages with plans for a boat similar to what Walter wanted. It would be a fifty foot boat with two cabins, holding six to eight people comfortably, with a well-equipped galley, and a large cooler to keep a stock of food fresh.

Walter studied the plans with Arnold, and decided it would be about perfect for what he wanted to do.

Arnold, after considering what the wood, hardware, and gear for the build would cost, not to mention a proper engine, had another idea he put before Walter.

There were a number of boats beached in various locations around Seward and other coastal towns. He thought it might be financially more reasonable to do some searching, and see if they could find one in good enough condition to be rebuilt and modified to suit Walter's needs.

"We could spend some time before the weather gets too difficult, bring a boat up here, and work on it over the fall and winter. 'Course, it'd take some doing, but I believe we could save quite a bit of money that way. I know men who have the equipment to salvage and tow a beached vessel and get it dry-docked here. I made the shop tall enough to house a good-sized boat, as you know."

Walter thought it over, and though he'd considered a new boat, Arnold's idea made sense.

Two days later, they had the *Journey* out on the water again, looking for a suitable vessel, with Arnold coming along, apparently over his dread of being on open water. They found one beached on the west side of Fox Island, close to the Bay's entrance. There was a deep bay, sheltering enough to protect anything there from heavy weather, and even from the full power of the tidal waves from the '64 quake. It was tucked in behind a large rock projection which apparently had protected it as it lay keeled over, above high water for all but the heaviest tides.

Both Arnold and Walter decided it had been there since before the quake. The hull had sustained some damage, the rudder was gone, it needed a new prop, and the shaft was bent. Arnold, after a close inspection inside and out, determined it was worth repairing. It was a forty-six footer with a deep hull, large enough inside to rework into the boat Walter needed. Below decks was a rough jumble of gear, old supplies, and some personal possessions, clothing and the like. All the debris was damp and mildewed, slowly rotting. They would worry about the cleanup later.

It was named *Ocean's Bounty*, originally out of Homer, and it turned out to be fairly easy to find the owner, actually the owner's son, who was still living in Homer. He had no desire to refloat the vessel, and offered it to them at a low price, far less than the cost of new materials would have been. Arnold had told Walter that buying the boat outright would be the simplest way to obtain the craft, rather than going through the necessary details of salvaging her.

The repairing of the hull, and what they had to do to get it off the beach, hiring someone with an old landing barge, a bulldozer to set the boat upright, and getting it out to open water again was an adventure in itself. But after three weeks, it was blocked up on shore in front of Arnold's shop. The *Ocean's Bounty* turned out to be too tall, from keel to deckhouse, to fit comfortably inside the shop. After serious consideration and an inspection of how the deckhouse was built, Arnold and Walter gently removed it, careful to tag and make notes and diagrams of how it went together. Then, the boat slipped easily into the shop. Now they could work on it in relative comfort over the winter.

The first thing to do was to get the main hull in good order. It was in surprisingly good condition, with only a few places needing any heavy repairs. It took more time to scrape down the hull and repaint it than to make actual physical repairs. Once they were done, it could be cleaned inside, clearing all the trashed materials jumbled together in the hold.

The deck and all the brass hardware needed stripping, refinishing, or replacing, and the numerous wooden bins in Arnold's shop contained an amazing number of brass and iron pieces, cleats, brackets, hinges, and even some brass ship's lights.

The anchor was gone, but the chain winch was repairable. Tuckerman made some calls and a suitable anchor was found and delivered.

Once the deck and topsides were mostly redone, they spent days inside clearing out all the scrap, then removing the fish holding compartments, finally leaving a stripped-open hull for alterations. Tuckerman, once he had the dimensions and knew what would have to be put where inside for efficiency and client comfort, got to work on the design plans. When he finally showed them to Beaumont, Walter was amazed and pleased at how perfect the finished boat would be.

Arnold had great enthusiasm for the project. He was glad he still had tools and supplies to do his life's work after the quake had brought almost total destruction to Seward and his property.

Walter stayed alongside him while he was inspecting and redesigning the interior. The old man kept up a steady flow of words as he worked, relating to Beaumont what he was planning and why. Walter marveled at his vast knowledge, and absorbed everything he could, for future reference.

Once he had the plans laid out, Arnold endeavored to contact the people he knew who could help them with what they needed for the build. A number of them were no longer reachable, having changed their location after the quake, moved to another state, and were beyond Tuckerman's ability to find them. Still, there were enough left to help get the boat properly fitted out.

Miriam would visit them often as they worked. She was worried about the finances for reworking the boat, but had faith in her husband to do what was necessary to keep things going. She kept her own council, not bothering him with small concerns she knew wouldn't help make anything better.

Through the fall and winter, Arnold and Walter worked together as only men with a shared enthusiasm and commitment can. The old ship builder was truly his mentor, and the innately capable younger man could not have been instructed by a better source, Walter listening to what Arnold told him, learning something of value every day, continually absorbing the knowledge Tuckerman had taken many years to accumulate. For his part, Arnold was glad it was Beaumont he was teaching.

Every morning Arnold would wake up, work the kinks out, have coffee, and review what they'd last done to the vessel, readying himself for the new day. While waiting for Beaumont to come down to the shop, he'd usually make a list of things to do. Then they'd have a specific goal for the day, which made the rebuild move along steadily. Arnold never suggested Walter come in earlier. He knew having a family meant time spent in the mornings, appreciating what he had.

Besides enjoying his family, Walter would spend an hour each morning putting himself through exercises and practice, as his Uncle Aubrey once had, keeping his ability for self-defense sharp, though what Walter had learned in the military had far outstripped what his capable uncle had taught him. While living a peaceful, domestic existence, he did not allow himself to become complacent, wanting to remain prepared for any eventuality.

The first time Tuckerman saw him practicing his combat training, he got a chill down his back, thinking it was Aubrey he saw, still keeping fit. He was glad Beaumont was carrying on the tradition, if one could use the term. It made Arnold feel he still had his old friend around, in a small way.

They had gathered all the wood and metal hardware required to complete the boat, and most of it was already in place. Arnold's old pal, Kenny Bowen, came up from where he lived on the coast of the Kenai Peninsula. Bowen was a retired marine engineer, capable of building and maintaining any diesel or gas-powered marine engines. He told Arnold he would come out of retirement and do the job for him, but it would be the last thing he'd do. Arnold laughed, telling Kenny he'd never be able to refuse an interesting project, and Bowen couldn't argue the point.

After arriving at Tuckerman's shop, Bowen did a complete inspection of the six-cylinder GM diesel engine in the boat, pulling the head and inspecting the pistons and cylinders. Afterwards, he said it was in fair condition for having sat idle for so long a time, but did have many miles on it. It was decided he would rebuild the engine. Kenny completely stripped it, checking each part to determine whether it was worth reusing, arranging them neatly on the engine compartment floor, and putting the parts to be replaced in a separate row. Once he had a detailed list of what was needed, Beaumont gave him enough cash to buy the parts, and Kenny left to do so.

A week after Bowen left, Arnold told Walter he had found something. They walked up above the head of the Bay, to where there were half a dozen boats in various states of disrepair. They had been scavenged by needy people for parts to repair other boats. Arnold took Beaumont to a large pleasure boat, not a commercial vessel. Inside, there were a lot of interior materials to use for the unfinished cabins on their boat.

"Doesn't this boat belong to someone, Arnold?"

"Not someone in this world anymore, Walter. He has no more earthly worries."

Over the next week, they pulled any useable materials, and Arnold applied them wherever possible, filling in with new materials where necessary. Beaumont was amazed, seeing the below-decks area being transformed. Arnold was a wonder.

It still cost Walter a sizeable piece of change to get the boat redone. With any luck, everything would be ready to start the new charter tour season late the next spring. They had decided on a name. It would be called the *Emma Joy*.

Miriam had been taking a few reservations for the coming season, two from people who had already taken a tour and wanted to extend the experience. Walter, with Miriam's help, advertised in the back of outdoor magazines, noting the beauty of Prince William Sound, as well as the excellent animal sightings in the area, for those coming for the photographic opportunities.

Walter had become a licensed charter boat captain, studying and jumping through the necessary hoops to become one. He figured the charters he hoped to promote were probably more accessible for him if he were certified, and it was mentioned in the ads.

Winter came in with lots of snow and low temperatures. Arnold and Walter worked on the interior of the boat whenever weather allowed, keeping it warm with a woodstove they had installed in what would be the main cabin. They ran the stove pipe out a round hole, which would be used for a porthole later.

By the middle of winter, the interior was finished including the installation of appliances. But, an unexpected change of plans touched Beaumont once again.

Walter had gone down to the shop as usual one winter morning, after clearing snow from the driveway and doorways at home. His uncle's old army ambulance was parked next to the shop, coated with a thick layer of snow. The sturdy old rig seemed to keep going if given normal maintenance. Neither Beaumont nor Tuckerman had registered the vehicle since Aubrey had been taken by the quake, and the State Police in Seward never hassled them about it.

Walter drove his Ford pickup down to the shop. He walked into the place, which was cold inside. Seeing Arnold at his worktable, his head down on his arm lying across the table top, Walter called out to him, but got no response. He felt a chill run down his back. He remained still a while, not ready to come closer yet.

Beaumont was no stranger to death, but the thought of losing another person close to him stopped him in his tracks. Taking a half breath, he walked up to Arnold. There was still a pencil grasped in his right hand, as if he was simply resting while planning something new. A touch to his wrist confirmed he was gone. The old man had submitted to what a body does at its destined time, and left everyone else behind.

Walter remained there a while, holding Arnold's wrist and gently patting him on the back. He felt a void open in his midsection, as though a physical part of him had been removed.

A week later, a memorial service was held for Arnold Malcolm Tuckerman, aged 81 years, according to the torn and wrinkled birth certificate Walter found in an old sea chest in the back of the shop.

A lot of people turned out, some coming from as far as Anchorage, Kenai, and Homer. Walter had contacted as many people as he could to let them know. Arnold had many loyal friends.

They buried him on a ledge upon a low ridge overlooking the head of Resurrection Bay in a coffin Walter made himself, with a cross of heavy native spruce boards by a wood carver who knew Tuckerman well, hand-carving his name, birth, and death dates, and nothing more, no more being necessary for those who knew him.

It wasn't easy digging in the cold, hard ground with picks and shovels. Taking turns, Walter and several other men who came to attend the funeral got the job done the day before the burial. The man with the bulldozer had to clear a path to the site.

For a few days Walter stayed at home with Miriam and Emma Joy or hung around the shop, inspecting what Arnold had by way of tools and plans, hardware, and wood. He was amazed at how much had accumulated over the years. He thought the quake had disposed of most of it. Arnold, however, had several other places where he kept much gear, one of them an outbuilding on the land where Beaumont's home was located. Another was a rusty old Quonset hut located on another piece of property. Arnold had Walter help him clear it out when the new shop was built, to use for storage of any more items they would accumulate.

He was surprised to find there was a will written, signed, and notarized a year before Arnold had passed. Everything went to Walter. He knew Tuckerman had no family and they had become close, but he was touched to know he'd thought so highly of him.

The biggest surprise was when Beaumont discovered Tuckerman had a sizeable savings account, many thousands of dollars, also going to him. This was a real Godsend to Walter. It would give him financial breathing room once the boat was done.

He felt strange about the money. It was, for him, an unpleasant way to receive funds. Because the financial arrangement was as Tuckerman wished it to be, Beaumont ultimately accepted it. Though some people might have thought it found money without concern for the circumstances, this way of thinking was not in Walter's personality. He always considered it a blessing through Arnold.

There was also a short letter, a long note, actually. It said Arnold knew his time was short. He was always tired, and he had been dreaming a lot about people he loved, who had gone before him.

He had written:

It seems less like dreaming and more like visiting all those I love who have departed. Doing it while I am sleeping makes it easier, removing the distractions being awake brings.

All in all, the main thing I wanted to say to you is this: whatever else you do in the years to come, I hope you will continue to build sturdy skiffs, and perhaps other forms of boats. You have a gift for doing so, and in a way it would make me feel you are continuing on with my one big passion in life.

God bless you, Walter.

He had signed it, *Your good friend, Arnold Malcolm Tuckerman, boat builder*.

Walter stood with the note in his hands, which were trembling slightly. His emotions surged, and he stood there until he'd settled down.

Tears welled up in Miriam's eyes when Walter told her about Arnold's passing, and the note, which he let her read. She didn't say anything, but the look she gave him when she was done reading said it all. Words weren't always necessary between him and Miriam, because they were so strongly connected through their love for one another.

For him, and his delightful daughter, Emma Joy, there was a lot of playful time, laughter and giggles, hugs and smiles. It was as if she, and her mother too, could draw out a part of him rarely seen. The way he interacted with them was in real contrast to how he dealt with most others.

Beaumont was serious yet fair in dealing with people he didn't know well. He rarely spent much time with anyone other than his family, on a social level. He didn't need a lot of friends, and often saw things in others that kept him from getting close to them.

Beaumont was finishing a twenty-one foot skiff a design based on one of Arnold's boats, with a few modifications of his own to strengthen the inner structure of the bow and mid-ships, in case whoever purchased it wanted to run a set net or other similar fishing system.

He had not yet put a finish on the boat. As always, he liked the way the bare wood looked, despite having to paint skiffs according to customers' wishes.

This was the fourth skiff he'd brought to completion on his own, and the first to have more of his own concepts in it.

It had been two years since Mr. Tuckerman had passed, but whenever Walter was in the shop, he still felt his presence strongly. A time or two, he seemed to sense him watching as he worked diligently to bring a new boat to completion. He didn't mind the feeling.

Walter had finished the forty-six footer he and Arnold had refurbished from a beached vessel. He had his neighbor with the small bulldozer pull the boat out of the shop, first building ramps to do so, then reinstalled the deckhouse, with a few modifications. He silently thanked Tuckerman for his detailed notes, schematics, and tagged parts for putting it all back together correctly. It had proven to be a seaworthy, well-equipped boat. The next season he chartered a team of biologists who did a research study in the Sound. They paid him well, and had let him help out with what they were doing, studying marine mammals in the Sound, comparing their numbers and condition to previous years.

It was a one-month charter, and when it was over, Walter took several families around the Sound with a new wealth of knowledge about the sea life there, courtesy of the researchers.

Chapter 24

Brady

Walter had struck up a friendship with one of the Alaska State Police officers. They had connected right away on levels they understood, stemming from their backgrounds. ASP Officer Charles Brady had been in the army and gone to Korea to fight in that difficult, deadly campaign. He had joined the Territorial Police after the conflict had ended, and was in service when that law enforcement agency became the Alaska State Police, and would still be in uniform later with the Alaska State Troopers. In 1969, Officer Brady transferred to the Division of Wildlife Troopers. He had always loved hunting and fishing and simply being out in the wilds, so it suited him to a T. His knowledge of and experiences in the wilderness enabled him and Walter Beaumont to have a productive relationship built on mutual respect for each other, and their shared appreciation and love for Alaska.

He had met Beaumont out on the Gulf, when he was on patrol making sure people were following the laws controlling commercial and sport fishing. He had talked to him about things in general after finding out Walter wasn't fishing. He had eventually come to visit Beaumont at Tuckerman's shop out of curiosity, and because he already felt connected to this fellow.

Walter and Charlie never talked much about their military service, and of course Walter could not have because of his classified duty. It was understood they had both been in dire situations, and no story-telling was necessary. Brady came to recognize Beaumont's abilities in the wilds, his tracking and general woodcraft capabilities. He had talked to other Troopers who had worked with Walter through his coastal searches, leading to his taking part in several search and rescue missions, tracking down lost hunters and fishermen, or their remains. He always found who he had been assigned to search for, usually by branching off on his own. It was this knowledge and experience which ultimately led to Walter being asked by Brady to help the Troopers' wildlife unit. Socially, they had gone fishing together in Resurrection Bay several times on the *Journey*, though both were busy most of the time with their work.

One day, there was a knock on the shop door, though it was open, and he looked up to see Officer Brady.

"Hello Beaumont, how's it going?"

"Hey, Brady, fine, and you?"

"Oh, well as can be expected. You have a minute to talk?"

"Sure, no problem. I'm ready for a cup of coffee, how about you?"

The two men sipped from their mugs in silence for a while.

"We're having a problem with some poachers down on the Kenai, southeast of Tustumena Lake. We've been trying to catch up to them on and off for months. Unfortunately, they're good out in the woods. We came as close as running them off a fresh bear kill, recovering the hide and skull. They were in the middle of skinning the nine footer, and we got there before they had a chance to take off with the hide. They did get the gall bladder."

"Gall bladder? Why would they want that?"

"Though it's not well known here, they're sold in Asia where their medicinal use is highly prized, and the dried, ground-up bladder is quite valuable. Usually the body is left to rot, or be eaten by other bears, coyotes, wolves, and foxes. At any rate, would you have some time to help me nab the bastards?"

"Is that a law enforcement term?" Walter had a crooked little grin when he said it.

Charlie smiled too. "Purely a subjective comment."

236

"Well, count me in. Sounds like an interesting job. Will I be deputized in case I need to defend myself, or you?"

"With your working with us already, and past military experience, I can't see any problem with it. You know, you should consider becoming a Trooper. You'd get all the excitement you could want."

"Well, thanks for the suggestion, Charlie, but I've already had all the excitement I need, if that's what you want to call it. I'm happy to help out, though."

"I hear you, and understand. I think the main difference between where I was in the army, and where you were sent was I froze my butt off, and you had to watch out for heat prostration."

"If that had been the only thing I had to watch out for, I would have been fine."

As others had, Brady saw the look in Walter's eyes when he spoke, and knew all he needed to know.

He responded, saying, "Well, bullets are bullets and dead is dead, no other way to put it."

"That about covers it, Charlie." Beaumont looked down at the floor and was silent.

"Yeah, I understand, Walter. As long as you're willing to use your knowledge to help us out from time to time, no need to take it any further. I know you're great at tracking. Must have gotten a little technical training."

Walter smiled, and gave a little laugh, "You could say so, yeah. More coffee? Come look at this skiff I just finished."

Three days later, they were landing in a Cessna 182 on floats, coasting up to the southeast shore of Tustumena Lake. They unloaded the gear they had brought, then watched as the pilot taxied away, back up the lake.

They set up their camp inside the willows by the shore, for the sake of concealment. Their tent was waterproof camo material, the same colors and pattern as army fatigues.

Charlie was dressed in hunting clothing, including hip boots. Walter wore a heavy canvas shirt and pants, an insulated camo military jacket, and eight-inch hiking boots. They were dressed and equipped for chill weather. It was the end of September, and was turning cooler day by day, though no frost was appearing yet.

They built a small, smokeless fire, made coffee, and ate some moose meat sandwiches Miriam had insisted on making them, as well as some blueberry muffins. Neither man argued against the tasty provisions.

As soon as the plane was gone, both men went into quiet mode, using low-level voices to communicate, what some might call hunting whispers.

"O.K., the men we are looking for were sighted within five miles of this area three days ago. There's plenty of game here, as I'm sure you know. but these guys are only after bear. There are probably three of them, and it's more than likely they're a rough bunch. You comfortable with that?"

"Oh, don't be concerned about me; I was trained for this. We'll have no problem bringing these guys in, if they're around."

"Still, I would feel better if we had a couple more men along."

"This is better. Less chance of noise, better for catching them by surprise. When we do, we'll have them under control, no problem."

Charlie smiled, nodded, then checked in with the Trooper office in Kenai on the field radio he had brought to make sure contact was good. It was, a strong signal available.

The two men didn't find any fresh sign right away, though Walter was already getting an idea of the lawbreakers' pattern of movement, based on what Charlie had told him. He also saw a lot of old sign showing him what he needed to know. Even though Brady was good in the bush, an experienced outdoorsman and law enforcement officer, Beaumont was on a level above most. His instincts about human activity out in the wilds were still finely tuned, despite being out of military service for some years.

He had hunted for moose many times since he'd returned, never coming home empty-handed. When he'd come home from a hunt, Miriam always said, "My successful hunter husband brings us our meat again."

He never trapped any more. Though he had done his share with his uncle, having other ways to make a living allowed him to leave the beasts of the forest to their own ways, which he actually preferred.

The second day there, Beaumont asked Charlie to let him do some reconnoitering on his own. Brady realized it was probably a good idea, though he couldn't help being concerned. It turned out to be the best thing to do. He returned several hours later, Charlie not seeing him until he was by the tent.

"I know where they are, Charlie. I got a slight whiff of smoke, and meat cooking. Let's head over in that direction and see what we find."

Brady nodded his assent. He was confident in his own abilities, but trusted Beaumont's skills implicitly.

They had been slowly searching for any sign, and had seen several bits of evidence indicating someone had been in the area recently. There were some fresh boot tracks, and a cigarette butt crushed under someone's foot. There was little of the finished smoke left, but Walter had spotted a small edge of paper.

Squatting down to palaver, Walter handed Charlie a strip of moose jerky from a small cotton bag he had brought.

"We've been following some strong sign for the last hour, Charlie, and I think they may be nearby, maybe a few minutes away. So let's go silent now, okay? You still remember hand signs, yeah?"

"I do. You lead the way."

Beaumont was right. No more than fifteen minutes later he held up his fist, signaling stop. They stayed hunkered down, listening. It was obvious Walter had heard the quiet voices well before Brady did, and then Charlie picked up the sound too. Walter put his face right up to Charlie's ear and, whispered, "Somebody's there in front of us, about twenty-five yards away, by that trio of little spruce. How about if you move up out of sight through the willows on the left, and I'll come around on the right, and we'll have them dead to rights. Sounds like there's a creek just beyond them, and it might slow them down if they try to take off."

Brady had heard no water sounds, but he knew Walter wasn't mistaken. He nodded, and said, "Let's do it."

Five minutes later, Brady had slipped up to a point where he could see the camp. There were three men, and a suspicious-looking large lump wrapped in a canvas tarp. He ran his eyes over the bundle until he saw what looked like the vague outline of a bear's head in one corner of it. Deciding Walter must be in position, he called out to the three men, who seemed to be busy packing up their camp, identifying himself.

"State Wildlife Troopers, stand where you are!"

At Brady's call, they jerked upright, one of them picking up a bolt-action rifle from the ground. They all stood glaring at Charlie's position, obviously unhappy he had gotten the drop on them.

"Hey, take it easy, guys. We don't want any more trouble than necessary."

"Oh, yeah?" said the man with the rifle. "Maybe you ought to crawl away back to where you came from, so you won't have more trouble than you can handle. What we're doing ain't none of your business, Trooper."

Another voice called out from somewhere else close by, the person speaking also hidden by the willows, "If you've been taking game illegally, it is our business. Drop your guns!"

The man with the rifle hesitated, all three poachers turning to see where the voice came from.

Brady's .357 magnum service revolver was pointed at the man with the rifle. He said, "Better do as the man says, boys, he's a crack shot. We're State Trooper wildlife officers, and this is all our business, now drop 'em!" Then he came out from the willows.

There's no telling what a trapped man will do. Most have enough sense to give up when someone gets the drop on them, but not all. One of the men started to pull his pistol. Charlie couldn't see him because one of the other poachers was blocking the view, but Beaumont saw.

Walter yelled, "Don't!" The man didn't do the smart thing. He aimed in Brady's direction.

Charlie saw the man swing in his direction, pistol in hand. Before he could pull the trigger, a loud shot rang out from a rifle, and the man collapsed to the ground, his pistol going off once as he did. He was dead where he lay.

The other two poachers froze, not willing to take a chance on receiving the same treatment. They dropped their guns, waiting for whatever would come next.

A moment later, Walter came walking out of the nearby brush, his rifle still at the ready. The look in his eyes made the two men take a step back as he approached.

Brady holstered his Smith and Wesson and cuffed the two, making them sit on the ground. Walter kept watch as Brady went over to the canvas bag. Sure enough, there was a brown bear hide rolled up in it, with the gall bladder wrapped in a piece of cloth, tied with some string.

Charlie looked over at Walter and nodded, receiving the same in response.

Brady read the two men their rights, then had them use an extra piece of canvas as a carrier to haul their partner's body out, while Walter set up the bear hide package as a makeshift backpack. Charlie slipped the criminals' pistols into his small pack, and made the poachers shoulder their now-empty rifles, bolts removed, and they walked out. Even stopping several times to give the two a break, they made it back to their lake shore camp in good time. Charlie used cuffs to join the two men together back to back, sitting them down on the gravely shore before calling in a larger plane to take them down to the Kenai office, where the men would be held over.

Charlie thanked Walter for his help. "You probably saved my bacon back there, thanks."

Walter smiled, and pulled on the left shoulder of Brady's insulated coat. Charlie saw there was a fresh rip in it, insulation sticking out. He got a chill, realizing it must have been made by the bullet coming from the dead man's pistol. He smiled a hesitant smile, and drew a hand in jest across his brow.

"I'm sorry you had to take him down. You okay?"

"Yeah, he made his choice, and it was the wrong one. I'm glad you weren't hit."

Walter had to make a statement at the Trooper office and appear in court six months later as witness in the case. Even though he was on the right side of things, being in the courtroom made him feel uncomfortable. "Like being in a fishbowl," is the way he put it. He gave testimony, then put it behind him.

Over the next several years, Beaumont participated in more tracking jobs, one of them to find a burglary suspect, an Athabascan man who had escaped from jail out of Anchorage. He found him on his own in the dense bush country northwest of Point Mackenzie, and captured him without a hitch.

As the man was being led away by Troopers after Beaumont called in their position by field radio, the prisoner turned and asked how he'd found him. "I'm pretty good at being sneaky in the woods."

Walter had on his poker face, and after a moment he said, "You're a noisy walker. You broke lots of little sticks on the ground, and small branches along the way. I smelled the smoke from the cigarette you had when I caught you, and besides, I found the canoe you stole to get across the Arm, which was a good starting point. It all added up."

"Well, damn, guess you outfoxed me and caught me fair and square. Maybe I'll look you up when I get out and we can discuss it."

Despite the man's smile, Walter knew he wasn't being friendly. He said, "Fine by me. I might have another lesson to teach you, one you definitely wouldn't like."

The man's smile turned to a dark look, and they took him away. He never did visit Walter.

Miriam disliked him going off on potentially dangerous trips, but she trusted in her husband, and would never go against his decisions. She was always relieved when he came home safe and sound.

Chapter 25

Changes

Beaumont never actively looked for news about Viet Nam. Still, it was almost impossible to avoid hearing about it. He knew, before it was over, the war would not go as he and many others hoped it would, but not because those that served there weren't willing and able. He had done his duty, only coming home when he did because he was badly wounded.

The wounds Walter received caused him distress over the years. Sometimes after he'd been working too hard, his guts would flare up, and he'd have to sit or lie down and rest until the pain went away. A doctor he saw told him the rough inner scar tissue caused irritation after too much physical stress.

Being who he was, Beaumont didn't complain much. In that, he and his wife were well matched. She'd make him some broth from game meat, and chamomile tea to sooth his innards, and she'd sit by him until he felt better, unless Emma Joy or Nicolas needed attention.

Emma had grown into a pretty young girl, tall for her age, with a sharp wit. She did well in school, and was known for having a beautiful singing voice. She was Miriam and Walter's pride and joy.

The little Beaumont family entered into a time of true peace and contentment. Miriam became pregnant again, this time with a boy who they named Nicolas Benjamin Beaumont, Benjamin after his grandfather. She had none of the difficulties being pregnant with Nicolas she'd had with Emma Joy, much to their relief.

After Nicolas was born, Miriam wanted to take him and Emma and go visit some of her relatives on Kodiak Island, where they had settled after Chenega was hit by the tidal waves in '64.

Walter had no problems with her visiting, of course, and he decided it was high time to visit his folks, whom he hadn't seen in more than a year, though he tried to visit them once a year, as promised. So, while his wife and children were in Kodiak, he'd head back to the family home in Manhattan, Kansas, which to him, by then, seemed like going to a foreign country. It was late fall, and Beaumont didn't have a new project going, having finished a finely done skiff just a week before.

After seeing Miriam and the children off, he headed to Anchorage, catching a flight to his destination in the Midwest.

He was sitting in the crowded waiting area of the Anchorage Airport, crowded for him, at least, when he noticed an older man staring at him, a large fellow with a bushy gray beard and a beat-up, floppy brimmed hat. Almost at the same time, they recognized each other. It was Leonard Patterson, the man who, with his wife, Lizzie, had given Walter a ride and a place to stay his first night in Alaska. They shook hands and hello'd each other, then sat down to talk.

Leonard was headed down to California to see his eldest daughter and her husband, who owned and operated a small vineyard. Walter explained where his destination was, and why.

Leonard looked closely at Walter, the scar along his cheek. There was something about him the skookum old fellow detected.

"You been in the military, Walter? If you don't mind me asking."

"Yeah, Mr. Patterson, I have."

"I didn't mean to pry. From the looks of things, you saw some serious action. I'm glad you're here, is all."

They carried on some small talk, Walter sorry to hear his Lizzie had passed away two years before. Then Leonard's flight was called. They shook hands, and went through the ritual of promising to see each other again, when more than likely they wouldn't.

Walter was glad when his flight boarded. It wasn't full, and he could sit alone in one of the rows.

After take-off, he let his mind run through what had happened since he had last seen his parents. They had looked pretty much the same as when he had first left Kansas, except for having more gray hairs. It was a pleasant visit, and his parents were obviously glad to see him.

When he got to Kansas this time, it was chilly and raining hard. He spotted his mother waiting for him, without his father. This put a seed of doubt in his mind. The two hugged and smiled at each other, then set out for the Beaumont family home.

As his mother drove, chatting happily, Walter responded little, looking at Manhattan. It had grown, and a lot of small businesses had cropped up. What he noticed when they got to the house made him shake his head. Where the creek and small cottonwoods had been outside the old wooden fence, now there was a large tract of identically built houses, the only difference between them being the exterior colors.

When he and his mom entered the house, there was a heavy atmosphere, almost sad. His mom's facial expression had changed, too. Then his father came into the house from the garage, and Walter was shocked to see how much older he looked. His color was bad, a grayish hue revealing illness, and he moved slowly.

Ben Beaumont walked up to his son, saw the look on his face and said, "I know son, it is kind of shocking. Don't worry, I'll be getting better soon. Open heart surgery can be hard on you at first."

"I didn't know anything about this, dad, why didn't you two let me know. Maybe I could have helped."

"Well, we didn't want to worry you and take you away from your own concerns. As I say, I'll be better soon."

He turned to look at his mother, and the expression on her face told a different story. He took a moment to collect himself, smiled at his father, and patted him on the shoulder. On the inside, he was not feeling good about any of this.

The visit went well enough, all things considered. He told his folks all about what he'd been doing, and of Mr. Tuckerman's passing.

"He was a good man, treated me well. As I think you know, he taught me how to build boats, mainly skiffs. I've sold a few, and they've proven to be good, sturdy, and capable out on open water. He also worked with me to rebuild the larger boat I wrote you about, repairing and changing it to use for my charter business. Maybe sometime you can come up and take a tour with me. I think you'd both love seeing Prince William Sound. It's one of the most beautiful places I've ever experienced, and Alaska's full of amazing country. Oh, I've brought you both some blueberry and currant jam Miriam made. It's tasty stuff."

"How is she, by the way?" his mom asked. "I hope you brought some photos of those grandkids of mine."

He had brought some, and his mom and dad sat and looked at them for some time. He left the photos with them.

"She's on Kodiak Island right now, visiting. She took the kids too, to let them meet and get to know her side of the family."

"Speaking of family," Ben said, "has anything been found of Aubrey, maybe his boat somewhere?"

"No, nothing. The disaster took him away without a trace. Mr. Tuckerman and I held a little memorial service for him though, out on the Bay. We threw some flowers out on the water and said some prayers."

Much as he loved his parents, after three days he was already craving to return home. At the end of a full week, he was headed back to the airport to return to Alaska. He'd had a nice time with the folks, and they were glad to see him as well, though his mother had fretted over the scar on his face, saying it looked no better than it had during the visit several years before. His father made a remark, saying it added character to his face. "It's a wound declaring his willingness to fight for his country, for freedom."

Walter didn't respond.

Before he left, his mother brought out a little pouch, and gave it to Walter.

"This was your uncle's. I'm sure he'd like you to have them."

In the pouch were several medals, two purple hearts, a marksman's badge, and a bronze star. There was also, folded up, his honorable discharge, and a small photo of Aubrey with several of his G.I. buddies, standing in front of a jeep, shirts off, helmet straps unhooked, and their M1 Garand rifles held casually. It was a classic image of three warriors in a rare moment of relaxation. Of all the things in the pouch, this was the most important and valuable to him. In a flash thought, Beaumont realized he didn't have a photo of him and Everett, or anyone else he knew in the army. Because of their activities, they would not have been permitted anyway.

As always when he'd been away, Walter paused on the top of the airplane ladder at the Anchorage airport before leaving the plane, to gaze as far as he could past the visible city to the mountains beyond. And as usual someone behind him made impatient noises.

Walter took a taxi uptown and found what he planned to purchase upon returning to Alaska. It was an International Travelall, built in 1965. He bought it at the car dealership where the salesman had given him good advice years before, after the quake. He got himself a fair deal on it, low miles, and in excellent condition.

The Travelall was a good vehicle, four-wheel drive with a strong V-8 engine. It was also comfortable, with a good heater. It was actually the best rig he'd ever had. He enjoyed the ride down to Seward, actually sorry when it was over.

The old army ambulance his uncle had used for so long had finally worn out beyond what normal maintenance could do to keep it running right. It would take its place next to the outbuilding on the land he and Miriam had bought from Arnold. It would never be driven again, but he'd keep it cleaned up and on blocks, a fitting monument to Uncle Aubrey's memory.

Collecting the mail before going home, he sat in his new vehicle and leafed through the envelopes. There was a letter from Miriam, and Beaumont immediately opened it. He read:

Dearest Walter,

You must be home if you're reading this. I miss you a great deal, but being here with my people has been wonderful, even though the older ones are still grieving the great loss we suffered at Chenega. Emma loves playing with the other children in the village and learning about our traditions from the old ones. Nicolas absorbs everything happening around him. He smiles a lot. It is an important experience for them, as I am sure you will understand.

I know you will not want to hear what I write next, but I pray you will understand. I want to stay here a while longer. I can't honestly tell you how long. I have been doing some teaching for the children here, and it has been very satisfying. You know it's what I was schooled to do, and something my heart cries out for.

I know you were expecting to see me waiting for you when you got back. Please don't be too disappointed. You and I will always be as one, and I cherish our marriage. For now, I need to remain here. If I get into Kodiak town, I will try to reach you by phone. Please know I love you dearly.

I hope your parents are well, and the visit was a sweet one.

Your Loving wife,
Miriam

He sat in the Travelall digesting what he had read. He had no doubts about Miriam loving him. She was a totally honest person, and he knew what she wrote was true. It didn't diminish the sadness he felt because she and the children would be gone for some time. He'd hold back from going to the Kodiak village she was staying in. Much as he wanted to see her, he knew her well enough to leave things be, so strong was the love and understanding between them. Starting up the Travelall, he slowly drove home.

For several days, Beaumont didn't write back to her. He was in a turmoil, and needed to wait until he had a clear sense of how he felt about the situation.

The next morning after receiving the letter, Walter fueled up the *Journey*, provisioned himself for an extended trip, added some cold weather clothes to the forward cabin, and headed down the Bay without a clear plan of where he would go. He only knew he needed to get out on the water and away from their home and the shop, now empty except for him, to sort it all out.

The weather had become colder, but he was all right on the boat inside the cabin. The water was a little rough, a crisp chop on the surface. He decided to head back down to Kayak Island. He had given the place a good once over when he had been doing coastal searches for the State Police. This time he could have a pleasure run, and hopefully get the situation with Miriam put in a good place in his mind.

Kayak was still an interesting place for him. It had the steep pointed mountain in the middle, the lower reaches covered with dense growth making climbing difficult. He hove to, letting the bow anchor hold the *Journey* facing the incoming waves, and took the rubber raft onshore.

A drizzly rain was coming down. He didn't mind, wearing waterproof gear, including the sou'wester hat he had come to appreciate. Walter found something amusing. Despite the life and death situations he'd been in, a single drop of cold water down his neck was still very annoying.

The wind was blowing rain into his face, and he liked it, the forces of nature toying with him. Beaumont knew no matter what people thought of their abilities, their advanced sciences, and their theories of reality, that nature, which he knew was the visible power of God, always had the ability to turn life around, and change things in major ways, as it did in '64. A chill wind and light rain was merely a recognition of his existence by the natural world around him.

Walter froze in place, then slipped carefully behind a large boulder to his left. There was a large brown bear on the beach ahead of him, perhaps sixty yards away. The wind was blowing from the bear to him, so it hadn't caught his scent. He watched from concealment, as the bear explored along the shore, stopping to nibble or claw at something brought up by the water. Once in a while, the impressive animal would point his snout towards the gulf waters and sniff the air, shaking his head a few times to remove the rain building up on him. Walter realized this bruin was basically doing the same thing he was, looking around to see what he could see, though there was always the element of survival in whatever the bear did, mostly looking for something edible.

The wind seemed to swirl and shift, and a few moments later, the brownie lifted up on his hind legs and sniffed the air, trying to locate what Walter knew was where his scent was coming from. Finally, the bear trotted towards his hiding place, close enough for him to pull out the large caliber pistol from its holster under his raincoat.

When it was about fifty feet away, the bear turned off and ran into the heavy vegetation behind and above Beaumont's location.

Walter waited several minutes and headed right to the rubber raft to row it back to the boat. Rowing against the wind, it took longer than coming ashore had. He made the raft secure, and sat on the boat a while, digesting the situation he had left behind on the shore.

The water was getting rougher and the wind stronger, and he decided to head to Wingham Island again, to anchor on the lee side of the island as he had done once before. The weather had turned colder and heavier by the time he had brought the boat about behind the small, narrow island. He appreciated the Chevy V-8 engine having enough power to make headway. He anchored in, and as before, the island provided him sufficient protection from the worst of the storm, the rain having turned to sleet. He turned up the little oil burning stove in the cabin which kept him warm through the night, though sleep didn't come easily.

His guts were tender the next morning, his old wounds acting up. Walter had a cup of chamomile tea, which he knew was a soothing drink. Sitting with his feet up against the wheel housing, his XtraTuf boots off, he contemplated the several holes in his wool socks. If his wife was there when he got home, they would be neatly mended. Thinking of her just then, the storm blowing around him, he decided to write to her when he got back to the shop, his mind now set on how he would respond to her needs and desires.

When morning came, the water was relatively smooth, the storm having passed on. The skies were overcast, with no precipitation. On a whim, he decided to go find the boat which had been run aground on the island where he had rescued the marooned man.

Throttling up the engine after pulling anchor, he came around the north end of Wingham and dropped the anchor again off the western shore where he had first seen the fellow waving his arms to get his attention.

The situation had left a tiny seed of doubt in his mind about the story the guy had told him, how he'd lost his two friends from a tidal wave which had run the boat up into the underbrush. He had no reason to think the man had lied to him, but it didn't ring true, though he never tried to find out what might have actually happened.

After coming ashore in the raft, he found the boat where it sat unnaturally in the brush, looking as it had when Billy Weaks had first led him there.

A few small birds flew out of the glassless windows of the wheelhouse. The boat had an eerie feel to it, hidden as it was in the willows and alders, dead to the world. Beaumont climbed up and over the stern, then worked his way to the open hold, the hatch cover missing.

The hold had no living creatures in it, save some flies and other bugs. Looking around, he found nothing of any interest, only a lot of jumbled debris, ropes, cans, and other now-useless bits. There was enough water inside to be a definite layer in the hold where he walked, and the smell of mold and mildew was strong. He was going to leave, when he caught sight of a small door leading to a compartment set inside the bow. He clambered over the trash, and reached out to open the low door. He hesitated with a bad feeling in his gut, but still felt compelled to open the compartment. The door was stuck, and he had to yank on the loop handle with both hands, then fell backwards into a sitting position when it broke free. A small swarm of flies flew out the open door and then a stench the likes of which he had never smelled emanated from the small space now exposed. Beaumont's tough disposition gave way to a desire to run up and out of the boat, to be away from what was in the bow.

There, lying across each other, were two decomposed bodies. He leaned forward, hand over his nose and mouth for one quick look. They appeared to be two men, one wearing rain gear, the other in a heavy coat and rubber boots. Walter had seen enough, and he shut the door again, went out on deck, and sucked in several deep breaths of clear air. He stood a few minutes, letting his mind settle down, then headed right back to the rubber raft and put out for the *Journey*, wanting to be away from the gruesome scene as quickly as possible. He tied down the raft, hoisted anchor, cranked up the engine, and headed straight back to Seward.

It took a while before Walter had settled down from his discovery. Despite his experiences in the past, this had gotten to him. This wasn't several enemies put down during war time. It was two working men, fisherman, who were murdered, Beaumont was certain. He figured Billy Weaks must be the murderer, maybe for the sake of his own survival. He must have been desperate, to kill the two men.

When he got back to Seward, running the boat at higher speed than usual, he stopped at the pay phone by the grocery store in town, and called the Troopers.

Trooper Michael Trask was the one who answered, and Walter gave him the whole story, finally saying he'd be willing to go out with the investigating officers to guide them to the boat, which he did the next day. He only guided them to the vessel, refusing to go back aboard. He went back to the shore, sat on a rock, and waited.

The two officers, Trask and a new Trooper, came back to shore about half an hour later. The new man was looking a little gray, and Walter made a remark about the smell on board the beached boat. The young officer nodded, without saying a word.

They took down the full details of his rescue of Billy Weaks on the way back to Seward, including what Weaks had told him happened to the two other men on board. They thanked him for his help and left, saying he might have to give testimony, if necessary.

When Trask asked him if he had inspected the corpses, he said he hadn't.

"Then you probably didn't see the hole in one of the skulls, correct?"

"Correct. Did it look like a bullet hole?"

"Well, there's no doubt in my mind, though it will have to be investigated further. We'll get someone from the Anchorage Coroner's Office out here. He must have wanted to be caught, leaving them there like that."

Back in the peace and quiet of his cabin home, a cup of hot coffee on the table before him, Walter Beaumont knew the proper moment had come. He let out a long sigh. Taking pen in hand, he started writing.

Dear Miriam,

I have taken time before writing back to you because I wanted to be sure of how I felt about your decision to stay on Kodiak with the kids.

One thing I seriously considered was how you waited for me while I was in the army, and how for long there was no communication between us. And yet, you remained loyal, patiently waiting. I know you expected the same faithfulness from me, and I want you to know your belief was right. I was always true to our love.

I am accepting your decision to stay and help your people. I actually think it is a wonderful thing for you to do. I am missing you and the children a lot, as I'm sure you know, and am hoping we will be together again soon. It's what I'll be living for while you all are gone.

We will communicate whenever we can, and perhaps time will pass more quickly than I now think it will.

Give my love to Emma Joy and Nicolas. You already know you have mine, forever.

Walter

Reading it through twice, Beaumont folded the letter and put it in an envelope. After a meal of halibut and chips at Jim Bigelow's restaurant, he walked up to the post office and dropped it in the box outside. His heart twinged a little when he did, but he was a man who always did what needed to be done, no matter the consequences.

Chapter 26

A Family Again

Walter Beaumont hung up the phone after he had talked to his wife on Kodiak, always a bittersweet moment.

It was New Years, 1971, and it had been a long time since his wife had told him she was staying on Kodiak. She was teaching Native students the three Rs, as well as their people's traditions, something they wouldn't learn in a regular public school. Miriam had written to Walter, telling him she had also been helping some of the older people with their daily chores. It seemed she had established herself as a much-needed member of the village.

Though his love was as strong as ever, the intense loneliness he had felt during her initial absence had dulled with time, and it seemed now as if the separation had become the normal way to be, Beaumont in Seward, while Miriam was on Kodiak with the children.

He had built several more skiffs for customers who had come from various parts of the state, and his reputation had grown as a man who created fine watercraft, dories, as Arnold Tuckerman had called them.

He was doing well enough financially just building boats, and it was almost all he did now. Without Miriam's help, keeping the charter business going was more than Walter wanted to deal with. Because the constant contact with strangers during tour season wasn't something he liked as much as he had earlier in the business, deciding to stick mostly to boat building wasn't a difficult decision. He did a half-dozen one-day tours to fill in when finances were a little thin, though he didn't need much money to get along.

He kept the *Emma Joy* for any extended travels, which were few, while using *Beaumont's Journey* for shorter runs, such as cruising around Prince William Sound for one-day tours, or a pleasure run by himself anywhere he felt like going. It had been on one of these runs when he'd finally found evidence of his uncle.

He was cruising the Sound, running right off the shore of Smith Island, which was off the eastern tip of Eleanor Island, when something caught his eye. It was a large piece of debris looking as if it had just washed up on the rocky beach. There had been several recent storms, and they'd stirred up the bottom near the islands, releasing pieces of wreckage.

Looking through his binoculars, he thought he saw a few letters on the flat piece of material which might be part of a boat. Walter got a funny chill down his back. Running up as close as he could, he could see letters on the stained, broken section of what must have been a boat's transom. He dropped anchor, and rowed over in the fourteen-foot skiff he now towed instead of the rubber raft. It had finally given out, no longer reliably staying inflated. He had built the skiff himself of course, to use for running in to a shore, or for emergencies.

Once on the beach, he pulled the skiff up to keep it grounded, and slowly walked over to the object he had seen.

After years of wondering about his uncle, Walter now had a basic idea of where he might have ended his time on earth. The debris was indeed a piece of a boat's transom, and with the three letters still visible, could be nothing else than the remaining part of Aubrey's boat.

On the stained wood, with barnacles and seaweed attached, were three letters, still visible as black with gold trim which read, "ODE," as in the ending of the name, *Mother Lode*. Uncle Aubrey had finally returned, at least in spirit.

With some effort, he loaded the heavy piece onto the skiff, and rowed it back to the *Journey*. He would put it up on one of the walls of the shop, as he knew Arnold would have liked.

The run back to Seward was a thoughtful trip, the piece of the *Mother Lode* lying on the stern deck. He considered that at his age, a still young twenty-nine years, he had already lost his share of people, and he remembered his uncle telling him, "As time goes on, it's possible you might end up the last one standing, though there's no guarantee of anything, least of all longevity." Walter shook his mind loose from his current train of thought, and focused on looking at the natural scenic wonders around him, the forests on the islands and the animals he always viewed in the Sound and along Resurrection Bay, which always brought him some peace. Being in Alaska, barring any fateful incidents, always calmed his mind and kept him looking forward.

As he drove up to the shop, the broken piece of the *Mother Lode* in back of the Travelall, he saw a Trooper vehicle parked nearby. It was Officer Brady. Walter prayed it was only a friendly visit.

They shook hands, and Charlie told him he was being transferred up to the area between Fairbanks and Salcha to serve as a replacement for a wildlife Trooper who had retired.

"I've been up there hunting several times, and to explore the country. It's a beautiful area, so when I heard a posting was available, I jumped at it. Since I'll be leaving in a week, I thought I'd come by and offer to buy you dinner. There's a new restaurant open. What do you say?"

Beaumont smiled, congratulated Brady, and told him he'd enjoy having dinner with him. He showed Charlie the piece of debris he'd found, and Brady agreed with Walter, it was surely evidence of Aubrey's boat.

The two men walked to the eatery to work up an appetite. They liked talking together, and would miss one another's company.

They didn't talk much about personal things, though Charlie did ask if Miriam was coming home soon. Walter didn't look up, staring at his plate a while before shrugging his shoulders. Brady asked no more questions.

The men parted late in the evening, promising to stay in touch. As is not always the case, they meant it.

"Listen, Beaumont, maybe you would consider coming up to go moose hunting with me this year. There are some fine bulls up there."

"If you're serious, I'd love too."

"'Course I'm serious; I wouldn't kid about hunting, and there's no one else I'd rather go with. That way, I'd be guaranteed a good bull."

As Brady was walking to his vehicle, he remembered something, turned and said, "I almost forgot, Billy Weaks confessed to killing the two fishermen on the boat, about two weeks after they had been marooned. He said he was worried there weren't enough supplies, food and water to survive on until they might be rescued. He had a history of violence too, aggravated assault, bar brawls, and the like. It's good he's behind bars now, instead of in one."

Walter went back to his routine of building boats and working on the building he was erecting on his property. He had added onto the cabin already, making it more suitable for raising a family, and now he was erecting a new shop, smaller than Tuckerman's, built in a way he thought most efficient.

Several weeks after his last communication with Miriam, he had come home after a long day getting a twenty-one-foot boat with enclosed wheelhouse finished, to meet the deadline he had agreed to. He saw a light on in the cabin, and, as he walked closer, heard the obvious sounds of children laughing. Walter's heart leapt and he trotted to the cabin door. He opened it to find Miriam cooking something on the stove, with Emma and Nicolas playing a tickling game, his son rolling on the floor laughing, while Emma tickled his stomach and ribs unmercifully.

At his entrance into the cabin, the children stopped what they were doing, quietly looking at the bearded man with stained overalls and wood chips caught in his hair. Miriam turned from the stove, wiped her hands on the apron she was wearing, and walked up to Walter, wrapping her arms around him, putting her cheek against his chest.

Beaumont needed a moment to get his mind into this sudden change of reality. It only took a few seconds for him to put his arms around her slim body. The children moved to their parents and hugged them too. In an instant, life became complete again, all the needed elements in place once more. Walter felt fully alive again.

Later that evening, the two happy adults, lying contentedly side by side, talked for hours, catching up on what had occurred while they were apart.

Miriam had finally felt her need to be back with Walter more important than staying on Kodiak. A young woman who had teaching credentials had come to the island, and she had made it possible for Miriam to return to Seward without feeling she was leaving her people high and dry.

Now, lying together in their bed, she felt the completeness of their bond, and was happy to be continuing their life together again. Miriam was a loyal and devoted wife, despite her long absence.

Having his family back, after working in the shop, he looked forward to coming home to a warm cabin, and an even warmer reception from wife and children. He found his boat building went smoother and faster, too.

Several months after his family had come back, Walter finished up a one-of-a-kind skiff, large at twenty-four feet long. He had taken to working on more than one boat at a time, alternating between them. He had a number of orders to fill, and this way he could tell customers he was working on their boat, instead of telling them they'd have to wait.

As with a number of the boats he had built, this one had a centrally located wheelhouse enclosure, a high, wide bow, with an engine Douglas Padgett, his client, had brought him to use. It was a four-cylinder engine manufactured in Japan, and he'd paid good money to have a professional marine engine builder convert it for boat use. Walter was impressed. It seemed a cleanly designed engine, and would easily fit in the big skiff as an inboard set-up.

He called Padgett to let him know the boat was done, and was told he would be down from Anchorage with a boat trailer in three or four days.

"I'm looking forward to seeing her, and taking the *Yowza* out on her maiden voyage."

He told Beaumont it was a word his father had used when he was in a good mood about something positive happening. So, *Yowza* it would be.

The *Yowza*, as with all Beaumont's craft, handled well, running smoothly, cutting cleanly through the water. Though relatively small, the engine put out good power and, all in all, the first run went well. Padgett insisted on giving Walter a big bonus for doing a fine job, and having it done on time. The two men had taken to each other right away, and Douglas invited Walter to go on a fishing trip in a remote area.

"We'll fly in with my Dehavilland Beaver. There's a sweet lake northeast of Anchorage, about an hour and a half out. Been there several times, never anyone else around, and we always bring in some good trout. I fly a canoe in, strapped to one of the pontoons. I'm taking my nephew, my sister's boy with me sometime early next summer. He's kind of an urban hippie type, bead necklace, head band, without much outdoors experience, which is why my sister wants me to get him up here, away from the city life he's used to, give him a different perspective. What do you think?"

Walter thought it would be a good trip, and he'd never been in the area before. He took Padgett up on his offer and shook his hand. He didn't think the nephew would be too intolerable, and if he was, there were ways to adjust the situation.

"I'll get in touch with you, Walter, and let you know when."

The next few months slipped by quickly. Miriam and the children would bring him lunch most days, and visit while he ate. Occasionally, Emma would stay and visit with him while he worked. She was smart, and mature enough to stay out of trouble, sitting and watching him or making drawings at the workbench. Walter was impressed with her sketches of animals, puffins, and sea beavers, even a good rendering of a black bear seen roaming lately through the area near the shop, though causing no trouble. Emma Joy captured the bear's individuality well, its body shape and distinguishing physical characteristics. He realized she had real artistic ability, more than most children her age, and planned on quietly motivating her to keep up her artwork. Miriam was glad he had noticed her talent, and encouraged Emma to continue creating.

Tuckerman's wide, tall shop was hard to keep warm in winter. Beaumont had to take time to gather a full load of firewood to feed the two wood stoves, the larger one set in a back corner and a smaller one nearer to where he actually worked. Beaumont was always careful to keep any wood chips and scraps away from the heat. He would be glad when the new shop was finished, as it would be easier to keep heated.

There was quite a deep snowfall in the winter of '71, and he had hired a man with a small bulldozer to keep the area around the shop and a path to drive in to it clear.

As was sometimes the case with people who were offering a product or service to Beaumont, the man with the dozer wanted a skiff built, a relatively small, narrow one, sixteen feet in length, for use with oars only. The man was a New Englander as Tuckerman had been, and he recognized the basic shape of the craft Walter was constructing at the time as being similar to the dories he used to see off the eastern coastline of New England. The fellow had to have one. They worked out a deal where he would always keep the snow plowed in succeeding winters in exchange for the dory, plus any odd work Beaumont would find his dozer handy to accomplish. But, Walter would still have to climb up on the roof himself to clear it off so it wouldn't collapse, a wearying task, but necessary.

The following spring, Walter intended to complete the new shop on his home property. It was made all the more necessary when he found out Tuckerman did not own the property he had built his shop on, and there was the strong possibility the City of Seward would want to make use of the land. Nobody had minded Arnold being there in the past, considering him an asset to the city. Things had changed since he'd arrived in Seward years before, and building a structure anywhere one wanted to was not acceptable as in earlier times. As wild and vast as Alaska was, the civilized centers were becoming more like towns in the Lower 48, which was to be expected. More people were coming north because it was much easier now, even though there were still rough stretches on the Alcan, for those who drove.

Chapter 27

Reid

Walter gave Miriam a heartfelt kiss, hugged both his children, hoisted his pack onto one shoulder, and walked out to his Travelall.

Miriam's Chevy sedan, reliable despite having some age to it, sat waiting next to the more practical truck. He tossed the pack in the back cargo section, laid the rifle case down next to his two rods and reels and a small tackle box, got in, started the engine, and drove down to Tuckerman's Shop.

Douglas Padgett's Dehavilland Beaver was waiting at the shore's edge down below the shop. He was sitting on the end of a log up above water line. His sixteen-year-old nephew was a dozen feet away, tossing stones into the water, with a sullen look on his face.

Beaumont registered a first impression of the young man. He had a slouched posture, shaggy, unkempt hair, with a colorful cloth headband around his forehead, torn Levis, and old tennis shoes. All in all, to Walter, a picture of unused potential and a slothful nature. He was curious to see how this week-long trip was going to pan out. They were going to mainly fish for trout, rainbows in particular, along with Dolly Varden and perhaps some grayling. He suspected the nephew hadn't much if any experience fishing, nor would he be interested.

Beaumont mentally shrugged. Didn't matter to him, as long as the youngster didn't interfere with his fishing. He was Padgett's nephew, after all. Walter had a sneaking suspicion Douglas was half expecting him to spark some interest of the natural world in the boy.

Douglas greeted him heartily, obviously looking forward to going out in the wilderness with this man he knew to be more experienced than he was in the wilds.

"Mr. Beaumont."

"Walter will do, Douglas."

"Well then, Doug works for me. This is my nephew, Reid."

Reid did not respond to the introduction, merely tossing more stones into the edge of the Bay.

Walter, not particularly irritated at the boy's expected rudeness, walked over in front of him, until they were face to face, a couple of feet apart.

Raising his right hand, he said, "Reid, it's good to meet you." He remained there, unmoving, until the young man felt compelled to shake his hand. His grip was only what one could call soggy, and Walter slipped his hand from the slack grasp, walked back to Doug, and suggested they get loaded up and head out. Padgett was more than happy to do so. It took little time for them to become airborne, headed towards the lake they would be fishing. It was a fine day for flying, until the engine started sputtering.

Beaumont woke up, and nothing was right. Everything seemed upside down, and in truth, it was. Instantly, it all came back to him, the sound of the engine sputtering as they were flying above the center of a wide, deeply forested valley. He heard Douglas Padgett cursing under his breath before yelling out, "Seat belts! Seat belts!" He knew this was big trouble, and then the engine went silent. Padgett was desperately working controls to try and get the engine going again, to no avail. They were losing altitude fast, and Doug was trying to find some less heavily wooded spot in which to come down. There were none.

Walter tried to stay relaxed, while Padgett's nephew, from a back seat, was yelling, "Oh great! Just great!"

The first tree top they connected with ripped off the right pontoon along with the canoe, causing the plane to twist violently to the right.

It was turned sideways when the rear of the fuselage crashed into several large spruce trees. The impact tore the tail section off, which was the last thing Walter remembered before regaining consciousness.

He couldn't see out of his right eye, and his hand came away from it covered with blood. He thought his eye had been damaged, until he felt along a gash above his eye, and knew the blood was coming from there.

He started to lift his left arm, but the pain it caused made him yell out. It felt like his shoulder had been broken, and he saw a shattered piece of tree branch lying between him and the empty pilot's seat, which he thought might have impacted his shoulder.

Douglas Padgett was nowhere to be seen. He had yelled for them to fasten their belts, but the empty left front seat made it clear he had not made his own secure. Beaumont could only let out a little sigh.

Feeling on the right side of his pants belt, he found the knife, the one his uncle had given him, was still there. Taking it out of the sheath, he reached up and easily sliced through the seat belt holding him upside down. He dropped suddenly to the roof of the Beaver, coming down partly on his injured shoulder. The pain made him see stars, and he almost passed out.

Turning around as much as he could in the disrupted fuselage, he saw Reid, unconscious, hanging from his own belt. A careful cut and he was down too. As soon as the younger man fell, he snapped out of his unconscious state with a yell, which sounded as if it was the tail end of one he let out as they were crashing. Walter was amazed to see only a goose egg on the side of his forehead.

Walter said, "Does anything hurt badly, arms, legs or anything?"

"No, nothing. Where's my uncle?"

"I don't know. He isn't in the plane and I only got out of my belt a moment ago. We'll look for him soon. For now, I need to wipe this blood out of my eye."

He climbed out of the plane through the door after kicking it several times to free it up. Getting outside, he could see they were on an eastern-facing slope off the valley floor. There was no stream or river running through the valley, and he didn't remember seeing one before the crash. The cargo compartment was still intact, the missing tail end of the plane having snapped off aft of it. He had carefully tucked his left hand into his belt to ease the pain and avoid hurting it further while checking things out. The attempt was only partially successful.

Letting the upside-down compartment door swing open, he pulled out his pack, and searched inside for a piece of cotton cloth. He always brought some, finding it useful. Taking one corner in his teeth, he ripped off a strip and wiped his eye off until he could see reasonably well. Then he wiped off around the gash. It probably needed several stitches, which, of course, would have to wait.

Tearing off another, wider band of cotton, he made a sling for his left arm. Getting it into position burned like fire. Once it was resting in the adjusted sling, the major part of the pain subsided, to his relief.

It was then he noticed Reid standing a few yards away, touching the bump on his head, offering no help. Walter knew he could only depend on himself, but he determined to make him do something.

"I want you to tear off a strip of this cloth and help me wrap it around my head to cover the cut I have. Think you can do that?"

"Of course I can, I'm no dummy."

"Well, the way you were standing there watching me, I couldn't be sure."

The teenager's face turned red, and he got a petulant look on his face. Reluctantly, he stepped over and did as Beaumont said.

"O.K., let's see if we can find your uncle."

They searched all around the plane in ever-widening circles. It took a while, until they found Padgett's body sitting up against the base of a tree. At first, Walter thought he had been alive briefly and had crawled over to the spruce, then he realized the impact had left him in the sitting position. Doug had several large cuts, one across his right arm, and the other across his left cheek, extending up and across his ear. He had probably gone right through the pilot side door when the plane impacted the trees while sideways. Beaumont discovered major damage to the back of his head, possibly from impacting the tree. He felt the back of his skull and there was movement when he pressed it. He felt for a pulse, and checked for breath. There was nothing he could do.

"Is he dead?" Reid asked.

"I'm afraid so. Sorry for your loss."

"I didn't know him," said the nephew. Walter suddenly felt hot at the boy's callous remark. He took several quick steps up to him, his jaw muscles working. Reid took a step back, startled by Walter's quick movement.

"He was your mother's brother. Show some respect. Look, you and I are in a tough situation here. I'm hurt, and you don't know anything about anything. This is my country, even though I have never been to this specific place. So, in order to get out of here, you will listen to what I tell you, and dump this attitude of yours. What you do once we're good again is your business. Until then, you will follow my lead, do you understand?"

Reid didn't say a word, only nodding in response. His attitude had faded right away after Beaumont had approached him.

"Now, I'm going to check out the radio to see if it's still working so I can call in our situation. Stick close to the plane and see if you can find anything useful."

"Like what?"

"Never mind, just stay close."

The radio was out of commission. No way to make a call to anyone. Rummaging around in the back area of the remaining fuselage, Beaumont found a large metal container with a good first aid kit, a flare gun with six flares, some C-rations, and two one-quart containers of potable water.

Strapped to the floor of the fuselage under the second row of seats was a hard gun case. It held a short-barreled shotgun, a twelve-gauge Remington Model 870. Also in the case was a cartridge belt with twenty-four rounds of ammunition for the shotgun, six with double ought buckshot, a dozen slug shells, and six more with birdshot, good for small game or bird hunting.

Beaumont was familiar with the shotgun, and the ammunition was right for their situation. He walked over to Reid.

"Have you ever handled small arms?"

Reid looked puzzled. "Small arms?"

"Yes, rifles, pistols, shotguns."

"Well, I have a pellet gun at home I'm pretty good with."

Walter showed him how to work the 870. He made sure to impress on him the need for safety. He watched the young man work the pump action shotgun, going through the drill of firing and reloading it. He seemed to get it.

"Okay, we're going to use two of the buckshot shells to check you out. See the piece of metal over there, about five yards away? Aim with the bead on the front of the barrel, keeping your face down firmly on the gun's stock. Aim for the middle of the target, and squeeze off a shot, and then another. It's got some recoil. Go ahead."

Walter was pleased to see Reid hit the piece of metal dead center, twice, then had him load the magazine with slugs.

"Okay, now we do what we have to do."

"What do you mean?"

"We have to bury your uncle."

"We do?"

"Did you think we were going to leave him there, the way he is?"

"Well, kinda."

"Right. Find something to dig with, and we'll put him in the ground."

The soil there was loose and sandy, easy to remove. Reid made a half-hearted attempt, while Beaumont could only use one arm, and slowly. It took a while to dig it deep enough to properly put Doug to rest, but they got it done. Reid started to walk away when they had refilled the grave.

"Wait a minute, I want to say a few words over him, if you don't mind."

Reid shrugged, and Walter realized his reality included little, if any, religion. The boy stayed at a short distance while Beaumont recited the 23rd Psalm.

They spent the evening next to the fuselage. The mosquitoes weren't too bad, and Walter had some military bug dope, which helped. The boy grumbled about everything, and Walter blocked him out, thinking about what to do the next day. He knew his left shoulder was dislocated, and suspected there was something else wrong with it. He wasn't going to try and put it back in place, concerned it might cause more damage.

His pain kept him from getting much sleep, though Reid snored loudly all night.

The next morning they heated water in a small pan Walter had brought, and made some instant coffee. His sullen companion had several peanut butter and jelly sandwiches in the small pack he had with him, and they ate them for breakfast along with the coffee. Reid complained about the taste of the instant. Walter took the tin cup from him and was going to pour it out, but Reid stopped him, saying he'd drink it anyway.

Beaumont explained their present reality to the snotty kid, and as with most of what he said to the resistant youngster, he spoke in a way that made Reid listen, telling him not much was going to be fun or easy while they were walking out, and he might as well get used to it. "Or, you can wait here with your uncle until someone finds you, which would be pure luck, considering where we are."

Reid didn't respond, but he was ready to go when Beaumont told him they were heading out.

On Beaumont's belt was a large revolver in a plain leather holster. Walter had purchased it some months before at a store in Seward. It was a Ruger .44 Magnum, the old-style, single-action revolver looking similar to the Colt Peacemaker, popular in the Old West. He was impressed when he saw it in the case. Not familiar with the .44 Magnum, he was interested in what the store clerk told him about the cartridge.

"One thing for sure, be ready for the kick from it when you first shoot it. It's a real powerhouse."

Walter had practiced with it half a dozen times before putting it in his pack for this ill-fated fishing trip. He figured, when he bought it, a pistol was easier to handle while fishing, only one hand being needed to shoot it, and it was easier to carry than a rifle or shotgun.

Fate had been kind to him, since his left shoulder had been injured. Right-handed, he could still defend himself if necessary.

Reid asked him, "So, where do you think we are?"

"Well, from what I can tell, we're somewhere on the west side of the Talkeetna Range. I can't find any maps, and foolishly didn't bring one myself. I know we were traveling north and east from Anchorage. So, wherever we are, we'll travel south and west, and get out of the deep forest to have a better chance to see and be seen. Come on, let's start moving."

The two men, one older and experienced, the other without any connection to the world he now wandered in, worked their way along the slope, away from the plane wreck and the unfortunate man left behind.

It was cold, though not like it would be later in the year, and there were still tiny patches of snow beneath some of the more heavily branched spruce, from the previous winter. It would remain there through much of the summer.

By early afternoon, they had traveled off the slope, out of the deep woods, to the outside edge of the valley, and headed south.

Walter followed the direction he thought would get them closer to help and safety. The sun was moving low in the sky this far north, and it was not easy to be guided to a specific direction by its path over a day's time because there was virtually no rise and fall. At least the amount of light at this time of year did lend itself to traveling.

Reid followed closely behind, too close in the beginning of their trek, several times bumping into Walter when he stopped to take his bearings. He finally told him to back away ten steps or more to avoid making contact. He hadn't been paying much attention to the distance between himself and Walter, looking all around while walking, worried about bears and wolves waiting to jump on and bite him.

Through the rest of the day they walked, until Reid started complaining about his feet hurting. In pain, and ready to rest himself, Beaumont decided they could set up a camp. They were walking a short distance from a long strip of trees, and he found a relatively smooth place under a birch tree. Walter had Reid go through his pack, as his shoulder was hurting more than he wanted to admit. There was a small hatchet, a short folding saw, and some parachute cord. He told the younger man, still mumbling about his feet, how to set up a proper shelter. Since they didn't have a tarp, spruce branches were needed to cover their shelter. After tying a horizontal pole between two small trees, he had Reid tie several more poles coming down from the top pole, and two more across the others, making a simple framework. Then he cut a bunch of spruce branches to lay on top of the poles, gathering armfuls of drier sphagnum moss from the nearby tundra for a bed.

Walter told him to sit down under the shelter and take his shoes off.

He said, "I'll be back with dinner shortly," and, after picking up a spruce stick about three feet long, he walked away. Forty-five minutes later, he came back with two ptarmigan, the stick having done its job.

Reid watched with a slightly queasy look on his face as Walter took his knife, made an incision in the bird's skin, and bared the breasts, which he pulled off with his fingers.

"Here, take what's left of the birds and toss them far from us."

He stared at Beaumont, obviously unhappy about having to pick up the butchered birds.

"Either you do it, or you don't eat, your choice."

Reid did as he was told, walking gingerly away with his sore, bare feet, a frown on his face.

There was little conversation between them. Reid sat whittling shavings from a dry spruce stick with a Swiss Army knife containing many blades, screwdrivers, a tiny pair of scissors, tweezers, and other bits. He collected wood for the fire after Beaumont threatened to withhold food again.

Walter had started to boil water in the pan for instant coffee, and sharpened two green willow sticks to cook the minimal dinner of ptarmigan breasts, placing the can of corn he had brought along on the edge of the fire, the lid cut open.

Canned vegetables weren't something he'd usually carry into the wilds. It was more a joke to himself. Now, it seemed a better idea than it was originally meant to be.

"Reid, think you could carve a simple spoon from a piece of wood for eating the corn?"

"He glared at him and said, "No, I don't think so. Why don't you do it, you're the mountain man."

Walter held his temper, though he felt like roughing up the arrogant kid as a reality check. Instead, he took the stick with the two bird breasts from Reid's side of the fire and put it over the fire next to the one he had cooking for himself.

Reid stared at him, a mixture of shock and anger somehow mixing in him. He got the point, and started carving a crude wooden spoon. Beaumont closed his eyes and tried to rest.

An hour later, the two mismatched people sat back, the meal over. Reid had actually done a good job of shaping a primitive spoon. Walter told him so, and for spite, the boy tossed it into the fire. Beaumont could only shake his head and turn in for the night. Minutes later, the foolish boy did the same.

Early the next morning, Beaumont sat up to see Reid walking away with the partial roll of toilet paper he had brought in his pack.

"Where are you going?"

"I'm going to poop, okay?" His response was full of grouchiness.

"Well, don't go too far."

A few minutes later, Walter heard him making noises as though he was in pain. Worried, he started to get up but Reid came hopping and jumping into camp with his pants half down, a pained expression replacing the cranky one he had left with.

"What happened?"

"I don't know. I think something stung me. It hurts!"

Beaumont turned him around, to the boy's complaints, and pulled his pants down further. There was a big patch of rash on his backside. Walter couldn't help smiling.

"Show me where this happened."

Reid took him over to where he had squatted down in the bushes. Sure enough, there were several stinging nettles where he had planted his backside. Walter pointed to them and told him what they were.

"Don't worry, the stinging will go away soon. Give it some time, remember what they look like, and be glad there wasn't more of you involved."

Reid stared at him and gave an involuntary little shudder.

They walked back to camp. The suffering boy had such a pained look on his face, Walter had a hard time holding back a smile, knowing it wasn't a serious situation.

For the next two days, Beaumont and his unhappy companion continued to work their way back to civilization. They had to move slowly, to decrease the discomfort on Beaumont's injuries.

The boy had stopped being openly rude to Walter, even though it was obvious his attitude hadn't changed. Not once did he ask how he was doing, dealing with his serious injury. He seemed oblivious to the fact that Beaumont was the reason he'd probably get back home. He saw him as another adult he didn't want to listen to and depend on for help, even though without him, he might never be heard from again. But, unlike Beaumont at his age, Reid showed little if any common sense or desire to learn about the world around him.

Walter, for his part, understood the young man's feelings. As a child, he never liked anyone telling him what to do, though he never found a need to be rude, or spiteful. In the military, he rarely if ever got in trouble for not obeying orders. It was a combination of learning things that appealed to his desire to be cunning and stealthy, and because he knew he'd be doing work of real importance.

They had come to a place where the mosquitoes were seriously thick. The maddening flying insects were swarming there in great numbers.

He told Reid, who was already getting crazy from the bloodthirsty insects attacking him despite the bug dope he had lavishly spread on his exposed skin, they'd need to go to higher ground to avoid the bugs as much as possible, just as caribou herds would head to the hills to escape them.

Reid yelled, "I'm tired, and I won't climb anywhere, damn you!"

The childish remark finally did it. Walter strode over to the boy wildly swinging his arms to thwart the flying insects, mosquitoes and biting flies, grabbed him by the neck, and pulled him over to the base of the nearby hill.

"I'm only going to say this once: you have no chance to survive here without my help. I have no real obligation to help you survive, and I'm about ready to let you do it on your own, and you won't last long. I don't care if you respect me or not, I don't want to have to explain what a little jackass you were, and why you didn't come back with me. So, you can either follow me up this slope into a less bug-filled zone, or good-bye and good luck!"

Reid had stopped his wild gyrations when Beaumont grabbed and explained reality to him in no uncertain terms, the look in Walter's eyes and the tightening grip around his neck causing him to stand still. There was no way to not see he meant every word. Without another sound, the subdued young man followed his guide up the slope. He had renewed his efforts to chase the insects away, swinging his arms until he couldn't anymore.

The hill they climbed was actually a small mountain. As Beaumont had told him, the insects were much fewer higher up. It was a real relief to be out of their range. Reid was so glad to be bug free, he actually began behaving better. He started asking Walter about the country they were in as they worked their way in a southerly direction, trying to stay on his good side. Even though Beaumont wasn't in a mood to give the young man a nature lesson, he liked him more this way, so he told him what he wanted to know.

Walter stopped walking. Something didn't feel right. He pulled his binoculars from the upper outside pocket of his pack and glassed all around. At first he didn't see anything, then he did. A large grizzly bear was sniffing around and moving as though tracking something. The breezes were coming directly from the two men and heading back towards the bear. He knew it was following them. The hairs on his neck stirred, as if in confirmation of his thoughts.

The bear was a mile or a little less from them, so he didn't say anything to Reid, in case things changed. Ten minutes later, he spotted the bear, much closer, and it looked pretty lean. Walter figured this was an older bear who had made it through last winter's hibernation, barely. Now it was looking for an easy meal, and decided they might fill the bill.

He had no idea if this bruin had experience with people or not, and he didn't wish to find out.

"Listen Reid, a grizzly bear is following, and I think he's interested in us. I don't know how determined he is, but we're going to find a good spot and wait for him. He'll either turn off and leave, or we might have to deal with him. Let's go to this knob over here and wait."

The weary boy's face had gone pale. "A grizzly bear? Shouldn't we try to get away from him?"

"Nope, he's way too fast for us. Better to see what happens, and face him if we have to. Besides, you've got the shotgun and I have my .44. Together we can handle it." Beaumont changed his tone, needing the boy to accept and believe. "Listen to me, you have to overcome your fear enough to function properly, understand? We have no choice. I know you can do this. The bear is old, and not in good shape, which is a big advantage. It's only an animal, after all."

He could actually see the boy somehow strengthen his resolve. The color came back to his face and his eyes took on a different aspect."

"Okay, Mr. Beaumont, I can do it."

"I know you can. Let's get ready"

It took less than five minutes for the bear to come upon them, and it stopped about thirty yards away. It stood on its hind legs to sniff and survey the area where they were, then dropped down to all fours and stopped in place, just staring at the two humans in front of him. Walter knew they were as ready as they could be. There were slug loads in the shotgun, and five of the heavy bear loads in his revolver.

Reid was standing about ten feet to his left, as Walter had told him to do, shotgun at the ready. When the bear had come into view, he whispered to Reid, knowing the bear was, in all likelihood, going to charge them, to aim for the middle of its body. With a roar, the beast went for them, covering the distance in a flash. Walter had the opportunity to fire two rounds, and knew he had hit the bear both times, though to what effect remained to be seen. He heard the shotgun go off once. The bear dropped to the ground, but it wasn't finished. It couldn't rise again, turning in a circle on the ground, pivoting on its shoulder, moaning loudly. Then the shotgun went off again, and the animal was still.

Beaumont and the boy remained where they were, Reid breathing hard. They looked at each other and Walter nodded. Cautiously approaching, he saw the bear's eyes were open. It was dead.

He looked at Reid. The brief moment of great danger had obviously pulled the lad onto another level of reality, giving him a different perspective.

He looked at Walter, who, gun holstered, held out his hand. After a moment's hesitation, Reid shook it, firmly.

Beaumont said, "You handled it well, thanks."

Not knowing what to say, the young man smiled. Suddenly, he threw up a little. Walter said nothing about it. He removed two claws from the bear's front paw, and gave them to Reid to remember the moment, to remind him what he was capable of when necessity called.

They camped by the Susitna River that night. It had been a hard hike getting there, but Walter had felt the need to continue on to where help might be close by. His shoulder was causing him great pain, and he needed to get it fixed. He was feeling feverish, and, remembering how it had gone with his uncle's broken leg, knew they had to get help soon.

They were both hungry, so they heated up some of the C-rations from the survival supplies they had found on the plane. Reid made a remark about the flavor, but instead of getting irritated Walter smiled, telling the young man how many of these he had eaten in the army while in country. The two talked about many different things, a lot of them relating to living in Alaska. It seemed to Beaumont as if the whole rough trek, from the crash to them sitting now by a warming campfire in the chilly evening, had forcibly brought his young companion into a larger world he had not yet experienced, a wild world many never knew about. He seemed to have discarded his childlike self-importance and started looking beyond himself. Walter was sorry Doug was not there to see it.

As they were turning in, they heard a boat motor coming closer from down river. They both saw the boat, a long, wide, flat-bottomed rig. It caught Walter's attention as a boat builder, despite the painful circumstances. They waved the boat in, and explained the situation. Wherever the men in the boat were headed, they took the two survivors on board and ran them to Talkeetna, where they could get help and call the Troopers.

The Troopers showed up in Talkeetna two hours later, to find Walter and Reid in a small cafe where they had been given shelter. The two survivors got to eat burgers and fries, which tasted like a gourmet meal to both of them. They were also given slices of pie, washed down with real coffee, to Reid's delight.

Beaumont explained in detail to the Troopers what had transpired, showing them on a map they provided where the crash site was located, and where Douglas Padgett was buried. They would initiate a search by plane.

He wanted to go back and show them the spot, but they insisted he be flown up to Anchorage to get hospital care. Walter accepted the situation, and Reid went with him. Walter smiled and asked him if he needed treatment for the injury he had sustained on that earlier morning. Reid smiled back at him and said, "Yeah, sure."

Beaumont had been right. His shoulder had been dislocated in the crash, and the clavicle had been badly broken. If he had tried to reset the shoulder joint, it could well have caused more damage to the soft tissue. It would all be repaired in the Anchorage hospital.

He had asked a Trooper to call his wife and let her know what had happened. The next morning when he awoke in his hospital bed, there was Miriam sitting in a chair next to him. He smiled, and asked what she was doing there.

"Funny, Walter Beaumont, very funny," she said, before she gently laid her hand against his chest and bowed her head.

With his good arm, he lifted her face to kiss her and saw she was crying. He told her it would be fine, he'd heal quickly, and things would be back to normal soon. They both knew it would take quite some time for him to heal.

Beaumont, being who he was, didn't plan on taking any longer than necessary. He had things to do.

Reid had called his mother, and told her what had happened. She was devastated by the news of her brother's death. Her son, surprisingly, comforted her on the phone, saying his uncle hadn't been in pain, dying immediately. He would stay until his aunt had his remains, and could make arrangements.

Reid's mother would come up as soon as she could to help her sister-in-law. She asked her son if he needed anything, and he said no, he would be fine.

His mother paused a moment, not expecting this response from him. She said, "Alaska must be quite a place to visit."

He smiled to himself before saying, "You have no idea, Mom, it's amazing. I plan on coming back here some day. I wish you could meet Mr. Beaumont. He's an amazing guy, a true wilderness man. He saved my life!"

After he hung up, Reid went to see Walter. He was glad to see him all patched up, and was happy to meet Miriam. She told the young man he was lucky Walter was there to help him out of trouble.

Reid looked right at Beaumont and said, "For sure, Mrs. B, for sure."

Miriam looked at her husband. "Mrs. B?"

"Actually," said Walter, smiling, "Mrs. B sounds good."

"Don't even think about it," his wife said, giving him a hard look.

Chapter 28

Boat Builder

Six months after he had led Reid out of the forest, Walter was back at work building his version of the flat-bottomed river boat in which they had ridden to safety. Unlike that boat, which was aluminum, he was experimenting with a fiberglass-coated wooden hull design. He had read up on what was already being done, and he thought it would be a good way to go.

He used marine-quality plywood, which would function well because of the shape of the boats, flat bottomed and flat nosed. Afterwards, he would coat it with fiberglass, a thick covering to help make it impervious to harsh conditions, gravel bars, and snags. Working with fiberglass was an art in itself, and he decided, after several failed attempts, he'd better stick to wood only, at least until he could learn from someone who already knew what to do.

Miriam showed up early one afternoon with a couple of sandwiches and a thermos of coffee, to make sure Walter remembered to eat.

He took a break, and they sat together near the warmth of the wood stove in the shop on his home property. He'd had to remove Tuckerman's shop, hiring a team of three guys from Seward to do the job, bringing the used wood and metal up to the site of the new shop he was building near his house. He hired them to get the shop finished there, too. He had already done much of the building, a good roof already over the unsheathed walls.

They wanted to trade a large skiff for the work they did, one they could go fishing with in the Bay. He agreed, smiling, knowing they knew there was a skiff already made, a twenty-one footer, which had been in the old shop, and was now stored next to the new one. The three men had walked around the boat, inspecting it from stem to stern. It was obvious to Beaumont they were impressed, and he had an idea they would make him an offer. He was right.

With the new shop done and a proper wood stove installed, Walter started working on designing and building a drift boat. A man from down on the Kenai Peninsula near Cooper's Landing had contacted him about the project. Walter told him he had never built one. The fellow, named Granger, drove up to see him, and they spent three days talking about drift boats and what they were required to do. He taught Walter about the character of a proper drift boat, easily moved on the river, controlled by oars only, and a man's experience. Granger called it a "helo" boat, because a good fishing guide could hold it steady, even in the main current, like a hovering helicopter.

Beaumont and Granger struck up a good working relationship, and by the time the fishing guide left to go back south, Walter knew what he would do. The drift boat would perform as expected. He had told Granger it would take a while, as his shoulder was not properly healed yet. The fishing guide was fine with waiting, certain it would be a fine boat.

So, Walter took his time, stopping to rest whenever it felt best to do so, and the boat soon took shape. It would prove to be the first of many he would build over time. Granger made sure to mention who built the drift boat whenever he was in the company of other fishing guides and avid sport fishermen. His help proved to be a great source of orders for more boats. Beaumont made wooden-hulled boats only, which worked well. There were many customers who appreciated his traditional ways of building.

Of course, it was Arnold Tuckerman who instilled this concept in him, his wonderful designs proving to be a solid basis for Walter's boats. In truth, Walter could wholeheartedly state there was some Tuckerman in the boats he built, and he was proud to say so.

Chapter 29

Fathers and Sons

Walter and Miriam had returned home from driving Emma Joy up to Anchorage. They had taken her to the airport, where she would fly down to Washington State to begin her college education. They could have let her fly out of Seward, except they wanted the extra time with her, knowing it would probably be quite a while before they saw her again. It was a quiet run back to Seward.

Emma did extremely well in high school, and had won a scholarship. She'd worked every summer since she was fifteen, doing fish processing to save money for college, knowing early on she wanted to be a nurse and would have to go somewhere for the right education.

Her parents supported their eldest child's ambitions, and had built up a college fund for her. Miriam had started teaching at the elementary school in Seward once the children were grown enough to be on their own. The money from her teaching and what Beaumont made building boats had made it possible.

The two sad parents spoke little as they headed back down to Seward after saying good-bye to their daughter.

Halfway home, Miriam spoke about Nicolas to Walter. The boy was like his father, not fully domesticated, always wandering off to see what he could see in the forests and slopes around Seward. This concerned them both, as he never felt the need for protection, despite the abundance of predatory animals. There were never any problems, even though he made contact with a number of animals on his jaunts, more than he mentioned to his parents.

Walter decided it was payback for how he worried his parents as a child.

Miriam spoke, "Nicolas has mentioned a few times how he doesn't want to go to school anymore, and he isn't interested in college either. Has he mentioned it to you?"

"Not directly, no, but I've known for a while how he feels. He's naturally smart, and I'm not sure it's a bad idea, Miriam. He likes helping me with the boats when he comes around the shop, and I think he has good hands. Actually, I plan on talking to him soon about things."

Putting her hand on his leg, she said, "I think you two will work it out to his benefit, yes?"

"Yeah, it will be fine. And, I feel that whatever he decides to do, the way will be provided."

"I think you're right, my husband. Let's just accept and think in a positive way. Something will show him the right trail to follow."

Beaumont began taking Nicolas for trips into the forest and around Prince William sound, teaching him the ways of the bush. His son paid attention to whatever he told him, and to what was around him. A few times, a chill ran down Beaumont's back when the boy did something the way he would have as a child.

Nicolas never wanted to learn trapping, once he knew what was involved. He didn't feel right about it, just as his father preferred to trail and watch animals as they went about their lives, surviving in the ways their species had since they'd first existed.

Walter was fine with Nicolas' feelings. Hunting for food though, taking moose, black bear, and deer, was acceptable to them both.

Walter had given him a new .22 rifle for his ninth birthday, teaching him to shoot it well, and handle it safely. By the time he was eleven, he would go off on his own, hunting small game.

One day, Nicolas came home later than usual. He had a black eye and a split lip. Miriam was very upset, but tried not to make too much out of it. Beaumont could see he was all right. After his mom cleaned up his lip and gave him some ice for his eye, father and son went outside to sit by the fire pit.

"So, what happened?"

"I was walking home past the old warehouse a little ways up from our road. I was looking for spruce hens, and after I didn't find any, I headed for home. Three older guys stopped me, and told me to let them shoot my twenty-two."

"And what did you do then?"

"I told them no, tried to walk away, and one of them grabbed my arm. I did like you showed me, punched him straight in the nose, then kicked him in the leg, and he backed away. He didn't know what to grab first. I was gonna run, but one of the other guys grabbed me from behind, and the third one punched me a few times after grabbing the rifle. There was nothing I could do, dad. I'm sorry. They took my rifle."

"Would you recognize them if you saw them again?"

"Oh, I know two of them and where they live, including the one who took the rifle."

In the morning, a Saturday, Nicolas took his father over to where he knew the boy lived. There was a small group sitting on the porch of the house, including the boy, his father, and several other people. The men were all drinking beer. Nicolas pointed to the boy, who saw him and stood up, acting nervous.

Beaumont asked who was the boy's father, then introduced himself and repeated what Nicolas had told him.

"I would appreciate it if you would ask your son where the rifle is, so we can take it home, and no hard feelings."

"Oh yeah? How do you know it's your kid's gun?"

"His initials, N.B. are stamped into the bottom of the stock, in front of the trigger guard."

The man sized Walter up, then told his son to get the rifle which he had told him he'd found in the woods. Sure enough, when the boy handed his father the rifle, there were Nicolas' initials, small, right where Walter said they would be.

Setting the twenty-two against the wall of the house, he told Beaumont if he could take it, he could have it back. A couple of the people there started chuckling. The boy's father had Walter by twenty-five pounds and seemed fit.

Walter sighed, and told the man, "This isn't necessary, but if that's how you want it, fine. Though you need to understand something: one of us won't be standing for long." He was looking the man in the eyes, unblinking, a picture of confidence and determination.

The man tried to hold his gaze, except the more he looked into Beaumont's eyes, the less comfortable he was. Finally, he grabbed the rifle and tossed it at Walter, who caught it deftly in his left hand.

He turned to tell Nicolas to come with him, but the father made a leap off the porch. Beaumont heard the man's feet shift on the porch boards as he made his move, and side-stepped, pushing Nicolas away.

The man stumbled but kept his feet, turned around, and a few seconds later was lying unconscious on his back.

"Pick up your rifle, Nicolas, and let's go home."

They walked quietly back down the road, until Walter spoke.

"I know what you're thinking, and you need to understand, what happened back there was not a good thing. The man acted stupidly, and I didn't want to hurt him. Sometimes, though, we have no choice. Remember, you do what you have to do, like you did hitting the one who grabbed you, but take no pleasure in it. One other thing, say nothing to your mother. She would not be happy.

Speaking of which, I need you to do something, for your mom, me, and most of all, you. You have to go to and finish high school, and do it well, because I know you can. You may not necessarily think what you are being taught is of any value, but believe me when I tell you, it is. Someday, you may want to apply for a job, say, as a marine biologist, or as a Fish and Wildlife agent, or even to become a famous ship designer, not skiffs either. Without a high school diploma, you don't stand a chance. So, think about it, okay?"

Nicolas nodded, took his dad's hand, and smiled a little smile.

Chapter 30

Empty Nest

Beaumont looked up from where he'd been peeling a new log to replace a bad one from his Uncle Aubrey's cabin. He saw his son, Nicolas, working to even up the window frame in the rebuilt south wall. The boy had grown into a strapping young man, capable and confident. He had graduated high school a month ago, despite struggling to pass a number of the classes he had taken. It wasn't because he didn't have the intelligence to do it, far from it. He was much like his father, more interested in the natural world around him than in most of what his school books taught him.

His father had stuck with Nicolas, keeping him on an even keel, making him work when he least wanted to, reminding him more than once of what was at stake, his future. He still thought working with his father building boats was all he needed. The boy had a real talent for working with his hands, whatever he put them to.

As his uncle had done, Walter had told him if he graduated school in good shape, he could become his partner in the business. Like his dad, Nicolas always kept his word, promising to do his best.

Beaumont had made a run with Nicolas down to the site of Aubrey's old cabin several years before, and the boy instantly fell in love with the place, despite its ruined condition. He had convinced his father to restore the place, to use it for hunting and having it to stay in as a way to be out on the land, with the true luxury of solid walls and a dry roof.

They had worked on it when they could for the last two years, and with any luck it would be done by summer's end.

They had rebuilt the old shower system too, though Nicolas definitely didn't like the cold water at first. Seeing his father actually enjoying it made him determined to do the same. Walter smiled to himself, seeing Nicolas trying to put up with the chill water, as he had with Uncle Aubrey. It gave him peace of mind to know some good things continued on.

Something had impressed and surprised Walter. There was an encounter with an old brown bear while hunting for deer on the coast of Hinchinbrook Island. Sitting behind some debris, a fallen tree and rocks, waiting for deer to show, they both turned around in unison, hearing a deep grunting noise. The old bear was only about thirty-five yards away, eyeing them seriously.

Nicolas started talking quietly to the massive bruin, making it clear they weren't looking for any trouble. After a minute, the bear dropped his head, still keeping an eye on them, then slowly turned and walked away.

Walter smiled at Nicolas and said, "For me, whistling seemed to work to calm the big ones. I'm glad you knew to do what you did."

"Oh, I've talked to bears before, pop."

"You have? When?"

"Oh, uh, when I was younger."

"I'm glad you never told your mom. She used to give me grief about letting you go off on your own."

He and Nicolas looked at each other, smiling, sharing their father-son connection.

Their time working on the cabin over for a while, Walter and Nicolas were aboard the *Journey* heading into Prince William Sound between Eleanor and Montague Islands, on the way back to Seward. Beaumont had taught his boy to be as familiar with the Sound, its landmarks, animals, and islands as he was. On his part, Nicolas loved going anywhere with his father, and the Sound did draw him, being an incredible wild place. He was constantly observing, as they ran up through the islands.

Nicolas tapped his father on the shoulder and told him there was something about two-hundred yards off the port bow.

"I think it's an overturned boat, dad."

It was a capsized boat, and by the time they were within twenty yards, Nicolas, with his sharp eyesight, saw what looked like a pair of hands hanging onto the keel. A moment later, the hands slipped away. Nicolas waited until they had halved the distance, and, taking off his boots and shirt, dove into the icy cold waters, swimming quickly over to the other side of the capsized hull.

By the time his father had run the boat around far enough to see the other side, he saw Nicolas coming up for another big gulp of air and then he went under again. Fifteen seconds later he reappeared on the surface, holding a man in front of him who appeared unconscious. Walter gave a big pull up and backward and had the fellow, a teenager from the looks of him, onto the deck. He helped Nicolas, shivering cold, onto the deck, and gave him a blanket to wrap up in.

Walter laid the young man on his stomach, face turned to the side, and started pushing on his back, to get rid of any swallowed water. He was about to give up when the guy started coughing up water and moaning. Walter had Nicolas get a sleeping bag, opened it, and wrapped the young man up. He was coming around, and started yelling, "My brother, my brother! Help him, please!"

Nicolas told him there was no one else around the boat. "No, he's under the boat, we were yelling to each other, please!"

Without hesitation and before Walter could stop him, Nicolas dove back into the water, and swam under the hull. It was pitch black there. He yelled out and got a response.

"Okay, I'm here to help you, but we've got to hurry. My body's slowing down. Why didn't you swim out to your brother?"

"Because I can't swim, okay? That's why I'm hanging onto this crossboard, staying out of the water."

"Darned good reason. All right, slide over to me, take a deep breath, and we'll go out together. Don't worry, I've got you."

A few seconds later, they were up and out. Luckily the guy didn't panic, and soon they were both aboard and covered up, warming in the cabin. The two brothers, Chad and Rice, hugged each other, then thanked the Beaumonts.

"No problem," said Walter, "Let's get you two up to Seward for now. We'll come back tomorrow to see if we can salvage your boat, and tow it up to Seward." Beaumont came about, pushed the throttle forward, and headed back to Seward. Once there, they drove the boys up to the Beaumont cabin, got them some dry clothes, and sat them near the wood stove. It took a while for them to fully recover.

Miriam cooked up a pot of chicken and dumplings and served it with home-made bread. It was obvious the incident had not diminished their appetites, far from it, the food disappearing quickly. Miriam brought out a jar of berry jam, and they slathered it on some more bread.

Walter asked them what had happened, and Chad told him the engine on the boat had failed about where they found them. The open boat was in the wrong position when two waves, not very big according to Rice, had come one right after the other, rolling the boat over.

"Well, you two can bunk out in the guest cabin. It's warm and comfortable. In the morning, we'll have some breakfast and go after your boat."

"Sounds great, Mr. Beaumont. Uh, did we eat all the wonderful bread?"

Miriam laughed and cut them each another thick slice, put butter and jam on them, and they went off for the night.

By eleven a.m. the next day, they were back where the boat had rolled over. It took a couple of hours to find it, currents there being what they were. They spotted the boat on a rocky patch off the northeast corner of Montague Island. Luckily the tide was quite low. Taking the dory from behind the *Emma Joy*, they ran over to the wreck, and, using a block and tackle, attached to a nearby tree, turned the boat right side up. On closer inspection, they didn't see any broken places in the hull. There was no way the motor would start, so, fastening it to the *Emma Joy* with a line, they waited for the tide to rise. When the boat was truly afloat, they hauled it in closer and towed it back to Seward, to the upper shore near where the old shop had been. There was over a foot and a half of water in the twenty-one footer, meaning there was a leak they hadn't spotted. They were relieved the trip had not been longer.

Using a pair of hand pumps, taking turns, they got it drained out. The boys brought their truck and trailer around, and soon the boat was set for its run home.

"Our dad isn't going to be happy, Mr. Beaumont. We didn't tell him where we were going. Guess we'll have to face the music."

"Oh, I imagine you'll survive it, boys. I'm sure he'll be glad you're okay."

"Well, thanks for all your help and your hospitality. Tell Mrs. Beaumont for us she's a great cook."

"You're welcome, and I'll tell her. You know, I've always believed that if you see someone in trouble and don't stop to help them, you're not living right. It may seem like a simple thing to understand, but some don't. Maybe someday you can extend the favor to someone else."

They shook hands all around, and the two fortunate brothers headed home to Anchorage.

In the evening, Nicolas came over to his father at the workbench in the shop, where he was working on another river boat design, and asked to talk to him.

Surprised at the formality, Walter saw the seriousness in his eyes, poured them each a cup of coffee from the pot on the woodstove, and sat down again facing him.

"Well, what's on your mind, Nicolas?"

"When I dove into the water to save Chad, I knew it was a dangerous thing to do, but I didn't think twice about it. I knew it was the only thing to do. It seemed, well, natural to me. And then, going back in to get his brother, if anything, felt even righter. I've been thinking about something for a while, even before the situation out there. I've never given much thought to the military, but, I realize now I should join the Coast Guard. I think it would be the perfect outfit for me, what with all their search and rescue work up here. What do you think, dad?"

Walter hadn't said anything to Nicolas about the military. Certainly being in the Coast Guard wouldn't put him in the positions he had found himself in during Viet Nam, though he would find himself in dangerous situations nonetheless, doing worthwhile work.

"Nicolas, if it feels right to you, then I'll support you one-hundred percent. Your mom will too, though she won't like you leaving, of course. It's a mother's worry. Me, I have plenty of faith in you. You're a fine young man, Nicolas."

That was all Nicolas needed to hear, and it was settled. Several days later, he went over to the Coast Guard cutter currently moored in the harbor, and managed to get some time with one of the ship's officers, who was more than happy to discuss the Guard with the enthusiastic young man. He didn't sugar coat anything, but gave Nicolas the straight scoop on what it took to be a competent Coast Guard member.

Walter and Nicolas drove up to the Coast Guard recruiter in Anchorage. Three months later, he was on his way to the training base at Cape May, New Jersey. It all went very fast, and without a hitch.

With both their children gone, Miriam certainly was feeling the empty-nest condition. The night after Nicolas left, she and Walter talked quietly in bed.

Walter told her, "I guess life keeps moving along, and the kids will find their own paths to follow. They'll do fine, my dear, you've raised them well."

"As have you, my husband, as have you."

It was not as hard for Walter to adjust. He had learned to be more accepting of changes. He built boats, fished, hunted, and generally enjoyed his life alone with her.

Miriam, on the other hand, had an empty place in her, and she was having a hard time filling it. She hadn't been teaching in Seward for a while, and needed something to fulfill her desire to be useful. Miriam knew what would make her whole again. Her Aleut people who had been removed from Chenega Island after the '64 good Friday quake had been resettling on Evans Island from the other places where they had relocated. It had started with one family, and had now become Chenega Bay.

Walter and Miriam had taken a run out to see how things were going in the new village. Walter saw how being there had immediately perked up his saddened wife, and he knew what would follow. A week after the visit, she spoke about it to Walter. She had waited a while out of respect for him, while he patiently waited for her to broach the subject.

"Walter, since the children have been gone, I have wanted to do something to satisfy my need to be useful, helpful to someone. I love caring for you, but I need to spend time with my people again, perhaps a month or maybe even two, out of the year. I'm not sure what I can do. I would love to be able to teach the children there again. If this would be too much for you, I will forget the whole idea, and we'll be all right."

"I know how you've been feeling. Our hearts do beat as one, so how could I not know? I will back you completely, and if spending time in Chenega Bay with your people will make you happy again, I won't stand in your way."

Miriam, tears in her eyes, hugged Beaumont tightly. "I am a lucky woman."

After Beaumont had taken his wife over to Evans Island and returned to Seward the next day, he was sitting in the shop, working on plans for a new boat. He was okay spending time alone. Besides, he had plenty to do, with the boats and finishing up Aubrey's cabin, which was close to being livable again.

He thought about his daughter, Emma Rose. She was now an RN, working in a hospital in Seattle. She had met a young doctor doing his residency there to become an orthopedic surgeon. Emma and Gregory had visited the winter before, and Walter found him to be a solid, competent, and considerate fellow, a good find for Emma. The two men found each other's company satisfying. He was originally from Minnesota, had hunted and fished there, and as a teenager had trapped muskrat for extra pocket money. They got along well, swapping stories and discussing hunting and fishing techniques. He wished they would come live in Alaska, and even mentioned the idea in his last letter to them. Family meant more to him now than ever before.

Walter had come to a necessary decision. He needed help building boats. The shoulder injured in the plane crash had never healed one-hundred per cent. Walter had not given it enough time to do so, before becoming active again. Now, after a few hours working, he had to give it a rest. Miriam had made some willow tincture, which helped ease the pain but didn't cure the problem. He would never own up to the fact he had started working sooner than he should have, but that was Beaumont. So, he decided to find someone to help him in the business, if he could locate an experienced, competent person.

He went through half a dozen candidates before he found one who seemed to be right. His name was Ralph Hansen, from Cordova. Ralph knew of Walter's boats, having seen several around the southeast portion of the state he worked in doing finish carpentry. He'd always wanted to build boats, and he'd restored several, including the one he ran up to Seward. Beaumont's ad seemed a Godsend to him.

He and Walter clicked right away, and by afternoon, with Walter satisfied he knew what he was doing, it was settled. Ralph would come up in two weeks, and he'd stay in the small cabin until he could get himself a place.

He showed Walter the twenty-eight-foot cabin cruiser he had restored, and used to make the trip. He had re-glassed the boat himself, and inspecting the hull, Beaumont was impressed. When he mentioned he'd considered using fiberglass for a river boat he'd designed, Ralph told him if he wanted to set up the boat with glass, he'd be glad to work on it with him.

It came up in conversation that Hansen had done two tours in Viet Nam. When Ralph asked Walter if he had served, Walter nodded and told him when he had been there, doing forward recon, mentioning the general area, the year, and nothing else.

Ralph said, "Early times, Mr. Beaumont. I had heard rumors there were several units doing recon early on, to see how things were building up. I guess you were involved."

Walter nodded, they shook hands, and no more was said about it. The connection between the two had been solidified in one short, specific conversation.

Ralph proved to be the perfect match for Beaumont. They seemed to know instinctively what was needed to work together smoothly, and Hansen was a fast worker, while keeping the quality of work up to Walter's high standards. Beaumont talked to him about appreciating the way wood lent itself to boat construction, even though fiberglass and aluminum were becoming more popular.

Walter didn't like aluminum because it was noisy to move around on. It didn't mean it wasn't good material for boats, he just didn't like the way it sounded when walked on or had something bang up against it.

Ralph convinced him a sheathing of fiberglass over wood was a good surface, strong and long-lasting, especially in colder climates, where the lower temperatures made the fiberglass less likely to degrade.

When Miriam had come home from Chenega, it was obvious the two would get along fine. Walter hadn't thought about it, but it turned out Ralph was half Native. Miriam knew right away, though it was never an issue. Eventually, Hansen was like family, in all the good ways.

After three months, Walter told him they'd build the flat-bottomed river boat he had started to create at an earlier time, with fiberglass sheathing. It proved to be an opportune project. Walter saw, watching Ralph, all the mistakes he had initially made.

They tested the first boat on the rivers abounding in Alaska, traveling to various areas and different river environments. The boat was shallow draft, which suited the debris-strewn rivers and streams they encountered. Even getting grounded at times on sand and gravel bars did not prove too difficult to get free from, the flat bottom and smooth glass coating being positive factors.

They kept the first build and made a duplicate. It sold quickly. Ralph helped Walter put up an ad for the boats, including photographs he had taken. By the end of the year, a number of orders had been placed. Business was good. Walter decided to make Ralph a partner a year later. He even offered to give Ralph a corner of land on the family property. However, Hansen had a five-acre parcel he had purchased about three miles from the Beaumont's place, and showed Walter the layouts for the home he wanted to build. Times were good, and Walter didn't intend to let anything change that.

Chapter 31

Trouble in the Sound

Walter put down the letter he had received from Nicolas. His son had been doing well in the Coast Guard, training as a rescue diver to do search and rescue in helicopters, saving individuals and full boat crews on the often stormy waters of the North Atlantic. He had fallen in love with the New England coast, and had requested permanent duty there.

Though Walter was disappointed his son would not be returning home, he accepted Nicolas was where he wanted to be. He had to smile, seeing how life had put him in the position he had put his own parents in when he himself had insisted on leaving home because he loved Alaska so much. He was pleased to learn Nicolas had advanced quickly in the Guard, receiving several commendations for his rescue work. Of course, he hadn't expected less from him.

In the letter, Nicolas had enclosed a picture of the girl he had been dating for over a year, and who was now his fiancée. Arlene Thornton was a New England girl, originally from Vermont. Walter thought her pretty, though not as pretty as Miriam had been when he met her. He hoped his son would have as much good fortune and closeness with her as he had with his wife.

Ralph came in, a serious look on his face. He often brought Walter news, since Beaumont never had adopted the habit of reading the newspapers or listening to the radio. They didn't own a television.

"Walter, there's trouble down in the Sound." A big tanker has gone aground on Bligh Reef, a full oil tanker. It's leaking badly."

Hearing the news felt like a punch in the gut to Walter. He knew large ships ran through Prince William, and had worried there might be a real incident some day.

"How bad is it, Ralph?"

"She's carrying millions of gallons of oil. It could be very bad, big."

Over the next week, more and more facts about the spill came out. The two friends sat and discussed the situation, deciding to play a part in the clean-up. Walter contacted the DEC and offered use of the *Emma Joy* to help in any way possible. Though he hadn't asked, he would be paid for the boat's use, and his piloting services.

Beaumont went to work to help save the place he loved more than any other, hoping to restore the Sound back to the way it had been. Ralph worked with Walter on the *Emma Joy*. This dire situation took precedence over everything else.

The oil spill proved to be of such a magnitude, results were never more than partially successful. Walter and Ralph spent days on end ferrying workers and equipment around the Sound, in mostly futile attempts to fully rid the land and water of the poisonous oil.

In the end, only a small percentage of the oil was actually removed. There were dead sea animals and birds everywhere. It broke Beaumont's heart to see the effects of what he could only call major negligence, incompetence, and lack of responsible behavior on Exxon's part.

It took months for Walter to get fully paid for his services, and the more he learned about what Exxon was doing to avoid penalties, the more he hated that some people cared so little for a magnificent piece of the earth.

Exhausted from his efforts and disconsolate over the effects of the spill, Walter stopped working in the Sound. He knew there was little more he could do. In years to come he would do his own exploration of Prince William Sound, and he found, below the surface, there was still much residue.

Finally he stopped going to the Sound, the results of the catastrophe too much for him to keep awakening in his mind and heart.

Miriam had come home right after the Exxon Valdez had run aground. Walter had sped down to get her out of the area, and to let her people know what was going on, but learned they already knew. The oil spill devastated Chenega Bay and its fishing industry. They would eventually turn to investments from the funds they were given for the damage done. They had wondered what else could come to ruin their home after the big quake. Now they knew.

Walter and Ralph continued to build boats, even though, for a year after the spill, business was slow. Time passes, and blurs even the worst of situations. The people of Alaska are, by and large, not the kind to give up the life they love. The boats began selling again.

In 1996, Walter and Miriam moved to Cooper Landing, on the Kenai River. An army buddy of Ralph's, visiting in the spring, told him about a large shop and cabin being sold by an acquaintance there, at a fair price. The man needed to move out of state because of his wife's health. She needed the dry warm climate desert country would provide.

Ralph talked to Walter and Miriam, and they, along with Ralph's new wife, Greta, drove down to look at the place. It was ten acres in size, and the shop could be easily set up for small boat building. The cabin was roomy, two story, well built, wired for electricity. It had a woodstove and an oil heater. Two big windows faced the river, and the view was incredible.

After several hours of negotiating, mixed with good conversation and cups of strong coffee, a deal had been struck. Ralph let the Beaumonts have the cabin, as he wanted to build the house he had been planning for some time, but never built on the Seward land he owned.

If not for the oil spill and how it affected Walter, they might never have moved. Things were as they were, however, and Miriam knew a change of area would be best for her husband. By the end of summer they were all moved in. Their place in Seward had sold quickly, as had the *Emma Joy*. They kept *Beaumont's Journey*.

The way the whole change of location had gone quickly and smoothly made Walter and Miriam feel it was the right thing to do. No obstacles had been placed in their way to slow or halt the process.

Ralph's new home went up quickly. It was a beautiful frame house, designed to look like one from a hundred years ago, two story, wood siding, a large roofed over front porch, and a big stone fireplace.

Walter learned to love the Kenai River and Cooper's Landing. They were welcomed by the folks living there, and it didn't hurt that Walter and Ralph built excellent boats, especially drift boats, so useful on the Kenai. Neither man had considered breaking away from the business after the move. They were content, both wise enough to appreciate a good thing when they had it. Besides, they were good friends who found working together greatly satisfying. Miriam and Ralph's wife, Greta, also became close, Miriam even helping Greta through her first pregnancy.

Hannah was not doing well. Ben had passed in 1995, his heart finally giving out. In 1997, Walter went down to see her, and ended up bringing her back with him. He did it because she told him she knew her time was short, and Hannah was right. There was room for her in the large home at Cooper's Landing, and she loved living by the river, having never had one where she'd lived in the past. She said it felt like life itself flowing by her door. Living together worked well for all of them. Sadly, one short month later, Miriam found her passed away in her bed, a peaceful smile on her face. They scattered her ashes on the river, as she had wished. Beaumont contented himself with knowing she was with family at the end.

Walter's shoulder had worsened, and he had to accept his boat building days were all but over. He discussed it with Ralph, who agreed to buy him out for a continuing percentage of the business, in lieu of a cash amount. Walter, for his part, would still work with Hansen, consulting with him on new boat designs, and anything else he might need from him.

Though he was still young in mind, he retired from boat-building at the age of 64. Miriam smiled when he mumbled he didn't know what he was going to do.

"Why, Walter Beaumont, don't you worry about a thing. I'll see to it you'll always have something to keep you busy, count on it." Then she gave him a kiss on the cheek and went back to making some of her good sourdough bread.

He'd never visited with his friend Charlie Brady as much as either of them had wanted. Charlie was with the Wildlife Troopers until he retired in 1988. For several years after, he would come visit Walter and they'd go fishing, and hunting for moose, though not every year. They did go on a brown bear hunt on Kodiak. Charlie wasn't usually a trophy hunter, but he'd always wanted a brown bear hide for a rug or wall covering. It wasn't too difficult for the old Wildlife Trooper to get a bear hunting tag. Walter went with him for back-up. After a long hunt, Charlie took a bear, not huge, but with a beautiful coat. Beaumont never faulted him for it.

When he retired, Charlie chose to live in Salcha, on the Richardson Highway, in the general area where he had been on duty for years. He loved the place, and was strongly attached to it.

Needing an anchor for his life, he bought a small diner on the highway, The North Star Cafe, right in the tiny town. He cooked well enough, chili, burgers, and fried fish, and it gave him something to do. Travelers coming through, and locals, ensured him enough business to keep things going. Truth to tell, even when business was quiet he was fine, getting to chew the fat with the residents of Salcha he had come to know well.

Charlie Brady looked up one mid-June morning to see a familiar person walk into the North Star Cafe. It was Walter Beaumont, who he hadn't seen in quite some time. Both men had more gray hairs than they were willing to mention. Age had caught up with them, though they were healthy all the same, save for Walter's bad shoulder.

It was quiet in the cafe, as often occurred, so the two had time to catch up. Walter told him about the fishing on the Kenai, and the moose he had taken barely a hundred yards behind his place in Cooper's landing. Charlie suggested it was probably the easiest moose hunt Beaumont had ever been on, until Walter told him about the moose in the meadow when he was trapping. "Believe me, Charlie, the cow in the meadow was truly the easiest.

"Miriam is visiting at Chenega Bay, so I figured it would be a good time to come visit. The weather is fine, and the skeeters are barely out yet."

Charlie invited him to stay a few days. "I've got a house across the street now, a lot more room than the old cabin out back. I'd enjoy your company."

Walter smiled, and said, "Sounds fine to me."

"So, you up for a good burger? If you're hungry, I have one called the Homesteader Burger I invented for an old friend who lives way down the Salcha River, off a small tributary. He's an interesting guy. I think you two would take to each other."

"I'd love a burger, Charlie, if you've learned to cook yet. Does it come with fries?"

"Of course it does," Charlie said in a scoffing tone. "And don't start complaining again. I told you before, the soup you had last time you visited was supposed to be spicy."

"Yeah, but it took a while for the top of my tongue to grow back."

In the evening, sitting with beers in hand, the two men shared stories and important happenings since the last time they saw each other.

Walter told Charlie he would like to take a long hike in the area.

"I've brought all my gear, so tell me, where does this homesteader live? How long would it take to get there by foot, and would I be welcome?"

"Well heck, Walter, I've got a brand new ATV you could use. Make traveling a lot easier. He's definitely a solitary soul, but he'd be fine if you told him we knew each other."

"Thanks, but I'd prefer going by shanks's mare. Get to see more, no noise or smell either."

Brady shrugged and brought out a map of the area, marking the trail to show him the way. Charlie knew, of course, what a great woodsman Walter was. He had no worry about him having a good hike in and staying safe, though he saw Beaumont was obviously getting on. He did have one warning for him.

"Be aware, there is a small wolf pack out along the river which seems to have no fear of humans, and one guy's dog team was attacked last winter. No reports lately, but I thought you'd like to know."

Walter woke up early and saw Charlie had gone across to open the cafe. He walked over, had an egg sandwich and coffee, visited for a little while, then grabbed his gear and started out to the trailhead, more than ready to explore this area he had never been in before.

Chapter 32

Kindred Spirits

Leaving the road, it only took him a short distance to become immersed in the wilds, away from the structures, smells, and noise of the civilized zone. His mind opened right up to the natural world around him. Despite his passion for boat-building and the love he had for his family, there were periods when being alone in the trees was the only time he felt truly free. All his senses became heightened, the farther he walked into the bush.

The first thing he noticed was how the trail Charlie described seemed unlike the trail as it appeared to him. Brady, himself a capable woodsman, had mentioned how difficult it would be to stay on, because of the underbrush. For Walter, it was incredibly easy to follow.

Whoever traveled on it had been using the same route for years, and it looked to Beaumont like a highway in the forest. It was obvious a wheeler had been run. Branches had been removed to protect a rider from being scratched and poked, and some brush had been intentionally cleared, though in a naturally seeming way.

It was a beautiful area, as Charlie had said. The forest was healthy and lush, more spruce than any other trees, giving a strong, deep feeling to the area alongside the trail. The Salcha River ran close to the path most of the way, and he much enjoyed the sounds as the water ran its course. Sometimes he could hear rocks in the swiftly moving river, bumping along under the surface, as the fast current rearranged what lay on its bed. The water level was still quite high as spring run-off had not yet fully subsided.

There was lots of animal sign, tracks and scat from moose, bear, and fox. He'd not yet seen any wolf tracks, and figured the wolves might be farther in, knowing they could roam for many miles while hunting.

Walter didn't miss a thing. About five miles in, he thought he heard some scrabbling noises, as if some creature were climbing a tree. He pulled his light wool jacket back, leaving the .44 magnum exposed in its holster. He hadn't brought a long gun, not expecting to take down any large animal for food, and he didn't anticipate any need for a defensive situation. Besides, he practiced regularly and was proficient with it, easily hitting a target out to fifty yards. He had brought some special ammunition with him.

Walter had bought it in Anchorage at a gun store where he had gone to replace some gun cleaning supplies. The salesman told him they were unusual .44 magnum loads, more powerful than standard factory cartridges, with heavier, 300 grain bullets, but they were safe to use in his Ruger revolver. He called them bear loads. Beaumont asked a few questions and ultimately bought fifty rounds.

He had fired half for practice, finding them to be accurate and definitely more powerful. He had fired into a thick tree stump, and both rounds went right through. It was all he needed to know. His revolver would always be loaded with these bullets when he was out and about.

He heard some noises over his head, and looked up to see a small female black bear with one cub, hanging onto a spruce trunk about twenty feet up. After observing briefly, he went on his way, leaving them to their lives.

Around seven in the evening Walter made camp. He built his usual shelter with a tarp and willow poles, laid down some spruce boughs and started a small fire in front. Tying a hook onto a hand line with a small shot weight about six inches above it, he baited it with several cured salmon eggs, and tossed the twenty feet of line into a patch of slower water, and waited. In less than a minute, he had a grayling on the hook. He brought it in, pierced its head with his knife's tip, and laid it on the bank. Rebaiting the hook, he again tossed the line and it only took seconds before the line went tight, and a rainbow trout was fighting on the line. He cleaned it and the grayling by the river, tossing the gurry into the water for other fish to feed on.

After cooking and eating the delicious fish with a piece of fry bread, Beaumont leaned back under the tarp, a cup of instant coffee in his hand. He felt blissed out, being where he loved to be, stomach full of good eats. Walter removed a small flask from his pack for his evening nip of good bourbon. Raising the flask in a silent toast to all he knew and loved who were no longer around, he thought, "If you were with me now, you'd love this wonderful place."

Beaumont sighed, screwed the cap back on the flask, and snuggled into his sleeping bag, the .44 lying next to him, folded jacket beneath his head, and fell into the semi-conscious sleeping mode he had long ago adopted while in the wilds.

When Walter woke up, he took a few minutes to work out the kinks from his achy bones and sore muscles, grumbling to himself. While getting old, in and of itself, didn't bother him, the aches and pains that had come along due to an active, physically challenging life did annoy him.

The second day was much like the first, except there was more open country to walk through, the brush less dense. The river wandered off a bit, though never far away.

On this day he found fresh sign from a large bear. He came across a deep, wide pile of bear plop, so large he was actually amused by it. Walter figured it was quite a meal the bruin must have had, displaying a lot of gloppy bunches of fur, likely moose. Might have been a winter kill it had found somewhere. He knew bears didn't mind eating spoiled, fetid meat. He'd always thought they actually savored it.

He came across some wolf prints, and noted there were three animals, one leaving visibly larger tracks. They ran across the trail, headed to the left away from the river. Perhaps they had stopped there for a drink. His mind more alert than usual, he continued on. Beaumont knew there had been few recorded attacks on people by wolves, usually occurring in winter when their food was scarcer. At this time of the year he didn't think they'd be inclined to want humans for food; he'd be cautious, nonetheless.

In the afternoon, Walter stopped, seeing an odd sight in this wild place. There was a wooden pole-and-slab bridge over a stream running from the left into the Salcha, now close to the trail again. He walked up onto it for a closer inspection. It was a sturdy bridge, high enough to keep break-up waters from rising over it and washing it out. There was a foot-and-a-half clearance between the bridge poles and the top of the water.

He decided he was getting closer to his destination, as the homesteader had surely been the one who built the bridge. He walked over it and moved on.

Beaumont made camp a little early, his right knee feeling sore. He easily caught another trout, and repeated the enjoyable evening he'd had the night before.

Walter had brought a book with him, not something he normally did when in country. This one, however, had stirred his interest. It was about a man, Dick Proenneke, living alone in the Alaska wilderness, in a cabin he had built by a lake, a beautiful little home judging by the photos. The man was a true conservationist, and he made a lot of worthwhile observations about the land, the animals, and the seasons there. Beaumont felt immediately connected to this fellow, a kindred spirit, and also one who was very creative, building by hand with real craftsmanship.

He was reading the book after eating, sitting quietly under the tarp, until a unique scent caught his attention. Looking up he saw a pair of staring, golden-yellow eyes visible to him through some willows. As soon as he saw them, the head became visible. A wolf, a large one, was observing him, and two others were there with the first.

Walter sat quietly, staring back at them. They didn't seem aggressive, but these were great predators, and he hoped that, their curiosity satisfied, they'd leave. They didn't. Almost in unison, the largest wolf and the two others moved forward, no growling, no charging, out in the open now. Walter still hadn't moved. The larger wolf took two more steps towards him, and Beaumont jumped up and out from under the tarp, .44 in hand. The two lesser wolves dashed away into the willows again, but not the leader. He bared his teeth and growled in a low warning way. Walter pointed his gun and fired a warning shot right between the wolf's front feet, and in an instant it had spun and disappeared.

He got little sleep that night, even though he never saw any more eyes in the willows, and assumed they had gone looking elsewhere for prey. He'd let the Wildlife Troopers know about the aggressive animals when he got back to Salcha.

Despite himself, Beaumont had dozed off in the early morning hours. Fortunately, nothing happened to disturb his slumber, though he wasn't pleased with his inability to stay awake. Having a cup of instant, another piece of fry bread, and some moose jerky, he broke camp, killing the fire and leaving the spot as he had found it.

Around four in the afternoon, Walter took the trail around a little bend to the right. He had smelled wood smoke. Another fifty yards and he was in view of a expertly built log cabin, smoke coming from the stone chimney. An old plywood outbuilding with a lean-to built onto it stood off to the right, closer to the creek that had branched off from the river a mile or so back. A little log outhouse was behind the cabin, and across from it, a high cache on log supports. He was sure he had arrived at the right place.

Hearing the sound of wood being split with a maul, coming from behind the cabin, He yelled out, "Hello, the cabin!"

Immediately, two dogs, one old, the other younger though full grown, came running out barking. When they got close, Walter knelt down and extended his right hand, palm up, and whistled at the two dogs, the three-note whistle he'd used before. They calmed and sat down, the younger one whining.

A voice spoke out, "Hello yourself. Passing through?"

Walter looked up to see a man just shy of his age, shirt off, wiping his face with a bandana. The fellow was lean as a rail, and he looked tough, as though he was pared down to just what was needed. Beaumont also saw a bullet wound on his upper left abdomen. His hair was shaggy, and his beard full. His eyes caught Walter's attention. Even at a distance, they seemed to take hold of anything in their range until the eyes released whatever they were gazing upon.

"No, actually, I was told to come visit you while I was hiking the country. My name is Walter John Beaumont, I live down on the Kenai, and I'm a friend of Charlie Brady."

Walter advanced slowly, in a non-aggressive way. No sense putting off this man he'd never met, a remote homesteader who just wanted to be sure of this stranger.

Extending his hand, Walter waited until the fellow offered his, at which point a firm handshake settled things.

"Denny Caraway. Charlie has mentioned you a couple of times. I'm pretty much done with splitting firewood for now. Never can have too much on hand. Maybe you know that already. Yeah, I think you do."

"You'd be right, Mr. Caraway."

"Denny, if you don't mind. My dogs don't usually take to anyone this quickly. Guess you have a feel for animals. What was that whistling?"

"The few times I've disturbed a big bear, it seemed to calm them down."

"Interesting. Yeah, you never know about bears."

Walter noticed the three old scars on Denny's left upper arm. "Looks like you're aware of all sides of a bear's nature."

Denny touched his arm and smiled slightly. "Yeah, the old hungry ones, they can be tricky. Come on in and sit. You drink coffee? I've got a pot going."

"I do, and a cup would be fine, thanks."

When the two men walked inside the cabin, Walter was impressed. After Denny poured him a cup, he went outside to wash off in the Creek. Beaumont did a quick visual inspection of the interior. It was properly done, with built-in cabinets and shelves. A loft with natural poles as uprights was at the back end. What caught his attention was the fireplace. He suddenly realized why. It was almost exactly like the one he'd seen in Proenneke's book.

Caraway walked back in. He put on a light flannel shirt, and poured himself a cup.

"Seeing your fireplace, I have the feeling you've read Dick Proenneke's book, Denny. You did a fine job building it. I've only started reading it, and I'm already impressed with the man."

"As am I. He has certainly been an inspiration to me."

And so, the visit between the two long-time Alaskans was off to a good start. Walter ended up spending a week visiting, which was unusual for Caraway to tolerate well, being a solitary fellow, but Charlie had been right.

They came to know each other in quite a personal way, even though there wasn't a lot of verbal discussion of everything. Some things between these woodsmen were just understood.

They played cribbage that first evening after dinner. While Walter had never played the game before, he took to it quickly, and by the time the visit was over, Denny told him he was regretting teaching him, asking with a smile if he was sure he'd never played before.

On a whim, Caraway asked him if he'd like to do a little exploring, maybe stay out a night, and Walter readily agreed. The next morning, they crossed over a narrow point in Lanyard creek, thigh deep, and cold as could be. They hiked across three miles of flat, sparsely treed country, then up a relatively short, steep, more thickly wooded slope. Near the top, Beaumont saw what was obviously mine tailings.

"I've been doing a little playing around with the old mine up there, because the timbers are still good. There's color, though I don't plan on getting too serious about it."

The two dogs started growling. They were looking at the mine opening.

"Don't worry, there's no bear in there. You'll see why they're growling when we get up there."

Attached to the crossbeam over the opening was the skull of a large brown bear.

"They always growl at it whenever we come up here. It came from the sick old bear who left me these reminders on my arm to never be complacent."

Walter was enjoying his visit with Caraway. He was easy going, confident, and very woods-wise, from years spent living the life. During the visit, Caraway told Beaumont how he had come to be there, and what had lead him to Lanyard Creek.

They were sitting on two stumps, a small stone fire pit between them. There wasn't much conversation. It was a beautiful night, and the view from the mine was truly amazing, thick, lush forest beyond the flatlands below, several lakes visible, including the one past Caraway's homestead. There were some wispy clouds in the blue sky. It was a serene display, belying the constant struggle for survival going on in the country below.

"Denny, does the solitary life ever get to you? Do you ever want to break camp and head to town?"

Caraway said, without hesitation, "No, never." He looked at Walter a long moment with that penetrating stare, and seemed to come to some kind of decision. He continued speaking.

"I was married to a woman when I was living out here some years back. We had it good together, and she was the best partner a man could have. She succumbed to cancer and was lost to me all too quickly. I brought her home as she wished, after the doctors said they could do nothing more for her. She's buried on the little ridge between the cabin and the lake. I feel her here all the time. Of course, it doesn't replace her actually being by my side.

"Her death hit me hard, and I actually went away, deeper into the forest. That's all I want to say about it. Thing is, if I were to ever go back to the noise and stink of civilization, I would have done it then. No, this is my life. I accept and love it for what it gives me, as well as for what it takes away." He smiled, and said, "Besides, I can always go into Salcha and have one of Charlie's good burgers and coffee, and some pleasant conversation."

Rip, the older dog, slipped over and lay with his head on Caraway's foot. The old homesteader patted his head. "See, I'm not alone."

Walter thought a while. "I can appreciate what you've told me. I know if my wife was gone from me, I'd be living by myself in a cabin down on the southern coast. I can understand you two were close, like my Miriam and I are."

"Yes, we were. Well, think I'll turn in. Maybe I'll take you tomorrow to where I got these little scratches on my arm. Night."

Caraway walked into the mine a short way and wrapped up in his bedroll. He was apparently asleep in a few minutes, judging by his snoring, the two dogs lying by his side. Walter sat by the fire a while, chewing over some of their conversation. He decided Denny had more of real value in his life than others had, surrounded by all the distractions a populated city and surplus money could offer.

They did some more hiking around the next day, and Denny showed Beaumont the slope where the starving old winter bear had tried to make a meal of him, only succeeding in leaving him a reminder of how close he had come to being gone. There were a few big, heavy bones lying around, the only evidence of the near-death incident. The skull of course, was now above the mine opening.

Walter showed Denny his .44 and Caraway laughed. "Same gun I'm carrying," he patted the holster on his right hip, "and the one I was wearing when the old grizz jumped me. So, you know it'll do its job if you aim right, and get lucky."

They returned to the homestead the next day. Walter helped Denny split and stack some firewood, but he realized he should leave the next morning. He knew he'd already kept company with Caraway longer than he normally allowed.

The next morning, he was all packed and set to go when they heard a wolf call close by.

Denny said, "I do believe I'll have to take care of that one. He's come around with his two thugs, wanting to take my dogs out, and I think they'd try for me, too, if they had the chance. The big one has a chip on his shoulder, maybe 'cause I took down two of his pack when they got close once too often.

You know, I owe Charlie a visit. I'm going to throw a few things together and run you back in on the wheeler. No sense taking a chance on being waylaid by those howlers. Besides, you may like it and buy one of these trusty machines."

Beaumont smiled and accepted the offer. Maybe not having to walk back out would be all right. His knees had been unhappy since before he'd arrived at Caraway's 'stead.

They left early in the morning. Walter was amazed they could get into Salcha in one full day, even with Denny taking it relatively easy. Much of the trail required them to keep their speed down, but there were several places in more open areas where they scooted right along. By the time they got to the highway, Walter was actually considering buying one. It seated the two men side by side, with a little shelter from a half windshield and a canvas roof overhead. There was a good-sized storage bed in the back, filled with some gear and two happy dogs.

Evening found the three old woodsmen in the cafe, sipping coffee after having a good meal. Charlie closed down the cafe a little early, and they went over to his house across the road. Charlie offered them the use of his shower. "For my sake, as well as yours." was the way he kiddingly put it.

In the middle of the night, Walter got up to answer nature's call, and passed by the living room. He saw Denny lying on several blankets on the floor, snoring soundly.

Though Beaumont regretted having to leave, he needed to get back home. Ralph was in the middle of working out the last little kinks in the design for a medium-size bay cruiser he was building, similar to the *Journey*, except a few feet longer with greater cabin space. It was actually their joint design, based on some of Tuckerman's concepts. He shared one more meal, a good breakfast at the cafe, before leaving.

"Well, gentlemen, time to go. Always a pleasure to see you Charlie, and Denny, it was good visiting with you. Perhaps you could come down to Cooper's Landing to visit Miriam and me some time, maybe do a little fishing on the Kenai. Here's my phone number in case you want to call."

"Thanks Walter. Chances are it would be more likely you and your wife would come see me. Might be best if you bought a wheeler and came in with her. A lot more comfortable. You take care." The two men shook hands.

They walked Beaumont out to the parking lot. He smiled, and headed his old Travelall down the road.

He was glad to get home, even though it had been a fine trip. As he pulled up to the house, he figured he'd wash up, have a bite to eat, and go over to the shop to help Ralph. He noticed some smoke was coming from the house's chimney, and saw an old white car, a beater, parked nearby. It was an old Chevy, with a cracked windshield, and all the fenders rusted out. He knew the car, but had no clue as to why it was parked there.

Walking up carefully, he swung open the door to his house and saw Miriam sitting in her rocker and knitting, a big smile on her face. She got up and gave Beaumont a big kiss and a hug.

"Why, I didn't expect to see you for at least three more weeks, Miriam. Are you okay?"

"Hello to you too, Mr. Beaumont. I'm fine. I was sitting on the front porch of the place I was staying in at Chenega Bay. I had been watching some Orcas moving through, and they made me realize that at this time in our lives, I should be with you, as much as I love my people. I decided it was time to come home to stay. So, I had my cousin run me up in his boat to our old home in Seward. I bought my old Chevy back from our neighbor Harlan, who was happy to sell it, cheap, and I drove it down here. It burped and hiccupped a few times going over the pass, and the brakes were kinda soft, but it got me home."

"Miriam, the old Chevy isn't safe, you shouldn't have driven it."

"Well then, I won't drive it anymore. Nowhere else I want to go anyways. I'll get supper started."

Finis

www.ingramcontent.com/pod-product-compliance
Lightning Source LLC
Chambersburg PA
CBHW051518260626
47170CB00003B/679